JOHN MASON

The Voyage of the Hesperia

BARBARA J. ROBERTSON

JOHN MASON

Copyright © 2016 by Barbara J. Robertson

DEDICATION

The "Legend of John Mason" series is dedicated to the men and women of the United States Marines, Navy, Army, Air Force, and Coast Guard, whose hard work and sacrifice continues to provide us with the freedoms we enjoy, and hold so dear.
Thank you for your service!

CONTENTS

CONTENTS

ACKNOWLEDGMENTS

Many thanks are owed to my close friends and sisters:
To RMCM Marie Vellis, for her inspiration and support for this project.
Her loyalty and dedication to duty during an exemplary 30-year career in the
US Navy helped open the doors for women to achieve ranks and careers
previously not available to them. She is a champion, and a great leader to all
who know her. Thank you for your friendship.
To Bonnie Copeland for reading my works, and providing commentary and
gentle criticism during the creation process. Her encouragement spurred me
to develop the series. Thank you, thank you!
To Denise Robertson, RN, and Debbie Hilst, RN, my sisters, for patiently
providing medical advice during the creation of this book, and for reading
the finished work. Love You!
To Mara Kalcheim, for her encouragement and support, and for holding
my feet to the fire. Thank you!

PROLOGUE

In the 24th Century, all the population of Earth is united under the United Republics of Earth (URE) flag of red, white, blue, and gold. The one world government controls all food production, all fresh water supplies, and all natural resources of the planet.

All banking is controlled by Regional Banks, answering to the Central Bank, with one currency: the freedom dollar. All of the working people are paid by freedom dollars directly deposited to their mandatory banking accounts, and withdrawals from those accounts are by bio-plastic encrypted crystals, fully programmable, commonly known as a "slice," or charge crystal. No paper currency or coins are in use. Credit is no longer a function of banking, not available to private individuals.

Before all countries became united under the URE banner, there were hundreds of separate countries, and over eight billion people on the Earth. Terrible atrocities were committed by governments' armies upon their enemies, culminating in a series of three World Wars. Each war was more destructive and horrible than the previous one, until humankind finally realized they were close to the destruction of their own species, and perhaps Earth, itself.

World War III was not begun by one country attacking another, as in the previous two world wars, but by acts of terrorism. Radical atheistic anarchists, called the Offenders, activated their long-held plans to overthrow all governments by using traditional weaponry and crudely-fashioned nuclear devices known as "dirty bombs," to blow up government buildings, churches, mosques, synagogues, and population centers, killing millions of citizens, and blaming religious zealots for the carnage. These previously unknown terrorists, seeking to overthrow all governments and abolish all religion, were highly organized and well-funded, living in many countries all over the world. Their goal was to coerce the most developed nations to destroy one another, then step in and take control of their governments, while eradicating all religions.

Many of the capitals of the New Millennium were destroyed or left uninhabitable for over a hundred years because of radiation: London, Washington D.C., Moscow, Mumbai, Tokyo, and Paris were bombed by these Offender terrorists. The Offenders proudly claimed their victories with obscene revelry, and live displays of the torture and murder of men, women and children, via the world's public news systems and internet. They outraged the peoples of the Earth to action.

The great powers of the Earth, Russia and United States of America, united together in military campaigns to eradicate the government leaders of countries who openly sponsored the Offenders anarchist terrorists. China was finally pulled into the chaos when Hong Kong was devastated by dirty bombs; and Shanghai damaged, as well. No mercy was shown to the Offenders fighters, and no quarter given governmental officials from their supporting countries. The fighting continued on every land, on every sea, and in the air, for more than twelve years.

On every continent, armies, militias, and common people fought the Offenders terrorists and their sympathizers, until they were driven out or killed. The Offenders claimed responsibility for the destruction of Vatican City, Jerusalem, Mecca and Medina; all were completely destroyed by dirty nuclear bombs.

The ultimate destruction of the Middle Eastern region was so complete, and the loss of life so great, there were few survivors. The fires from the burning oil fields sent smoke and soot into the atmosphere for two decades, until they finally burned out. It took more than twenty years for the air to clear around Earth from the burning oil's smoke and pollution. More than three billion lives were lost in World War III, and the peoples of the Earth decided there would never again be a war amongst themselves.

This horrible war ended, not with celebrations and parades, but with starvation, radiation sickness, and myriad viruses and plagues affecting millions of the survivors. Nearly another billion people died in the twenty years after the war ended. The leaders of the greatest nations of Earth joined together and formed the United Republics of Earth. One nation, one government, one people, united in peace and equality for all citizens. No one leader ruled the Earth, but a High Council of eleven members. All civilian medical professions and medical services came under URE governmental control, for treatment of the survivors, and the best allocation of resources. The URE utilized remaining military forces for protection and control of land still usable for agriculture, and all fresh water supplies.

Every able-bodied man and woman was called to work, according to their ability, training and education. Those with business experience were placed into jobs within either the vast government, or in the six large corporations that survived the war, and were given URE approval to continue to operate: Sony General Electric; ALB (Aventis Lilly Bayer) Pharmaceutical; Coca Cola; Nestles; Toyota; and InBev. Ten unions were formed under the URE charter for the trade workers. The armies of all former countries were combined together to form the URE Army; all navies were now URE Naval Forces; and all air forces became the URE Air Force, and the elite Space Forces. The United States Marines and the Royal Marines of the United Kingdom became the Space Marines.

Under URE law, every man and woman were equal, deserving of work, justice, protection, and fair treatment. Worship of God was encouraged, and local churches, mosques, synagogues and temples soon sprang up to meet the survivors' spiritual needs. Everyone had a basic education provided, and individual testing provided the means to select those with above-average abilities for higher education. All health care was free, all transportation necessary for work was free, and all workers had free basic housing, according to their job. Private individuals could own property and homes, but the taxes were very high, and no mortgage was ever offered.

Many of the natural resources of Earth were either partially or completely destroyed in World War III. The ravaged fields of the Middle East would not produce a crop for over one hundred years. Fortunately, the great plains of the States Region, the Russian Region, and the Argentine Region, continued to produce the finest grains for food. The Asian Region continued to produce rice and soybeans. The oceans produced fish, and seaweed. The people could eat. However, the oil from the Middle East was gone, and the energy catastrophe many prophesized for decades had arrived. Transportation by automobiles and long-haul trucks was impossible, and those vehicles fell prey to the crusher. The railroads and electric-powered transportation were packed with people, trying to get to work and to food distribution centers, twenty-four hours a day. People were forced to walk or bicycle every day to survive. Suburban communities grew into small towns, ringing the larger cities. The first fifty or more years after World War III were a struggle to survive.

The mining of metals and minerals was, like all natural resource-related industry, taken over by the URE. Human power had to take over for years in the mines, until the machinery could be replaced by equipment that did not require fossil fuel to function. The power grids of the URE were eventually converted to hydrogen fuel cells, in addition to solar and wind power, over the subsequent decades.

The URE established the Metals, Mining, and Exploration Division approximately sixty years after the end of World War III. New sources for raw ore to produce refined metals were required, since most of Earth's mines were closed from over-production. It was decided to harvest asteroids from space to obtain the necessary iron and other metals for building materials, and ships were built at the enlarged space stations in orbit around Earth to make the long journey.

For the first few mining missions, asteroids from the asteroid belt in our own solar system were used, but scientific research came to prove that the delicate balance in our solar system of orbiting planets and their moons might become adversely affected by further disturbance of the asteroid belt. The mining journeys eventually went further out, into deep space.

Space stations for shipbuilding were constructed between the moon and Mars, and colonies on Mars were established under a plex-dome to house their engineers, workers, and support communities. Mars Colony III grew into a highly desirable place to live, and the largest colony off-Earth for the URE. After over 250 years of mining missions in space, the mining freighter ships grew into massive ships, combining the bridge and engineering sections of military cargo freighters with humongous refineries and harvester bays. Hundreds of trained miners and technicians were required to operate the harvester and crushers at the end of the ships, while the refineries in the center of the vessels smelted the crushed asteroids all the way back to Earth.

There have always been special elite units of highly trained personnel within the ranks of the military who exhibit superior talent and ability, and perform dangerous or seemingly impossible tasks with excellence. The Praetorian Guard of Rome; Assassins of the Ottoman Empire; United States' Delta Force, Green Berets, and Navy SEALS, to name a few. The elite fighting men and women of the URE military forces were the Space Marines, tasked with being the first line of defense and the first responders, and were stationed on every military base and space station. Only the best within the Space Marines could qualify as a Prime Marine, the most highly trained military personnel in the entire URE, a coveted achievement.

After successfully completing the harsh, extreme, and rigid training qualifying for the Prime Marines required, the graduated Prime Marines were bio-enhanced for superior strength and endurance, and their natural eyes replaced with bionic eyes that could see in both light and dark conditions. Their other senses were enhanced, as well, with spinal and brain implants. They became masters of every form of martial arts and weapons usage, and their way was the way of the warrior. They were the most respected members of the military forces. This series introduces the reader to Staff Sergeant John Mason, Prime Marine, of the Space Marines.

I

The day was dawning over the California coast; the sun's light illuminating the water of the deep Pacific. The deep azure began to come into view, teasing the eyes and senses with all its beckoning glory. Nowhere in the quadrant was there any sight as beautiful as the Earth, with her blues and swirling clouds. As the ship flew farther and farther away from Earth and Moon Base, John Mason became lonesome for his birthplace, knowing that it would be seven years before he would see Earth again. But before he let that emotion fill him, and grab hold of his heart, he stiffened his back, and told himself to keep the memory, and ditch the feeling. No time for that here, no place for self-indulgence. He had to have his wits about him, and engage his senses in the tasks at hand.

He had been assigned to the mining freighter "Hesperia," as Special Security Chief. She had a mixed crew of 800: military officers and crew manning the bridge and engineering; medical officers, nurses and med tech staff; other assorted officers and crew assigned throughout the ship; totaling 200 Space Forces members. Also on board were the United Republics of Earth Mining Minerals and Exploration civilian research scientists for research projects to be carried out during the long haul; a few civilians, for the limited number of company stores on board; and miners, for the real dirty work. The miners were all union members working under contract for the seven-year flight duration, with little or no education or training in ships' flight techniques or engineering. They knew mining operations, mining machine maintenance, and all that those duties entailed. They also knew that, once the ship was outside the solar system patrols, they outnumbered the rest of the crew three to one, and ruled the roost.

Six months ago, the Excelon, the last mining freighter returning from a deep space mission suffered mutiny by the miners, who slaughtered the entire crew, except for those officers absolutely necessary for ship's flight.

They held out near Titan One, until their demands for a tripling of their contract payouts, and a get-away ship, were met. Although they were eventually caught and punished, their notoriety quickly circulated through the entire solar system. There had never been an uprising on a mining freighter before this event. The high cost of lives and lost materials demanded that no such occurrence take place ever again. The URE would not tolerate another disaster of that magnitude. This mission must be successful.

Lessons learned from that ill-fated flight were applied on Mason's ship. The miners were a necessary evil, not to be trusted. A full contingent of thirty-two Space Marines was assigned to the Hesperia, including Staff Sergeant John Mason, Prime Marine. He reported only to Captain Kouras, the ship's captain, and Executive Officer (XO), Commander Baines. The Space Marines were stationed on the bridge, in engineering, in the hospital, mess halls, and even the lounges. Fully armed and resolute, the Marines were determined to have a safe flight, with no crew casualties.

John Mason joined the Space Marines at seventeen, and had advanced his career at a quick pace. He qualified for the Prime Marines at 20. The Prime Marines were the best of the best, the top caliber Space Marines, trained to master every known martial art, proficient with every weapon, mentally and physically superior. They were specifically bio-modified for deep space missions, capable of enduring extreme periods of solitude, cold, and confinement that drove most men insane. They could survive on minimal rations three times longer than an average man. Few wanted to apply for their ranks, for the billets were usually long, top secret assignments, no frills. Yet, a Prime Marine, whatever his or her rank, was the most highly regarded of all service members. Their life was the "way of the warrior." Every service specialty was minimum requirement for completing their training, whether it was sharp-shooting, piloting various spacecraft and aircraft, high altitude jumping and insertion behind enemy lines, diffusing bombs, deep sea diving, or deep space missions. Every ship's captain asked for a Prime Marine for bridge duty; few requests were honored. Staff Sergeant John Mason was the bridge Special Security Chief for the Hesperia, and her bridge crew knew they were safer with him in their midst.

Mason spent one very full month preparing for this journey, studying the technical diagrams of the Hesperia. She was a standard mining freighter class vessel, designed for deep space mining and refining, and specially modified for this mission. Only the garbage haulers were uglier, Mason thought, when he first saw her docked. The mining freighters were the largest ships in the URE fleet, built exclusively for work and service, with few human comforts provided.

She was made of four main sections. The bow contained self-defense weapons, shields, cargo storage and shuttle bays; followed by the engineering decks; nine decks of crew quarters, hospital, science labs, gyms, kitchens and mess halls; the bridge and communications towers rose from the top. Her mid-section was for refined metals storage. The last two sections were three times the height and twice the width of the first two. The center section was the furnaces and refinery, "Hell," the miners called it. The stern section was the largest, where the giant arms and claws of the monster gathered and stored raw materials, for crushing and preparation for the refinery. The Hesperia was truly a magnificent beast, and Mason studied her until he could traverse the entire ship, stem to stern, by lifts, ladders, or service tubes.

She had something no other mining freighter could boast of before her recent outfitting; she had a full armory, defensive as well as offensive weapons, and Space Marines who knew how to use them. Mason was disappointed there were none of the big battle droids for defense, or any of the larger weapons he was used to using. Most of the weapons were laser rifles and side arms, along with an assortment of flasher sets, incendiaries and other smaller arms. At least they had hand shields, metal sticks eight centimeters long that would form a full body shield against laser blasts at the touch of a button.

The seven year mission required seventeen months' travel from Space Station Ten, the "Last Stop." It was the last outpost before deep space. All ships must stop there for final checks, refueling, restocking, and personnel changes. If an error had been made in rations, life support, water, fuel, or crew, too bad. Too late, for many ships. The majority of the crew, and all but a handful of the miners' supervisors were placed in cryonic hibernation before the Hesperia reached Titan One.

After SS10, all remaining crew and personnel would be in cryonic hibernation for seventeen months, monitored by the life support computers. They would arrive at the hunting area, where the dead planets and asteroids floated, devoid of any life, or light. That would be their hunting grounds for four years, harvesting asteroids and chunks of space rocks for their minerals. This region was determined to have asteroids containing not only iron and gold, but also titanium. The research vessels which first discovered this region also detected traces of platinum, and other metals not disclosed to him, trace metals for scientific research. They would gather as much material as the ship could hold, and refine it all the way back to Earth. They would be put back into cryo-hybernation for the last twelve months, and be awakened two months before returning home. That was the plan.

The Hesperia moved slowly at half-standard speed, on trajectory towards the outer rim of the solar system and the heliosphere, passing Mars and the colonies established there, where Mason's remaining family now lived. He watched the red planet in the distance, and determined to see his sister and her family again, one day. His memory of her was interrupted by a call from Captain Kouras, "Marine!"

"Staff Sergeant Mason reporting, sir," he said.

"Yes, Mason, listen up now. We will be stopping over on Titan One briefly to pick up the last containers of equipment for the research staff in two days. No one gets off this ship, understood? When we reach Space Station 10, you will supervise disembarkation and re-boarding of personnel. We don't want any new miners getting on board, is that clear? No substitutes, no more union reps. No one gets on board this flight who did not initially get checked out through Earth security and begin this mission, is that clear?"

"Sir, yes sir. Perfectly clear. No surprises," Mason replied. He stood his watch, observing everyone and everything, silently, mentally noting details of the bridge crew and their actions. He did not smile; he did not show any emotion at all. They were all under his protection. The crew was an efficient team of seasoned professionals, except for young Lieutenant Urz, the communications officer. Mason could smell fear in him, the kind of fear that might cause bad decisions at the wrong time in panic situations. He would keep an eye on him, to detect any flaws, errors, or even the potential for covering up any mistakes. Deep space affected some men severely, and he was going to ascertain Lieutenant Urz's condition at regular intervals, even more so than the rest of the crew.

The Hesperia docked alongside the space station, and locked down, connected to its life support transport tubes. Amazing how a ship the size of a small town could be maneuvered so effortlessly. Such a graceful effort for a behemoth this ugly. Mason was amazed at the crew's handling of the Hesperia as she docked at Space Station 10. That ship was humongous, yet they docked her like a shuttle, smooth as silk. Nice to be among the pros, Mason mused. It was on SS10 that the mutinied freighter unknowingly picked up several "union reps," men who were not on the pre-approved roster of miners originally assigned to make that voyage. It was discovered by the investigating URE authorities that they were the instigators of the mutiny that cost so many lives, and not union men. SS10 crews were on the alert now, as were the captain and crew of the Hesperia. When the ship approached SS10, Captain Kouras announced:

"All hands now hear this. For security reasons, all personnel requesting leave on Space Station 10 must submit their requests in writing to ship security by ten-hundred the day prior to docking. Due to time constraints, all personnel leaving the ship for Space Station 10 will be limited to eight hours' leave, and will not be permitted to bring onboard the Hesperia any packages, containers, luggage, or other equipment or personal items purchased or picked up on SS10. All returning personnel must be willing to submit to full body searches, if requested, upon re-entering the Hesperia. There will be no exceptions to this order. Captain Kouras out." Mason heard the chorus of responses to this announcement from the ship's communications console, and young Lt. Urz struggled to handle the numerous incoming calls. The guy can't handle a couple of whiners. What will he do if things get rough? Mason made a mental note of the Lieutenant's actions. If unable to help him should a situation arise, Mason would render him unconscious, to protect the rest of the crew, as well as Lieutenant Urz.

Everyone on board the Hesperia felt the need to get off the ship one last time before leaving the solar system, of course. Thank God they went and returned in shifts, else tracking them on such a big station would have been too time-consuming. After supervising the disembarkation of the personnel for their last "hurrah," Mason over saw the refueling of the Hesperia. The new fuel cells were trucked on board, and the depleted ones returned, back and forth, until the storage areas were fully stocked. They had enough fuel cells for eight years, Mason noted, not just seven. This made him wonder at the rationale of this action. It was not the usual procedure to overstock fuel cells for a full year, even for a mission this long. He personally inspected the water stores, to make doubly sure they had plenty for the trip. The water treatment plant onboard was working perfectly, but since water was vital to all their survival, Mason left no questions unanswered about its proper storage, and quantity.

Mason chose to visit the space station for only four hours, just enough time to send off a message home, and get some food from the best restaurant he could find. The restaurant he picked had real beer and wine, for an inflated price, of course. There were no real alcoholic beverages served on the Hesperia, so he wanted a real beer now, even if it did cost more than his meal. The waiter offered packaged liquor to him to take back to the ship, but he knew that no packages would be allowed back onboard. Too bad. Mason wondered if the Captain had his own stash in his private quarters. He ate every bit of food on his plate, and every crumb of bread and butter, like it was his last meal. After washing the meal down with another beer, he paid his tab, and headed out to check out the stores. Nothing to spend his money on here, just the usual tourist crap sold in every space station. He headed back to the ship early.

He was just in time to break up a minor altercation between miners and security personnel, arguing about bringing onboard cases of beer they had just purchased. "No packages of any kind. You heard the Captain. Leave them over there," the corporal told them. There was a huge stack of beer and liquor cases growing in the corner. They spent their hard-earned money on booze they were not allowed to bring on board, and the miners did not like it one bit. Mason bulled his way through the rough crowd to the security desk, asking, "Do you have a problem, Corporal Johnson?"

"No, Staff Sergeant, no problem at all. We were just explaining to these men that they could not bring these cases of liquor on board the Hesperia." A lot of shouting soon erupted, and Mason turned to the growing crowd, quickly raising and arming his laser rifle.

"You all have exactly one-half hour to return these cases of liquor to wherever they were purchased, and get your money back, before the Hesperia prepares for final roll call. Any packages not returned must be left here. They will not be allowed on board. Is this clear? Do it!" Mason's last words were shouted at the crowd, and had the intended effect of quieting them down. Most just grumbled their way through the security line, while some grabbed their liquor and headed back down the hall to try for a refund. Another potentially physical situation averted, Mason thought. Another fight won before it began. He hoped all their situations would be that way, but experience taught him to be prepared for other outcomes.

Their implanted identification bugs made re-boarding fairly simple. Mason and Space Marine security details conducted unannounced neck inspections at re-entry stations, looking for any new marks where someone might have tried to get a new ID bug implanted to gain access to the ship. The necks of all the miners were checked for security. That made for a slower process, but the captain appreciated Mason's thoroughness.

Two hours later, all personnel were back on board, and the Hesperia was ready for release of the docking gear. After successful release, the ship rotated towards her planned course in the blackness, and slowly maneuvered forward. Less than one hour later, XO Baines announced everyone was to prepare for hyper-drive, and they were off, streaking through space.

Mason went to check the capsules containing the majority of the 800 people, kept in a state of cryonic hibernation for seventeen months. Some deep space crews had to "cryo-sleep" for years. The longest he had been in cryo-sleep was fourteen months, and he did not like it at all. Handing over his life functions to computers never sat well with him, or his stomach. This time, four corpsmen and three science droids would stay awake, watching over the sleepers.

Last minute cleaning and preparations took place quickly over the next couple of days. Unlike former freighters, the Hesperia featured separate areas for cryo-hybernation for different personnel. Miners were the first to be put into their capsules on Section 2, in the huge hall below their sleeping quarters. The remaining crew began their own cryo-hybernation process in their respective areas. The bridge officers' capsules were in the primary hibernation room, directly off the bridge, for quick access in any urgent situation. The Space Marines had their own area, and their capsules were mounted directly in the walls, in special compartments containing eight capsules each. The final life support and cryo-hybernation checks were completed, by Captain Kouras. Finally, it was the bridge officers' turn to get into their capsules. The corpsman helped him get his heavy, muscular frame into the tight capsule. Mason folded his hands across his body, and felt the gases enter; relaxing his muscles and mind, and went to sleep. Then he was gone, like all the rest, into the abyss.

II

"Wake up, Mason!" Captain Kouras ordered.

"Mason, wake up! Please wake up!" Commander Baines cried.

"Why isn't he waking up? Mason, we need you NOW! Wake up!" Captain Kouras yelled.

The alert sirens were shrieking and whooping, as the blackness began to part into the light. "Staff Sergeant Mason, wake up! That's an order! Wake up! Mason, Mason, I order you to wake up now! Staff Sergeant, wake...there he is! Mason!" Commander Baines was nearly frantic.

John Mason opened his eyes to the flashing red light, quickly blinking away the blackness of his cryo-sleep. "What? What's going on? I'm here." He sat up too abruptly, and got immediately dizzy, feeling the all-too-familiar wooziness, and leaned over just in time to vomit on the floor, several times.

"Good God, man, this is no time to puke! We're in an emergency here! Mason! Oh crap, he hit my pants! Mason, stop that and get up now!" The XO was yelling at the top of his voice. They helped him out of the cryo-cocoon, and stood him up, slowly. "OK, now, big guy, snap to. That's it, get yourself pulled together. There's a serious situation going on here. You with us now, Staff Sergeant?"

"Sir, yes sir! Staff Sergeant John Mason at your serv..." Mason mumbled, and then passed out. He lay like a rag doll in the arms of Commander Baines and Captain Kouras. They laid him on the floor until the corpsman came over and gave him an injection of stimulants. Mason blinked and rolled his head side to side, as they scanned him electronically with the hand-held medical scanner.

"Captain, he's loaded with opiated sleep inducers. He is not able to fully gain consciousness and awareness in this state. We've got to get him to the hospital and transfuse him immediately, or he'll fall right back into deep sleep," the corpsman said. Several crewmen picked up Mason's limp, large frame, got him onto the anti-gravity gurney, and he was taken as quickly as possible to the hospital down the lift and through the corridor.

Captain Kouras bellowed out, "I want that Prime Marine fully functional and on the bridge in the shortest time possible, do you understand? Baines, come with me now, and let the Doctor bring him out of this. I want to know why he was loaded with sleep inducers. This voyage cryo time was not long enough for sleep inducers. I want answers. We need that man now!" He broke into a run towards the lift, with the XO and two security officers trailing behind him.

In the hospital, the nurses and corpsmen lifted Mason off the anti-gravity gurney onto the scan table, and started the IV on him. The analysis screens showed five times a normal dose of sleep inducers still present in his system. "Why was he given sleep inducers for only seventeen months' cryo time? He shouldn't have had any! Doctor, we need to start the transfusion now," Nurse Cohen urged.

"Go ahead, but draw blood for analysis first, and monitor him closely, Nurse Cohen. Start the drug neutralizer and plasma now. Get those drugs out of his system." Doctor Hassan leaned over Mason, looked up at the analysis screens again, and asked, "Corpsman, were any other crew members showing signs of sleep inducing medication?"

"No Dr. Hassan, only Staff Sergeant Mason. No one else, sir. Everyone else woke up normally, alert and responsive," the corpsman stated. "I wonder why him? Why was he dosed?"

"Why him, indeed. Corpsman, notify Captain Kouras of his condition, and that we will expedite his recovery as soon as medically possible. Also, advise the Captain that I recommend Mason's cryo-cocoon be isolated until it can be fully examined by security and myself. It should not be touched by anyone, is that clear?" Doctor Hassan ordered. He inspected the IV and new blood flowing from the packets into Mason's vein. He read the handheld scanner's information, and said to Nurse Cohen, "I want a complete analysis on the blood drawn from this man prior to transfusion, stat. The Captain will need to know everything we can give him about the patient's condition, and he'll want it as soon as we can get it analyzed. Let's not waste any time getting him up and moving."

Mason was in the field playing with his dog, when he heard, "Mason, can you hear me? Can you hear me Staff Sergeant? I think he's beginning to come around, Doctor. Mason? John? There you are, come on now," Nurse Cohen said with a soft, concerned voice. Mason suddenly felt the dreamed grassy field morph into light, bright light, and then saw the lovely face of his Nurse.

"Hi, I'm John. Where am I? Oh, you are so beautiful!" The Nurse blushed immediately, and began talking Mason back to reality, gently, slowly, "OK, Staff Sergeant John Mason, you are here on board the Hesperia. Doctor Hassan and I have been very worried about you. Come back to me, John. Come on back to me. We are in danger, and we need our Prime Marine to protect us now, more than ever. Are you with us, Staff Sergeant?" As Mason started coming back to the real time, real place, real life, he jerked his torso straight up, looked around at the staff, and noticed the IV dripping new, pure plasma-enriched blood into his vein.

"What's going on here? What is happening to me?" He reached for the IV, but his hand was stopped by Dr. Hassan. Mason was slowly achieving full consciousness. "Can you tell me what's happening, Doctor?"

"Staff Sergeant Mason, the ship's computers woke up the primary bridge and life support crews, because of some emergency. Everyone awoke normally, except you. It appears you were given sleep inducers prior to or during cryo-sleep. Do you remember anything? Did you dose yourself?"

"Emergency? What is happening to the ship? Is everyone all right? I have to report to the XO and Captain Kouras immediately." He stood and turned to face the Doctor, and stated, "No, sir, I did not dose myself. Why would I jeopardize my career for mere drugs?" Then, with more volume and emphasis in his tone, Mason said, "Would someone get me out of this rig so I can report to the Captain?"

Doctor Hassan said, "Stop the transfusion, Nurse Cohen, our Staff Sergeant is in a hurry, so pull out the IV, and let this man go." Nurse Cohen did as she was instructed, and stood back out of Mason's way, as he bolted to the lift.

"Staff Sergeant Mason reporting as ordered, sir."

"'Bout time, Mason. We're in an emergency situation here. Lieutenant Davis, report your findings to the Staff Sergeant," the Captain ordered, turning his attention back to the tactical screens at the back of the bridge.

Lieutenant Davis proceeded to update Mason on their findings, scant as they were. "The computer detected an anomaly within scanner range in the dark sector, fully armed with nuclear and long-range particle beam capabilities, on course to intercept the Hesperia in six hours. It seems to have just popped up on the screens, out of nowhere. Its shape, size, intentions all unknown. No other craft have ever been reported in this sector by our buoys. Except our mining freighters, of course. Captain has ordered probes sent out to investigate the anomaly. We are on red alert. Communications dispatched to URE command and SS10. No reply yet. The ship's bridge and medical crews and security forces have been awakened, just two months into our voyage. We came out of hyper-space, and are now at quarter-standard speed."

"Miners still in stasis? What about the research teams, sir?" Mason enquired.

"Both still in cryo-sleep. Only the medical, life support, and military crews activated, Staff Sergeant," the Lieutenant replied.

Mason surveyed the bridge personnel to assess their mental, physical, and emotional states. The heightened tension ran through the bridge, but everyone was on task. He remembered his mental notes on Lieutenant Urz, and looked toward the communications station. The officer was in control, checking all channels for incoming messages, from SS10, Earth Command, or one of the probes.

Captain Kouras returned to his chair, determined to discover what or who was threatening his ship. "Engineering, this is the Captain. I want all defensive systems fully functional, and all shields at full capacity. Acknowledge."

"Engineering to Captain Kouras, all defensive systems fully armed and at the ready, sir. Shields at full power. Awaiting further orders, sir." The voice belonged to Lt. Commander Powers, a twenty-year man with no sense of humor. Short on speak, long on action, Mason mused. Perfect.

The probes suddenly started signaling their beeps and blips to the communications and tactical consoles, and Captain Kouras spun around and jumped out of his chair, bolting to see what was coming in. Suddenly, the brightest flash of light Mason had ever seen blinded him for a split second, as the first of the probes exploded. "All hands, battle stations!" Captain Kouras commanded, getting back into his chair. One by one, the probes exploded, by means unknown. No weapons appeared to have been fired from the anomaly. It remained invisible, hidden, lurking just out of sight, menacing.

"What is it, Captain? Do we know if it's a ship, or a battle station, or an inhabited asteroid, sir?" Mason asked.

"Unknown," Captain Kouras quietly said. "All we know is that it's armed to the teeth, it's invisible, and it doesn't like our probes."

For the next few minutes, the crew was silent, listening, watching, at the ready. An orange-green cloud slowly formed on the distance, as the alarms went off again. "Red Alert! Warning! Unidentified intruder alert! All hands. Red alert!" The computer voice announced, followed by sirens and flashing strobe lights.

"Cut that off now! I want total silence!" Captain Kouras demanded. He sat straight up, forward, straining for any movement, any sound, anything...

The cloud undulated for a minute, then retreated into the blackness, as silently and slowly as it appeared, swirling in orange-green and yellow colors. "All clear," the computer said, in a calm, hollow, electronic voice. "Stand down. All clear."

"Go to yellow alert, and give me some goddamn answers!" Captain Kouras ordered, leaving his chair. He got into the lift and left the bridge. Mason stayed at his post, ever at the ready. He wasn't standing down. Not until the Captain ordered. He looked at the bridge officers, and not one of them had relaxed.

What was hiding behind that orange-green cloud? That cloud looked like the sick color of the clouds of chemicals exploding in the old World War III films, billowing and expanding over the troops, choking unprotected noncombatants and soldiers alike. It moved like Death itself, coming out of nowhere, forming its undulating shapes, and then withdrawing. Was this a warning to not advance the Hesperia any further? Why did it destroy the unarmed probes? If there were intelligent life forms doing these maneuvers, why didn't they communicate with our ship? Or, was the cloud formation itself the communication it sent? Mason's mind was full of questions, just like the rest of the crew.

A real 'riddle inside an enigma,' or whatever that old saying was. Whatever it was or is, Mason knew his job was to protect the bridge crew. Against any threat, real, perceived, or otherwise. His laser rifle rested lightly in his arms, safety off. What good was a laser rifle against something that could make itself appear from the deep emptiness of space, form into a cloud, then disappear, as silently as it had come into being? He remained for hours, until the XO ordered him relieved by a full security detail.

"Staff Sergeant Mason, you are relieved. Report back to the hospital for further testing. And get some sleep in your quarters tonight." The XO, Commander Baines, looked tired, as did the entire bridge crew. Mason was surprised to find the Captain in the hospital. Doctor Hassan, Captain Kouras, and two security crew members were inspecting a cryogenic capsule, a "cryo-cocoon," to the crew. Mason's name was on the nameplate.

"Ah Mason, glad you've come. Look at this, would you? Nothing out of the ordinary, at first glance. But what's this tiny blue tube, here, above the hatch lid, by the cranial rest? See it? We are testing it for foreign substances. I think it's how you received those opiated sleep inducers, through the blue tube, next to your nose." Doctor Hassan was visibly excited to have discovered his "culprit."

Captain Kouras noted, "This tube is not present in any of the other cocoons we observed, and all were checked. Only yours, Mason. Someone did not want you to wake up for a long time, Prime Marine."

"And, if he had not been bio-altered for deep space, Mason would most likely have never been resuscitated. Whoever did this did not do his or her homework properly, or you'd be dead now," the Doctor offered, matter-of-factly. "You're a very lucky man, Mason."

"My grandmother always said it's better to be lucky than smart, Doctor. Guess that she was right, this time," said Mason, looking around the room, suspecting everyone. Everyone, except Nurse Cohen. She was over in the opposite side of the room, tending gently to a crewman's bandaged arm. She looked over at him, and smiled. Aw shit, Mason thought, why did she have to do that? Why'd she have to smile like that? She was so beautiful, and kind to him. She was the only female on this crate to notice him, to give him the smallest kindness, to care whether he was dead or alive.

"I don't know anything about luck, but I know the fact is, Mason, with you having survived this dosing, you'd do well to assume that another attempt may be made on your life. I think that we'd better work together to determine the reason for that unsuccessful attempt on your life. I'm not certain it was related to our discovery of the anomaly, but it cannot be ruled out. Better watch your back, Staff Sergeant," the Captain warned. "I can't afford to lose my only Prime Marine. I want any and every suspicious activity reported to me or the XO immediately, is that clear? Any evidence you or the security team discover, I want to know."

Mason nodded and said, "Sir, yes sir. I will immediately report any findings to you or the XO." The Captain left the hospital. Mason stared into the cocoon where he trustingly laid down only two months ago. Never again. He'd check out those puppies' internal components completely before getting back inside, you better believe it.

Mason completed his full blood transfusion with one of the corpsmen. He was disappointed that Nurse Cohen wasn't in the room to talk with him. He had to admit, she was one fine looking woman. Red hair, gray-green eyes, fine, full figure. And she smiled at him. Did she just feel sorry for him? Who cares why, Mason admitted to himself; she helped him come back to the land of the living. She actually cared, at least for a moment, whether he lived or died. Too bad she was an officer.

Activity to identify and analyze the anomaly continued for the next several weeks. Mason never got used to the scientific lingo, but he was very aware of tactical interpretations of the data. The Hesperia resumed hyper-speed on orange alert as she continued on her course in that sector. It would be a long cruise, having been in cryo-sleep for only two months, instead of the planned seventeen months. Some crew members were placed back into their cryo-cocoons, to preserve food, water, and life support, for the rest of the planned sleep time. The little probes did manage to send over some data before being blown to bits and that data was analyzed nine ways to Sunday. The crux of the matter was that they could no longer afford to assume the Hesperia was alone in the sector. They were most likely being shadowed by the mysterious cloud anomaly, and the crew could not indulge themselves with a false sense of security. Mason had to be watchful for the crew, as well as for himself.

The big ship felt suddenly very foreign. He no longer felt safe or comfortable in any part of the ship. They were a huge, streaking target, on course to the mining fields. Mason knew they were being followed by something or someone, whose intentions were entirely unknown. His battle-tested instincts never steered him wrong. He slept in his bunk-drawer fully clothed in his uniform, boots and all, rifle at the ready, in his arms. His side-arms and weapons belt were rolled around his left arm for quick access. He checked his quarters thoroughly every night, inspecting every centimeter of space. He left nothing to chance, and took nothing for granted.

After a few weeks, the ship stood down from yellow alert. But the only person onboard Mason relaxed even a little with was Nurse Cohen. She accepted Mason's offer to share dinner in the enlisted personnel's mess hall one night, a food rations dinner consisting of three different colors of food paste in tubes. How romantic. They laughed at their situation, dining with food tubes, with several security officers watching. She was so genuine and friendly, so relaxed, and so disinterested in the food fare. It did not matter what or where they ate, as long as they had each other for company. Mason wanted to spend as much time with her as possible, but he was cautious. If someone really was out to get him, they might try to hurt her, as well. He let her know his concern, and they agreed to briefly see each other on rare occasions, to be safe. He ordered a security team to inspect her quarters, and the living quarters of Doctor Hassan. No such thing as too much caution to protect his friends.

III

Dr. Mohammed Hassan, Chief Medical Officer of the Hesperia, had been a good surgeon his entire career. He joined the URE Space Forces after graduation from Stanford Medical School to follow in his father's footsteps, and care for those who serve.

His career already spanned over two decades before accepting this post. Earth Command recommended him for this mission because of his exemplary record serving aboard deep space missions, with combined military and mixed crews. He was outgoing and friendly, and well-liked by most of his patients. The rank of his patients was of little consequence to Dr. Hassan; he treated everyone with care and expertise, and their health was all that mattered to him. You couldn't see any stars or bars under the surgery sheets.

The matter of Staff Sergeant Mason's drugging with opiated sleep inducers posed a real challenge for him. He was determined to solve this mystery, by himself, if necessary, and discover who the attempted murderer was, before he or she managed to accomplish the deed the next time.

Every centimeter of Mason's cryonic capsule was examined, scanned, analyzed, and tested for DNA, without a trace of evidence as to who the perpetrator could be. No information on who planted the blue tube into the capsule, with its tiny pressurized gas canister so skillfully mounted inside the lid that it went unnoticed through all inspections. There was enough opiated sleep inducers passed into Mason's lungs to kill an average man, but that Prime Marine was anything but average.

John Mason stood a full head taller than Dr. Hassan, who was no small man himself. His med files showed he scored off the charts during his pre-mission physical, and his body fat was less than 4%. Mason had bio-enhanced skeletal and muscular abilities. He could even see in the dark with his special bionic eyes. Those Prime Marines were given every physical enhancement available, including plasma-enriched blood, which gradually increased their overall strength, ability to heal, and tolerance for enduring pain. His brain implants were primarily sensory-enhancing. He had the best instincts of any two-legged creature on Earth, with hearing and sense of smell nearly as good as a dog. Dr. Hassan wanted to not only discover the perpetrator of this offense; he wanted to catch him first, before Mason got hold of him. He needed to know how and why. Mason just wanted to kill him. The race was on.

The cryonic capsules were of standard manufacture, delivered to the Hesperia during the four months of special outfitting for her current mission, on Moon Base. All capsules were inspected and tested on Moon Base by the cryonics teams, and had to have passed 100% before being loaded on board. Each capsule was identical to all the others, and weren't assigned to any specific deck or crew until the Hesperia left Moon Base. There was no way any tampering took place before the ship left on her mission, since the assigned location of any one capsule or its eventual occupant was unknown. Even the nameplates were not affixed to the capsule's lid until departure. It had to have been someone on board the Hesperia.

Dr. Hassan thought the best time and place to tamper with Mason's capsule would have been during the visit to Space Station 10. With so many coming and going, it may have been a good time to implant the little blue tube and mini-canister into Mason's capsule, stored inside the room next to the bridge. The only access to that room was from the bridge, or from the emergency crawl way. The bridge was never totally unmanned, so that meant that either a bridge crewman was responsible, or some agile person crawled up the emergency ladder from one of the decks or cargo holds below.

Lieutenant Davis had command of the bridge for the midnight watch, until he was abruptly interrupted by Commander Baines. "Lieutenant Davis, you are relieved. Meet up with Staff Sergeant Mason in engineering for a security check on sections one and two. I want a complete analysis of all primary areas, with special details reported of the status of our water and food supplies."

Mason was discussing the possibilities of breaching the engineering decks with Lt. Commander Powers, as Lieutenant Davis got off the lift in main engineering. "Lt. Commander, I am certain that, on your watch, no one has ever gained access to engineering without your approval. I meant no disrespect, sir. But, sir, it is my job to keep this ship secure. I am requesting permission to attempt to breach your engineering security, and take command of ship's systems, in order to discover any weakness the designers of this ship may have overlooked. You are aware that the mutiny on the last mining freighter began in engineering, Lt. Commander. We don't want that to happen here, sir." Mason was not making any friends in engineering now. The engineering room crew members were listening to every word of this conversation.

"Go ahead and try to breach our security, Staff Sergeant. You won't get within five meters of the main computers, or the engine room," Lt. Commander Powers threatened. This enlisted man was getting on his nerves, now. Inspecting his engine room was one thing, but this was bordering on the ridiculous, a sheer waste of time.

"Lt. Commander, thank you for giving me permission to test the security systems in place on your deck. You will not know the time of my attempted attack, until it has been stopped, or I have taken over ship's computers and the engine room. Only Captain Kouras will know the time," Mason concluded.

That arrogant son-of-a-bitch, Powers thought. "If you have nothing better to do until we reach the hunting area, then be my guest. You will forgive my crew for not cooperating with you, however."

"Understood, Lt. Commander Powers. Thank you, sir." Mason knew the importance of an attempted breach in engineering. Better his security team, with their weapons on stun, than real mutineers. He knew the Lt. Commander would not make it easy, though. Taking over his engineering deck would require more stealth and split-second timing than most breach-tests he had conducted.

"Am I interrupting anything, Lt. Commander Powers? Commander Baines ordered me to meet up with Staff Sergeant Mason and the security team for full systems checks," Lieutenant Davis said. He thoroughly enjoyed what he overheard of their conversation. Not just anyone could get a rise out of Powers, and the man's red face belied his calm demeanor.

"No, you're not interrupting anything important, Lieutenant Davis, carry on." Lt. Commander Powers walked back to his command console, with very deliberate steps. Lieutenant Davis did all he could to keep a smile off his face, until he and Mason got into the lift. "Good job, Mason. Keeping us all on our toes, whether we like it, or not."

Lieutenant Davis and Mason began their security sweep of the areas. Checking out the engineering decks took nearly five hours in itself. They found nothing out of order, and moved on to the food and water stores. Each container and water tank was thoroughly checked. Mason had them check every seam in those tanks; we'll be at this for-ev-er, Davis moaned to himself.

After what seemed an eternity to Lieutenant Davis, the security team checked out the empty mess halls, unused kitchens, and waste disposal areas. All clear. We are on food rations until the mess crews are awakened, Davis noted, why would there be any problem? He was beginning to get frustrated at the Staff Sergeant's diligent inspections of every bloody nook and cranny. Great, we're on to the walk-in freezers now. Maybe he could snatch some ice cream bars…

"Lieutenant Davis, please come here, sir," Corporal Johnson requested.

"Don't tell me you've found a rat turd, Corporal. I couldn't bear any more excitement tonight," the Lieutenant quipped.

"No sir. It looks like a body," the Corporal offered.

"What the… Oh, shit! Mason come look at this!" Lieutenant Davis was wide-awake now. "Do not touch anything, just get in as close as you can, and take video shots of the body to show Commander Baines."

"Lieutenant Davis, I am afraid I do not recognize this man. Do you, sir?" Mason enquired. "He is naked, frozen stiff, and covered in ice particles. I can't tell if he was wounded without moving him, sir."

"Don't touch him, I said. Corporal Johnson, did you get those shots? Then send them to the bridge for further instructions immediately."

The Corporal did as ordered, and then Mason said, "Lieutenant Davis, whoever did this probably assumed this body would not be discovered until the mess crew was awakened, about twelve months from now. Do you agree, sir?"

"Undoubtedly, you're correct. They thought they had a year or more before their criminal act would be uncovered. When was the last time this freezer was inspected, Mason? Do you know?" Lieutenant Davis asked.

"The security log says it was inspected at Titan One, after loading final meat and supplies. It was signed by Chief Dawson, Mess Chief. No other entries since then, Lieutenant Davis."

"Lieutenant Davis, this is Commander Baines. What's going on down there? Where's Mason?" The voice coming over the comm speaker was that of a man who did not want to hear any problems on his watch. "I'm sending the gurney and med team down there, along with Dr. Hassan. I want a complete assessment of this situation."

Mason and the security team cleared away as much of the frozen meat and food as they could, without disturbing what would soon be designated as a crime scene. The video cams hovered above them, taking pictures of everything, and their every move. When Dr. Hassan arrived, red-eyed and wearing a wrinkled lab coat, he and the med team crouched over the body with their scanners, being careful to not touch any part of him. "Male, around 30 to 35, I think. I can't see any wounds yet. There's severe frostbite; be careful not to touch him. His eyes are still open. Who did this to you, my friend?" Doctor Hassan's voice trailed off, as he scanned the body. "The autopsy room is ready, whenever we can take the body to the hospital."

The security team scoured the big freezer for any and all evidence, but it appeared that the body was dumped there after the killing took place. When the dead man's body was eventually put onto the anti-gravity gurney and removed, more forensic work was performed on the surrounding area. The Commander ordered all meat and frozen food kept in quarantine, until the cause of death could be determined. In a few minutes, the body was identified as that of Dr. Richard Reese, one of the research scientists on board the Hesperia. He was supposed to have been in cryonic sleep.

Captain Kouras drank a cup of coffee straight down, trying to jolt himself awake. Commander Baines and Dr. Hassan sat at his table with him, while Mason and the security team four stood at the back of the captain's ready-room. "All right gentlemen; let's hear what we currently know about Dr. Reese. Leave out not a single detail." Lieutenant Davis proceeded to give the details of their discovery, and accompanied his written report with video.

"Dr. Hassan, what do the autopsy findings tell us? What was the cause of death? In plain English, please."

"The cause of death was blunt trauma, a blow to the head. Only one blow, in the right place, with a heavy object leaving an octagonal imprint in the skull, above the right ear." Dr. Hassan spoke very matter-of-factly, continuing on about pooled blood behind the right eye, and so on. "I very much doubt if the man even saw his attacker. It appears to be a blow from behind, from the angle of the skull imprint. The man was completely naked, without any jewelry or wedding ring. He did have some curious tattoos, and I have documented them on this video for you to take a look at."

The tattoos were indeed curious. On his back and shoulders was the head and upper body of some sort of winged reptile, like a dragon, mouth agape, and teeth bared in an attack position. "Dr. Hassan, that looks like a prehistoric raptor to me. What do you make of it?" Mason asked.

"I really can't be certain without seeing the full body. Raptors had a large hooked claw on their feet, and the feet of this creature have not been drawn. Only the upper body and wings, as you can see, Mason." The doctor watched the video for another second or two, and then slowed the playback down. "Look here, on the base of his neck. There are two markings there, like perhaps an etching for a future tattoo or something. Anyone have any idea what that's about?"

"Commander Baines, make sure all this gets sent to URE and Earth Command. They will need to direct us in any further investigation of this matter. Mason, I want your security inspections completed first thing tomorrow. It's late, and we all need some sleep. Nothing further can be done at this point. We will reconvene this inquiry after receiving orders from Earth Command." The Captain stood up, took the video record, and retreated to his quarters.

Mason was not satisfied, however. First his opiate-doping, then the orange cloud, and now, this death. The research staff was there to conduct deep-space experiments on metals, right? Why would someone murder a science geek? Why would a science geek have such intricate, detailed tattoos? Mason was irritated at the preponderance of unanswered questions swarming in his brain. He could not afford to let the investigation of these matters drag on. There was only a few months before the rest of the crew would be awakened from cryo-sleep, and then all the miners, as well. Eight hundred reasons to solve these riddles sooner, rather than later.

Security team four met on the cargo deck to continue their inspections. All cargo containers locks were unbroken, no tampering with their electronic seals. As they moved on to the shuttles stored in their bays, Mason split the team up into parties of two. "These shuttles were locked down on Titan One, and there should not be any records of activity since then. Check their operations records, and get the last date and time they were flown, and their destination. Let's be absolutely certain that these birds have been asleep here in their bays since Titan One." The men dispersed to check out the shuttles, as ordered. None had been used since Titan One, but unit one had been accessed for navigational coordinates. That shuttle's number was reported to the bridge, and the entire team converged on the little shuttle to check every system, each and every compartment and crevice on her. Nothing was found out of the ordinary.

The last areas to be inspected before crew's quarters were the gym and the lounges. Only one lounge was open for use now, and was not staffed. You could come up there and enjoy a drink for a while, entertain yourself with movies or video games, read, or just play cards. No real alcoholic beverages were served, although the synthehol gave you a brief buzz for a couple of hours. Mason checked the dispensers and fridges, and the team turned over all the furniture to check for anything unusual. All clear; Mason was on to the gyms.

He went straight to the weight-lifting room, to check out the free weights. They were all accounted for, and the ends did not have octagonal shapes. At least Dr. Reese was not chucked on the head with a free weight, Mason thought. The cardio room was occupied by Lieutenant Urz and Nurse Cohen, both working out diligently. Lieutenant Urz was drenched with sweat, in the zone. Mason nodded at them, and the team continued its sweep in the other rooms of the big gym. The court room could be used for many kinds of sports, since it was computer-controlled and fully adjustable. Mason noticed the most frequently used formations were for racquet ball, two players. He had one of the security team to download the video monitor recordings since departure from SS 10, to see who visited the court, and when. Racquet ball racquets had hexagonal and octagonal handles. Maybe someone didn't like losing to Dr. Reese.

The security team checked the crew's quarter's deck. This would be the easiest inspection on this deck for the entire journey, as they were all in cryo-sleep. Their cryogenic cocoons were stacked twelve-high in racks in the cryonics chamber, all present, and all functions normal. All their sleeping quarters were checked, inspected, and locked down when they reported for cryo-sleep. Their access doors were monitored 24 hours per day, and no incidents of tampering were reported.

Mason and the team were on the lifts to their last checkpoint, the research labs. Two techs were on duty, one in each of the labs, monitoring the computerized experiments, and were visibly startled when security team members opened the lab doors to speak with them. Captain Kouras had given strict orders that word of Dr. Reese's death was not to be mentioned to either of the lab techs, without permission from Earth Command. The experiments were taking place in pressurized containers, and could not be opened. Whatever was inside the metal containers would have to remain there until the Hesperia came out of hyper-space. The team checked what spaces they could, thanked the lab techs, and left.

With the full inspection completed, Mason dismissed the security team, and went up to the bridge to report their findings. He relayed the information about the shuttle whose computer system had been accessed, and his recommendations for the sensors to be installed. Captain Kouras agreed, and also ordered the visible mounting of large security cameras to be placed in the shuttle bay. He wanted whoever was going to the ship to know, without any doubt, that their identity had been discovered. "Staff Sergeant, your next full security inspection is not due for two more months, but let's move that time frame up to thirty days. And I want the security teams rotated. I want each security team member to know this ship like the back of his own hand, understood?"

"Yes, Captain. Understood, sir, like the back of his hand." At least they would be kept busy, Mason thought.

Mason enjoyed the observation deck lounge of the Hesperia the most. He could let his mind wander, or plan the next days' activities without being interrupted, usually. Today, he was busy planning how to breach the engineering deck, and take over the main computers. He was deep in thought, when he noticed Nurse Cohen come off the lift, and sit down across from him. "Hello, Staff Sergeant Mason. I didn't know you were up here. Am I bothering you?"

Of course you're bothering me, Mason thought, in all the right ways. "No, ma'am, I appreciate the company. How goes your day?" That was so lame.

"My day is just fine. Dr. Hassan has decided to inventory the entire medical stores and supplies in the hospital, and I've been let off the hook. I think he's just trying to keep the med techs busy, if you want to know the truth. The last two times we inventoried everything, I had to help. So, I ran away before he had time to change his mind!" She laughed, and Mason laughed with her. They chatted about little everyday things, and Mason got them some tea, and joined her on the couch. She was so comfortable to be with, Mason thought. For an hour they forgot all about being on a mining freighter with eight hundred other people, albeit in cryo-sleep. They were in their own sphere of enjoyment, laughing and flirting with each other. Sometimes, the best times happen by accident, and this was one of the best times of John Mason's life. He was enjoying the company of a beautiful woman, and she was enjoying being with him. They were the only people in the universe for the short time they were together; it felt like magic. In another place and time, this conversation might be continued in the bedroom.

This wonderful moment ended, as most truly special moments do, with the sudden appearance of several other people entering their formerly private space. The crewmen entering the lounge were from engineering, and recognized Mason. His demeanor immediately changed, and he felt his defenses go up. They were polite to Nurse Cohen, sitting next to Mason, and acknowledged him, as well, but it was blatantly apparent something made her friend edgy.

"I guess it's time I got back to the hospital. Dr. Hassan is probably looking for me. Thank you for the tea, Staff Sergeant. I needed a little break," she said, standing up to leave.

"No, the thanks go to you, for giving me some company, Nurse Cohen. Mind if I escort you back to the hospital?" Mason asked. He walked with her into the lift, and stood as far apart as the walls of the lift would allow, knowing what would happen if they got any closer to each other. He realized he'd been holding his breath the entire ride down to the hospital deck, and didn't exhale until she walked off the lift. She slowly turned to him.

"You can breathe now, John," she said with a smile.

"Not really, ma'am," Mason admitted, and watched her walk down the corridor, and disappear around the corner. Damn, he was crazy about her. Why'd she have to be an officer?

IV

Rachel Cohen spent most of her adult life as a military nurse, serving on Moon Base, Mars Colony III, and on two space cruisers. She had heard every pick-up line a hundred times, and was immune to men who were cruising for the quick sexual encounter, no matter how handsome they were. That immunity was the result of a time when she was young and inexperienced, and stationed on Moon Base with over fourteen hundred men. She fell for one of those lines, from her CO, no less. She was deeply in love with him. He used her love for the duration of his time on the base, and then dumped her. She suffered in terrible pain, and nearly resigned her commission. When she realized how she had been used, and his feelings for her were not real, she was crushed emotionally, and determined never to let any man get close to her again.

Rachel never married, although she had been in relationships with a few men over the years. The first time, she gave herself totally and completely, and got thrown away like an old pair of shoes. The experience caused her to be overly cautious with potential suitors for many years. Thankfully, she grew out of that stage. She was born beautiful, with a great figure, bewitching hazel eyes, and an infectious smile. More than once she overheard fellow officers refer to the "Ice Queen" in sick bay, and it bothered her, even if the nickname was somewhat accurate.

Now that she was on the last space tour of her nursing career, she was happy she stayed in the service. She enjoyed helping other people, was an excellent caregiver and a true healer. She preferred to be called simply "Nurse Cohen," and not by her rank, while she was in her white lab coat. Knowing only a handful of the crew was awake now made her more relaxed. Most of the senior officers she met on the Hesperia were on their last deep space detail, same as she was, and they showed her courtesy and respect. She had no idea what the miners were like, but they had their own medical staff, and she was promised they had no access to the officers' quarters or lounge areas.

She was a full Commander, the same rank as Dr. Hassan, but he was the Medical Chief of Staff and her boss. She was the Head Surgical Nurse, and second in command. She was disturbed by the early events that took place on board the Hesperia. Everyone knew about the mutiny that befell the last mining ship coming in from this sector, the Excelon, and how the few military officers who were not slaughtered were the ones necessary to pilot the ship home. That ship had only one hospital for everyone, and little separation of crew and mining personnel. This mining mission is very different, she reminded herself; there were separate areas for military and mining personnel. Knowing that made her feel somewhat safer.

What really made her feel safe was being around Staff Sergeant John Mason. Whoever dosed him with opiated sleep inducers had better never be discovered, she decided. He was a Prime Marine, a highly trained killer, and sworn protector of the officers on the Hesperia. He was her protector, at least when he was near her. She liked John a lot; too much, especially when he relaxed and could step outside his Prime Marine role for a while. Those times were rare. She was very attracted to him, and felt dangerously fond of him; she loved him, if the truth be told, but she was forced to not consider him, because she was a command medical officer, and he an enlisted man. She was too close to completing her career as a nurse and moving into biological research afterwards to throw it all away at this point in her life. Thankfully, Mason understood this age-old separation of officers and enlisted, and they agreed they could not be together other than as friends. But she cherished his friendship, and cared deeply for him.

She read the autopsy report on the dead man found in the freezer. What troubled her was the fact that no one from the bridge security crews knew him at all. Indeed, research scientists, especially civilians like Dr. Reese, had very little in common with the military crew members, but someone should know him. She did not know if the lab techs had been told of his death at this time. The other researchers were still in cryogenic sleep, not to be awakened until the Hesperia reached the mining area. The scientists all worked for URE. Surely the researchers knew him.

She finished reading the autopsy notes when Dr. Hassan appeared in her office doorway. "Good morning, Doctor. Mind if we go over this autopsy report for a few minutes?"

"Absolutely. I'm more than a bit intrigued by that case myself. If you wouldn't mind, I think we might benefit from your seeing the body of our late Dr. Reese. His tattoos are so unusual. Shall we go now?" Dr. Hassan led her to the tiny morgue, where they removed Dr. Reese's body from cold storage. After donning their aprons and gloves, the doctor unsealed the body bag, and asked, "Nurse Cohen, please help me turn him on his side."

They gently rolled him onto his side for a better look at the tattoos. "You see this? The markings resemble those of traditional tattoos, but the ink looks all wrong. I sent skin samples of the inked areas to our med lab for full analysis. We should be getting that report soon." He traced the longest line of the drawing in the air with his pen. "Something's just not right. I've seen hundreds of tattoos, but nothing quite like this."

"What about those markings on his neck? They don't look like tattoos at all. Do you think it could have been a laser etching, Doctor?" She asked.

"Not sure. I have spent half the night studying tattoos and skin painting, and I still don't know. We need those skin sample reports to be certain," he replied.

Nurse Cohen felt it was time to ask the question that bothered her more than strange tattoos. "Dr. Hassan, there were only four research scientists assigned to the Hesperia. Now I know they were civilian government employees, but no one remembers Dr. Richard Reese."

"What do you mean 'no one remembers' him? He boarded the ship from Moon Base like the rest of us. Didn't he? Did you check the records?" Now Dr. Hassan was beginning to understand his Head Nurse's concern. "No one got on the ship on Titan One, only cargo."

"His name was on the manifest as Chief Research Scientist. He boarded the Hesperia at Moon Base with the rest of the crew, two days before the mining personnel boarded. I checked the ship's records. But no one remembers meeting him, no one awake that is." She sighed and said, "Maybe I'm just making something out of nothing. But you and I met the other three research scientists, and the two lab assistants, at the welcome dinner hosted by Captain Kouras the very first night on board. Attendance was required by all, no exceptions. So, where was he?"

"The Captain would have been made aware of anyone's absence. I think it's time we brought our concerns to Captain Kouras directly." With that, Dr. Hassan closed the body in the bag, resealed it, and rolled the table back into the cold storage locker. He went to the comm link, and signaled the bridge. "Dr. Hassan to Captain Kouras."

"This is the Captain."

"Captain Kouras, Nurse Cohen and I need to speak with you briefly about Dr. Reese. May we come to the bridge?" Dr. Hassan requested.

"In my ready room in one half hour," Kouras answered.

"Thank you, sir." Dr. Hassan nodded at Nurse Cohen, and they left the morgue. They later went to the Captain's ready room to wait for him. They stood at attention as Captain Kouras quickly entered the room.

"At ease. Please be seated. Would you like something to drink? I'm having coffee." He sat at his command console, while the server robot came in with coffee service for them. "Since this is the first time we have all met in my office, I thought we could enjoy a little refreshment." The

Captain served them each coffee and small cakes, and then sat back in his chair. "Now, what concerns my Chief Medical Officer and Head Nurse today?"

Dr. Hassan began. "Captain, I have shared my concern about our late Dr. Reese and his body markings with you earlier. Today Nurse Cohen and I re-examined his body markings and have made another interesting discovery. At first look, the body markings appeared to be tattoos. But closer observation questions that assumption."

"They're not tattoos? Are they temporary drawings?" The Captain queried.

"No, not temporary at all. The analysis of skin that bore those markings was just completed a few minutes ago. The drawings appear to have been machine-etched laser markings. A permanent organic dye was added on top of the laser etchings. Not really tattoos at all. This process is frequently used with livestock to identify herd ownership," the Doctor said.

"You mean he was branded? Like cattle?" Captain Kouras nearly choked on his cake. "Why would any man allow a laser etching on his own skin? Then permanent ink? Now that is interesting. Must've taken more than a couple days to burn a dinosaur on his back. Bet that hurt." The Captain looked at them both and asked, "What else?"

It was Nurse Cohen's turn. "Captain Kouras, did you know Dr. Richard Reese?"

"I knew he was the Chief Research Scientist from URE government."

"But did you know him, sir? What I'm trying to say is, no one I've talked to can recall meeting him. No one who is awake, that is," she enquired.

"He was on the manifest, I'm certain of that!" The Captain seemed peeved at the turn the conversation had taken. He pulled up the manifest, checked it, and then referenced his personnel files. "Yes, he checked in prior to boarding; checked in at boarding security; he had to have his security badge to get on board."

"Excuse me, sir, but did Dr. Reese attend your first night party in the Officer's Lounge?" Nurse Cohen persisted.

"No, it says he did not attend my party. The notes say his living quarters were locked when the security officer I sent to fetch him arrived, and the privacy light was on. Hmmm," Kouras pondered.

"Captain, did we receive permission from URE to inform the research lab techs of Dr. Reese's death?" Dr. Hassan asked. "Perhaps they knew Dr. Reese."

"No, as a matter of fact we have not received any response from Earth Command. We will resend those communiqués right now." The Captain then called Lieutenant Marston, and instructed him to resend all communiqués to Earth Command immediately, and request acknowledgement of their receipt. He finished his coffee, and said to them,

"If these incidents had to have happened, I feel fortunate they happened while only five percent of our passengers are awake. We've had too many unsolved mysteries take place on the Hesperia in a very short time. I want to..." his discourse was interrupted by Lt. Marston on the comm-link:

"Captain Kouras, Earth Command acknowledges our transmissions are received. Permission is granted to inform such crew members as have a need to know of Dr. Richard Reese's demise. The Captain is instructed to inform Admiral Tomiko directly of any and all findings related to the investigation of Dr. Richard Reese's death. Also, you have permission to increase hyper-space speed to a factor of four. End of transmission."

"Engineering, this is Captain Kouras. Powers, we have permission to increase to hyper- speed of four. Acknowledge."

"Aye-aye, Captain. Hyper-speed four it is, sir. Powers out."

The Captain leaned forward and looked directly at his medical chiefs. "Dr. Reese must have been an important man for the Admiral to order direct input on his investigation. Nurse Cohen, my apology for not initially regarding your concern as relevant. I assure you my mind has been changed. Thank you for bringing the matter to my attention. Let me know if there are any further developments on this case from either of you, right away." The Captain stood, and came around his desk to show them out. "Thank you both for coming."

Dr. Hassan gave a knowing smile to Nurse Cohen as they rode down in the lift together. "That took courage. Glad we're on the same team."

Captain Kouras studied the files on Dr. Reese for several minutes. How did he let this man get away with not showing up at his first dinner? Was he still alive the first night? He decided to inform the Staff Sergeant of the new developments in the case, and order him to take a team to the research labs and inform the techs of Dr. Reese's death. He wanted a detailed description of their reactions and response to the news. Mason was the natural choice for this. The man recognized each and every body sign.

No wonder Nurse Cohen has that silver maple leaf on her uniform, he thought. No one else on this ship had the balls to challenge him.

Mason took Corporal Johnson and Corporal Milton with him to the research labs to deliver the news about Dr. Reese. The Captain gave orders to read, notate, and report on each lab tech's response to the news. The security detail entered Lab 1, and greeted Dr. Jenkins, the lab technician. Corporal Johnson relayed the news of Dr. Reese's death as Mason watched.

"Earth Command and Captain Kouras have instructed me to inform you that there has been an incident on board the Hesperia involving Dr. Richard Reese, your Chief of Research. Dr. Reese is dead. We are sorry for the loss of your colleague."

Dr. Jenkins immediately put both his hands to his mouth. "Oh my God!

He's dead? Oh my God - no!" He exclaimed. "Wait. You said 'incident,' not 'accident.' What exactly does that mean?"

"It means that, apparently, Dr. Reese was killed by person or persons unknown. We are at present investigating his death as a murder. I am not at liberty to share any more details with you at this time," Corporal Johnson said gently.

Dr. Jenkins was visibly distraught. "Killed? Why? Who could have done this? Tell me, is someone working to figure out who did this? Are you?" He looked squarely at Mason.

"Yes, sir, the entire matter is under investigation as we speak," Mason said. "Did you know Dr. Reese personally?"

"Yes, I knew him. We all knew him. He was our Chief of Research at MM&E. He is, or was, in charge of these experiments we're conducting."

"Did you see him onboard the Hesperia, Dr. Jenkins?" Mason asked.

"I saw him on Moon Base, and I think I saw him here. Wait, maybe not. Oh, I'm just not sure now. Poor Dr. Reese!"

"Thank you, Dr. Jenkins. We appreciate your help. We may need to ask you questions at a later time. Once again, we are sorry for your loss." Corporal Johnson was really good at delivering bad news, Mason thought to himself.

They left Lab 1, and went to inform Dr. Honig in Lab 2 of the news. He was more reserved upon receiving the news of Dr. Reese's death. Too reserved. "How was he killed?" Dr. Honig asked.

"We are not at liberty to answer questions, Dr. Honig," said Corporal Johnson.

"That's too bad," he responded.

"Dr. Honig, did you know Dr. Reese? Did you see him on board the Hesperia?" Mason questioned.

"Yes, I knew him. I had him as my doctoral sponsor at university, and he's head man at MM&E, you know," he responded.

"Did you see him on board?" Mason asked.

"Not really. I barely had time to drop off my things in my room and start to get familiar with this lab, when we all had to attend the Captain's party. I drank a little too much, and went straight to bed. Don't recall seeing him at the party. Would you please keep me informed?"

"We will advise you on what we can, Doctor," Mason replied.

"Thank you," Dr. Honig said, as the security team left.

When they were well away from the labs, Corporal Milton said, "My money's on Honig. He didn't seem to care one way or another that Reese was dead."

"And he was ambivalent to the news that his boss, the man who helped him get his doctoral degree, was dead. He showed little emotion," Mason added. "Remember what he asked? He asked how Reese was killed, not how did he die. That doesn't mean he's guilty, it just means he is a person of interest. Let's write up our reports and give them to the Captain ASAP."

They all did as Mason ordered, and gave their reports over to Captain Kouras within the hour. Mason accompanied the Captain to the ready room. He watched in silence as the Captain read the reports. "Have these entered into the log, Mason. Now, tell me how they appeared to you. Anything suspicious about either man? Honig bears watching, don't you agree?"

"I think they both should be observed, sir. Both men have something to gain with their Chief gone, as do the other researchers still in cryo-sleep. I could have micro cameras installed in their quarters, if you wish, sir, and in the labs," Mason offered.

"They will be expecting the cameras in the labs, and maybe in their quarters. I need their rooms swept for any electronic devices, anything they could have brought on board that's not on the approved list. This may be part of a larger scheme, Mason, and we need to find that out. We need to know much more about this case as soon as we can. Earth Command has accelerated our speed to hyper-speed four, so we'll be at the hunting grounds six weeks earlier, after a detour."

Mason asked, "Detour, sir?"

"Yes, detour, Mason. We're not that far from the first deep-space colony, GK-356. No ship has called there for several years."

"Purgatory," Mason said, referring to its nickname among the Space Patrol. "Is anyone still alive on that asteroid, Captain? I haven't heard anything about that place in a long time."

"Yes, Mason, there are still some hardy souls alive on that rock. Let's get to work," Captain Kouras told him.

Mason took security team two out the next day for inspection of the aft compartment. They navigated the maze of halls through the ship's second and third sections on a transport, to save time. Hundreds of crevices small enough to hide a murder weapon. It took fifteen minutes just to get to the beginning of section four. It was a huge, open bay, with retracting claws, clamping arms, and rock crushers for breaking apart and retrieving pieces of asteroids, and floating chunks of anything containing metals. The rock chunks were loaded onto cargo cars here to be sent to the furnaces. Tracks for the cargo cars led from the end of the ship to the refinery in section three, one track going out to the furnaces, one coming back to pick up more rock.

Now Mason realized why so many miners were necessary. They worked three shifts a day, not two, like the military crews. Once the refinery started up, its furnaces would blaze during the four years in the mining areas, and all the way back to Moon Base. The miners had the technical staff to keep everything operating efficiently, and at peak capacity.

With the bay doors closed, they could be in section four without being suited up. After checking for adequate air and pressurization, the team began their search for anything that did not belong there. The section was very open, but compartments along the walls provided ample space for hiding something as small as the weapon that killed Dr. Reese. They must be thorough and inspect the claws and arms of the big rigs. That meant climbing up the equipment by hand, a dangerous and tedious job. Although each man wore a safety belt, no one liked crawling along the steel beams at those heights, inspecting the massive claws, their bodies dangling over the bay floor. "Let's do this right the first time. I don't want to spend all night filling out injury reports," Mason warned.

They finally finished their inspection, and headed back to the crew quarters to report and rest. Either they were all blind and could not see the possible murder weapon, or it was hidden in section two or three. Or, Mason suddenly realized, in an outside compartment.

"Commander Baines, sir, permission to speak," Mason asked.

"Permission granted Staff Sergeant. What is it?" The Commander was anxious to finish reading the inspection reports and get some shut-eye. He'd been up for over thirty hours, and was more than a little cranky.

"Sir, could anything have been left behind on Titan One while we were docked there? Or would it have been possible to plant something on the outside of the ship at Titan One when we stopped to pick up cargo?" Mason asked.

"Nothing was taken off the ship at Titan One. No personnel were allowed to leave the ship," Baines replied.

"Commander, I am still investigating the death of Dr. Reese. He was killed by a single blow to the head with a blunt object having an octagonal end. It could've been a hand tool, a support rod, a racquet ball racquet, several things, sir. I'm attempting to consider all possibilities, especially since none of our teams have come up with anything, sir," Mason explained.

"I see, Mason. No, I don't think anything could have been moved off our ship at Titan One, as everything would have gone through the scanners prior to being allowed off ship. Any part, or hand tool, or racquet, would have been picked up by the scanners and stopped for inspection," the Commander said.

"What about outside the ship, sir? There are several tool boxes, equipment holds, and other storage places that might serve as a hiding place," Mason asked.

Baines was losing patience. "Staff Sergeant, after your security crews have checked every centimeter of this ship, and we've come out of hyperspace, if you want to inspect the outer hull of the Hesperia, be my guest. Until then, I suggest you continue looking for the weapon inside the ship. That's where all the people are, and that's most likely where the weapon is."

"Yes, sir. We will continue our search. Thank you sir," Mason said, and went down the lift to the gym. He had to find a nice large bot to spar with soon, or he was going to tear something apart. He changed out of his uniform, programmed a sparring bot for twenty rounds of mixed martial arts, and proceeded to take out his frustration on the robot. A couple of hours later, bruised and exhausted, Mason went to the showers and then a massage. Thirty days until inspections continued. He decided it was time to focus on breaching the engineering deck.

V

Nearly two months passed since the Hesperia encountered the orange cloud. They were no closer to identifying that mysterious anomaly than they were the day it appeared from the void. The probes sent to analyze the anomaly gathered data for only a few seconds before being obliterated, and most of that data was inconclusive. The only significant bit of information collected was that there were traces of tachyon particles identified near the anomaly. Those particles indicated the anomaly utilized some type of hyper-space engine drive. The orange cloud was some sort of machine. Who made that machine, and for what purpose - those were the primary questions needing to be answered.

Commander Victor Baines was determined to find answers to these questions before the Hesperia came out of hyper-space. With so little data available, identification of the anomaly was proving extremely difficult. He was positive the orange cloud was following the Hesperia.

Commander Baines served as navigator and tactical officer for most of his assignments in his Space Forces career. His mathematical achievements at Harvard University in his doctoral research presented him with two very different career paths: a military career in the URE Space Forces; or an academic career, teaching and researching higher mathematics. He had been pressured by his family to pursue a career in academia, but he chose a military officer's life; he entered the Space Forces at age twenty-eight, after he completed all his post-doctoral work and published his dissertation. Both his parents were Harvard University professors, highly regarded in their respective fields. His father was an astrophysicist, and his mother was a physician, teaching neurology.

Victor never married, although there were several women along the way who would've jumped at the chance to be his wife. He was blessed with arresting good looks: tall, slim, with a swimmer's build, and had thick platinum blonde hair and blue eyes. He usually refrained from getting involved with any female on board ship in order to not have any potential problems during his tour of duty. Being highly reserved as a rule, he was not comfortable in social situations where there were many girls looking for boyfriends; he didn't like "easy girls," the kind his fraternity brothers specialized in during his first four years at Harvard. He wanted to marry a woman who was beautiful and intelligent, someone he could build a life with, and be proud to introduce as his wife. He was willing to wait for the right woman to enter his life.

As Executive Officer of the Hesperia, he had many duties to perform, including mundane tasks that actually helped relieve the pressure to solve the riddle of the orange cloud. He had an obsessive desire to solve the "orange cloud equation," and it caused him to sleep or eat very little, and be less patient with the crew. He was growing more intolerant of any shortcomings in the crew's performance, and it was obvious to everyone on the bridge that he was withdrawing from any sort of camaraderie.

Fortunately for the Hesperia, what Commander Baines lacked in people management skills, he more than made up for in problem solving. Captain Kouras worked with a few truly brilliant science officers in the past, but none had achieved line command rank, like Commander Baines. The Commander needed to be challenged to both occupy his mathematical mind, and improve his interactive skills, if he was going to make captain of his own ship someday. Captain Kouras assigned Commander Baines the task of improving the crew's qualifications for promotion. He himself was working to make Admiral upon completion of this seven-year mission. The Captain believed that the way to the top was best achieved by raising up everyone around you, not by stepping on their backs. He wanted to take full advantage of the unplanned fifteen months the working members of his crew would spend awake.

Each active crewman's file was analyzed by Baines to determine what areas of weaknesses existed, officer and enlisted alike. He designed specific learning paths for each one. He assigned a score to quantify their accomplishments, incorporating the university degrees attained, their service background and levels of experience, and their physical fitness. Extra credit was given for non-military proficiencies such as playing one or more musical instruments (music was, at its purest level, mathematical in nature, of course). He also studied their psychological tests to identify strengths in logic, intuitive reasoning, and powers of deduction.

The Captain, although impressed by his XO's thoroughness in designing learning paths for the officers, made an additional demand of Baines. "Commander, these paths for learning and self-improvement you designed for the officers are incomplete."

"Sir, incomplete? How so? I have analyzed each officer's file, performance history, mission background, and education, and determined precisely what each of them need to attain top scores in all categories for promotion consideration. I fail to see what is incomplete," Baines said defensively.

"Did you meet with each officer individually, and ask them what they wanted to achieve? No, you did not. What motivates them? What made them sign up for a seven-year assignment, away from family, friends, and their homes? Find out what makes them tick. The files will never tell you who someone really is, and what their goals are. Find out what their dreams are, Commander." The Captain paused briefly, and then said, "The officers already know you are a genius. Show them you are a great leader of men, someone who will inspire them to greatness." He watched Baines, waiting for his response.

"Yes, Captain, I think I know what you mean. I have more work to do, if you will excuse me, sir." With that said, the Commander tucked his report under his arm, and headed off for his quarters. Captain Kouras knew he had just achieved a breakthrough with Commander Baines. He hoped his faith in his second in command would be justified.

One by one, each bridge officer met privately with Baines to go over his learning path. The first few meetings did not go as smoothly as he would have liked, but he was determined to get better. The officers were uncomfortable knowing he had so deeply studied their files. He needed help with these meetings, so he sought out the best "people persons" he knew on the ship.

Commander Baines invited Dr. Hassan and Nurse Cohen to dine with him in his quarters, and they graciously accepted. He openly shared his frustration with his special assignment from the Captain. "I know the crew is defensive, and we both feel very uncomfortable in these one on one meetings. How can I convince them that I want to help them advance their careers, and that I have a genuine interest in their success?"

Nurse Cohen looked directly at the Commander, and asked, "Are you really trying to advance their careers, or your own?"

"Well, both, actually," he admitted.

"Have you spent much off-duty time with the other officers?" Dr. Hassan asked. "Have you ever shared dinner or had conversation over a few drinks with them, just to get to know them?"

"No, not really. I've been attempting to identify the orange cloud anomaly we encountered. I am certain it is following the Hesperia," Baines revealed.

"You need to get to know the officers on a more social level. Perhaps you could plan a few team-building activities with them. You know, not necessarily a party, but something to do together that would be fun and challenging, and give them a chance to know you better. On a different level," Nurse Cohen offered. "How about a team sport, like a basketball game?"

"Or card games, like bridge? Or a chess tournament? Or a party?" The Doctor suggested.

"Can't throw much of a party with food pouch rations," the Commander grumbled.

Nurse Cohen suddenly lit up. "Why not have two teams, and, instead of a competitive sport, have the teams compete to build something!"

He was intrigued. "Build what?"

Now Dr. Hassan got on the bandwagon. "Let each team decide what to build. You give them a purpose, and let them design and build their solution! The Captain could give out an award to the best accomplishment."

"Or maybe break out the ice cream," Nurse Cohen said wishfully. "No cooks needed for that treat!" Baines enjoyed watching her excitement. There was something about her that fascinated him suddenly.

The Commander's guests left his quarters more excited than he about a team competition. Baines gave the matter a lot of thought, met with the Captain for his approval, and made the announcement to the crew one week later: "Now hear this. We will be kicking off our exciting new learning paths program with a special challenge. All members of the bridge and engineering crews will be divided into two teams for this competition. Each team will elect one team leader of their choosing. You will be assigned a project to complete. Each team will be allowed time off-duty to design and build their own project, in secret, without sharing their design with the other team. You will have three weeks to complete your projects. The completed projects will be judged by Captain Kouras, and the winning team will receive a wonderful prize."

"What's the prize?" Lieutenant Urz asked.

"The prize consists of three components. The first is an extra day off-duty. The second is a lavish party held in the Officers' mess after the rest of the crew is awakened. The third component is a mystery prize to be shared with the entire winning team," the XO answered.

"So, what's the project?" Lieutenant Davis asked, suspiciously.

Commander Baines let the suspense build for a moment. "The project for the two teams is to build - a one-man ship."

"A ship? In three weeks? Impossible!"

"A space ship? Where will we get the parts for construction?"

The comments and questions were coming in hot and heavy from both the bridge and engineering crews, and the Commander was happy with the active responses. "The project is to build a one-man ship. Each team will design and build it to their specifications. Remember, you are to work completely in secret. I will be the only one to know the designs of both teams. Everyone will draw for their teams tonight at dinner. Good luck to both teams!" The Commander created quite a stir with the crew, and smiled at the Captain, knowing full well that he had successfully kicked the entire crew out of their comfort zones.

The Captain exempted the Space Marines from the competition. Their top priority was the security of the crew of the Hesperia. Mason was more than happy to be excused. He needed to continue investigating the death of Dr. Reese.

Commander Baines actually enjoyed attending the meetings of both teams, sometimes as a referee, and frequently as a contributor. He resisted the temptation to play one team against the other, or show favoritism. He could tell that the crew was becoming more relaxed with him, and the feeling was mutual.

When the day arrived for the judging of the completed projects, Commander Baines assembled as many of the entire crew as was available in the main lounge. Team A built a mini-shuttle that could actually fly inside the ship. Captain Kouras insisted on taking it for a spin, and flew it around the lounge for a test. He had it transported to section four, where he flew it around the large bay, enjoying himself immensely.

Team B took an entirely different approach, and built a sailboat. It was a one-man ship, to be sure, and she was a beauty! She was painted white, with red sails, and a real wooden ship's wheel. The Captain hoisted her up to one of the recesses in the front of the general assembly hall for all to see and enjoy. The entire crew talked about the two very different ships built for the competition, each one having their own opinion of which team was the prize winner.

Captain Kouras generously awarded the prize to both teams for their efforts, two magnums each of red and white wine from California. Mason nodded his head; the Captain did have his own stash. The bottles were uncorked immediately, and everyone savored their glass of wine as if it were the best wine they had ever tasted. It would probably be their only glass of real wine for a long time.

Commander Baines had a much easier time relating with the crew after the ship-building competition. He gave a personal note of thanks to both Dr. Hassan and Nurse Cohen, promising them a steak dinner when they all returned home. He was especially interested in getting better acquainted with Nurse Cohen. Baines realized there was more to her than he initially thought when they first met. Although Nurse Cohen was beautiful at first glance, she seemed definitely worth getting to know, on many levels.

VI

Day after day, the Hesperia flew through hyper-space towards her destination in the outer asteroid sector. Mason checked and double-checked every possible hiding place on board the massive ship, and no murder weapon could be found. The perpetrator was most likely in cryo-sleep, evading discovery, for the time being. Images of any potential blunt object with an octagonal end were captured and stored for reference in his files titled, "Dr. R. Reese Murder Investigation." Mason felt that Dr. Reese's murder and his own dosing in the cryo-capsule were related, but he did not see how either of those events could be tied to the orange cloud.

The Captain requested they gather in the observation lounge today, and Mason knew the reason for this change of venue. When they had gone over most of the agenda items, Captain Kouras told them Earth Command had given him the choice to decide whether or not to detour the Hesperia to the URE's first deep-space colony on asteroid GK-356. "As most of you know, we will pass very close by the asteroid on our way to the mining area. Earth Command would like us to make a short stop to visit the colony there, and assess their situation, prior to continuing on to the hunting grounds. We will orbit the asteroid, and descend to the surface in shuttles to call on the colony. This is your opportunity for input on the mission."

Dr. Hassan spoke up first. "Have we already been in contact with the colony? Are we sure they are still alive on that rock? I had not heard anything about the colonists in such a long time, I thought they had been brought home, or were dead."

"That would be the primary reason for going there, to ascertain the answers to those very questions, Dr. Hassan," Captain Kouras said. "Earth Command has had little contact with the colony in the last year. If I were on that asteroid, I would be very appreciative of any attention from one of our ships. If they are in need of food or other supplies, the Hesperia could be very helpful."

"When do we make the course change?" Commander Baines asked.

"Tomorrow. We have their coordinates already loaded in the computer," the Captain said. "Staff Sergeant Mason will assemble two security teams to accompany the landing groups, led by Commander Baines and Dr. Hassan. You will take all four of the shuttles to the surface, and establish a base camp there. We will make contact with the colonists, determine their immediate needs, and provide supplies and assistance to them. I will make the announcement to the crew tomorrow, prior to altering our course. No discussion is to be held on this decision until the announcement is made, is that understood?" Captain Kouras watched for their agreement. "We will be going here," he said, standing at the front observation window and pointing to the targeted region where GK-356 would be. "We will all need to familiarize ourselves with any and all available information on the asteroid, as well as our colony, and the colonists. Dismissed."

Mason studied all the information on the asteroid that the ship had available, but it was mostly the kind of general information found in any library. When he asked for more information on GK-356, the Commander told him he would be given detailed specifics one week away from the asteroid, and not before. "The shuttles will be landing in the staging area, directly north of the actual colony village. For security reasons, those coordinates, and any other details about that location are classified top secret, Staff Sergeant. I understand you need to plan the security and base camp details, but I am not able to give you any more information right now."

"Yes, sir. Will the Commander advise me when I might have the information needed to provide security for the landing parties?" Mason asked.

"Yes, of course, Staff Sergeant. I will advise you myself," Baines answered.

"Thank you, sir." Mason was intrigued by the ambiguity of the side trip to GK-356. Why the secrecy? What is going on at the colony? All he could find out was that the colony was a research facility, but what they were researching was never disclosed in the available information. Any place called "Purgatory" had to be full of secrets.

GK-356 was an orbiting large asteroid, the size of a small planet, with a deep sheet of ice covering two thirds of its surface. Ice meant a chance for life; hence, the rock was a natural target for research and exploration. The colony was established twelve years ago, led by Dr. Maxim and thirty additional researchers. They were living under a large plex-dome, in a man-made atmosphere. Whether or not they managed to successfully seed the asteroid outside the dome with blue-green algae was unknown. The thought of eating food rations for twelve years made Mason shudder; that, in itself, would be purgatory to him. Algae wafers might seem to be a delicacy, in certain situations.

After the Captain made the announcement of their detour to GK-356, the Hesperia was slowed over the next two days to sub-hyper-speed, and her course changed. She was boosted back to hyper-speed four for the duration of her detour to the asteroid. They would continue on this course for another five weeks, and then gradually slow to sub-hyper-speed until the ship reached the asteroid.

Mason decided to enact his plan to breach engineering during this time, and he received approval for his maneuvers from Captain Kouras. "I understand you are trying to catch Lt. Commander Powers off guard, since he'll be busy making adjustments for these course corrections and speed variances. But he'll be expecting you to try now, don't you think? It's the logical time for sabotage, when everyone is busy doing something not anticipated in their pre-flight planning."

"Sir, was Lt. Commander Powers ever briefed on the possibility of the Hesperia making this detour to GK-356?" Mason asked.

"No one was briefed except me, and Commander Baines. It was my choice to make, assuming everything was running smoothly up to this point in our flight." Mason mentally disagreed with the Captain's statement of the ship running 'smoothly.' Murder of one of the leading research scientists in the URE did not equate to smooth running, in his book. But he was not the Captain.

Mason continued his questioning, "Has the Chief Engineer requested any other crewmen be taken out of cryo-sleep to assist with the new course changes, sir?"

"Yes, Powers has requested four more of his engineering staff be awakened, and I approved his request. And, I'll answer your next question by telling you they will be awakened this Thursday at o-seven hundred hours," Captain Kouras said, smiling.

"Thank you, Captain. Does the Captain need to know the exact time the breach attempt will take place?" Mason checked.

"No, Mason. You make that call without telling me, or the XO. Best if the attempt is as realistic as possible. But be careful, Staff Sergeant. Stick to your plan. I don't want any serious injuries in this exercise, understand? We don't need to cripple our engineering or security crews, or have any accidents to report. Is that clear, Prime Marine?"

"Aye-aye, Captain, no serious injuries, sir," Mason acknowledged. Damn, I never get to have any fun, Mason thought to himself as he walked out of the ready room.

When the Excelon was attacked and taken over by the miners, they accessed engineering through the emergency crawl spaces. The crawl tubes on the Hesperia were monitored by the many cameras installed by Mason and the security teams to prevent another event of that type from taking place. Captain Kouras assumed that, since Mason had installed and programmed those cameras, he would take a small Space Marine team and use the same crawl tubes again, after having tricked or disabled the cameras.

But Mason didn't think like the Captain. He found a possible weakness to be exploited in the engine room, in the conduit shafts adjacent to the viewing portholes where engineers monitored the exhaust ports of the engines themselves. The narrow shafts required a horizontal climb of twenty meters, if one did not use the walkway that ran alongside them from the main engineering bridge to the engine room. Then a vertical climb of twenty meters to the engine control console. The cables could not be stepped on, or alarms would sound; the small, narrow ladder inside the shaft must be used. Not an easy series of climbing, but doable. They would disable one of the hyper-speed engines, and take over the engineering command console. He hand-picked the six Space Marines to assist him, and each one had a specific role in the breach attempt. Their timing must be perfect for his plan to work. They practiced their physical maneuvers during the second work shift in section two, the refined metal storage area, with the privacy locks in place to avoid any detection. They rehearsed their actions step by step with holographic models of their assigned areas until each man was overly familiar with his job.

"There will be at least twelve engineers on deck, maybe sixteen. The Chief Engineer has requested another four crewmen be pulled out of cryo-sleep to assist with the course corrections. Those men are supposed to be awakened next Thursday, but I am assuming they are already awake and functional, and will be posted in the main engineering bridge. We must assume that our attempt is being anticipated by those in engineering," Mason cautioned.

He handed each of them special apparatuses for breathing, saying, "These are masks of super-thin material for breathing and eye protection during a chemical attack. Your faces must be entirely covered for them to function properly, so be sure to put them on at the appropriate time. They are new to the field for the Space Marines, standard issue for Prime Marines. Leave them in their containers until time to use them, and do not take them out to inspect them. They are one-time use only." They looked like cigar tubes.

Mason continued. "We will meet for dinner in the mess hall, as usual, at seventeen hundred. It is imperative that everything look normal, so act that way. Bitch and complain like you always do, Milton, or others in the mess hall will get suspicious." That comment added some much-needed levity to the secret meeting in section two. "Then we will begin our assignments at precisely nineteen-thirty. Are there any questions?"

At nineteen-thirty, Mason's team was wearing full camouflage and face paint, scattered in their positions to start their maneuvers. Corporal Milton, the shortest, thinnest member of the team, easily slipped into main engineering when the crewmen left to take their dinner breaks. He immediately dropped to the floor, and crawled on all fours behind the large server towers to the conduit shaft access panel. He silently opened the panel, slipped inside, and began the long horizontal climb. Mason reprogrammed the shaft cameras to replay yesterday's feed, so Milton was virtually invisible, as long as he did not step on any cables inside the shaft.

Corporal Johnson and four other Space Marines were noisily loading equipment onto the shuttles, located in the hangar bay directly below the main engineering deck, for all to hear. Then they pretended to leave, and turned the lighting off. They headed to the walls of the hangar, and climbed the conduit tubes up to the ceiling, removed the lighting panels, and hoisted themselves up into the sub-floor of engineering. There they waited for the signal.

Corporal Milton harbored a grudge against the day-shift engineers, for making fun of his thin, short stature at the Captain's first night dinner: "Hey, we've got a baby Space Marine, isn't he cute!" He would now make them pay for those embarrassing remarks. Mason couldn't even get his broad shoulders in this tube when they were inspecting it, but short and thin Milton had no problem. He climbed along the underside of the tube's ladder, using both his hands and feet. Like a schoolboy shimmying along the horizontal playground bars, he quickly covered the distance, and then transferred to the vertical ladder at the conduit ninety degree bend. This was a little more difficult, as the cables in the shaft were double the number of the horizontal conduit, but he was careful and quick, and reached the access point in less than one minute. Carefully checking for other crewmen in the area before proceeding, he opened the access panel, and was behind the engine console in a second. He keyed in the code sequence that the Staff Sergeant had given him, then hit "Enter," and passed back through the access panel to climb back down. He was all the way down the vertical shaft, half-way across the horizontal shaft, before the warning lights and bells went off all over the ship. That was the signal to action for the other four team members.

"Warning! Warning! Engine three misfire. Emergency deceleration! Emergency deceleration! Warning! Warning!" The computer kept repeating the warnings until the Assistant Chief Engineer located the source of the malfunction, but it was too late to prevent deceleration. The huge ship lurched violently as it came out of hyper-speed four, directly to sub-hyper-speed, sending many crewmen all over the ship into the walls and each other. Powers ran from the officer's mess back to his engineering bridge, followed by his engineers. They were greeted by a face full of stun gas, courtesy of the masked Space Marines. The crewmen in engineering became so absorbed in finding the cause of the malfunction they never noticed the Marines running into their main deck, spraying stun gas at them. Mason quickly reprogrammed the misfiring engine three to normal function, sub-speed, while his Space Marines deftly bound the engine crewmen and officers, and arranged them to lie side by side.

"Mason to the Captain," he called, using the engineering comm link. "We have control of the command console in engineering. Do you surrender your ship?"

"Captain Kouras to engineering. We surrender. Good job, Prime Marine. Now, release the men in engineering at once. Call the corpsmen to check for inhalation injuries. You and Lt. Commander Powers report to me in my ready room in one hour."

The extremely agitated engineering officers were released from their bindings, and hurried to their consoles to check the engines and computer systems. "How did you manage to use the crawl space? I've got three men assigned in the juncture sections waiting to stop anyone in there," Powers barked at Mason.

"We did not utilize the crawl spaces, sir. Your men are still inside. In fact, they are sealed inside the crawl spaces. Temporarily, of course, sir," Mason stated.

"Then how in hell did you access my engine console without being seen?" The Lieutenant Commander looked as if he would break a blood vessel.

"The conduit shafts, sir," Mason quietly replied.

"You can't get through those conduit shafts, Staff Sergeant. They're too small. You'd get stuck," Powers argued.

"The Chief Engineer is correct; I would not fit inside those narrow tubes. But Corporal Milton did, and he navigated both the horizontal and vertical shafts easily. This is the design flaw we need to correct, sir." Mason showed little emotion speaking with Lt. Commander Powers. He already breached his engineering deck and engine room. There was no need to agitate the officer any further, and risk an accusation of insubordination. "If the Chief Engineer will permit, I will call for the corpsmen, and my men will remove themselves from your bridge, sir."

"Permission granted!" Powers was beside himself, apoplectic. He knew Mason would try something during these unscheduled course corrections, and he was confident he would capture him red-handed in the crawl space. He was given a wide berth by his crewmen as he walked back to his command console to determine what, if any, damage had been done to his engines.

Later at the debriefing in the Captain's ready room, Mason explained the squad's detailed moves to everyone present. Lt. Commander Powers was in disbelief about Corporal Milton's ability to navigate through the conduit shafts. "Are you telling me that man made it from our engineering deck, crawled twenty meters upside down, then twenty meters vertically, programmed a false set of instructions on engine three's computer, then retraced his path, and got back to engineering in less than ten minutes? Impossible! I don't believe it for one minute. Captain this is absurd!"

"No, it's neither impossible nor absurd, Powers, it is history. You must remember that the goal of this exercise was to exploit a fatal design flaw in the Hesperia's engineering decks, not in your men. Mason came to me with his plan, and explained their every move, and I approved it. We must now take advantage of those Marines' efforts, and shore up the security in engineering. I have contacted Earth Command with the information gathered from this exercise, and they are pleased with the results. They are awaiting our recommendations to increase security in the engineering deck. URE scientists and ship designers are working to correct the design flaw."

"My engineering bridge still reeks from the stun gas. It has permeated the entire deck, all the way to the engine rooms." Powers glared at Mason.

"Captain Kouras placed restrictions on our team's handling of the crewmen on the engineering bridge, sir. No lasers or hand weapons were used, and no hand-to-hand combat was permitted. We were able to incapacitate the crewmen with a diluted form of stun gas, and no one was hurt, sir." Mason spoke somberly, looking at the Captain, and did not challenge the Chief Engineer with either his eye contact or his tone of voice.

"There were several minor injuries incurred from the ship coming out of hyper-speed so quickly, though. The hospital treated eleven crewmen for deep bruises, and one young man suffered a dislocation of his shoulder," Doctor Hassan offered.

"I am sorry for their minor injuries, Doctor Hassan, but this was a very important exercise. No damage was done to the ship or her engines. Thank you, Staff Sergeant Mason, for the hard work you and your Space Marines put into exploiting this design flaw. Your recommendations for increasing security in engineering will be taken into consideration. Your request for a special commendation for Corporal Milton has been granted. You are dismissed."

"Yes, sir. Thank you." Mason left the meeting, noticing that the XO was smiling at him.

"That enlisted man has stepped over the line, Captain. He made me look like a fool, and I think he deserves a reprimand for his behavior. I think..." the Chief Engineer was interrupted by Captain Kouras.

"He didn't make you look like a fool, Powers, you did that yourself. He came to me after the security team's first inspection of the engineering deck, with concerns for the safety of your crewmen and this ship. He was concerned that, if these sleeping six hundred miners were inspired to attempt mutiny on board the Hesperia, there would be little defense against them if they used the conduit shafts. I agreed with him, and ordered him to devise a plan to breach engineering, and take control of the ship. His plan originally did not involve using stun gas, but using laser guns set to stun. I did not allow weapons to be used. I think they did a hell of a job taking control of the engineering command console without firing a shot, or anyone getting hurt. I am writing a commendation for Mason for his successful efforts. You should thank him, Lt. Commander Powers, for identifying this flaw in the ship design, and possibly saving you, your crewmen, and everyone on board from being slaughtered, like the poor bastards on the Excelon. Now let's talk about the recommendations to increase security in the engineering deck."

Mason walked to the lift, heading for his quarters, when he decided to check in on the guys in sick bay. He did feel bad for the kid with the dislocated shoulder. Nurse Cohen greeted him with her usual beautiful smile.

"Hello, Staff Sergeant Mason. Are you planning any more attacks on our ship in the near future, or are we safe now?"

He returned her smile, and said, "Sorry to make more work for you and the med staff, ma'am. We attempted to hurt no one. How's the kid with the dislocated shoulder?"

"Lieutenant Urz is just fine. I'll tell him of your concern. I'd love to chat, but I'm rather busy now, so if you'll excuse me?" She could even tell me to leave, and I feel great, Mason admitted.

"Begging your pardon, ma'am." Mason left for his quarters.

VII

The ship was coming out of hyper-speed slowly, this time, towards GK-356. Mason and Dr. Hassan were checking the shuttles' life support systems while their cargo holds were loaded to capacity with new equipment, food, clothing, and medical supplies. Shuttle one was loaded with a new computer to upgrade their communications systems. All of the equipment on the colony was original, over twelve years old. In technology, that made their systems dinosaurs.

"Has anyone visited those colonists during the twelve years they've been on that asteroid, Dr. Hassan? The records are very sparse with information about them, sir," Mason asked.

"I think there were a couple of ships that made contact with them a few years ago. Research vessels, and a mining exploration ship, I think. You have to respect their tenacity. I couldn't have stayed on that rock for twelve years," Hassan replied.

"I would not have voluntarily done that either, Doctor. Couldn't they come home on leave for a few months? Or maybe exchange duties with someone else after a few years? It almost seems like cruel punishment to leave them there for so long." Mason could not fathom how thirty-one people could survive well on GK-356, even with an endless supply of water from the ice sheet covering most of the asteroid's surface.

"Earth Command thinks we need colonies established in the regions we wish to eventually call home, Staff Sergeant. Someone has to start them, from the ground up, you know what I mean," the Doctor said. It was imperialism at work, then. You could have substituted the word "control" for "call home," and you'd be right, Mason thought to himself.

"Yes, sir." Mason left to check that the base camp supplies were properly loaded and stored on shuttle three. Commander Baines was satisfied that everything was in order and ready to launch when ordered.

The Hesperia entered orbit with the asteroid in a few hours. All landing parties were ordered to their shuttles, and the trip to the surface began. Mason was on board shuttle two with the small contingent of armed Space Marines, for the protection of the landing parties, and base camp. No one knew exactly what to expect. The Captain made several attempts to communicate with the colony, and there had been no response. Would there even be anyone alive there? No one knew for certain.

The shuttles completed their short trip, and landed at the assigned staging area in a circular pattern, all facing outward. In case of a quick getaway, Mason assumed. Base camp was quickly set up, and the official greeting entourage gathered. "We will proceed to the colony, and be escorted by the Space Marines. Hopefully, we will be welcomed by the thirty-one colonists. Our intent is to reestablish contact with the colonists, ascertain their immediate needs, and offer any assistance needed. We will not engage anyone in the colony, unless it is to defend ourselves, is that perfectly clear?"

The landing group members acknowledged the Commander's instructions, and started the long walk towards the colony, through the dome's hatch. Why would the colonists engage us, Mason wondered? All ships bore the URE symbols, and everyone in the landing groups wore their uniforms. As they got closer to the colony, they saw an unkempt village, littered with trash, and discarded pieces of equipment. There were a few lights on; someone was watching their group approaching.

The Commander signaled for all stop, then called out, "Colony GK-356, we are from the ship Hesperia. We have attempted to communicate with you many times, with no response. We are here to help you. Please show yourselves."

No response. Mason saw some movement in one of the small buildings, and told the Commander. The XO motioned for him to move out, and the group stayed behind while the Marines slowly advanced.

"We are here to help. Please show yourselves. We mean you no harm. Dr. Maxim, are you there? Please come out, Dr. Maxim." The XO waited for their response, and, getting nothing, used his comm link with the Hesperia and notified the Captain of their situation.

Mason slowly moved toward the building where he had seen movement. His eyes were better than those of the rest of his party, he knew, but he wasn't sure what he had seen. He entered the building through a broken window, and dropped to the floor. He saw someone slowly raise up their head to look out the window in the next room. He crawled along the filthy floor to the next room, and saw a woman peeking out a corner of the window. Standing and raising his rifle, he said, "Don't be afraid, ma'am, we're not here to harm anyone. Where are the others?" She ran out of the room, through the door, and into the waiting arms of Corporal Johnson, who restrained her. "Got her. We have one female, Commander. She's pretty scared, sir."

"Hold her, Corporal. Ask her where the others are hiding," Baines ordered.

"Ma'am, we are here to help you. Please tell me where the others are. We are from the ship Hesperia, from Earth Command. We are here to help," Johnson said.

"Who are you? Why are you here? Are you with them? I won't tell, I won't tell, I won't tell." She wrestled in his hold, but he didn't let her go.

"I am Corporal Johnson, and the man who found you is Staff Sergeant Mason. We and others are here to help you, and the other colonists. Can you take us to Dr. Maxim?"

She struggled to get free of his hold, and Mason said, "We'd better put restraints on her, until we find the others. Take her to the Commander. I'll continue the search for the other colonists." The Corporal did as instructed, and took the terrified woman to the Commander.

She was told again they were sent to help her, and the other colonists. She held up her bound hands, and said, "This doesn't help me." The Commander ordered her restraints removed, and she bolted for an outcropping of icy rocks close to them.

"Let her go. We don't want to hurt anyone," the Commander said.

The Marines searched every building, and found the power supply for the compound. They threw the switch for the outdoor lighting, and it worked perfectly. The room where they were was virtually destroyed, all furniture broken and scattered everywhere. It was the same in every building. The lights made the compound look like a war zone. No one else was found. The XO sent the medical team back to base camp with a security team, and continued the search for anyone who could explain what happened.

"Staff Sergeant, find the communications center, and let's see what we can do to establish a link with the Hesperia in the compound," Commander Baines ordered over his comm link.

"I think this is the main building, Commander. Computers, storage systems; here's the communications station, sir," Mason reported. "Commander, the comm system is dead, sir."

"OK, Staff Sergeant. We'll deal with that later. Continue searching for other survivors. Widen your search perimeter only by one hundred meters, and report immediately if you find anyone else, especially Dr. Maxim," Baines instructed.

"I'm Dr. Maxim." The Commander was startled. "You don't need that gun here; it won't be of any value to you in this place." The man looked like he was a zombie.

"Dr. Maxim, I'm sorry. I'm Commander Baines of the mining freighter

Hesperia. We've come to render any assistance to your group that you may require. Food, medical supplies, new communications equipment. How may we help you, Dr. Maxim?"

The ragged man looked intensely at the Commander, and said, "It has been a very long time since we received any visitors. Please come inside." He led the Commander and his group inside the farthest lit building, went inside, and went to a microphone. "It's all right. These men are here to help us. Everyone come out and meet them."

The colonists looked like World War III survivors, ragged, so thin they could not walk properly, and filthy. They looked and smelled like it had been years since they bathed. The Commander ordered the med team to return. He ordered portable showers set up, and fresh clothing for them. And crates of food rations, as many as his men could carry. "What happened here, Dr. Maxim? How long since anyone visited to bring food and supplies to the colony?"

"I think it's been three years or more. I'm not sure. I kept a log for so long, but I stopped. We thought we had been forgotten, left to starve," Maxim said.

"You were not able to successfully seed the asteroid with blue-green algae?" The Commander asked.

Dr. Maxim laughed at that question, a hideous laugh that shook his entire body. "Oh yes, the blue-green algae. They loved that. It bloomed, and was consumed in one week. An incredible waste of time and effort."

"It was consumed in one week? By your people?" The Commander asked, innocently.

"No, not by my people, sir. You see, we are not alone on this cursed rock. Our initial readings were faulty. We are not alone," and the Doctor's voice slowly trailed off. He lowered his head, and closed his eyes, asleep, it seemed.

Commander Baines persisted. "Dr. Maxim, if you could not grow your own food, and no supply ship has been here in over three years, how have you survived? Sir?"

"We have survived on our wills, our wits, and water. It is truly amazing what you can eat and digest, is it not? When all the food was gone, we ate paper. Then, our shoes. Boiled our belts and the cushions from all the chairs. Ate the insulation off the computer wiring. Scavenged our arrival ship until everything we could chew was gone. Even tried crushing some of the rocks. We ate all our clothing except for what we have on. And more," Dr. Maxim answered.

The Commander was afraid to ask what "more" meant. "What about your research?"

"We abandoned the research after the first of us died from starvation. Too weak to do research. We lived off the agar in the test jars for months.

We did what we had to do, you must understand. But you cannot understand." Dr. Maxim looked at his fellow colonists, and lowered his head. "I'm responsible. I brought everyone here. I'm responsible."

Dr. Hassan came in with the med techs, and stopped in their tracks at the sight of the colonists. They set up IV's in the fifteen colonists as soon as possible, and gently laid them on what tables they could find for emergency treatment. The colonists were given as many protein food tubes as they could eat, and they sucked them down in an instant. No one was talking except Dr. Maxim, a strange situation. They looked at the corpsmen with fear and trepidation, yet allowed them to pump fluids and plasma into their weak veins. Their eyes were those of starving, terrified people, not research scientists.

Mason reported finding no other colonists, and was instructed to come to the main building and assist. The Space Marines tried to straighten up the larger rooms so they could be useable for interviewing the colonists. They set up the portable showers, and helped the colonists one by one into the cabinets for their first showers in years. Mason nearly puked from those people's stench. They smelled like rotting eggs; some of them, worse. Each one received their own soap and shampoo kit, razor, washcloth, and towel. The Marines handed out fresh, new clothing to them. Some of them just stood in the shower with their mouths open, drinking in the water, like baby turkeys on Earth. Some had to be cajoled into cleaning their bodies, like they were in a dream they didn't really believe.

Hours later, when they all were washed and dressed in new clothing, Dr. Maxim asked them to assemble in the rearranged conference room in the main building for a meeting. There were signs of life coming into their faces, after many food tubes were eaten, and fresh water being drunk. "These men have come to help us. They are from the Hesperia mining ship. They want us to tell them what happened." Not a single sound was heard.

Mason wondered if Dr. Maxim had some kind of hypnotic hold on them. Or, were they still afraid of them? Dr. Hassan broke the ice, and asked, "It is my understanding that there were originally thirty-one colonists here. There are only fifteen of you now, in this room. Can you tell me what happened to your fellow colonists?"

Finally, one woman spoke. "They all died, except for us, and Dr. James. He went away with them."

"Dr. James went away with whom, ma'am?" Mason asked politely.

"The men from the cloud. He wanted to go. They took him. He went back with them," she said feebly. She hung her head, and said no more.

"Can you tell us the name of their ship, the one who took Dr. James away?" Mason asked.

"It was the red cloud, or something close to that," a man in the back offered.

"Corporal Johnson will help fill up your new air beds. You can all sleep on them tonight. Which building do you sleep in?" Mason asked. It turned out that, since they'd tried to eat their mattresses long ago, and had no beds, they just wandered around the compound area, and slept wherever they landed.

The crewmen found the sleeping quarters, and tried to clean and straighten it out for the colonists. They inflated their air beds for them, and laid them out in an orderly fashion. The colonists picked up their beds, and wandered off in all directions, with only one man choosing to sleep in the cleaned room.

The landing groups from the Hesperia stayed for the day with the colonists, trying to get them in better health. The crewmen replaced their useless computer and communications system with the new equipment they'd brought down for them, so they could connect with Earth again. They brought enough food rations for thirty-one people for one year. Each man and woman asked to go back with them to the Hesperia, and leave the asteroid. Each shuttle could take perhaps one or two of the colonists, but no more. Captain Kouras was waiting for authorization from Earth Command to bring seven or eight colonists on board.

Dr. Hassan asked Dr. Maxim, "You said you were not alone on this asteroid. What exactly did you mean, Doctor?"

"I mean we found life here, on this asteroid. It lives below the ice sheets. It is a kind of bacteria we've never seen on Earth, extremely virulent, and resistant to freezing cold and boiling water. It ate all the blue-green algae. We had to be careful not to cut too far down into the ice sheets, or we'd pick up the bacteria. That's what killed the other colonists. They thought that boiling the deep ice water would kill anything, and the water would then be safe to drink. The rest of us were not certain, and were testing the bacteria in the labs. We didn't drink the boiled water, they did. We are alive; they died, within hours. The bacteria consumed them from the inside out. It is very voracious."

Dr. Hassan became immediately concerned about bringing any of the colonists on board. They all went through the bio filters upon boarding the ship, of course, but the scanners were programmed for known viruses and bacteria. A voracious, virulent strain of unknown bacteria that could eat a man alive from the inside out could decimate the Hesperia. He left the building, found Commander Baines, and immediately called the Captain on the comm link.

"Captain Kouras, this is Dr. Hassan. I don't think we would be wise to bring any colony survivors on board the Hesperia, sir." He proceeded to tell him what Dr. Maxim said.

"OK, I wonder when Dr. Maxim planned to tell us this little detail. You are to leave every piece of food, supplies, and equipment you brought down there in the compound, or in base camp. All of it! I want you all on board your shuttles immediately and headed back to the Hesperia. No colonists. Just get back here now, is that clear?" The Captain was adamant. "Are you still there Doctor? Commander? Get going now! That's an order!"

The Commander immediately ordered everyone back to base camp, on the double. Dr. Hassan gave them all antibacterial wipes to use prior to entering the shuttles. As if that would kill unknown bacteria, he thought. They launched immediately when everyone was on board.

No one in the landing group but the XO and Dr. Hassan knew why they were ordered to leave immediately, and the crewmen were never told about the bacteria. Upon returning to the Hesperia, the men were all put through the bio filters three times, and given antibiotics intravenously and orally. The clothes they wore down to the surface were burned and jettisoned, and they were placed in quarantine inside section two for one week. The shuttles were sprayed with antibacterial agents and wiped down by hazmat teams in the bay. Then they were subjected to infrared lighting for one week, until their interior wiring disintegrated.

Earth Command placed the asteroid GK-356 on full quarantine. At Captain Kouras' request, humanitarian food drops would take place whenever a ship passed by. No other Earth ship would ever land there, on "Purgatory." The colonists were really on their own, now.

VIII

No one who went down to the GK-356 asteroid believed that their forced quarantine was for their own protection, as they were told. But no one complained about being segregated from the rest of the crew. They knew something happened to force their departure so quickly, something they weren't told, something they'd probably never know. The men were racked with guilt from leaving the colonists behind, seeing their gaunt, desperate faces, pleading and crying for help getting off that rock. Mason would never forget their faces, and the fact that he was ordered to abandon those he was brought in to help.

The Hesperia was taken out of the asteroid's orbit as soon as the shuttles were back on board in their bay. They launched a missile container to the surface packed with medical supplies, more clothing and food rations, and then the ship left for the mining fields without delay.

Upon release from his quarantine, Mason turned his attention to preparing for the remaining passengers awakening. Their orders specifically provided the date and time the rest of the sleeping crew would be awakened from cryo-sleep. The full crew was to be up and fully functional before a single miner was awakened. First, the remaining crewmen would be awakened, according to duty station, staggered over a period of two weeks. Then the research scientists, and finally, the last contingent of Space Marines. After these personnel were all back to full duty, eating normally, and able to sleep a full seven hours each night, the six hundred miners' awakening would begin.

There was a very specific hierarchy of which civilians would be brought out of cryonic sleep first, second, and so on. The Captain had been made aware that any change to this schedule might result in a contract "violation" with the miners' union, a situation no one wanted to happen. They could not afford to be in deep space with six hundred miners on strike.

First to be awakened was the URE Mission Director, Harold Keene, followed by the URE Mission Coordinator, Alfredo Garcia. Their own medical staff was next. Then the two union reps, the supervisors, and Chief Technician. The rest of the men would be awakened by duty and seniority, a task supervised by the Mission Coordinator and the union reps. The corpsmen charged with bringing the men out of cryonic sleep would only awaken the men on that day's roster provided by the union reps. The entire process would be managed by the Mission Director.

After the Mission Director was awakened, Mason would be at his station on the bridge for the duration of the four years that the Hesperia would be mining and refining. Mason's orders were to protect the bridge, defend the officers and crew of the Hesperia, and prevent the takeover of the ship at all costs. No civilian was to set foot on that bridge. The miners were not to even cross over into section one. They had their own mess hall, gym, lounge areas, and hospital. There was to be as little interaction between the military crew and the miners as possible. The Captain and Commander would interact only with the Mission Director and Mission Coordinator. Mason was ready for the general awakenings, starting in five weeks from now

The security team accompanied Mason day after day through the various sections of the Hesperia, looking for anything that appeared out of the ordinary, or simply out of place. No one attempted to board one of the shuttles to check navigational coordinates or for any other reason, since the monitors were installed. All of the very large equipment was undisturbed in section four. The foundries and furnaces of section three were eerily quiet.

Mason took one more climb up the crawl tubes into engineering, and sent roving video cameras into the shafts where Corporal Milton had so deftly hurried just a few weeks ago. All clear. Lt. Commander Powers helped them check out the computer systems access panels, and all were free and clear. Next came the crews' quarters' deck, which should have been quick work for the security team, since the majority of the crew members were still in cryo-sleep.

The security team members broke into two-man teams and proceeded to check every assigned room for locked doors; all locked, as before. Then Mason decided to check inside the few unassigned rooms, and sweep them for any bugging devices, booby traps, or incendiaries. Every room was clean and all clear. As the teams were heading towards the lift and the next deck, something caught Mason's bionic eye, a reflection, or a small flash, where none should be. He halted their steps, scanning the top and sides of the corridor with his electronic scanner. Nothing. Maybe he was just tired. But, maybe not. He reversed his steps for six or seven paces, and then resumed walking straight for the lift, and there it was again! "Corporal Johnson, let's remove that ceiling panel very carefully." The tall Corporal did as requested, holding the panel by both ends, and gently moving it along its track for a better look.

"Wait, stop right there! Don't move!" Mason exclaimed. "Just hold it right there. Men, get over there and help him hold that panel still." Mason shined the light from his flashlight into the newly-opened crevice, onto something shiny and metallic. "Corporal Milton, get a ladder for us on the double."

The Corporal ran down the corridor, and was back with a ladder in a short time. "Staff Sergeant, do you want me to..." he began to ask.

"I want you to set it up right here for me. Now Johnson, I told you not to move!" Mason climbed up two rungs of the ladder quickly, above the low ceiling panel, stuck his head above the panel into the ceiling, and saw the object reflecting the light in the corridor. He put on his gloves, and then slowly removed the metal object from the ceiling support truss, being as careful as he could be to not drop it. He stepped down the ladder, holding an octagonal tube, decorated with strange and unusual symbols carved or etched into its metallic surface, approximately one half meter long. "Well, well, well, what have we here? Corporal Johnson, check up there for anything else in the ceiling that doesn't belong there. Corporal Milton, notify Captain Kouras that the team has made a discovery he will definitely want to see. Let's go."

Mason and the team went straight to the bridge to meet with the Captain, explaining how the octagonal tube was spotted and recovered. "Captain, do you think this metallic tube could have been the weapon that killed Dr. Reese?" Mason asked.

"Possibly. Commander Baines, ask Doctor Hassan to come up here and take a look at this thing," Kouras requested.

"Yes, Captain," Baines responded.

"Any of you know what language this is, or what these symbols mean?" Captain Kouras asked, turning the tube in his gloved hands. "I've never seen any writing like it. I can't even positively identify the type of metal it is. Baines, can you figure this out?"

He looked at the tube curiously. "No, Captain, but I'd like the opportunity to study it."

"It's mine first," Dr. Hassan said, running from the lift. "I've got to see if it is a match for our murder weapon. Where was it found?" He offered a tray to the Captain, who gently placed the tube on the tray, and the Doctor covered it with a clear lid. "Where did you find it?"

"Hidden in the ceiling in a corridor on the crew's deck, sir," Mason answered.

"How did you know it was in the ceiling, Staff Sergeant?" The Doctor asked, bewildered.

"I saw a glint of light in the ceiling. When we removed the panel in the ceiling where the light was being reflected, we found this object," Mason stated. "The panel had obviously been improperly replaced in a hurry by whoever put the tube up there, and it was enough for the tube to reflect light, and catch my eye."

The Captain was pleased. "Good catch, Mason. We'll notify you of our findings. Have you completed your inspection?"

"Not quite finished, Captain. Permission to resume our inspection, sir."

"Permission granted, Staff Sergeant. Carry on." The team left the bridge, and Captain Kouras said to the Doctor, "I want a full analysis on this thing. Any prints, DNA, whatever. Is it our murder weapon? I also want to know what it's made of, and what language this writing is. What do these symbols mean?"

"I have no idea what they mean, Captain. We'll run a thorough analysis on it right away, and notify you as soon as the information is available." The Doctor carefully took the tray and went to the hospital.

"Nurse Cohen, will you assist me with an analysis of this object?" He asked.

"Yes, of course, Doctor. What is it?" She looked at the strange tube.

"I'm pretty certain it is the weapon that killed Dr. Reese. Other than that, I have no idea what it is," Doctor Hassan said. "Let's get it under the scanners."

The octagonal tube was placed under the scanners for analysis. The readings were helpful only in that they told them what the object was not. There was no DNA residue, no fingerprints. The object was sealed at both ends, and they didn't know how to get into the tube. Nurse Cohen asked, "Why can't we take this up to the research labs? Aren't the doctors there working on some kind of metal analysis? Perhaps they would have scanners more adept for this kind of work. Our scanners are designed for medical analysis and diagnosis, primarily for human tissue, not strange metallic objects. Doctor?"

Dr. Hassan nodded his head in agreement. "Yes, you are correct. I thought we could get some kind of data on this octagonal tube before turning it over to someone else. The only thing we know is that the ends of this object are a 90% match for our murder weapon. Since the injury did not leave any residue or traces of any particular type of metal, we cannot say with absolute certainty that this was the weapon that was used to inflict the deadly blow to his skull. We'll have to notify the Captain," he sighed, disappointed with their lack of information. "Captain Kouras, this is Dr. Hassan."

"This is the Captain, what did you find out, Doctor?"

"Captain, I am sorry to report that our analysis is insufficient. It has shown only that this is most likely the weapon that was used on Dr. Reese, but even that conclusion is only 90% certain. We recommend that our MM

& E research scientists assist us, utilizing whatever means of analysis they have at their disposal."

There was a slight pause before the Captain responded. "I see. I am assigning this task to Commander Baines, and your Head Nurse, if you can spare her, Doctor. I am not simply handing this object over to the civilian research lab for analysis without our own people there to supervise and observe every step of their procedures. Nurse Cohen, meet me and Commander Baines in my ready room in fifteen minutes, and bring the tube with you in a sealed, transparent container. Kouras out."

Commander Baines and Captain Kouras discussed protocol concerning the MM & E research scientists. "They are still conducting their experiments, Captain, but I think they would be honored to assist in analyzing the weapon that killed their Chief Scientist. Don't you agree, sir?"

"Baines, careful of trusting the research scientists too much. They have their own agenda, remember. And, one or both of them could be involved in Dr. Reese's demise," the Captain cautioned.

"Are we to treat them as suspects, then, Captain?" The Commander asked incuriously.

"No, I didn't say that. They have not been named as suspects, but they are "persons of interest," as Mason would say. Not everyone in research has a conscience as white as their lab coats, Commander," the Captain said.

Commander Cohen walked into the ready room, and both men stopped talking when she came in. "If I'm interrupting your conversation, I can wait outside."

"No, no, we were just discussing protocol in dealing with the research scientists, Commander Cohen, please be seated," the Captain urged. "I was just cautioning Commander Baines about trusting the researchers too much, so soon. We must enlist their cooperation in our investigation of this object, but we cannot leave it with them. I don't want this tube in anyone's possession but our own."

"Absolutely, Captain. I met the doctors at your first night party, but neither that introduction nor professional courtesy entitles them to have temporary control of such an important object." She held up the octagonal tube in its protective container. "I know there is no absolute proof that this octagonal tube was used as a murder weapon, but it fits the skull injury site markings perfectly. We must discover all we can about it."

"I wasn't saying that we should just hand over the tube to them, sir. But I doubt that we would be familiar enough with their equipment to know exactly what test they were performing on it, assuming they will help us," the Commander said, in his defense. "I am not a metallurgist, sir."

"No, you are not; however, I want you and Commander Cohen to be in charge of this investigation because you both have displayed superior analytical skills, and deductive reasoning. And, they will help us, if for no other reason than they have to!" The Captain stood up and told them, "It is in the best interests of this mission to find who the perpetrator of this murder is, the murder of MM & E's own Chief of Research. Earth Command has instructed us that they cannot refuse to help us in this matter, period. Good luck, Commanders."

The Commanders left the ready room for the research labs. "Do you have a preference as to which of the doctors we should approach first with this matter, Commander?" Baines asked.

"Why don't we ask them to meet with us together? They can recommend which tests they can perform on the tube, and how long the tests will take. Also, what is their procedure for interpreting the analytical data? We need to know and document their methods, as well as their analytical results," she replied.

"Precisely! I'm glad we're working on this together," Commander Baines said, a smile coming to his face. They soon entered the corridor where the labs were, and Dr. Honig's lab came up first. After a quick knock on the lab door, the Commanders entered and introduced themselves to Dr. Honig.

"I'm Commander Baines, Executive Officer, and this is Commander Cohen. We'd like to meet with you and Dr. Jenkins about this object." He pointed to the long container where the octagonal tube rested.

Dr. Honig got up from his chair and came over to look at the object in the container. "What is it? Oh, you don't know what it is, else you wouldn't have come to us, isn't that right?"

"We need to know exactly what it is, and what methods you and Dr. Jenkins will use to determine its composition, and hopefully, its intended use," Commander Cohen said, holding the container for Dr. Honig to see. "Would you please call Dr. Jenkins and ask him to join us?"

"It is unusual," Dr. Honig said, looking intensely at the object. "Yes, let me get Dr. Jenkins in on this. Dr. Jenkins, Honig here. Would you come into Lab A for a minute? There are a couple of officers with a very interesting metallic object looking for our help."

"Really? OK, be right there," Dr. Jenkins said over the comm-link. He appeared at the doorway in an instant. "What do you have?" He came over to Commander Cohen, and looked at the metallic tube inside its protective container. "Let's take it out for a look."

"If you don't mind, we would like to discuss what tests you would perform on it for analysis. Is there a meeting room nearby?" Commander Baines asked.

"Yes, certainly. Right this way." Dr. Jenkins led everyone to their small conference room, and sat down at the farthest end of the table. "It would probably be the most proper thing for us to ask if there's any hurry with this. Reason being, our team lead doctors are still in cryonic sleep for another two weeks or so. They should really be the ones to ask for help. I don't know if we are allowed to use our equipment for anyone else's projects."

"Yes, we'll have to check it out with our team leaders. Why not just leave it with us, and we'll get back to you in a few weeks. We are in the middle of our experiments, you know," Dr. Honig said dryly. "We can't take on any more assignments now."

"This is not one of your assignments, Doctors. This is a matter of primary importance to the Space Force, as well as to this particular mission," Commander Baines said, getting irritated at their attitudes.

"It's not one of *our* primary important experiments, officer," Dr. Honig said arrogantly, and stood up abruptly. "So, I guess we're done here."

"No, we are just beginning," Commander Cohen said firmly. "Please sit down, Dr. Honig. If you'd prefer, we can have this meeting in Captain Kouras' ready room, and we'd be more than happy to explain to him and Earth Command that you are refusing to assist us with our request." Commander Cohen stared him back down into his chair. "First of all, we cannot afford the luxury of waiting a week or more for your research team leaders to be awakened. We need to accurately analyze and identify this octagonal tube as soon as possible. Our scanners in the med lab could only provide limited information from their analysis. They are programmed primarily for human tissue analysis and diagnosis, not metallurgy. That is why we have come to you. You are the experts in this field, and we need your help. Now, not at some later date."

Commander Baines was seeing a side of Commander Cohen he had not seen at any time before, and his respect for her shot off the charts. "The Commander is quite correct. Time is of the essence. How will we proceed in the analysis of this tube?"

"We?" asked Dr. Jenkins. "I thought you wanted us to analyze it for you." He looked at Commander Cohen.

"This metallic object is so important that we cannot let it out of our sights, Dr. Jenkins. I am not at liberty to tell you why, for now, but we must be present to observe and document any and all procedures and tests performed on this octagonal tube in your labs. I assure you both that we are here as observers, relying on your expertise." Commander Cohen looked at both of the researchers, and asked, "Shall we get started, then?"

The young research scientists settled down, after Commander Cohen successfully "unruffled their feathers." They recommended three basic analytical tests to determine the type of metals the tube was made of, and its approximate age.

"I have never seen these symbols before, have you, Dr. Honig?" Jenkins asked.

"No. Never. Have you run them through your ship's computers for language analysis and translation?" Dr. Honig was finally getting on board the investigation.

"Yes, and we have come up empty. The symbols are still being analyzed by the computers, checking symbology in astronomy, all known languages, formulaic transcriptions, and all scientific applications, as well as higher mathematics, of course," Commander Baines offered. "My specialty."

"We think it is some kind of hollow tube, but what it is, and what it contains, we do not know. You'll note that both ends are identically sealed so perfectly that it appears at first to be solid. Do you see the seals?" Commander Cohen put on a glove and lifted the tube out of the container, and handed it to Dr. Honig. He and Jenkins also donned sterile gloves.

He examined the tube closely, turning it around several times, before giving it to Dr. Jenkins. "Yes, I see what you mean. Can you at least tell us where you found such an object?"

"No, we can only tell you it was discovered on board the Hesperia yesterday," Commander Baines said, watching their curiosity grow.

"Then let's get the analysis underway. Jenkins, want to start with your photo macrographs and photo micrographs? I'll prepare the computer for the vacuum impregnation mounting, heat and cold treatment conditions."

"I'm on it. And I'll do the grain analysis, for compositional determination, as well."

The young researchers went to their respective laboratories to program their analytical computers. "Why don't I go with Dr. Honig, Commander?" Commander Cohen was very perceptive, and noticed that Honig seem to enjoy baiting Baines into confrontational situations. She went with Honig into his lab, and sat down to watch him prepare the computers for their analysis.

"How soon before we have the analysis on its micro structural constituents, Dr. Jenkins?" asked Commander Baines. "We need to know the process by which this tube was formed, if possible."

"Will you be attempting to reverse engineer that process, because determining that analysis will take more than a couple of hours? Probably several days, if the basic components can be identified now," Jenkins enquired.

"Well, that's not my call to make, Dr. Jenkins, although it is intriguing. No, for now, let's just get the basic analysis. That should give us what we need at this juncture." Commander Baines liked this young man. Not only was he capable and intelligent, he anticipated the needs of the situation, and suggested the next possible direction the analysis might take.

In the other lab, Dr. Honig took the tube from Commander Cohen. "I assume we cannot take samples of this tube, is that right? I could try to take a very small sample for the heat and cold treatment conditional analysis, if you'll permit." She definitely liked Honig better when he was not in the same room with Commander Baines.

"If it's possible to take a very small sample, then go ahead. But please record your attempt, would you? We need to record as much as possible, you understand, Dr. Honig."

"Yes, I understand. OK, let's obtain a sample." He turned and placed the tube onto the round analysis table, and operated the micro laser carefully. "It is not cutting a sample. In fact, look here. The laser didn't even leave a mark on it. Interesting. I'll increase the intensity a bit." He keyed in the instructions, and returned back to the micro laser. "Now, let's see. Now that's really interesting. Not even a micro etching on the tube. This material is very hard." Dr. Honig picked up the tube and held it in his hand. "Not the slightest heat on it, anywhere. I wonder..." and he went to one of his side cabinets along the wall, and returned with a bulky hand tool. "This is a diamond saw. Old school. With your permission?"

"Go ahead," Commander Cohen said, as captivated as the young doctor was with the tube's resistance to being cut.

"OK, here goes the diamond saw, the sharpest substance on Earth. It can cut anything." He clamped down the tube, with an edge protruding over the edge of the table, and confidently lowered the diamond saw blade on the edge of the tube. He started the noisy saw, holding it on the tube edge for a few seconds, and then stopped the saw. "Now that's impossible! Look, Commander, it didn't even scratch the tube!"

"What does that tell you, Dr. Honig?" She asked.

"I am not one to rush to judgment, ma'am, but I seriously doubt that what we're dealing with is composed with Earth metals." Dr. Honig replaced the saw into the cabinet, and went back to his computer to finalize his analysis. He handed her the stored analysis. "It is impossible to conduct any further analysis of the materials in this tube without subjecting the entire tube to extreme heat and cold, which could possible destroy the tube, or its contents. I hope Dr. Jenkins' tests can provide more usable data for you, Commander. I'm sorry to disappoint you."

"You have not disappointed me at all, Dr. Honig. To be quite truthful, I expected as much. Thank you for your time and your analyses. I'll notify Captain Kouras that you were most cooperative and helpful." She smiled, and left his lab, heading for the next lab, where Commander Baines and Dr. Jenkins waited for the tube. "Your turn, gentlemen." She handed the tube to Commander Baines. "I'll just sit over here and make some notes."

Dr. Jenkins placed the tube under the photomicrography computer. He turned the scanner on, and ran the analysis of the tube, then turned it over, and re-ran the analysis on the other side. "OK, now for the photomacrography." He took the tube to the other side of the lab, and placed it under the lens of that computer. First one side, then the other side, as before. He went back to the main computer control console, and watched the 3D images of the octagonal tube, rotating the image over and over. When the analysis finished running for both tests, he brought the stored information to Commander Baines. "I can honestly say I have no idea what is in this tube's composition. I can't even run a grain analysis. Our scanners cannot penetrate the outer shell. I can see the seals at each end, but not how they were sealed. I doubt we can open it without destroying its contents completely, if at all. Any chance I can have the opportunity to test it when my team leader is here?"

"I'll let you know later, Dr. Jenkins. Thank you for your work. We appreciate your cooperation," Commander Baines said. He and Commander Cohen both left the lab, and headed for the lift. "I'd like to write a summary of these analyses before presenting them to the Captain. Would you care to join me for a boring, tasteless lunch of food rations, while we discuss our conclusions, Commander Cohen?"

She looked at his twinkling blue eyes, and his smiling face, then said, "Now, how could I refuse such an invitation, Commander Baines?" They both were laughing as they walked towards the Officers' Mess.

IX

"Ninety percent certain," that was what Dr. Hassan told Mason. But ninety percent certain would not fly in a court of law, civilian or military. He decided to continue his search for the 100% certain murder weapon. He and his security teams scoured every hall and corridor, every panel and storage area, locker, container, and every hold on the Hesperia. All four main sections of the ship were meticulously searched for over a year. The octagonal tube seemed to be the likely murder weapon, but without any DNA or prints, it was not a fool-proof piece of evidence.

Mason asked himself a hundred times how he would have disposed of the murder weapon. Of course, there would have been no weapon found if he would have killed someone. There would have been no body found either. He would have disposed of both cleanly and efficiently as ash in space.

Two days before the general awakenings for the crew, scientists, and his remaining Space Marines, Mason decided to consult the XO. "Commander Baines, permission to speak with you, sir, in confidence, privately," Mason asked.

"Certainly, Staff Sergeant. We can use the Captain's ready room." He gave the chair to Lieutenant Davis, and led Mason to the ready room. "What's on your mind, Mason?"

"Sir, we have searched this ship dozens of times in the past year for the weapon used to murder Dr. Reese," Mason stated.

"You found that octagonal tube. Dr. Hassan is almost positive that is what was used to kill him. What's your point?" Baines asked.

Mason answered firmly. "My point is, sir, that the Doctor is ninety percent certain, not one hundred percent. We both know that a court of law, civilian or military, would throw that tube out as evidence at ninety percent, lacking any DNA or prints. So I have continued searching."

"I see, Staff Sergeant. How may I assist you? You're not still wanting to walk outside the hull are you?" The Commander queried.

"Yes, sir, but that's not what I want to ask you," Mason said. He began, "Commander, if you had used some sort of weapon to kill Dr. Reese, in the short amount of time available before the ship went into hyper-space and everyone went into cryo-sleep, where would you have hidden or disposed of that weapon?"

The Commander sat bolt upright in his chair. "Are you accusing me, Staff Sergeant?"

"Absolutely not, sir. My reason for asking you this question is that I think whoever committed this act of murder was a scientist, like Dr. Reese, and a man of above-average intellect. But not a man used to killing, and definitely not someone with military training. A trained killer would not need a weapon, just his hands. Killing him with a blow to the head from behind is not the way an expert would have done it."

The Commander relaxed a bit. "I see what you mean. A blow from behind would not be the style for you - or me. I am trained in some martial arts; black belts in Tai kwon do, in fact."

"Sir, I meant no disrespect to you. I'm just trying to profile the killer. I wanted to get your opinion of what someone else would do." Don't you dare piss off another officer, especially the XO, Mason told himself.

"OK, Mason, I understand. You and I both have to improve our communication and people skills." The Commander sat back and chuckled.

Mason felt relieved. "Yes, sir, I'm aware I don't always approach people the best way. I just want to solve this case, or at least have exhausted every possibility, before the general awakenings."

"And I'm doing all I can to solve the orange cloud mystery before the awakenings, as well. We both must be willing to admit that the lack of evidence has caused our efforts to be stifled," Baines sighed. "At least we will not be stone-walled from lack of trying, Mason."

"A bitter pill to swallow, sir," Mason admitted.

"Yes, indeed. So, let's go over what we do know. Dr. Reese did board the ship properly, at all the security checkpoints." Baines referred to the ship's logs. "He did enter his quarters the first night. He would have to use his full handprint to set the entry code. We checked it out; the handprint matches the one we have on file for him, and also matches the post-mortem print."

"Check, sir." Mason looked at his notes. "But he was found naked, and his shower had not been used. There was no soap residue on the body. I checked the showers in the gym, and none were utilized the first night. Perhaps he undressed in preparation to take a shower, and was assaulted in his room. The privacy lock was activated when the Captain sent the security team to check on him when he was not in attendance at the first night party."

"That only leaves about a two to three hour window when he was killed." The Commander searched the computer for a moment, and then said, "But the killer put his body into the walk-in freezer soon after he died, according to Dr. Hassan's autopsy notes. There was no blood clotted on his head when he was found on the freezer floor."

"Commander, suppose Dr. Reese was confronted by someone who he knew, or knew of, who came to his quarters; they argued about something, and Dr. Reese was killed, fully clothed. The perp would have had enough time to take him to the mess hall and strip him before putting him in the freezer. He could've cleaned his wound with his clothing after stripping him. Then gone to the Captain's party, like nothing ever happened."

The Commander considered the hypothesis. "Yes, Mason, that does make sense, as well. The killer could've trashed the doctor's clothing down an incendiary trash chute, maybe along with the murder weapon."

"I thought about that too, Commander, but the trash chutes did not have their burners on while we were docked. They were not activated until after we left Titan One. I'm thinking the perp knew that little detail, and hid the weapon until he was certain it could be recovered, and destroyed. But, what if he could not go and retrieve it, without being noticed? The only persons allowed on board the first three nights were the military officers, bridge crew, security, and the Space Marines; and the URE scientists from the MM & E. No miners or their civilian crew." Mason was perplexed.

"Have your men checked inside the ceiling panels, where the octagonal tube was found?" Baines asked.

"Affirmative, sir. After the tube was discovered, we checked all hall and corridor ceilings on the crew quarters deck, engineering, the bridge, and cargo bays, both by men crawling up there, and with video cameras. Nothing else was discovered."

Baines sat back in his chair. "Quite a problem, Staff Sergeant."

Mason agreed, "Yes, sir. So, if I may ask again: if you had murdered Dr. Reese, where would you have hidden the murder weapon?"

Commander Baines thought briefly, and answered, "Probably somewhere in the mess hall. Maybe we're overlooking something. What if the blow to his head only stunned him or he was not killed instantly, and could walk? Then the killer could have taken Dr. Reese while he was able to walk somewhat, and led him to the mess hall to let him die in the freezer."

The two men looked at each other to let that scenario play in their thoughts for a moment. "There are a lot of cooking utensils in the mess hall, Commander," Mason said.

"Didn't you check the mess hall, Mason?"

"Yes, of course, sir. But, we're not cooks. There are hundreds of things in there I have no clue about as to their usage. Maybe the weapon was only part of another tool, separated, used to kill the doctor, then put back together, Commander Baines."

"Let's wake up Chief Dawson!" The Commander was on the comm-link to Captain Kouras in a flash, getting permission to wake Chief Dawson ahead of her scheduled awakening. "Yes, Captain, we're requesting the Chief be awakened as soon as possible; right now, in fact."

The two men rushed to the hospital and found Nurse Cohen on duty. They asked to have Chief Dawson awakened, and that they secured the Captain's permission to do so.

"May I ask why Chief Dawson is to be awakened early, Commander Baines? I'll have to enter the reason for your unusual request in the log." Nurse Cohen was suspicious regarding their request at such an hour.

"Let's just say that her expertise is necessary for a potentially new development in the investigation of Dr. Reese's murder, Nurse Cohen." The Commander had an excited look on his face Mason had not seen before; was he excited about a potential new development, or Nurse Cohen? "Would you kindly wake the Chief now?"

"OK, Commander Baines, as long as the Captain has signed the order. Let's locate her cryo-capsule first." She turned towards the computer.

"Deck 6, Room 3A, stack 14, ma'am," Mason quickly offered.

"Thank you for saving me the effort, Staff Sergeant. Then let's go." She shook her head, and led the way to the lift.

The stacks of cryo-cocoons were silent and ethereal in appearance. Mason was used to his cryo-cocoon being in vertical stacks with the Space Marines, not laying one just atop the other, with only one centimeter in between. Perfectly aligned white cocoons in column after column, with their individual computer screens providing small, pulsating red and green lights, indicating that all was well with their occupants. He recalled how the miners' stacks looked in their quarters, with their six hundred cocoons all lined up in columns and rows, keeping those men and women safely in hibernation. A cold and efficient process. His musings were interrupted when Nurse Cohen turned on the ambient lighting to operate the stack where Chief Dawson's cocoon was filed. Soon, the hibernation capsule containing Chief Dawson was lowered to a stop, then horizontally pushed out of the stack, and gently lowered onto the anti-gravity gurney that they brought with them from the front of the room. The stacking mechanism retracted, leaving the Chief's cocoon on the gurney. Nurse Cohen and the Commander slowly maneuvered the gurney to the end of the stacks, and onto the lift.

When they brought the cocoon into the hospital, they discovered a red-eyed and annoyed Dr. Hassan waiting for their arrival. "Looks like serious intrigue going on, here, Commanders. Mind telling me what you're doing with that hibernation capsule?"

Commander Baines quickly told the Doctor what they were doing and why it was necessary to awaken the Chief earlier than scheduled. Mason filled in the details for both Nurse Cohen and Dr. Hassan regarding the new theory concocted earlier by him and Commander Baines.

"So, let me see if I have this correctly. Because neither of you know your ass from your elbow with cooking utensils in the mess hall, you decided to wake up Chief Dawson, to test your hypothesis at four o'clock in the morning?" The Doctor asked.

"Yes, sir, that's pretty much it," Commander Baines said, trying to stifle a smile. "We had no intentions of waking you, Dr. Hassan."

"Intentions or not, it is my responsibility to be present when something this irregular occurs. Stop smiling, Baines, and help me get this thing up on the table." They moved the cocoon off the gurney onto the table. "All right, let's get on with it. Undo the electronic seals, Nurse Cohen, and prepare for cover release."

She did as ordered, and checked her scanner again. "All vital signs are good, and all functions normal, Doctor."

Dr. Hassan shooed Mason and Commander Baines away from the capsule. Then he keyed in the sequence of instructions on the side control panel, and touched the electronic release for the cover. With a loud sucking hiss, the cover opened automatically until it was at a right angel to the cocoon. As the gases dissipated, the icy face of Chief Dawson appeared, expressionless, at first. Then the Chief slowly blinked her eyes. Dr. Hassan gently helped her sit up, and said, "Chief Dawson, I am Dr. Hassan. You are in the hospital of the Hesperia. Your life functions are normal, and your vital signs are all good. How do you feel?"

"I'm fine, but if everything's okay, why am I in the hospital? Who are these people? Where's my mess crew?"

"There, there, you are quite well, Chief. You have been awakened a bit early, because these gentlemen need your help. But first, I want to make sure you are doing well, is that all right with you?"

The Chief nodded, looked at Commander Baines and Mason, and instantly put her arms up over her breasts. "Do those men have to see me like this, all exposed?"

"No, they don't, Chief Dawson," Nurse Cohen answered. "Now, Commander, will you two gentlemen kindly wait outside while we check out our patient, and she can get some clothing on her cold body. Thank you."

"My apologies, Chief Dawson, we'll be outside while you get checked out. Mason, in the hall." The Commander was blushing, a fact that did not escape notice from Nurse Cohen.

The Doctor indicated they were to leave the area. "Give her a few minutes to shower and get her uniform on, so she can feel at ease. This has been quite a shock for her, you know. It was her first cryo-sleep. Remember how you felt the first time you were awakened, Commander?"

The Commander gave the Doctor a knowing look, and said, "I'll never forget waking the first time, with all those faces staring in on me. I felt they were stealing all my oxygen and I started to hyperventilate. I came close to having a panic attack. I had to be sedated for a few hours, and then they woke me again. I handled waking up better after that episode. How about you, Staff Sergeant?"

"I awoke feeling threatened, and reached for the throat of the med tech. Fortunately for him, there were three other Space Marines there, and they got me to stop before I damaged him. Then I puked everywhere for nearly twenty minutes. Made a real embarrassing mess. My stomach still can't handle it any better," he admitted.

"Yes, I know," said the Commander, remembering how his new trousers and shoes were covered in vomit from Mason waking. They walked to the crew lounge, and sat, waiting for the Chief and Nurse Cohen to join them.

"Would you like some coffee, Commander Baines? Doctor Hassan? I'll get some for us. Wish we had some sweet rolls, too." Mason suddenly realized he hadn't eaten in who knows how long. "How about a protein tube, sirs?"

"If you can wait an hour, I'll fix breakfast for everyone, sirs," Chief Dawson offered, coming into the lounge. She was clean and spiffed up in her chief's utility uniform, and looking much better. "It'll taste better than that crap."

The offer of real, genuine food was something that made all of their stomachs start growling. They all followed the Chief to the mess hall, where the long explanation of why she was awakened early began in earnest. While she was getting the food from the freezer, she asked, "So the dead guy was put into my freezer? Was it sterilized afterwards? Will the meats be okay to cook? Was anything thrown away? We have just enough for six meals a day, two shifts, for the duration of this mission. I need to know if there is less of any food than we started with now, to make any menu adjustments, sir."

Commander Baines assured her that Dr. Reese's body was lying by the door, directly on the floor, not touching any food or meats. "We scanned everything in the frozen food locker thoroughly, to ascertain whether it had been contaminated, but all the food and meats were untouched, and clean of any foreign bacteria or pathogens. It's okay to cook and serve." She continued to prepare the food, and the crowd of hungry onlookers was growing.

The Captain soon joined them, having been notified by Mason where they were going. The Chief snapped a salute, and, after returning her salute, the Captain smiled and said, "Please carry on, Chief Dawson. I'm not sure if you're aware of this, but everyone you see around you has been awake since the second month of this mission. We've been living on food rations and crackers for over fifteen months. So, if we appear a little eager, please forgive us, won't you?"

"Fifteen months on food tubes and crackers, sir? I'm surprised you didn't wake me much earlier than today!" They all shared a laugh, as she poured hot coffee into mugs for everyone, and topped it off with real steaming milk. When she poured real sugar into the serving bowl for them to use, Mason smiled. "Here's a spoon for you, Staff Sergeant, go ahead." She smiled as he heaped three spoonfuls into his cup, stirred, and nearly gulped down the entire cup at once.

When the Chief oiled the grill and put the hash browns on to cook, the sizzle was the first of many great smells to come. She opened the big box of bacon she had just thawed, and turned the entire box down onto the grill to fry. Then she went to the pantry and came back with pancake dough, and put it into the mixer. She worked so quickly and proficiently, that it seemed almost like a dance. The Doctor looked at Nurse Cohen, and said, "She is a master of multitasking. I've never seen anything like it!"

The Chief started bringing out the platters of hash browns, pancakes, hot syrup and butter, scrambled eggs with cheese, sausage, and bacon. Mason knew this was the best day of the entire year for him. "Go ahead and start. Your steaks are coming up next, sirs," the Chief said with a smile. They ate and ate, and when they were finished, the Chief asked if everything was all right.

"All right? Chief, this was not merely 'all right;' it was superb!" Doctor Hassan had become a fan for life. The Chief was beaming with pride, well deserved.

"Captain, would you give your permission for me to cook breakfast for the rest of the crew? If you could just let me know how many are awake, I'll be happy to begin now, sir," she asked.

"Permission gladly granted, Chief Dawson, after we've all sat down and discussed kitchen utensils. Staff Sergeant, please tell the Chief what we're looking for, if you are finished." Mason was still chewing the last piece of bacon, when the Captain interrupted his savory bliss.

After swallowing a little too early, Mason told the Chief about the octagonal tube, its approximate size, and how it was used on Dr. Reese. "Anything with an octagonal handle or shape at the end could have done the job. The security teams looked around in the drawers, but we didn't see anything that would fit that description. Do you have any tool that might look like our murder weapon?"

The Chief leaned against the table across from them, thought for a minute, and said, "Not any kitchen utensil I can think of, except maybe..." She quickly jogged into the prep area, and started rummaging through the drawers. Mason got up to see what she was looking for, watching her rifle through dozens of utensils of all shapes and sizes. "Now, where is it? It's supposed to be in here, with the shears and rolling pins. It's definitely not here, where it should be."

"What isn't where it should be?" Mason asked.

"The meat tenderizer. You know, to pound lesser cuts of steak into thinner sheets. It has a mallet-like head with spikes, and an octagonal handle for easier gripping." She was perplexed, and squatted down to better look in the back of the lower cabinets. She was moving all the pans out of their shelves, and Mason kneeled down to assist. "It looks like a thick hammer, all steel. Why isn't it here so I can show you?" The Chief was getting frustrated at her inability to find her own kitchen tool.

Commander Baines walked behind the prep area towards her. "Chief Dawson, think for a moment with me, will you? If someone came down here and got into a fight, exactly where should that mallet have been?"

The Commander watched Chief Dawson go back to the first drawer next to the freezer, open it, and said, "It belongs in here, Commander Baines. Right here. And it's not here now." She stood with her hands on her hips, studying the drawer. Then she looked up, at the top of the shelves.

Mason saw her look up, and jumped onto the end of the shelves, hoisting himself up to the top shelf. "The security team searched every shelf and cabinet in here, Commander, for a likely murder weapon. I'm sure we would have noticed a mallet if there had been one up here."

"A meat tenderizer," the Chief corrected.

"Wait a minute. I recall looking at this thing, and wondering what it was." Mason was hanging onto the top shelf, moving the large baking pans and trays, and he pulled one down to show to the Chief. "Here it is. It just looks like a metal block, with a notched face."

"Mason, did you tell anyone about this finding?" Kouras asked.

"I put it into my report, along with a picture of it, Captain." Mason picked up the block, and showed it to the Chief. "Is this part of the meat tenderizer?"

"Yes, it's the head. Its handle screws into this hole here. It was in one piece when I conducted the inventory, Captain, I swear it," she said.

"I'm sure it was, Chief Dawson. So, we have a missing meat tenderizer handle, which just happens to be of an octagonal shape, made of steel, right, Chief?"

"Yes, sir."

"Staff Sergeant, let's get another security team down here tonight, and search this kitchen and prep area again, now that we have a better idea what we're looking for. Right after the Chief makes that breakfast for the rest of the crew. Let's get out of her way now. Commander Baines, in my ready room." The Captain headed out the kitchen door with Commander Baines following right behind him. Dr. Hassan and Nurse Cohen thanked the Chief for breakfast, and urged her to come to the hospital if she had any ill feelings still bothering her from the cryo-sleep.

Mason waited until everyone left the kitchen except himself and the Chief. "Chief, is there any other utensil, or pan with an octagonal handle, that we should be looking for around your area? We conducted search after search throughout this entire mammoth ship, for over a year. We did find that strange, octagonal tube in the crews quarters hall ceiling, but no one was totally positive that tube was the actual murder weapon. We scanned this entire mess hall for DNA or tissue particles. Can you think of anything else that someone may have quickly grabbed to strike Dr. Reese?"

She looked at him, and said, "No, Staff Sergeant, I can't think of anything else now. But, it doesn't make sense to me. If they grabbed the meat tenderizer to kill that poor bastard, why not hit him with the big end? Why use the handle?"

"That's exactly what I'm wondering, Chief. It doesn't make sense. Thank you for your help. And for the best breakfast I ever ate in my life!" Mason did not even try to hide his smile.

"You are most welcome, Staff Sergeant. Now, unless you want to help me wash these pans and dishes, you'd better get going!" The Chief didn't have to threaten him twice. He has such a nice smile, she thought to herself.

"Aye-aye, Chief. Thank you, again." Mason left her domain, with a full stomach, and a head full of questions.

What a good day, Mason thought. Real food. Real good food and lots of it. The Chief seemed like a very nice lady, tall and slender, and strong. He liked her blonde hair, at least what he got to see of it. It was hidden under her hair net, as was required. She had crazy blue eyes, the kind of bright blue like the ocean in the Gulf, on Earth. And the Chief helped find another missing piece to this damned puzzle, although he did not believe that it was used as the murder weapon. He would have to wait for Dr. Hassan's forensic analysis to prove him wrong, or right.

X

Dr. Hassan completed his forensic analysis of the meat tenderizer head. He called Captain Kouras on the comm-link. "Captain, Dr. Hassan here. I have completed the analysis of the metal kitchen tool. No DNA, but there is a smeared partial print. Obviously, whoever used it attempted to wipe his prints off before tossing it on the top shelf inside the pans. The spiky surface caught just enough of a print to be read; not enough to be registered and identified. I'm sorry to disappoint you again."

"Yes, it's another disappointment, but you did not do it, Doctor. Have it brought to Commander Baines in a sealed container. Get some rest. Tomorrow we begin awakening the remaining crew, and I would like you and Nurse Cohen to supervise the procedures. If possible, have your entire staff there to assist. I need everyone fully functional as soon as possible." Captain Kouras added, "Doctor, I have also given the order that each cryo-cocoon be inspected immediately by security after their occupants are out. They are not to be moved and cleaned until they are checked out."

"Yes, Captain, I will personally make sure none are tampered with until they are fully inspected. You can count on me, sir," Dr. Hassan assured.

"Great. Now see to it that you and Nurse Cohen get some shut-eye. Kouras out."

The Doctor gave the meat tenderizer head to his med tech to be sealed in a container and taken to Commander Baines. He signed the lab slip, and stuck it onto the container before sending it up to the bridge for safe storage. Got to keep the chain of evidence intact, he thought. More clues and evidence, less understanding of the murder mystery.

Dr. Hassan and Nurse Cohen went into the crews' quarters the next morning, and into the cocoon storage room. The cryo-containers were off-loaded one by one, until a full stack was emptied. Then, Dr. Hassan made certain that their computer indicators all read the proper life function markers, and had the corpsmen scan them. Once the scanning was done and their readings were good, he broke the electronic seals, and opened the container. The crewmen woke up all in a similar way: eyes blinking; rising up out of their cocoons; some stretching before they got up and out, and stood. Just like clockwork. The security teams of two then picked up the containers individually, and laid them side by side for inspection.

Nurse Cohen and Mason inspected every cryo-container, together, with the entire inspection being recorded by floating cameras, capturing every possible angle. After each container was inspected and recorded, the security crew placed them on a transport outside the storage room, to be taken down to the cargo hold and cleaned. The cleaned and sterilized containers would be replaced in their respective stacks as before, waiting to be used for the journey home, in four years.

"Dr. Hassan, this is the Captain. I'm sending down a relief team, so you can all take a break. You've been at this for several hours. Exactly how many are awake now?" Kouras asked.

"Eighty-six crew are awakened. All of your bridge crew, and engineering," the Doctor answered.

The Captain ordered, "After the mess crew are up, skip over to the Space Marines' quarters. Wake them next. That'll make time to catch up on the cocoon inspections. Tomorrow, we can complete the awakenings for the balance of the crew."

"Yes, Captain." With those instructions, the Doctor became very curious. Why must the Space Marines be up and working tonight? What was he planning or, perhaps, what was the Captain expecting to happen?

After an hour break, everyone returned to the storage room. All the emptied cocoons were moved out and onto transports for cleaning and sterilization.

In the Space Marines' quarters, the corpsmen asked the Doctor which cocoon to begin with. The Doctor deferred that decision to the Prime Marine. "Staff Sergeant Mason, please choose which cryo-containers to open first."

"Yes, Dr. Hassan. Corpsman, help me release this cocoon." Mason immediately went to the cryo-container of Lieutenant Cheung. They initiated the release mechanism for the cocoon, and it pushed forward, past its recess in the wall, and held there until Mason and the corpsman took the container by its handles, gently laying it down on the floor. "Doctor, this is the officer in-charge, 2nd Lieutenant Cheung."

Mason went across the room, selected the cocoon of Master Sergeant Alta, and followed the identical procedure to remove the container from its hold, onto the floor. Sergeant Lucas was next, followed by Corporals Gomez and Waters; the remaining Space Marines followed. The containers were taken to the center of the room, inspected and recorded, as was previously done in the crews' quarters. Since there were only thirty-two containers to be opened here, the procedure went fairly quickly, especially after Master Sergeant Alta came awake.

"Get up and get going, Space Marine. Stretch on your own time, you slacker. Your ass has been asleep for over a year, now let's get moving." The Master Sergeant asked, "Staff Sergeant, where's Lieutenant Cheung?"

Mason answered, "He's up and gone to his quarters to shower and dress, Master Sergeant." A little "humph" was his reply.

"Where are Corporals Johnson and Milton? I don't see their cocoons," Alta asked.

Mason answered, "Corporals Johnson and Milton have been awake with me since the second month of the mission, Master Sergeant."

"What? Why wasn't I awakened and informed of this? Who made this decision, Staff Sergeant?" Master Sergeant Alta was in his face.

"It was the Captain's orders, Master Sergeant." Dr. Hassan stepped into the discussion. "And I'm sure he'll want you informed as to the reason for his decision at a later time. Let's just get everyone up for now." Dr. Hassan ordered.

"Yes, sir." Master Sergeant Alta complied, and, once everyone in his command was up and awake, he led them to their quarters to clean up and get into their uniforms. Mason made sure that the containers were all inspected and loaded onto the transports.

The Captain called Mason and said, "Staff Sergeant, inform the Space Marines to assemble in the mess hall for a briefing after dinner, at eighteen-thirty. I want to see you on the bridge as soon as possible."

"Sir, yes sir." Mason quickly left for the Space Marines' quarters, to deliver the message to Lieutenant Cheung and the Master Sergeant.

"Our Staff Sergeant never changes his composure, does he, Nurse Cohen? Always the same, strictly business," Dr. Hassan commented as they were walking back to the officers' quarters.

"Oh, I think he may let his guard down occasionally," Nurse Cohen remarked. "But definitely not around that Master Sergeant!" They both chuckled.

Nurse Cohen said goodnight to the Doctor, as she went into her quarters. She was tired, and wanted to shower off the reeking stench of the hundred-plus cryo-cocoons she inspected. She thought about the strange markings on the octagonal tube again. Those symbols somehow seemed familiar. She quickly finished washing, before her three minutes of water shut off automatically. Putting on her long pajamas, she had a new thought: what if the symbols were actually instructions for opening the tube? She quickly went to her computer console, and called to Commander Baines. "Commander Cohen here. Have you deciphered those symbols on the octagonal tube yet?"

He sighed deeply. "No, not yet. The computer is still searching for anything related to them in its libraries. Why do you ask?"

"Perhaps we've been making too much of those symbols. What if they are the actual instructions to open it? One of the symbols looks like some sort of key to me," she said.

"Are you sure?" Baines asked.

"I'm not sure of anything right now, except that I'm tired. It's been a very long day. Maybe I'm just crazy, but I think we need to look at that tube in another way." Her voice was a little deeper than it usually was, because of her being tired, working for so long.

The Commander agreed with her. "Fine with me. Why don't we go over this tomorrow morning, before you start the other crew awakenings?"

"No, the Doctor promised the Space Marines we'd start at o-six hundred hours. How about afterwards, at dinner? I'd really like to examine the symbols firsthand on that octagonal tube again, and with both of us discussing them, Commander Baines."

"Okay, so it's dinner and the octagonal tube. Call me when you're ready to meet me in the officers' mess, Commander Cohen."

"Thank you, Commander Baines. Cohen out."

"G'night. Baines out." Now, why didn't he offer to meet her in her quarters, instead? God, her voice sounded sexy. He started to call her back and change the location for their meeting, but he thought better of it. Fool, get some shut-eye yourself.

At the meeting with the Space Marines, Commander Baines began by saying, "Welcome to the Hesperia, Space Marines. Captain Kouras and Earth Command have authorized me to brief all of you on the events that took place on this ship since we left Titan One, and why some of your fellow Marines have been awakened early, and stayed awake since the second month of this mission." He gave information to them regarding the enigmatic orange cloud; the death of Dr. Richard Reese; and their diversion to GK-359. He spoke succinctly, and with brevity, and gave them just enough information to make them understand that this mission was not at all "business as usual." He then introduced Captain Kouras.

"Welcome, Space Marines. Commander Baines has given you the background of our situation. I will now tell you our present state of affairs. Tomorrow, the remaining crew members will be awakened. Once everyone is up and fully functional, the general awakenings of the six hundred miners will commence, according to a very strict schedule. But, before that happens, we will have completed another full ship's inspection, supervised by Commander Baines. You must thoroughly search every part of this ship, stem to stern. You will search for an octagonal-shaped weapon, used to commit murder. The searches are to be recorded by vid-cams, and documented." He added, "We have a murderer and an attempted-murderer on board the Hesperia. I want every potential piece of evidence, no matter how unusual, large, or small, discovered, and brought to the attention of Commander Baines, Staff Sergeant Mason, or myself, immediately. Is that understood?"

They unanimously shouted, "Sir, yes sir!"

"Excellent. We will begin immediately. Commander Baines will take over from here. Good hunting, Marines." The Captain left the mess hall, leaving Baines with the anxious Space Marines. They searched all night, recorded every movement, and looked into every hold, panel, nook and cranny, and found nothing.

The next morning saw the rest of the crew begin their awakenings, much like those from the previous day. Dr. Hassan changed jobs with Nurse Cohen, letting her unseal the cryo-containers and wake up the crewmen, while he conducted the inspections with Mason. The last of the cocoons to be opened belonged to the research scientists from URE.

As they prepared to open the last three cocoons, Nurse Cohen noticed the sound of an irregular blip begin on the computer monitor of Dr. Ed Wise. She called for Dr. Hassan, and immediately scanned the container and the body inside. "His monitor began sounding an irregular blip, when we off-loaded his container onto the floor. He may be waking early, Doctor."

"Let's get him out of there now." He unsealed the container, and keyed in the opening sequence quickly.

Nurse Cohen reported, "His heartbeat is very erratic, blood pressure climbing to 193 over eighty-three. Life functions off the chart. He is going into cardiac arrest!"

Doctor Hassan opened the container unassisted, and began chest compressions while the corpsmen ran for the gear and stimulus shots. "Administer CPR, stat," the Doctor ordered. They gave the body two intravenous stimulus shots, with anti-coagulants. There was no change. They used the shocks on him. No response. Then he gave him a shot directly into his heart. There was still no response. The scanner held by Nurse Cohen yielded a steady tone, no life signs read. The team worked on his body for several minutes, before Dr. Hassan gave in to the obvious: Dr. Ed Wise was dead.

The vid cams recorded the entire episode, from the cryo-container being off-loaded from the stack onto the floor, to Dr. Hassan's calling the time of death. They notified Captain Kouras, who ordered the body left in the container, and moved to the morgue for an immediate autopsy.

Captain Kouras ordered an inquisition immediately, and told Dr. Hassan, Nurse Cohen, and the attending corpsmen to meet in his ready room in two hours. He reported the death of a second research scientist to Earth Command, feeling his credibility erode all the while.

Nurse Cohen called Commander Baines on the comm-link. "Commander, this is Nurse Cohen. I'm afraid I'll have to ask you to take a rain check on our dinner and the discussion on the symbols on the octagonal tube. I am sorry, though, to miss our dinner together," she said disappointedly.

"Me, too. We'll talk later. Baines, out." Dammit! What happened, he wondered? Just then, his comm-link buzzed again.

"Commander, this is the Captain. I need you to join in a meeting with the med staff in about an hour, in my ready room."

"I'll be there, sir. Baines, out."

The meeting in the ready room took place as scheduled, with Dr. Hassan, Nurse Cohen, and the attending corpsmen all entering the room together, and finding the Captain, Commander Baines, and Mason already discussing the situation. "Ah, here are our medical experts now," the Captain said. Mason immediately jumped to his feet, and offered Nurse Cohen his chair. "We were discussing the possible suspects in this case, or 'persons of interest,' to be accurate. Our Staff Sergeant is of the mind that the remaining research scientists have the most to gain from the deaths of their two colleagues, both politically, within the MM & E, and perhaps financially. The Commander thinks somehow the management staff of the miners may be involved, as well. What is your hypothesis, Dr. Hassan?"

"I have not been able to gather enough credible data to postulate a hypothesis yet, Captain. There are too many unknown variables at this juncture. What about you, Nurse Cohen? Any theories?" The Doctor looked at her, and she thought for a moment before answering.

"I would not eliminate the research scientists as persons of interest, or the miners' managers, or anyone else who might have obtained access to the containers. The number of suspects is very large, at this time; it includes anyone and everyone who was put into cryonic hibernation after Dr. Wise. And, there's also the matter of our Staff Sergeant, as well. Let's not forget his attempted murder." She looked over at Mason, who was listening to her every word. At least she cared enough to remember the attempt on his life, Mason mused.

"However, I do think we should consider the octagonal tube as being connected somehow to all three events. It was most likely the murder weapon of Dr. Reese, and we need to know what it is, what the symbols mean, and exactly what it was designed to contain." Nurse Cohen continued, "It may indeed play a larger role in these mysteries than we know. It may be somehow associated with the orange cloud anomaly. It is not constructed from any Earth metals."

Commander Baines realized he had been staring at Nurse Cohen a little too long while she was speaking. He turned in his chair, and spoke to the Captain. "Nurse Cohen and I were planning to discuss the strange symbols on the tube, comparing and contrasting what our ship's computer has suggested, with our own theories about what they could possible mean."

"I don't see how that bloody tube is connected to Dr. Wise's murder, or the orange cloud anomaly. I want to discuss a possible list of suspects for the killings, and attempted killings. Earth Command wants to know who we have under suspicion, and if we have sufficient evidence to bring charges against anyone. They have given us the authorization to conduct a trial on board the Hesperia, during live communication with Earth Command. They are anxious to get this investigation concluded, and move on with the mission, as am I." The Captain was obviously being pressured by his superiors to bring an end to the entire matter.

"Permission to speak, sir." Mason stepped forward, one step closer to the table.

"Yes, Staff Sergeant?"

"Captain, the desire for a quick conclusion to the investigation at hand is understandable, sir, but it is this Marine's humble opinion that doing so may inadvertently cause more damage to the crew and passengers on this ship." Mason, don't lose your control, look straight ahead, he told himself.

"How is that, Staff Sergeant?" The Captain was trying to be patient with Mason. "What additional damage may be caused to this ship?"

"Sir, since Cain killed Abel, three basic things are necessary to prove the guilt of an accused murderer: motive, opportunity, and means. We are not positive about the time frame for the opportunity to commit the two murders. We are not even one hundred percent certain what weapon was used to kill Dr. Reese. But the primary factor we lack is motive; what was the motive behind the two killings? If we rush to judgment with evidence this shaky, I am certain – without a doubt – that this case will be dismissed, regardless of whom we will bring it before, civilian or military judge. I have no desire to risk the credibility of anyone on board the Hesperia, including myself, sir. We may even jeopardize our mission, sir," Mason concluded. He then stepped back.

"Staff Sergeant Mason, you are right, dammit, you are right. We cannot let political pressure determine our actions in this case. I want this investigation continued, until we have credible and substantial evidence to bring against anyone charged with these murders. We will very soon have another six hundred persons awake on the Hesperia, and, although I hoped for a swift conclusion of this situation, it is not to be. We will discover the facts, and determine the perpetrators of these crimes in due time. You will come to me directly with any new information, is that understood?"

"Sir, yes, sir!" Mason said briskly.

"Commander Baines will now take a statement from each of you individually, regarding the inspection of Dr. Ed Wise's cryo-cocoon. Mason, on the bridge." They all stood, and the Captain left the room with Mason.

"Well, our Staff Sergeant may have just saved us all from a very rocky road, indeed," Doctor Hassan observed.

Baines added, "The Space Marines are getting their investment back from Mason and his criminal forensics master's degree. He had a good argument, and proved his point."

"Yes, he made his point, but none of us has proven anything, at least not yet, Commander Baines." Nurse Cohen sighed, and looked at the Commander.

Dr. Hassan offered, "I'll go first, since mine will be the shortest, I think." The Commander took individual statements from each of them, describing the events of Dr. Ed Wise's death, and the inspection of his cryonic container. When each had given their statements for the official log, the Commander dismissed them; Nurse Cohen lagged behind to speak with him.

"Commander, I hope we can still discuss the strange symbols on the octagonal tube sometime. I don't want to overlook anything, especially something we have found, but do not understand," she said, putting her hands inside her lab coat pockets.

"Certainly. I look forward to taking up your offer of a rain check for dinner and a discussion. Sooner, rather than later, Nurse Cohen." His voice was softer, and somewhat suggestive.

"Of, course, Commander Baines, sooner rather than later, it is." Nurse Cohen smiled and left the ready room.

Commander Baines finished signing the log entries, left the ready room, and went on the bridge. As he settled in, he checked the positioning of the ship, and ran checks on all systems from the chair's hand controls, built directly into its arm rests and attached monitors. He busied himself for four hours, totally absorbed in the duties at hand, until Lieutenant Davis relieved him. As he entered the lift to go back to his quarters, he realized it would be another long night, thinking of the orange cloud anomaly, and trying to not think of Commander Rachel Cohen.

XI

Early the next morning, Captain Kouras called for a general assembly. Captain Kouras quickly strode to the podium, followed by his command officers. "Be seated. I am Captain Kouras, your Commanding Officer. To my right is the Executive Officer, Commander Baines, Commander Hassan, Commander Cohen, and Lt. Commander Powers. We want to welcome you all to the Hesperia. Commander Baines will brief you regarding the recent events that have occurred on this ship since we left Moon Base. The command officers you see before you, and several of your crew members, have been awake and functional for the entire seventeen months you were in cryo-sleep. I ask that you give your undivided attention to each of our speakers this morning."

Commander Baines stepped up to the podium, and began to briefly describe the last seventeen month's unusual events to the seated group: the appearance of the enigmatic orange cloud; the death of Dr. Richard Reese, Chief Research Scientist; and the side trip to colony GK-356. He ended his remarks to them with the following: "It should be apparent to everyone that the initial phase of this mission has been extraordinary and not at all business as usual. We can expect no less from our remaining five and one-half years on board. We must all be mindful of our duties and vigilant with the enhanced security measures to be put into place, for everyone's safety. Lt. Commander Powers will brief you regarding the security rules and regulations."

Powers spoke, "Earth Command has ordered the following security measures to be implemented immediately. No civilians are permitted to cross over from Sections 2, 3 or 4 into Section One, unless accompanied by one of the command staff you see here, and a full security team. The only military personnel allowed in Sections 2, 3, and 4 are the shuttle pilots, Captain Kouras, Commander Baines, and Prime Marine Staff Sergeant

Mason, and the Space Marines, who will be accompanying as security teams, at all times. You are not to interact with the miners in any way, including socially. You are not to accept anything from them, including any gifts, souvenirs, packages, notes, or verbal requests. Any such requests are to be reported to your crew leaders immediately. No civilians are allowed on the bridge or in any part of the engineering deck at any time, with or without escort. No exceptions. Any violations of these rules and regulations are to be reported immediately to your commanding officer. Are there any questions?" He paused, looked around the crowded room, and said, "Very good. Now our Chief Medical Officer, Dr. Hassan."

Dr. Hassan spoke very briefly about the need to be observant of each other's physical and mental conditions for the next few days, then turned the podium back to Captain Kouras. "Thank you, Doctor. It is readily apparent that this mission has been challenging in its opening phases. Tomorrow, we begin the general awakenings of the miners and their managers. Our mission is to provide safe transport to the six hundred miners who are our passengers, assist them whenever necessary with locating and securing their targeted asteroids during the four years we will be in the mining areas, and return everyone safely to Moon Base."

The Captain paused, and then continued. "But, I also realize that seven years on any assignment can be long and arduous, therefore we will allow each crew member five minutes' communications transmission to family and friends, beginning at twelve-hundred hours. Also, I have planned a get-acquainted party for everyone tonight, at eighteen-hundred hours, in this general assembly hall. Mess Chief Dawson and her crew have been busy making a very special menu for us to enjoy. There will be music, a few party games, perhaps a surprise or two, and you will be served by your officers." He smiled, and waited for the outbursts of shouting and applause to die down before closing. "Attendance is mandatory for all personnel, and the uniform is class A. See everyone tonight!"

Master Sergeant Alta sought out Mason after the assembly members started to leave the room, in search of their duty stations. "Staff Sergeant Mason, what do you make of the Captain's party tonight? Very unusual, don't you think?"

"Not really, Master Sergeant. I think the Captain wants everyone to see the faces of those supposed to be in Section 1, and get acquainted with each other."

"It's unheard of, being served by an officer." The Master Sergeant wouldn't let it go.

"Master Sergeant, the Captain's no man's fool, and not the type to give anyone slack. He's a real disciplinarian, that man. Had us all working twelve hours or more every day, while you were asleep. I'm just glad there are more of the crew awake, now." Mason tried to placate the gruff Master

Sergeant.

"At least you earned your pay, Mason." Alta quickly left for his quarters.

Nurse Cohen asked Mason to assist her in the storage area where Dr. Wise's cocoon was stored. They started the floating vid cams, and proceeded with the inspection. She was taking the lead, and was nearly upside down inside the container. Mason was trying desperately not to look at her wonderful ass, and failing miserably. She said, "Where is it? Where's the delivery system? It has to be here. There you are, you little bugger!" She pulled up the head cushion for Mason and the cameras to see the little blue tube. "He hid it under the head cushion this time. It was more elaborately concealed than the one in your cocoon, John. Let's get the scanner in here for an initial analysis on the traces of gases present." She used the medical scanner inside the cocoon, and the indicator flashed a bright green. "It contains the same opiated sleep inducers used on you, plus nitrous oxide, and with a few other interesting chemicals. The slightest disturbance would send his entire nervous system into shock."

"The poor guy probably never had a chance," Mason observed.

"He was not in the same excellent health as you, nor did he have bio-enhanced lungs and blood. When his cryonic container was moved, even the slightest, his heart became erratic, and he went into shock, then a full-blown major heart attack. As you said, he had no chance." She very carefully removed the blue tube and its tiny cartridge with forceps, being sure that her movements were captured by the cameras, placed the delivery system inside a plastic sample bag, and sealed it. "The container inspection is completed, Staff Sergeant. It is good for cleaning and storage. I'll be going back to the hospital." She smiled at him and left.

"Yes, ma'am. I'll take the cocoon now, ma'am," Mason said, watching her walk away. Hopefully, she hadn't seen him looking at her fanny.

Mason thought about his own cocoon, how the tube was jury-rigged close to his nose. This installation of the drug delivery system was more professional, while his was either done by a second party not as skilled, or installed in haste, or both. He was certain the killer was awake and aware that Dr. Ed Wise was dead, and he was still alive. Mason had more reason that ever to be cautious, and to persevere with his investigations.

After moving the cocoon down to the storage area for cleaning and sterilization, Mason went to his room. He needed to get out his class A uniform, and make sure it was perfect. Like most of the enlisted Space Marines, he wore his belted one-piece working uniform while on daily duty. The Space Marine daily uniform was olive green, gray, and black colored camouflage. Mason's working uniform was all black, with many pockets and pouches, where he carried his gear necessary for the tasks at hand. His hat was a squared, formed, billed cap, with the Prime Marine badge and his Staff Sergeant insignia. His weapons belt held his long blade and sheath, his laser handgun and holster, and many compartments for various tools and smaller weapons, and several loops to secure a xenon flashlight, stun spray, and so on. His uniform was made of a special waterproof nano-fabric type of material to repel laser blasts, and was impenetrable to knives and sharp weapons' attacks. It was also made of the type of nano-fibers that would keep his body at a regular temperature, whether the outside weather was cold or hot. He loved it.

His duty boots kept his feet warm and dry in all types of weather, and formed a tight but non-binding seal around his mid-calf whenever he was in water above their tops. Their composition was rugged, supportive and supple, at the same time. He preferred them over any other type of footwear he had ever worn, especially the shiny boots that went with his class A's. Those boots made him look great, but they went right up to the bend in his knees, and continually bugged him. They had higher heels than his daily boots. They were stiff, and made him look even taller than he was, and that was all right when he was walking or marching, but they were hell to wear if he had to run for any length of time.

His class A uniform looked much different than that of his Space Marine brothers. Their dress uniform was somewhat similar to that of the Space Force: full-length black trousers with black double-piping down the sides, ankle-high zip dress black boots, and hip-length jacket. The Space Force jackets were single breasted black with open lapels, while the Space Marine jackets were crimson red, with open lapels and single breasted gold buttons bearing the Space Marines insignia. Mason's Prime Marine class A uniform's black trousers came just below the knee, and were tucked snugly inside the knee-high boots. They featured red double-piping down their sides, which he liked.

But the jacket was what made a Prime Marine immediately stand out from among any other services' class A uniforms. The crimson red jacket was tunic-length, worn closed, and featured gold buttons from the neck to the waist for its double-breasted front. His hat was even different than the crimson red traditional berets of the Space Marines: it was a black beret, with the Prime Marine insignia, also in pure gold.

Mason was proud to be a Prime Marine, and placed his many medals properly, measuring their alignment until they were displayed perfectly. He shined his tall boots until they gleamed, and polished his gold buttons to a mirror finish.

Mason hung up his readied uniform and put aside his boots, and went to the lounge area, where there was a long line for the five minute calls home. But the line moved quickly, and he made his call to his sister on Mars Colony III. "Hey, Babe!"

"Johnnie! How are you? We didn't think we'd hear from you this soon! Honey, get the kids, its Johnnie, calling from space. Where are you now

Johnnie?" His sister Sarah was tall, and slender, and looked like their mother, Mason thought.

"I've only got a couple of minutes. I just wanted to see if everyone was OK." He was trying to not look excited, in case any of the crew could see his face.

"We're all right here. The kids are getting bigger every day. Here's little Johnnie now." She picked up the toddler, and held him up to the monitor for Mason. "Say hi, Johnnie."

"Hi, Unka Johnnie. When you comin' home?" He was so cute!

"Not for several more years, sport. Now you grow up big, so we can go flying together when I come home, OK?" Cute kid, Mason thought. He's going to be tall, like me.

"Hello, Uncle Johnnie. Will you be home soon?" That charming little lady's voice belonged to Angela, his niece. Such a beautiful girl.

"No, honey, remember I told you I'd be away for seven years. You'll be all grown up when I come home. I hope you'll still have time to take your Uncle out for ice cream when I get back." John, you'd better not get all mushy now, he told himself.

"You betcha, Uncle Johnnie! Here's Daddy."

"Hey, old man, where the heck are you calling from? Pluto? We miss your ugly face around here." Dave was a great guy, a good father and husband. Sarah could have done a lot worse. He worked for the URE as Assistant Finance Minister for the Mars Colony III.

"We're just outside the solar system, can't say where. I miss you all. I'll call you again whenever I can, OK? Just wanted to say "Hi." The yellow warning light came on, letting him know he had ten seconds left on his call. "You kids be good, and do what your mom and dad tell you, OK? I love you all. Bye."

They all said good-bye, and Mason waved and watched them until the screen went to black, and read "Transmission Ended." He turned and left the booth, trying to hide the red in his eyes. I'm lucky to have a family like them, he thought.

Mason went back down to his quarters to shower and get ready for tonight's party. His comm-link beeped, and the XO called out to him, "Staff Sergeant, are you there? Mason, this is Commander Baines. The Captain wants all the officers in the general assembly hall at seventeen-hundred hours. Would you meet with us about fifteen minutes prior in the hall?"

"Yes, sir. I'll be there." Now what?

"Good man. See you there. Baines, out."

Mason hustled to get himself in top form, and made it to the general assembly hall right on time. As he approached the group in the back of the room, he noticed the Captain and Commander Baines were talking with Dr.

Hassan and Commander Cohen, and some guys in civilian clothes. As Mason got closer, he recognized the research scientists and lab techs from MM & E. "And here comes our Prime Marine, Staff Sergeant John Mason." Doctor Hassan was definitely "on" tonight. "Looking sharp, Prime Marine, looking sharp."

Mason stopped short of their group, snapped to attention, and saluted. "Sirs, Staff Sergeant Mason reporting, as ordered." His salute was returned by all the officers sharply.

"At ease, Prime Marine. Thank you for coming to meet with us early, Staff Sergeant. I wanted to formally introduce you to our guests from MM & E, Doctor Bergen and Doctor Moore. You are already acquainted with Doctor Honig and Doctor Jenkins." The Captain was handling the introductions well.

"Pleased to make you acquaintance, doctors. Hello, Doctor Jenkins, Doctor Honig." The chit chat went on for a couple of minutes more, and then the Captain got to the point.

"I have briefed our guests on the octagonal tube, and requested their help in determining what it actually is made of, and its possible uses. They understand it is valuable evidence in our on-going investigations, and will treat it with care." Mason was not surprised to hear the tube being discussed by the officers with the scientists present, but the large open forum did not seem at all appropriate for such an important topic.

"Dr. Jenkins and Dr. Honig said they made attempts to study the tube in our labs, but without much success," Dr. Moore said to Mason.

"Yes, sir, both Doctors rendered valuable assistance to us when approached for help." Mason noticed that the XO and Commander Cohen were being unusually quiet on this subject.

"But, it was my understanding that they were not able to determine exactly what made up the composition of the metal in the tube, or give much information at all," Doctor Bergen commented, looking right at Mason.

"That is correct, Doctor. But the process of identifying what something is also includes confirming what it is not, as well, and that they did for us. I can provide you both with their reports, if it is the Captain's wish," Mason offered.

"It is my wish to do so, Staff Sergeant. Since the procedures were recorded and documented for our use, it would be proper for us to share those reports with the MM & E team leaders. Please see to it that they have those reports in the morning, Staff Sergeant." The Captain looked very pleased.

Mason said, "Aye-aye, sir."

"Thank you Captain, Commanders. We'll be back in about an hour for the party. Thank you all very much." The scientists left the room, walking to the lift area.

Mason knew how a trained animal felt at that moment. He had been summoned, and performed well. Was there a treat coming, now?

"Well done, Staff Sergeant Mason. Your powers of observation were very astute. Let's just say for now that you effectively turned around a potentially awkward situation. You are an invaluable asset to this ship. Now, if you'll excuse us, we have to find our stations, don our white gloves, and prepare to serve you and the crew tonight's fine fare. Dismissed."

"Sir, yes sir." Mason saluted, at attention. The Captain gave a quick return salute, and the officers all went to the other end of the room, where serving tables were being set up and decorated. Now he was curious. Probably, the research scientists' team leaders were told about the examination of the strange tube by the little lab geeks the second they walked into their labs, and they got ticked off at the use of their equipment and lab time. All without getting billable hours, too. Let them get all puffed up. As far as he was concerned, they all had motive, opportunity, and the scientific knowledge necessary to commit the murder of both Doctors Reese and Wise, and his own attempted murder. They were all suspects in his investigation, and they just revealed more of their personas to him for profiling.

He started to head for the front doors, when the Captain called him over. "Staff Sergeant, I need you to do a personal favor for me. Round up your Corporals again, and meet me in about ten minutes in my personal storage locker in the cargo bay."

"Yes, sir." I hope this means what I think it means, Mason thought. He tapped his small comm-link on his wrist. "Corporal Johnson, Corporal Milton, this is Staff Sergeant Mason."

They were both ready for the party and just hanging out in the crew lounge when Mason called. They left the lounge, and met Mason in the cargo bay in record time. The Captain appeared in the cargo bay storage locker area, with an anti-gravity dolly in tow. "All right Space Marines, give an old man a hand with these cases, would you?"

"Sir, yes sir!" They loaded ten cases of silver 151 rum, triple-distilled vodka, and bourbon onto the dolly.

"Easy now boys, this precious cargo is worth more than gold out here, in deep friggin' space," the Captain said. "It's our last night to party."

They took the cases into the lift and up to the general assembly, and hid them under the tables where the punch bowls were sitting. He said, "I volunteered myself to serve the fruit punch!" He was smiling at them, ear to ear. "OK, boys. I'm all set. Mum's the word on this. Go help someone get set up, will you?" They obliged, and each went to help one of the officers. Mason went straight to his favorite nurse, Commander Cohen.

"Anything I can do to help, Ma'am?" Mason asked, with a big smile on his face. She looked him up and down, smiled and answered him.

"No, Staff Sergeant Mason. If I get any whipped cream on that uniform, the Captain will have my hide for sure!" They both laughed, and Mason chatted with her, keeping her company while she arranged all the cakes and pies to be served. Chief Dawson and two of her crew were slowly bringing in a spectacular cake on an anti-gravity table. The Chief was walking backwards towards the dessert table, guiding the huge cake slowly, and telling the crewmen just how to steer the table into position. "Chief Dawson! A cake with petit fours icing, with ribbons and flowers all around! It's so perfect! Isn't it simply magnificent, Staff Sergeant?" Her admiration was genuine. The cake was a work of art.

The Chief turned around to see Mason, and blushed. She had not seen him as they were approaching the dessert table. "Staff Sergeant Mason, I didn't see you at all! We didn't get anything on you did we?"

"No, Chief, you did not. It'll be my goal tonight to keep things that way, as well." The women had a good laugh with Mason, and enjoyed having him all to themselves. Both women were obviously impressed with Mason in his uniform, as they flirted and chatted with him for several minutes.

"Now, how can a guy compete with someone who looks like that, tell me now. It's not fair, I tell you!" Lieutenant Davis was watching Mason at the dessert table, and seeing both Commander Cohen and Chief Dawson fawn over him. "It's got to be that uniform. Anyone would look good in that uniform."

"Not as good as Staff Sergeant Mason looks in it, Lieutenant. He is tall, handsome, and in perfect physical condition," Commander Baines observed, coming over to join in the complaint session. He watched Commander Cohen arranging the same plates again and again, talking and laughing with him. It was innocent fun, but he realized he was getting jealous of that Prime Marine tonight. "Just ignore him, Davis. He'll be back in that ugly black uniform after tonight and no one will pay any attention to him again."

Davis wasn't so sure, but said, "Yes, Commander."

Chief Dawson walked back to the kitchen with her crew, and discovered she was blushing. Her face felt hot, and her pulse was up. Good God, that man! She thought he was good-looking the first night she met him, but tonight, he looked absolutely gorgeous! She wouldn't mind whipped cream on him at all. Get a grip on yourself, he's just another man, she told herself. But she knew better. She knew she was enamored with him, and had to be careful. She couldn't get involved with anyone on a mission this long. She'd be lost for good, if she did.

The signal was given, the music started over the sound system, and the great hall doors were opened. The entering crew members found a wonderfully decorated hall, arranged with festive bouquets of dried flowers and bows on the columns. No military hall ever looked so well decorated. The crew was fed a generous buffet of roasted beef, rotisserie chickens, baked hams, and more vegetables and side dishes than anyone could sample in one week. Before the meats were carved, the Captain made a brief announcement for everyone to enjoy his very special fruit punch, and held aloft one bottle each of vodka, 151 rum, and bourbon, and poured the entire contents of each bottle into the punch, as the crew applauded.

Baines couldn't help noticing Commander Cohen again. She looked over at him several times during the course of the evening, smiling at him. Even with her hair up, military fashion for the women, she was beautiful. She was so friendly, and actually seemed to be having a good time, serving cake and pies to the crewmen, and chatting with them. Her smile was warm, and she was charming. He was jealous of every man who had her attention. Something about that woman made him want to run away with her to an island in paradise for the rest of his life. He decided to tell her about it; no, he'd show her how he felt. Tonight, if he got the chance. It had to be tonight.

Mason was having a good time with everyone, and was careful not to have more than two cups of the Captain's punch, because he must remain in control of the evening. He never forgot his duty, to protect the bridge and its crew. The guests began to slowly clear out, so he moved his position by the main doors, where he could get a better look at everyone leaving the hall.

When only the Captain, Commander Baines, Commander Cohen, and Mason were left, they went to the lift together. Mason escorted the officers to their quarter's deck. They all said goodnight, and he went down to his deck, full and wanting to get out of his uniform. The Captain slipped him the last bottle of bourbon, and ordered him to take the day off tomorrow. He saved the bourbon, because you never know when a real drink might come in handy.

Commander Baines walked down the corridor with Commander Cohen towards their quarters, with Captain Kouras in tow. They both stopped, and Baines asked, "Captain, would you like for me to have the watch tonight, sir?"

"No, Baines, I'm feeling too wound up now to go to sleep. I'll take this watch. See you in the morning, Commanders." Kouras walked steadily to the bridge lift

"Commander Cohen, would you like a nightcap? I've a little brandy I'd love to share with you, if you'd like." She looked up at his shining blue eyes, that smiling, handsome face and platinum blonde hair, and walked with him to his room. He placed his palm on the pad to unlock and open the door, and they went inside. "Would you like some music and a few canapés, or just some brandy, Commander?" He was trying to remain calm and cool.

She heard the door close shut, and walked up to him, saying, "I'd like for you to call me Rachel, tonight." He opened his mouth to tell her how he felt about her, but he couldn't find any words. He took her hand and kissed it, drew her close to him and gazed in her eyes. She removed the pins holding up her thick, dark red hair, and shook it free. They kissed, softly at first, then he took her in a passionate embrace. They kissed over and over again, nearly tearing each other's uniforms off their bodies, until they were naked and driving each other to his bed. They were lost in a paradise of their own making, loving each other, and releasing the desire they suppressed for so long. There was no ship, no time, and no world but their own.

XII

The first day of the general awakenings arrived. Captain Kouras reviewed the protocol for the hierarchal awakening of the mission managers and mining crews with the medical staff, all covered by contractual agreements with the URE. Dr. Hassan and a corpsman would begin by awakening the Mission Director, Harold Keene. After Director Keene was awake and alert, the Mission Coordinator, Alfredo Garcia, would be awakened. The medical staff dedicated to the mining personnel and managers was next. Then the two union reps, the twelve supervisors, and Chief Technician would all be awakened. It was mandatory that these key passengers be awake, alert, and fully functional before any other mining personnel were brought out of cryonic hibernation, since they were tasked with making certain that all of the unionized miners and stewards were awakened in the proper sequence.

The rest of the men would be awakened during the following days by duty and seniority. The medical technicians belonging to the mining personnel were in charge of bringing their miners out of cryonic sleep. There were a certain number of miners to be awakened each day, and the day's roster was provided by the union reps.

The cryonic containers with the mission managers were stored in a room separate from the general mining population, the Mission Control room. Director Keene, Coordinator Garcia, the Chief Technician, their doctor, and three nurses were all in the main circle of cocoons. The twelve supervisors and two union representatives were in two short racks on either side of the control room.

Captain Kouras received written permission from Earth Command to inspect each of their cryonic containers, due to the ongoing murder investigations. They negotiated a contract amendment to allow for the transport of the newly-emptied containers to the cargo bay, where they would be inspected by the Space Marines, recorded by vid cams, and observed by two of the mining supervisors. Then the cryonic containers would be transported across the cargo bay to the cleaning station. The cleaned and sterilized containers were to be stored in their racks in the hibernation rooms, for re-use after the four years' mining schedule was completed.

Captain Kouras entered the Mission Control room, and logged into the computer at the main console there. He placed his palm print down onto the recognition pad, and his access was granted by the URE mining computer system. He entered the programming key crystal into the slot, and waited for acknowledgement. Finally, the computer said, "General awakening protocol, URE mining ship Hesperia, ready to commence recording."

Captain Kouras said only, "Captain Kouras, protocol acknowledged. Let the awakenings begin." He signaled for Dr. Hassan and the corpsman to approach and scan the cryonic container of Mission Director Keene, and he took his place at the computer console chair. The Doctor checked the scan's vital signs and life functions, and the container monitor. He keyed in the sequence to unseal the container, and it opened with the usual hissing "pop." Dr. Hassan opened the latches of the container, pushed back the lid fully, and began speaking to Director Keene. The man was older than most of the patients he had brought out of cryonic hibernation, so Dr. Hassan went very slowly with his awakening. When Keene's eyes finally began blinking, he rose up from the cocoon, and Dr. Hassan said, "Slowly, Director Keene, let's go slowly. I am Chief Medical Officer Dr. Hassan. You are fine, and you are on the Hesperia, inside your Mission Control room. Director Keene, are you awake?"

The older man did exactly as Dr. Hassan told him, and raised his torso up slowly. He shook his head a little, and looked around the control room at everyone. "I'm okay, I'm okay."

"Do you feel good enough to try to stand, Director?" Dr. Hassan was very reassuring with his new patient, and did not rush him at all.

The Director nodded, and rose up out of the cocoon, and stood up. "Thank you, Doctor. I feel a little fuzzy. Mind if I sit down for a while?"

The corpsman quickly brought the man a chair, and helped him sit down, and covered him with a blanket. The Doctor brought out his light scope, and checked his eyes, and then scanned him head to toe. "We older gents have to take these cryonic awakenings easy, Director Keene. It is a common symptom to be a little light-headed upon awakening, for either old or the young. Would you like us to wait further for you to recover more thoroughly before we begin awakening Coordinator Garcia, or may we proceed with opening his cryonic container now?"

"I'm okay," he responded, blinking his eyes. "Go ahead and wake

Garcia. See if he comes around any better," the Director said.

Dr. Hassan went to the Mission Coordinator's container, and began the same technique for opening Garcia's cocoon. When the lid was raised fully open, Coordinator Garcia began blinking his eyes. Garcia raised himself up quickly, and stood up. The Doctor urged him to take slower steps, but he stepped out of the container directly onto the floor, and stretched his arms wide. Then, his eyes began to roll, and he started to heave, and then vomited. The corpsman quickly went over to him, and produced a bag to give to him to contain his vomit, while Dr. Hassan administered an intramuscular shot to settle his stomach.

Director Keene stood up and walked over to Captain Kouras at the main computer console. "I'm Mission Director Keene, Captain, hope you don't mind if I skip the formalities, and go to my cabin, before he has me puking, too."

"That's quite all right, Director. We'll be in touch later," the Captain said. "Lieutenant Cheung, move his cocoon off the table, so Dr. Hassan can lay that man down." The Captain winched every time Garcia retched. Dr. Hassan and a corpsman took Garcia, and put him onto the table, and gave him another shot to knock him out, and the sickening noise stopped.

"Thank you, Doctor. Now, please proceed with waking the others, according to protocol." Captain Kouras was demonstrating patience, and control; there could be no mistakes. They woke everyone, according to the protocol. Coordinator Garcia was slowly coming awake again and was escorted to his quarters by a corpsman.

"All right, let's get that last container loaded onto the transport, and get back to Section One. We've had enough for one day," Captain Kouras announced. The Space Marines took all the containers down to the cargo bay for inspection, cleaning, and sterilization.

A corpsman asked, "What about the floor, Doctor? Don't we have to clean it up?"

Captain Kouras answered that question. "Leave it for their people to clean up. We did our job. Let's get out of here."

Mason went to the mess hall, to see the Chief, and grab some dinner. There she was, brushing herself off.

"Chief Dawson, how are you doing today?" Mason asked her.

"Staff Sergeant, why is it you always catch me looking my worst? We've been inventorying all our supplies today, checking the food stores against the manifest. I'm covered with flour, and you ask how I'm doing!" She looked like she had borne the brunt of some frat party prank.

"Looks to me like the flour sack won, Chief," he said with a grin.

She smiled through the layer of white flour. "I'll get a cook in here to rustle up something for your dinner. Just give us a minute, Staff Sergeant."

"I've got a better idea, Chief. Why don't I give you an hour or so, and we can have dinner together in the observation lounge? I'm off today." He smiled at her, and she hesitated.

Then she said a quick, "Okay. But I'll do the ordering."

"Fine by me, Chief Dawson. I'll meet you there in an hour." Mason walked out of the mess hall, laughing to himself. At least I've seen her at her worst, he thought.

Mason went to the ship's library, and sat down at the computer console. He checked the progress of the search still being conducted by the computer on the strange symbols on that octagonal tube. Why was it taking so long? He went into the search program to check out the search parameters, and attempted to pause the search when he saw what was written. He copied the file to his com tablet, and sent it to his private files. He then tapped his comm-link, and called for Nurse Cohen. "Nurse Cohen, Staff Sergeant Mason, ma'am."

"Yes, Staff Sergeant. How can I help you?" She was in her quarters, enjoying her free evening.

"Well ma'am, it seems that someone altered the original search parameters Commander Baines programmed for those symbols on the octagonal tube. That's probably why we have not found any information on the symbols. I was going to call the XO, but I know he's on the bridge, in command. Would you like to see this, Nurse Cohen?" Mason asked.

"I'll be there in ten minutes. Cohen out." She quickly changed into her uniform, went to the library, and found Mason. "Let's see what you've discovered."

Mason showed her the search parameter program currently running on the ship's computer. Then, he showed her his com tablet, with the original program designed by Commander Baines. "I'm no programmer, Ma'am, and certainly no math genius like the XO, but I know when something's been altered."

She looked closely at the original search parameter program, and then at the program currently running. She tapped her comm-link, and called Commander Baines. "Commander Baines, this is Commander Cohen. Mason has made a very interesting discovery in the ship's library. Can you come down here for just a minute?"

"On my way." He ordered Lieutenant Davis to take command, and went down the lift to the ship's library. When the lift doors opened, he nearly knocked Captain Kouras over. "Sorry sir, I didn't see you!"

"Is there a fire somewhere Baines? Who has the bridge?" He asked.

"Lieutenant Davis has the bridge, Captain. There's been some kind of discovery made by Mason and Commander Cohen, in the ship's library." The Captain turned to go with Baines, both men walking briskly down the hall, into the library.

"Captain Kouras, Commander Baines, our Staff Sergeant has once again made an interesting discovery. Show them, Mason." Commander Cohen stepped back so that the Captain could sit next to Mason, who was now standing at attention.

"Sit, man. Now, show us what you've discovered," Kouras said. Mason showed them the original search parameter programming saved to his com tablet, and then the current programming running on the ship's computer.

"That's not possible, Captain, without a command override. Whoever over-wrote my program has the computer searching every possible star system for xenoarcheologic evidence of macrobiotic life. That will run to infinity!" The Commander became suddenly anxious. "Sir, this program could tie up the resources of the computer so completely that it could potentially overload, and cause a total systems malfunction. And it was done under my authorization!"

The Captain stood and ran to engineering, with the Commander right behind him. Mason looked at Commander Cohen, and said, "Ma'am, I am no programmer, but I do recognize an attempted sabotage. I had no idea of the potential scope of this altered programming, but, now that I do, I'd say that someone really does not want us to decipher the codes on that octagonal tube. Those symbols have taken on a new importance, ma'am." She looked directly at him with a concerned look on her face.

"Someone is willing to cripple this entire ship in order to prevent us from knowing the meaning of those codes, Mason," she surmised.

"And probably what's inside that tube, ma'am." Mason turned to his notes, and pulled up the image of the octagonal tube. "What is it? What is inside the thing that's so important?"

"We have to find out. We must find the meaning of those symbols, and get inside that metal tube as soon as possible. Our very lives depend on it, Staff Sergeant." They looked at each other, realizing the ramifications of failure. "I'm going to the hospital to inform Dr. Hassan. Excellent job, John. Really excellent." She hurried to the hospital.

Mason looked at the time on the computer, and said, "Shit! I'm late!" He jumped up, collected everything on the desk, and ran to drop them off in his locker. He ran up to the observation lounge, and found a clean Chief Dawson pacing the floor.

"Sorry, Chief, truly, I'm sorry. I was in the ship's library, and got to reading some stuff, and forgot the time. It won't happen again." He had obviously run there, and was slightly out of breath. He felt really bad that he had made her wait for him.

"The library, really? Well, it happens. As long as you don't make it a habit." She nearly left when she discovered he was not in the observation lounge, but decided to wait a couple of minutes more for him. Seeing his apologetic attitude, she knew she made the right decision to wait. "Let's just have dinner, and start all over again."

"Great. I'm starved. What're we having tonight?" Mason was thankful she forgave him. He really liked her down to Earth personality. No ulterior motives, just one hard-working, really nice woman. He saw her smile, at last, and noticed what a nice smile she had. Long legs and lean, with shapely thighs, creamy white skin, lips and mouth perfect; she looked better than most fashion models, even in her khaki uniform.

"I figured you were at least as hungry as I am, so I ordered steaks and potatoes au gratin. Would you like a glass of wine?" The Chief asked him.

"Sure, I'll get the wine. Red?" Mason asked.

"Yes, a cabernet, if that thing can manufacture it." She used her wrist comm-link to give the go-ahead for their dinner to be delivered while Mason brought over two glasses of synthehol cabernet.

"It's not exactly from the California wine country, but it is red." He laughed a little, and sat the glasses down. "Have you been up here before?"

"No, this is my first time up top. I've not seen this view before," she admitted.

"The ship is coming out of hyper-drive very slowly, so everything looks kind of streaked. See?" He held out his hand to her, and took her over to the main window. "I kind of like the way it looks when we slow down, don't you?" She would not get too close to the window.

"Yes, it does look interesting. Like wet icing on a cake that's been cut by a knife." She cautiously stepped a little closer to the window. "How long does it take to come out of hyper-drive?"

"Well, sometimes it's a real quick maneuver, and the entire ship kind of throws everything forward. But this ship is so big, that it's better to do it slowly, and not cause any undo commotion." He remembered his breaching of the engineering deck and the sudden drop out of hyper-drive, and the ensuing chaos.

"Here's dinner! Come on Mason, and tell me more after we eat." She sat down very properly, like a lady, Mason noted. They ate their dinners while chatting about different steak cuts, and which each of them preferred. Then they drank more wine, settled on the couch together to watch the streaking stars for a little while longer, and spent a very relaxing evening with each other. She thought that everyone needs a friend, especially on a seven-year mission, with five and a half years to go. He knew how to make interesting conversation without dominating, and he had a good sense of humor. She was trying to not get caught up looking at his handsome face, but it was a real challenge for her. He was such a flirt!

While Mason and the Chief were having dinner in the observation lounge, Captain Kouras and Commander Baines were at the command console in engineering with Lt. Commander Powers. "Chief Engineer, I want you to tell me who changed the search program originally written and implemented by Commander Baines."

"I'm trying to find out for you, Captain, but that information is not available in the file." Powers was searching all the authoring files by date, time, and subject, and the name of the author; the overwritten search program was the only file without an author.

"What do you mean it's not available? Whoever did this had to have command authority to overwrite my instructions. There are only four people on this ship who have that authority: Captain Kouras; you; me; and Lt. Commander Westerly, who was awakened only yesterday." Baines was livid. He turned to the Captain, and asked, "Sir, has anyone else been given command authority by Earth Command since this ship left Moon Base?"

"Not that I'm aware of. Powers, can you cancel that program running now?"

"Yes, Captain. One moment, sir, and it'll be gone for good. Wait…it's not allowing me to cancel. Captain, we're going to have to contact Earth Command. We need higher authority than ours to cancel this program, sir," Powers replied.

"You two in my ready room in ten minutes!" The Captain left the engineering room, and ran straight for his ready room. He used the secure video comm-link and contacted Admiral Tomiko. "Hesperia ship's Captain Kouras, calling for Admiral Tomiko on a secure channel. Code Red. I need to speak with the Admiral immediately." The Captain was clenching his teeth in frustration. Finally, a response came.

"Tomiko here. What is your Code Red, Captain Kouras?" The Admiral had obviously just been awakened. He was in a robe.

The Captain explained the overwritten program's discovery, and the potential ramifications of its not being cancelled at once. "Admiral, our Chief Engineer has attempted to cancel this unauthorized program from the main control console in engineering, without success. The author of this program cannot be discovered. Will you authorize its cancellation immediately?"

"Absolutely, Captain. One moment." The Admiral switched channels, muted the volume on the comm-link with the Hesperia, and spoke with someone on another channel. "We seem to have an issue here, Captain Kouras. I will be back momentarily. Tomiko out."

Now, the Captain was having thoughts of conspiracy and possibly sabotage. He waited for the Admiral's response.

"Captain, we are here, as ordered," Commander Baines reported.

"Order Lt. Commander Westerly in here, on the double, Commander," he said.

"Aye aye, Captain." The Commander went out of the room, and quietly ordered Westerly to join them.

Lt. Commander Westerly had no clue as to what the reason could possibly be for this hastily called meeting. She looked at Baines and Powers, and saw no reaction in either officer. They were all waiting, at attention, for the Admiral.

"Captain Kouras, this is Admiral Tomiko."

"Yes, Admiral. I have asked our command officers to join us, with your permission, sir: Commander Baines, Lt. Commanders Powers and Westerly."

"Very well, Captain. It has been brought to my attention that several unauthorized communication transmissions have been made from the Hesperia to Earth Command headquarters, and Titan One. Are you aware of these transmissions, Captain Kouras?" The Admiral was fully dressed now, and in a very serious mood.

"No, sir, I was not. No transmissions have been made by me that were unauthorized, or not reported. Commander Baines, Lt. Commander Powers, and I have been awake since the second month of our mission. However, Lt. Commander Westerly was only awakened yesterday, Admiral. We are unaware of any unauthorized transmissions until this call." The Captain's neck blood vessels began to protrude. "I'm curious as to how those transmissions could have been made without our knowledge, Admiral."

"So am I, Captain. I have ordered a full scale inquiry into this matter. I have also ordered the cancellation of the search program you identified to me earlier. Please verify that it has been cancelled."

"Sir, with your permission...." The Captain nodded, and Powers left the room to check the status of the program currently running.

"Admiral, I am sure you are aware of the potential implications of any information sent in these transmissions. Whoever overwrote the Commander's original program had to have command authority," the Captain reported.

"Yes and also extensive knowledge of the ship's systems to make those transmissions and avoid detection. Possibly even systems developer status. Earth Command is very concerned, as you might well surmise. This mission may have been compromised, Captain Kouras." The Admiral spoke very emphatically, looking directly into his monitor. "All due care should be taken. You are to go to orange alert, but without making the Mission Director and Mission Coordinator aware of the change in status. Is that clear?"

"Yes, sir," Kouras answered.

The ready room door opened, and Powers spoke immediately. "Captain Kouras, the altered program running the search to infinity has been canceled, and deleted, sir."

"Which one of your officers discovered the altered program? I think a commendation is in order for this excellent work, don't you, Captain

Kouras?" The Admiral suggested.

"I wholeheartedly agree, Admiral, but it was not one of my officers, sir. Prime Marine Staff Sergeant John Mason made the discovery, sir," Kouras revealed.

"Really? That is remarkable." The Admiral looked at the command officers in the room again, and then at the Captain. "His Commandant will be pleased to hear the news. I will write the commendation myself. Tomiko, out."

"Captain Kouras to Staff Sergeant Mason."

"Staff Sergeant Mason here, Captain Kouras." Mason had been completely absorbed with flirting and chatting on the couch with the Chief when he got the Captain's call.

The Captain said firmly, "I need you in my ready room, Staff Sergeant. Now."

"Aye aye, Captain." Mason jumped off the couch, shrugged his shoulders, and said, "Another time, Chief?"

"Just go. Don't keep the Captain waiting." The Chief was disappointed to lose her evening companion in such a rush, but understood he had to leave her. He was so nice to her, and comfortable to be around. Most really handsome men she had known were vain and full of themselves. Mason was down to Earth and unpretentious, and fun to be around. She looked at the streaking stars, and wondered if they would actually have a chance to get together, in a non-platonic way. She definitely wanted him, no bones about that. Should she consider it so soon?

Mason made it up to the bridge as quickly as he could. He knocked on the ready room door, and heard "Enter!" He went inside, snapped to attention, and saluted the Captain. "Staff Sergeant Mason reporting as ordered, Captain Kouras."

"I have just spoken with Admiral Tomiko about your discovery of the altered program, Staff Sergeant. He has canceled the program, and deleted it. The Admiral has informed me there were several unauthorized communications transmissions made from the Hesperia to Earth Command, and Titan One, not detected by our equipment. You are to investigate these unauthorized transmissions, discover their content, if possible, and find out who made them. This is to be your top priority."

"Begging the Captain's pardon, sir, but the top priority of this Marine is the security and safety of the Captain, bridge officers, medical officers, and engineering officers on the Hesperia," Mason countered.

Kouras almost smiled. "You are correct, Staff Sergeant, but, now you have another priority. I want to know who sent those transmissions, and what exactly did they contain, as soon as possible."

"Sir, yes, sir," Mason responded.

"The Admiral is also informing your Commandant of the Space Marines that you are to receive a commendation directly from him, in appreciation of your excellent performance," the Captain informed him. "Your day off is ended, Staff Sergeant. Dismissed."

"Aye aye, Captain." Mason stepped back one step, made the half turn perfectly, and quickly walked out of the ready room. He went to the storage cabinet, took out his laser rifle and helmet, and assumed his place on the bridge.

"Lt. Commander Westerly, you are undoubtedly confused about these matters. You will be briefed on our situation, and the series of events that transpired during your cryo-hybernation. Lt. Commander Powers, you may return to engineering. I want to know how those communications transmissions evaded detection by our systems, and I want to know as soon as possible," Kouras ordered.

"Aye aye, sir." The Chief Engineer quickly left for his deck.

Kouras turned and said, "Commander Baines, you are to take our Science Officer down to the hospital. See to it that she is given a complete physical, and a thorough screening for post-hibernation sickness. She is as white as a ghost. We will all meet here tomorrow morning, for a special staff meeting to discuss our progress in investigating the situation at hand. I want answers! Dismissed!"

They all said, "Aye aye, sir," and left his ready room. Captain Kouras went to his quarters, and wrote the order for Dr. Hassan and Nurse Cohen to attend his special staff meeting, and Lieutenant Cheung, as well. They had not even awoken a single miner, and already the Hesperia's mission was threatened. Were the miners planning another mutiny, with the help of someone at Earth Command? But how did the murder of two research scientists figure into this scenario; or are they another completely different scheme? He held his head in his hands, pressing on his temples. His head felt like it would burst from the throbbing inside his skull. He knew this would be a challenging mission, but he already had more than what he bargained, just seventeen months into the mission. He pulled out an injection pen from the drawer, and shot himself with a tranquilizer in the thigh. He got ready for bed, before the drug hit.

Commander Baines took Lt. Commander Westerly down to the hospital, and did as he was ordered. "This is Dr. Hassan, Chief Medical Officer. Doctor, this is our Science Officer, Lt. Commander Westerly. She is showing signs of post-hibernation sickness."

"Hello, Lt. Commander, do you remember me? I helped you awaken from your cryonic hibernation." The Doctor smiled, and her face lit up somewhat, recognizing him. "You look pale, my dear. Let's have a look at you. Ah, here's our Head Nurse Cohen, and she'll help me check out your vital signs. This is our Science Officer, Lt. Commander Westerly." The Doctor continued to chatter on about the steps they would take to evaluate the Lt. Commander's physical, mental, and emotional condition. Baines left the exam room and waited outside.

In about fifteen minutes, Nurse Cohen came outside, and said, "Dr. Hassan has determined that the Lt. Commander is showing signs of hibernation sickness, and needs to stay in the hospital for tonight. He is informing the Captain now." She smiled at him, and he felt the sudden urge to charge at her. "Does she know what's happened on the Hesperia while she was in cryonic hibernation?"

He recovered from his brief animal impulse, and answered, "She has very scant information, and only regarding the altered program. Other than that, she's ignorant of our situation."

"I'll stay with her tonight, and make sure she recovers as much as she is able, so she can attend the meeting tomorrow, if possible." She noticed the disappointed look in his eyes, and smiled. "You should try to get some sleep. The general awakenings are tomorrow."

"Yes, they are. They cannot be delayed, or it might be interpreted as a contractual infraction." His voice trailed off as he looked at her. He accepted his fate for the night.

"Then I'll see you at the Captain's meeting tomorrow morning, Commander Baines." With a slight hesitation, she gently touched his arm, and went back inside to tend to her new patient. Westerly had been moved farther into the hospital, and was being helped into a gown by a corpsman. Nurse Cohen helped her finish dressing for her stay, and started her intravenous line of saline fluid, essential vitamins, and electrolytes. She explained what they would do for her through the night, and told her they would put her to sleep for a few hours. "You will feel much better in the morning after we get some fluids into your bloodstream."

Westerly watched Nurse Cohen inject something into her IV tube. "What was that for?"

"That was the injection to put you to sleep for a few hours. Now, can you count down from one hundred to one for me?" Nurse Cohen asked.

"Of course I can. One hundred, ninety-nine, ninety-eight, ninety-sev…" and she went out, gently rolling her head a bit to the side.

Nurse Cohen watched her go out, and scanned her completely, head to toes. She clipped analytical mini-clamps onto her forefingers and big toes, and placed a band over her forehead to record her brainwaves. She went to the panel behind the bed and lowered the lights, and pressed a switch that lowered a scanning panel completely over the length of her patient's body. She pulled up a chair next to the bed, and sat down to read the medical history of Lt. Commander Westerly, and spent the night studying her files, adjusting her meds dosage as necessary, and monitoring her progress, just as nurses have done for a thousand years.

The Captain held his meeting in the conference room, adjacent to the bridge. In attendance were his entire command staff, Lieutenant Cheung, and Staff Sergeant Mason. Lieutenant Cheung had obviously spent much of the night reading the ship's log, to familiarize himself with the events of the past seventeen months. He had written a long list of questions he hoped could be answered about the orange cloud, and the deaths of the scientists.

"Thank you all for coming. Let's welcome Lt. Commander Anna Westerly, our Science Officer. She assures me she is ready to take her station this morning, if that's approved by our medical staff members?" The Captain looked at Dr. Hassan.

"As long as she feels fit, and promises to return to sick bay in twelve hours for a booster, she has my permission to take her duty station, Captain Kouras," Dr. Hassan responded.

"Excellent. Then let's get started. Lt. Commander Powers, any results on the analysis of our computer systems' failure to detect those unauthorized communications transmissions?" The Captain went right for the jugular, Lt. Commander Westerly noticed.

"No sir. There are no records of any unauthorized or any unapproved communications transmissions made from the Hesperia to Earth Command, or Titan One. While I realize that the Admiral would not have said it if it were not true, there are no records at all," Powers reported.

"What about gaps in the information logs?" Commander Baines asked, trying not to sound accusatory to the Chief Engineer, who had also been up all night in his quest.

"No, Commander, no gaps in time. We checked for time lapses, or gaps in the information data feed, and came up empty-handed." Powers answered matter-of-factly, but it was clear that he was perplexed.

"Permission to speak, Captain?" Mason asked.

"Permission granted to speak freely, Staff Sergeant."

"Lt. Commander Powers, were the logs of the shuttles checked, sir?" Mason asked politely.

"No, because, while they are in the cargo bay, all shuttle transmissions would be monitored by the main computer," Powers answered.

"A landing group would have access to hand-held communicators kept in the shuttles' emergency kits. They could have been modified to send transmissions, sir." Mason had been on the bridge all night, and had not been relieved to check the shuttles out himself.

"That is highly unlikely, Staff Sergeant. Those communicators only work short-range. They'd never be capable of transmissions to Earth," Powers answered.

Lt. Commander Westerly said, "I think I know what the Staff Sergeant is getting at. The hand-helds could be modified to send data signal transmissions much farther than voice transmissions; in fact, you could use the shuttle itself as an optical transmission booster, and get a data transmission to one of our satellites on the rim of the solar system, if you knew the time and approximate quantity of the data to be sent or received. From the satellites, data could be sent anywhere within our solar system."

Commander Baines listened to this argument, and added, "In order to accomplish such a feat, both the sender and receiver would have to be in perfect sync for time, size, and duration of the data transmissions. They would have to plan these transmissions very carefully. One miscalculation and the data would be sent into space, or would have been received as incomplete scattered data packets."

"Powers, find any such scattered data packets that were perhaps returned to the hand-held communicators. Check out the communicators thoroughly, checking for records of transmissions." The Captain turned to Westerly, and said, "Contact Earth Command for records of any data-only transmissions received that coincide with the unauthorized communications transmissions from our ship."

"Sir, if the monitors are still in the cargo bay, we may have more information as to how those transmissions were sent, if they were to be checked again." Mason was happy they took his suggestion at face value this time. "We may also benefit from vid cams being put in the garbage bins, sir. It would be very easy to float a small transmitter outside the range of detection of the Hesperia that could transmit data to a satellite."

"Of course: no one pays attention to garbage once it's outside the ship. You could even free float a mini missile for several kilometers that would automatically activate at a certain distance, and broadcast its transmission out of the range of the Hesperia!" Baines was positively excited.

"But, now that we're out of hyper-drive, it will take much longer for a mini missile or a small transmitter to be outside the detection range of the Hesperia," Commander Cohen noted.

"They could utilize the shuttles working outside the ship in the mining fields!" Commander Baines exclaimed.

"Excellent. Baines, take Westerly down to engineering, and work with Powers on these hypotheses. Contact me immediately if anything turns up. Lieutenant Cheung, have a team of your Space Marines review every second of vid cam recordings, and check the sound levels for any sort of transmissions noises. Then, review the vid monitors' records to see if anyone accessed the shuttles since the day they were loaded onto the Hesperia. We know for a fact that someone got on shuttle one to access navigational coordinates. Perhaps that is related to the transmissions." The Captain raised an eyebrow.

"You have your orders. In ten minutes, we will begin the general awakenings. We will meet for a status update tomorrow at the same time. Dismissed." The Captain took his com tablet, and headed for the bridge. The medical staff went to the hospital, and began their "on call" status. The others dispersed according to their orders. Mason went back to the bridge, donned his helmet and his weapons belt, shouldered his laser rifle, and took his post. For the first time, he felt like a member of the bridge crew, and not merely their watchdog.

XIII

Everyone on the bridge was waiting for the notification from the Mission Director to begin the awakenings. Mason had not been present to watch general awakenings of six hundred people before. The vid cams provided live coverage of the entire operation in the miners' quarters. Rack after rack of cryonic containers was off-loaded, the containers placed on waiting anti-gravity gurneys. Once the miners were awake, they were raised up by their two medical personnel, helped to standing and stepping out of the containers. The lids were then closed, and the gurney pushed aside to waiting Hesperia crew technicians for loading onto transports. The containers were taken to a special inspection station on the cargo bays, where each container was subjected to a thorough inspection, which was recorded by vid cams. The reloading process was slower than usual, because of the inspections, but it was necessary to thoroughly check each container for any alteration, similar to Dr. Ed Wise's container, or Mason's; or to find any hidden contraband; or discover a possible murder weapon.

The awakening of the miners went like clockwork. Even the few miners who awoke with nausea were taken aside, out of the way of the technicians and the waiting cocoons. When each miner was up and walking, they reported to Coordinator Garcia and a union representative, and they were assigned a bunk, and told which corridor to take to their shower facilities. Their individual gear was awaiting their arrival in their private locker, having been stowed and palm-locked by each miner upon their initial boarding, seventeen months ago. Mason noted the continual stream of men, and a few women, dressed only in disposable diapers, shuffling down corridors and taking lifts to their quarters.

The only members of the mining personnel to have private quarters were Mission Director Keene, with a suite off the port side of the Mission Control room, and Mission Coordinator Garcia, whose smaller, junior suite was off the starboard side of the Mission Control room. The doctor and nurses also had individual, private rooms, but they were small, single rooms off their hospital area. Their Chief Technician had a small, private room, located some distance away from the Mission Control room, near Section Three.

Mason's regular duty on the bridge was two six-hour shifts per day, 6am to 6pm, with one day off every six days, which he rarely used. He would be relieved by two Space Marines during his lunch break, and after his shift. He was essentially on call for any other time his presence was ordered by the XO or the CO. The bridge of the Hesperia had only her skeleton crew awake and on duty for the initial part of their mission, the seventeen month's trip out to the mining fields outside the solar system. Now, the full crew complement was on duty: Captain Kouras in the command chair; Commander Baines directly behind him on the starboard side at his executive officer station; and Lt. Commander Westerly on the Captain's port side, at the main science station. These command stations formed the main triangle in the center of the bridge, raised at the highest point on the bridge deck.

The second level of the bridge formed a complete circle, with Lieutenant Fontenay at the bridge engineering station, and Lieutenant Davis at tactical, both below and behind the Captain; and, directly in front of and lower than the Captain, were Lieutenant Espinoza at the navigational control station; Lieutenant Kim at the helm; and Lieutenant Sukesh at defensive control. The lowest level featured observation windows, filling 200 degrees visibility from the Captain's chair, all the way up and over the top of the bridge. They delivered a full view for the bridge crew. The front windows could be converted into viewing screens at a touch. In between the main entrance to the bridge and the entrance to the ready room was Mason's station. Opposite those two entrances was a bank of computer screens for communications, flight control and operations, mission operations, and life support. Twelve officers on the bridge from 6 am to 6pm, and ten officers from 6pm to 6 am.

The only command-level officer not stationed on the bridge was Lt. Commander Powers, Chief Engineer, whose station was the engineering deck. His crew had multiplied four times in number after the crew awakenings. If one was to ask the Chief Engineer exactly what his area of responsibility was, he would answer, "Everything." With the Hesperia nearly reaching the mining fields, his engineering crew would soon have their duties increased ten-fold, managing the power supply for the huge mining machines in Sections Three and Four, and the mining crews' quarters and facilities in Section Two.

Mason kept his calm and controlled demeanor as the lone sentry on the bridge, silently keeping watch, and observing all that he could. He could request and receive more back-up from his Space Marines in a few seconds, if needed. They all hoped and prayed that call would not have to be made this mission. Crew security sentries were stationed outside the bridge entrance and the entrance to the engineering deck fully armed with laser rifles, hand lasers, and stun grenades. Security droids stood the watch at the lift entrances, and corridor transition points.

Mason, of course, was an armory all to himself, as the Prime Marine's definition of "fully armed" went beyond the scope of the Space Force general regulations manual. His weapons belt contained everything from a long-bladed knife, to kung fu throwing blades; a twelve-centimeter xenon flashlight that could double as a club; a hand energy shield; exploding gas pellets; a two-minute breathing tube; a grappling hook in a firing tube; a mini razor-wire garrote; several 3"x4" packs of explosives, small in size, but mighty in explosive force; and a few other "goodies," as he referred to his Prime Marine-only issued weapons. His extra ammo packs were on belts that crisscrossed his shielded torso and back. One could only guess as to what kind of fearsome gear he kept in his deep thigh pockets. If deadly force had a name, it was John Mason.

At the end of the twelfth hour of their awakenings, the Mission Coordinator, Garcia, contacted the Captain to announce they were stopping for the night. Captain Kouras completed his log entries, and gave Baines the chair. "I want you, Westerly, and Powers in my ready room at o-three thirty tomorrow morning, to discuss progress on your new theories, Commander."

"Aye aye, Captain," Baines said, taking the command chair. It had been a tense day for everyone, especially the Captain. They were all bleary-eyed from observing the live vid cam feeds of the general awakenings. Over three hundred miners were awakened today, an amazing feat of practiced coordination and perfection. No reports of any contraband or illegal substances were found in any of the cryonic containers. Yet.

He wondered how the medical staff was handling today's events, especially Nurse Cohen. Their duty was to be on call for any emergency, and they stood at the ready to serve the entire twelve hours. He invited Nurse Cohen to have dinner with him.

Chief Dawson served a dinner of chicken Kiev, with red parsley potatoes and broccoli with cheese sauce, to them. "Would you like some chardonnay?" She took a carafe of synthehol wine off the tray held by her crewman, and poured two glasses of the golden liquid for them. "I'll leave this full carafe for you. If you would like seconds of anything, please let us know." The Chief went back to her kitchen.

Commander Baines and Nurse Cohen finished dinner, and drank more wine silently. "There are so many things I want to say to you, Rachel," he said softly, trying his best to keep his voice down. They sat and sipped their wine, looking at each other, and said more than mere words, in total silence.

She broke the silence, speaking softly. "We'd best be going, Victor. We can't sit here all night." She smiled at him and stood up. "I can't drink any more of that synthehol wine, Commander," she said, with a little more volume in her voice, knowing that the other officers were listening. "I have a little pinot noir from Oregon that might interest you."

"Sure. I like pinot noir." They walked out of the officers' mess together.

"I'd like to try her pinot noir, myself," one of the officers at the nearby table said to his buddies. His dinner companions chuckled.

"We can't stay up the whole night, with your having a three-thirty meeting with the Captain, Victor," Commander Cohen said.

"I know, Rachel," he said, walking with her to her quarters. She opened her door with the palm lock, closed it, and secured it.

She turned to him, and said, "Meeting you was not on my radar, you know. We have a long mission ahead of us, Victor." He only said "uh-huh," as he covered her in kisses, picked her up in his arms, and took her to bed. They totally ignored the time, choosing instead to do what passionate men and women do with each other in private.

Hours later, she looked at her alarm clock, sighed upon seeing the time, and set it for two-thirty, with the loudest alarm available. She rolled over next to him, and he put his arm around her, holding her close, until she fell asleep. He lay there, wide awake, happier than he had ever been, with Rachel in his arms. He wanted it to be that way the rest of his life. Would she just think him a fool, if he told her how he felt? Was it too soon? She seemed to feel the same way about him; or was he just fooling himself? He looked at her, watching her sleep, as she breathed deeply, in and out. She was so beautiful. He knew he was in way too deep, and he never wanted his life to be the way it was before her. He finally fell asleep, holding Rachel, with her arm over his chest, in complete bliss.

Rachel awoke with a start as the alarm chimed loudly, announcing 2:30am. She took a deep breath and got up. No snooze alarms allowed this morning. She leaned down and touched his shoulder, saying gently, "Victor, time to get up. C'mon." She went into the bathroom, showered, and started getting herself ready, and noticed he was still asleep. She had to try another tact. "Rise and shine Commander Baines." That worked. The covers flew off him, exposing his slim, well-muscled, naked body.

He sat up, looked at her and laughed. "Thanks, Rachel. What time is it?"

"It's 2:45am, and your ass is grass if you're late for the Captain's meeting," she told him.

"Oh boy." He was up, dressing in a flash. He came over to her to give her a kiss, but she said, "No candy this morning. Better take these instead." She handed him a plastic bag with four pills inside.

"What are these?" He looked at them suspiciously.

"Vitamin B, C, and ginseng capsules. I'll call down to the officers' mess and have them whip up a protein shake for you. My own concoction. It'll be ready for you to pick up on your way up to the bridge." He stuffed the bag into his pocket, and started to leave.

As he was almost outside the door, he turned and gave her a quick kiss. "Ha! Gotcha!" He was laughing to himself as he jogged down the corridor to the lift.

Rachel watched him jog down the corridor, hoping he would still be in as good a mood at 6pm as he was now. She shook her head, and resolved they would not do this again when they had early duty. She went back inside to her desk, and called the officers' mess to order two of her special recipe protein shakes.

"Two shakes, ma'am?" Sammie checked.

"Yes, Sammie, two shakes this morning. I'll be there in twenty minutes," she said.

It was all she could do to hold onto her heart with Victor Baines. He was a very striking man. She was not attracted to him immediately; he was not her usual "type." She usually was attracted to men who resembled John Mason: tall, dark hair and eyes, and very muscular builds. Victor was tall, with a slender, well-muscled body; strength without the bulk. As she carefully brushed his blonde hairs off her jacket, she lost herself briefly, remembering last night. He was a powerful man, but gentle with her. That combination was new to her, and she liked it. A lot. She hoped their new romance would endure, this time.

She left her daydreams behind, and headed for the officers' mess hall, realizing their romance was no longer their secret anymore. The other officers in the mess hall noticed them leaving together last night; she heard them snickering. With over two hundred Space Force crew members now awake and running around, she and Victor were bound to get noticed sooner or later. Inside the empty officers' mess, she went up to the counter, and tapped the little bell.

Sammie, her favorite 3rd class cook, came out smiling with her two shakes. "Here you go, Commander. Just as you ordered them, ma'am."

"Thank you Sammie. I really need this today." She handed her a charge-crystal.

"So do I," said Commander Baines, suddenly appearing behind her, smiling. "What's in it? Does it have a flavor?"

"It's strawberry-banana sir, and it's Commander Cohen's secret recipe. If I tell anyone what's in it, I'll be washing dishes for a month!"

"Then mum's the word!" Baines took his shake and hurried out of the officers' mess to the lift, leaving Rachel shaking her head, and laughing softly. Sammie handed Nurse Cohen her charge-crystal back.

"Thanks, Sammie. See you tomorrow," Commander Cohen said, and left for the hospital. Yes, the word would definitely be out now.

At o-three thirty, the bridge command officers stood, chatting with Dr. Hassan, and waiting, as the Captain rushed into his ready room. "Good morning. Let's get started right away. We will have this meeting with Admiral Tomiko on the comm, joining us." The Captain looked intensely at the vid monitor, chewing his lower lip. His eyes were very red and watery.

The Earth Command operator announced, "Hold for Admiral Tomiko."

"Good morning everyone. I have some good news for you, and some not so good news. We have determined that our satellites on the outer rim of the solar system were indeed used in the unauthorized communications from your ship, Captain Kouras. We have not ascertained exactly how they were used, however, nor have we discovered what information was transmitted," the Admiral stated.

"Admiral, we have a theory on how the data was transmitted, if we may explain to you, sir," Captain Kouras offered.

"Go ahead, Captain."

Kouras said, "Lt. Commander Westerly, please."

She explained the handheld communicators' theory, and how they could have been modified for long-range data transmissions. She posited about the use of data packets, and how they would not be readily detected by modern computer systems. The Admiral seemed to understand, nodding as she spoke.

"Excellent, Lt. Commander. Your addition to the crew of the Hesperia is welcome, I'm sure. Your expertise is notable. Have you been able to gain any knowledge about what may have been communicated in those transmissions?" The Admiral asked the group.

"Not yet, Admiral," Captain Kouras answered, "but we are making every attempt to discover that information, as we speak, sir."

The Admiral just nodded, and continued speaking. "We have also pinpointed two of the locations where your ship's unauthorized communications were received. One is on Titan One; a small, remote bar and restaurant near the shuttle landing platform on the north side of the complex, popular with shuttle crews. The other location is far more disturbing. It is an empty training center building, located three blocks from Earth Command Central in Houston. For both locations, transmissions were received and sent out to the Hesperia. All were unauthorized. The first signal was sent from Titan One to the Hesperia upon her departure from SS10, just prior to engaging the hyper-drive. The transmissions all contained encrypted data, as your officers suspected. Every attempt is being made to recover the data packets, and break through the encryption." The Captain was silent, looking at his hands.

Commander Baines spoke. "Admiral, we have been able to prove our hypothesis on utilizing the emergency handheld communicators to transmit date to our satellites on the fringe; it is possible, and probable. However, we are continuing to search for any other type of unauthorized, and perhaps heretofore unknown, communications device."

"The Hesperia has become a cornucopia of riddles, crimes, and seemingly disassociated evidence that, for most intents and purposes, cannot be determined as related to each other," the Admiral said, frowning. The Captain said nothing.

Baines stated, "Admiral, we are dealing with very knowledgeable persons, possessing sophisticated, well designed methods for sabotage, and murder. It was our desire to have solved these crimes prior to the general awakening of the mining personnel, but it was not possible, sir."

The Admiral asked, "Captain Kouras, where is your Prime Marine, Staff Sergeant Mason?"

"He comes on bridge duty at 6am, Admiral," Kouras answered.

The Admiral was not pleased. "I want that Prime Marine available for my calls regarding this investigation in the future, Captain Kouras. While your command and medical officers have been exemplary in their methodology and technique, Mason is the only crew member on board with advanced education and training in criminal forensics, and he has demonstrated phenomenal insights into these matters."

"Yes, Admiral," the Captain said nervously.

"We must utilize every weapon in our arsenal. I fear something much larger than originally suspected is at play here." The Admiral leaned in closer to the screen to say, "We cannot allow word of this to reach the ears of your mining personnel or their managers. Is that clear?"

They answered in unison, "Yes, Admiral."

"Captain, what reason did you give the Mission Director for inspecting their cryo-cocoons?" Tomiko asked.

"We told them we were checking for contraband and drugs, sir," the Captain replied.

"Excellent, and true. The rebellious miners on the Excelon smuggled small knives and stun gas into their cocoons. I'm certain they are aware of that fact," the Admiral revealed to them.

"Yes, sir, they complained about the inspections slowing the progress of miners' awakenings, but acquiesced, nevertheless." Captain Kouras thought to himself, at least we did one thing right.

"Very good. I will expect weekly updates from you, Captain Kouras. Keep me informed as to your progress. Tomiko out."

The screen went thankfully blank. "Lt. Commander Westerly, have you caught up with the ship's logs and briefings yet?" The Captain asked.

"Yes, sir, but there's honestly more incomplete evidence and conjecture than hard science available, sir." Her comments set the Captain off.

"I concur with you, Lt. Commander Westerly. We have proven nothing. We have only formulated hypotheses at this time. But we shall all continue to do our best to gather more hard evidence to discover what exactly is going on here." He raised his voice and pounded on the table. "I want answers! Dismissed!"

They all went to their stations, except for Dr. Hassan. "Captain, a private word with you?"

"No, you'll have to wait for some other time. They'll be resuming the miners' general awakenings any minute now." The Captain started to head out of the room.

"No, it cannot wait. Please sit down, Captain Kouras." The Doctor blocked the doorway, reached over, and locked the door. "Please, Captain, sit down."

Captain Kouras was visibly upset. "No, I won't sit down. What's this about, Doctor? What's so damned important?" He was gritting his teeth.

"Our commanding officer's health, well-being, and mental stability are the prime concern for the Chief Medical Officer," he said firmly.

"I'm fine. Now get out of my way," the Captain yelled, pushing his way to the door.

"Please - sit - down!" Doctor Hassan pulled his handheld medical scanner from his lab coat, and quickly scanned Captain Kouras. "As I suspected, there is evidence of recent use of stimulants, tranquilizers, and sleep-inducers in your bloodstream, Captain. Did you think I would not notice? I am your doctor."

The Captain was seething. "Get out of here now, Doctor."

"Captain, I understand that Admiral Tomiko and Earth Command want answers. So do we all. But the Hesperia needs a healthy, strong, and mentally stable commanding officer. You must have immediate medical treatment, before your heart stops beating, or your brain fries." Dr. Hassan looked at him intensely. The Captain tried again to push the Doctor aside.

Dr. Hassan reached into his chest pocket, withdrew an injection pen, and hit the Captain's arm with a shot of tranquilizers. "Captain Kouras, you are temporarily relieved of duty. You will be taken down to the hospital for treatment, either with or without your cooperation."

"You can't do this to me, you bastard, I'll have you court-martialed and put into the bri…" the Captain ranted, as he began to collapse.

The Doctor steered him into a nearby chair, and quickly tapped his comm-link. "Commander Baines, please come to the ready room at once."

The Commander quickly entered the ready room. "What has happened to the Captain, Dr. Hassan?" He came over to the Captain, but was stopped short of getting too close.

"Close and lock the door. Our Captain is ill, Commander. As Chief Medical Officer, I am temporarily removing him from command. It has all

110

been recorded on the vid cams."

"Is this necessary, Dr. Hassan?" He saw the wild look in the Captain's red, teary eyes.

"Yes, in my medical judgment, it is. Please call the hospital and have two corpsmen get up here with an anti-gravity gurney. Tell them to enter the Captain's quarters, and use the door inside to the ready room. Let's not let the other bridge officers see this, Commander," the Doctor said.

"Yes, Doctor, I agree." Baines did as the Doctor ordered, and went inside the Captain's quarters to admit the corpsmen with the anti-gravity gurney. "This is not to be broadcast around the ship, gentlemen."

"Yes, sir, Commander," the corpsmen said.

Baines stood by the locked ready room door as the Captain was helped onto the gurney, and taken back through his quarters to the hospital.

"Help me search his quarters, Commander. Use these gloves. Release a floating vid cam to record our efforts." Baines did as instructed, and the two men searched the room. When they opened the desk drawers, they saw dozens of injector pens. Dr. Hassan used a glove to take them out of the drawer, and laid them out onto the desk. "Where did he get these? There are no drugs or injection pens missing from the hospital." After the pens were recorded, the Doctor put them into an envelope, and they continued searching the Captain's room. When they finished, they left his quarters and locked the door, and went back inside the ready room.

"We must notify the Admiral at once." The Doctor looked gravely at Commander Baines.

"I will." The Commander called up a secure channel on the ready room vid-comm link, and requested to speak with Admiral Tomiko.

"The nature of your call, Commander Baines?" The Earth Command operator asked.

"Red alert. Old man down. Urgent. Relay at once," he said firmly.

The Admiral finally came on screen. "What's happened to Captain Kouras?"

"He was taken suddenly ill, Admiral," Baines replied.

"This is Chief Medical Officer Dr. Hassan, Admiral. We have taken Captain Kouras to the hospital for testing and treatment, sir."

"What happened? We were speaking only half an hour ago," Tomiko said.

"Admiral, I believe he is suffering from extreme exhaustion, and an inability to sleep. We need to confine him to sick bay for several days, to run tests and analysis on him. He is temporarily unfit for duty, in his condition," Dr. Hassan said.

"Exhaustion? Is that all, Doctor?" The Admiral was trying to read between the lines.

Dr. Hassan reported, "Yes, that is all I can confirm at the present,

Admiral."

The Admiral stared at the Doctor, and heaved a great sigh. "This is your call, Dr. Hassan. Very well. Captain Kouras is temporarily relieved of command. Commander Baines, you are now Captain of the mining freighter Hesperia. You will immediately assume all duties and pay fitting your new rank. Congratulations, Captain Baines."

Baines merely said, "Thank you, Admiral."

"Keep me informed, gentlemen. My announcement to the crew will be made via vid-comm in one minute. Captain Baines, be at the ready. Tomiko, out." Baines unlocked the ready room door, and both men walked out together.

"Commander Baines, an urgent message is coming in from Earth Command, sir," Lieutenant Marston said.

Baines ordered, "Put it on Section One communications, Lieutenant."

"This is Admiral Tomiko, Earth Command. Until further notice, Captain Kouras is temporarily relieved of command. Commander Victor Baines is hereby promoted to Commanding Officer, Captain of the mining freighter Hesperia. Congratulations, Captain Baines. Tomiko out."

The bridge officers looked at their new Captain, and each other. Finally, Lt. Commander Westerly broke the brief, but awkward, silence. "Congratulations, Captain Baines."

The rest of the bridge officers offered their congratulations to their new CO, and then Dr. Hassan said, "I'll be in the hospital, on call for the miners' awakenings, if I'm needed. Congratulations, Captain Baines."

"Thank you all. Now, let's get back to work." Captain Baines brought up his command screens, as he had many times before. But now, the chair of command was his, at least until Captain Kouras was better and fully recovered.

The Captain's first order was for two Space Marines to guard each entrance to the hospital. He then called for the Captain's steward, and gave instructions to have mess crewman Sammie make him another "special recipe" high protein shake. He did not feel tired, or sleepy. He had worked hard, been prepared, and received the call to command. He would not let his crew, Admiral Tomiko, Earth Command, or Captain Kouras down.

When the corpsmen brought Captain Kouras into the hospital, Nurse Cohen quickly led the corpsmen to the quarantine room in the very back of the hospital, started the vid cams, and helped them move the Captain from the gurney onto the bed. She called for Nurse Jones to assist his undressing and getting the Captain into a gown, as he fought their attempts at removing his boots and uniform. Nurse Cohen was compelled to have his hands, feet, torso, and even his head restrained, to protect him from injuring himself, or her medical staff.

Nurse Cohen set up his IV, and took blood samples from him for analysis. He was still struggling inside the restraints so violently that she had Nurse Jones hold the Captain's arm still. "Captain Kouras, this is Nurse Cohen, and I'm trying to help you, sir."

"You are all trying to kill me! Let me out of here! I want out of these things! I'll kill you! I'll have you court-martialed for this! Let me out!" He continued yelling at them, and trying to break out of his restraints. Nurse Jones taped his arm with the IV securely to the bed side rail, and told the corpsman to hold his arm firmly, but not too tightly, as a saline and electrolyte drip started in his IV. "Captain, I am giving you fluids to help rehydrate your body. I am going to scan you now." She kept her voice low, firm and even, trying to relax him. She used the handheld scanner over his entire writhing body, and sent its analysis to her log.

They covered his body in warm blankets; that soothed him, and he stopped resisting for a while. Nurse Cohen described to him - and for the vid cams - every step she was taking, in a firm, soft voice. The Captain's extremities were beginning to shake, and he was sweating profusely.

The Admiral's general announcement came over their wall comm-link before she could cut the sound. The Captain yelled, "No! No! No!" at the top of his lungs, ranting over and over. She told him, "It is only a temporary change of assignment, sir. You are still our Captain Kouras. As soon as you are well, you will be back on the bridge." The delirious man kept screaming.

Doctor Hassan came running in from the lift to the back of the hospital room, scrubbed, and had a sterile gown put on him. Nurse Cohen brought him up to date on the Captain's condition, as he took her scanner to read its analysis. "We will need the overhead scanner used for him, but he'll have to be fully sedated first." He programmed a sedation mix from the IV controller. The Captain finally became quiet, and then his struggling stopped altogether. The corpsmen and Nurse Jones released their holds on his body. "Now, let's bring the body scanner down over him, and find out the whole story. We must all exercise maximum secrecy about the Captain's condition, is that clear?"

The corpsmen acknowledged, "Yes, sir," and the Doctor dismissed them. "Nurse Cohen, please stay and assist me with him."

Captain Baines settled into his command chair comfortably. Not so much difference now than yesterday's duty, so far, he thought. The bridge screens were monitoring the live vid cam feeds of the miners' awakenings, as well as the inspection of their cryonic containers.

"Staff Sergeant Mason, join me in the ready room. Westerly, you have the comm," Captain Baines said.

Baines said, "Please be seated. Much has happened very quickly this morning, Mason, as I'm sure you have noticed. I will tell you, in strictest confidence, that Captain Kouras is now in the hospital being treated. We expect his full and complete recovery shortly. In the meantime, Admiral Tomiko specifically requested your presence at the weekly meetings to report our on-going investigations."

"Captain, if I may ask; any sign of the orange anomaly yet? I know it's out there, watching the Hesperia, and waiting," Mason said with his voice lowered.

"No signs detected yet, but I feel it, too, Staff Sergeant. We have so little information on it," he said, frustrated.

"Captain, may I be permitted to see Captain Kouras, sir?" Mason asked.

"If Dr. Hassan and Nurse Cohen give their permission, yes. But keep everything confidential, you understand," Baines replied quietly.

"Yes sir," Mason answered. The Captain stood, and Mason stood up, donned his helmet, and asked, "Begging the Captain's pardon, sir," he asked stiffly. "Sir. It is this Prime Marine's duty to advise the Captain that he is out of uniform. Sir."

Baines chuckled, and said, "Yes, I am, Staff Sergeant. Thank you for reminding me. Dismissed." The Captain returned Mason's salute, and sat back down at the console. He called to the Base Exchange, and ordered a new captain's shirt and insignia, to be delivered as soon as possible to him on the bridge.

XIV

Captain Baines went to the hospital in the afternoon to check on Captain Kouras' progress. He still could not understand how the man became so ill in such a short time. He waited, pacing the small room. Sure, Kouras was under the gun from Earth Command to deliver results from their investigations, but that couldn't have been the only thing. The Old Man exercised, ate well, and was healthy as a horse, up to today.

He heard a familiar voice say, "Captain Baines," and turned to see Head Nurse Cohen, in surgical garb, taking off her gloves and cap, tossing them into the disposal.

"I've come to check on Captain Kouras, Nurse Cohen. How is he? Do you know what's wrong with him?" Baines asked.

She took off her gown, disposed of it, and said, "Come with me, Captain." She led him to the viewing room adjacent to the quarantine room where Captain Kouras lay, fully restrained, under the body scanner. Dr. Hassan was standing over him, checking his eyes with a light scope. "He is fully sedated at the moment, as you can see."

"Is he under quarantine? Why the restraints?" Captain Baines looked into the room from behind the thick glass at his Captain and implored, "What's wrong with him?"

"Dr. Hassan will give you the complete analysis when Nurse Jones has finished the blood panels. He is not quarantined. I brought him here for privacy, out of respect. He was restrained to prevent him from injuring himself, or the medical staff." She shared with him the Captain's violent behavior, and how he reacted when the Admiral's announcement was broadcast. "I could not reach the volume control switch in time to shut it off. He became very agitated upon hearing that announcement, and we had to restrain him."

He suddenly realized she could have been hurt. "Are you all right,

Rachel? Did he hurt you?" He turned and took her hand.

"I'm all right. Really, I'm okay, Captain." She squeezed his hand lightly, and removed her hand from his, turning back towards her patient. "He's in bad shape."

They both watched the scene inside the glass room, Dr. Hassan checking the indicator lights on the full body scanner, moving along the bed.

"Did you see what happened?" She asked.

"No. We were dismissed, and I went back to my station. The ready room door was closed. Next thing I know, Dr. Hassan told me to come in and lock the door. The Captain was sitting in a chair. You probably know the rest. In any case, I should let Dr. Hassan tell his side of the story." They looked at each other, each curious what the other would not or could not say.

Finally, Dr. Hassan turned around to see them, and said, "Give me a minute please, Captain. I'll be out shortly." He went over to the other side of the scanner, and made some adjustments while they watched, and waited. When he finished, he came into their viewing room, removing his mask, cap and gloves, and threw them into the trash sharply. He went to the console, and called the lab. "Finished with that blood panel yet, Nurse Jones?"

"Yes, Dr. Hassan. The results have just finished compiling. Here are the results, sir," Nurse Jones said, handing him the com tablet. "The initial results looked skewed, so I ran the panel again, just to be certain."

"Well, it is best to be certain," the Doctor admitted. "Thank you." He read the information, and then handed the com tablet to Nurse Cohen to read. "We'll need to find out where he got those drugs: Psychotropics, tranqs, and stims, plus. But, first things first. We will begin detox in two hours, assuming his heart has stabilized by then. Monitor his brain waves, too. He nearly had a stroke just now while lying there. Put Nurse Jones on first watch when he comes out of sedation. He's big enough to handle him."

The Doctor sat down and briefly told Nurse Cohen of their search of the Captain's quarters. "His heart rate and blood pressure were in very dangerous territory, Captain Baines. If we had not brought him here, he would most likely be dead now, or in a coma. Captain Kouras had massive amounts of psychotropic compounds and stimulants in his bloodstream this morning; enough to stop his heart. First I had to stabilize him," the Doctor said. "There's nothing to be done for a couple of hours but monitor him closely, and pray he doesn't stroke out, or have an MCI." Baines accepted the information, and returned to the bridge.

Mason decided on a half-sandwich and lemonade for lunch, to keep his stomach light. His intuition told him that something was getting ready to break, and he wanted to be fast on his feet for whatever would happen. He waved at Chief Dawson, and she came over to sit with him.

"So, how's bridge duty these days, Staff Sergeant?" She had a little twinkle in her eyes.

He laughed and answered, "Boring as ever, Chief." They both laughed softly. "Can we get dinner delivered in the main lounge for us in a couple of days? I'd like to see that show they're transmitting to us this weekend, if you're up for it. Some kind of musical."

"Okay, I'm definitely interested in getting out of here for a while. Tell me what day you have off, and I'll adjust my schedule," she said.

"My next day off is Friday." Mason noticed her strong, hard-working hands and nails. "And I'd like to treat you to something special, if you can get the whole day off."

"Like what?" She was getting more interested by the second.

"Let's do the spa thing, then dinner and the show. What'd you think?" He folded his arms and leaned closer to her, across the table. He looked into her bright blue eyes.

"I didn't even know we had a spa on board. I don't get out much, you know. But I would love it!" She looked at him in silence for several seconds. Was it as easy to read her mind as it was to read his? "No strings, John."

"No strings, Sherrie." They both smiled, and just stared at each other. "I got to get back to the bridge now. Pick you up Friday around 2 in the afternoon, okay?" She nodded. Mason stood, picked up his tray, said, "See you soon," and left, with her defenses crumbling.

Upon his return to the bridge, Lieutenant Marston advised Captain Baines that Mission Director Keene completed the general awakenings.

"Lieutenant Davis, call Lieutenant Cheung, and get a full status report on container inspections for me. Lt. Commander Westerly." Captain Baines turned his chair around to her.

"Yes, Captain," she answered.

"Thank you for volunteering to be my Executive Officer. Please take your station, update the log, and have Lieutenant Juarez and Lieutenant St. Marten report to the bridge immediately."

"Aye aye, sir." She went over to the XO's station, and made the calls.

Captain Baines checked the navigational maps, automatically recalculating in his mind their new speed and trajectory; arrival at the mining fields at 11:13am.

The ship's navigator, Lieutenant Espinoza, called out, "Captain, we will arrive at the mining fields…"

"At 11:13am, yes, thank you, Lieutenant Espinoza."

Mason smiled under his helmet, and thought, my Captain just beat the computer!

Captain Baines rearranged the bridge officers to fill the open positions, and summarized. "Excellent. Lieutenant St. Marten, you have the Flight and Mission Ops. Lieutenant Juarez, you are my new Science Officer. Take your stations now, and update your logs," Captain Baines, said, smiling. He then turned around to the tactical station. "Lieutenant Davis. You are invaluable at tactical. I want you to work with Lt. Commander Powers to thoroughly review the current tactical plans for the Hesperia, and recommendations you may have. You will present these recommendations at our next staff meeting, Friday morning, when we will be joined by Admiral Tomiko."

"Thank you, Captain Baines." Lieutenant Davis' face lit up. "I'll do my best, Captain."

"That's what I expect. Lieutenant Juarez, set your scans for any traces of tachyon particles, 360 degrees, when we reach the mining fields. If the scanners detect even the slightest traces, notify me immediately," the Captain ordered, knowing that Juarez had absolutely no comprehension of the reason why he needed to do so. The Captain returned his chair forward, and called Director Keene.

"Director Keene, Captain Baines here. My men should be finished with your cryonic container inspections in four hours. The Hesperia will reach the mining fields at 11:13 am. My suggestion is we discuss the plan to begin mining over dinner tonight. We want to make certain we're all on the same page," Captain Baines offered.

"Fine with me. We'll be ready to begin mining upon the 11:13am arrival at the hunting fields. Your mess hall or ours?" Keene asked.

"Let's meet in your Mission Control room, if possible. You can show me your initial plan for harvesting the first asteroids. I want to align our shuttle pilots' schedules to meet your needs."

"Sounds like a good idea to me. How's 5:30 pm for you?" Keene asked.

"Perfect. We'll be there on time. See you at 5:30. Captain out." He cut the comm link, and got up out of his chair. He stepped over to Westerly, and said, "We will meet at 5:15, in the lower corridor of Section One. You are not to cross over that threshold into Section Two by yourself. You will wait for Staff Sergeant Mason and me. Is that understood?" He was adamant about his instructions.

"Yes, sir. I will not cross the threshold into Section Two by myself," she acknowledged.

"Good, 5:15 then. You have the comm. Staff Sergeant Mason, come with me." He went to the door by Mason, and waited until the two Space Marines arrived, and they left the bridge.

They walked down the corridor from the bridge, to a room Mason had only been once before. Captain Baines held his palm up to the lock pad, and the door opened, and swiftly closed after they entered. The white room contained locked cabinets on all walls, and a table in the middle of the room with four chairs. The Captain opened a cabinet door and removed a deep box, and took out several tiny cameras, no bigger than the tip of a stylus. He put one on each of his lapels, one on each of his sleeve cuffs, and one at the tip of each boot.

He said to Mason, "Put a couple where their scanners will find them, like your collar. Put the others where they won't be detected without a body scan. Put one on the end of each boot. When you're sitting at the table, flex your feet casually once or twice, to check under the table."

Mason did as ordered. He was impressed with the Captain's subterfuge. "Who will be monitoring these cameras, Captain?"

"Lieutenant Davis will monitor them, alone. He will be told to begin monitoring our live feed at 5:25. Lt. Commander Westerly will be given only two to wear. We will each lose the top two, most likely, but I hope we can keep the other cameras going. I want you to walk next to Westerly every step of the way, Mason. She is young, female, and has never served on a mining freighter with six hundred miners. You are to escort her. Is that clear?" The Captain suddenly grabbed his head with both hands.

"What is it, Captain?" Mason asked, concerned. "Are you all right, sir?" His Captain reeled in his stance.

"Just a sudden headache, Mason. It started after my second shake today. It didn't taste as good as the first one, so I finished it after lunch. The headache comes and goes." He grimaced, and lowered his head.

"Captain, where did you get that shake from?" Mason asked, alarmed.

"I had the steward bring it to me. I asked for Sammie to make the special one she makes for Nurse Cohen. The first one tasted a lot better," Baines said weakly.

Mason went into action. "Staff Sergeant Mason to Nurse Cohen, urgent."

"Nurse Cohen here, Mason. What is it, Staff Sergeant?"

"Ma'am, please come up here to the Captain's storeroom with Dr. Hassan at once, and bring your scanner. It's Captain Baines, ma'am. Please hurry."

He heard her call for the Doctor and cut the comm link. The Captain was holding onto a chair so tightly that his hand was white. "Mason to Master Sergeant Alta, urgent."

"Alta, what's your situation, Mason?" He asked gruffly.

"Master Sergeant, I need you to come quietly to the Captain's storeroom, with a security detail immediately. The Captain is going down," Mason said.

The Space Marines arrived first. Master Sergeant Alta held the Captain steady in one of the chairs, while Mason directed the other Marines stand sentry at the door. Nurse Cohen ran into the room to Captain Baines, and asked him what was wrong.

"I've just got a headache, that's all. I've…" then his head dropped to the table. Dr. Hassan ran into the room, and immediately scanned him, while Nurse Cohen held his head. Master Sergeant Alta steadied his body while they scanned him.

"He said he'd had a headache since his second shake late this morning, that the steward brought to him, Dr. Hassan, ma'am. Said it didn't taste as good as the first one this morning. He grabbed his head like he wanted to crush it between his hands. Doctor, the Captain's steward is the only one other than the Captain and me who have access to the Captain's quarters," Mason said. Nurse Cohen looked at the Captain incredulously.

"He's got to be taken to the hospital, immediately. I think he's been poisoned. You men, can you carry him to the lift?" Dr. Hassan asked.

"Sir, yes sir," they answered, picking up the Captain in a fireman's carry, and moving him to the lift in seconds.

"I'll find that steward, Mason. You go with them," Master Sergeant Alta ordered.

Mason ran down the stairs, having just missed the lift with Captain Baines inside. He met them at the hospital, and stood guard on the inside hospital door, waiting for the news. Nurse Cohen stood back from the examination table, watching.

Master Sergeant Alta found the steward in the mess hall. Upon seeing the stern Master Sergeant head directly for him, he bolted from his seat, and ran. Alta caught him, and knocked him to the floor in the corridor past the mess hall. The steward was trying to put a large white capsule into his mouth, but Alta stopped him. Alta bound his hands behind his back, and called for backup. The steward was taken to the brig, placed in electronic shackles and collar, and chained to the wall of his cell. The Master Sergeant used all his self-control to not go inside and beat him to a pulp.

Lieutenant Cheung ordered Captain Kouras' quarters and Captain Baines' quarters locked, sealed, and posted armed Space Marine guards at the entrances. He quietly informed Lt. Commander Westerly of the nature of the situation, whispering in her ear while she sat in the command chair. Her eyes got as big as they could get, but she controlled her emotions, and did not react to the news. She casually got down, and ordered Lieutenant Davis to take the comm, and left with Lieutenant Cheung. She went into the ready room, went through the trash, and found the cup from which Captain Baines had drunk his shake. She took some papers and picked it up, careful not to touch it, and left the bridge with Lieutenant Cheung. They quickly went to the hospital with the cup, and gave it to Mason, still crudely, but effectively wrapped in papers from the trash can. He sat the cup down on the desk, and returned to his guard duty.

Mason soon heard the results of Captain Baines' stomach being pumped. The only weak part of him was his stomach, and he fought hard to keep it together. He breathed in deeply, held his breath for a count of ten, and let the breath out as slowly as he could. Every time the Captain retched, he did his breathing exercise, and exhaled loudly, to keep from hearing those sounds. He tried to concentrate on his next steps. Interview that steward, and find out who he was working for. Whatever was in that shake nearly killed his Captain, his friend, the same day that Captain Kouras was taken off of the bridge on a gurney. He would get the truth out of that steward.

Nurse Cohen came over to him, shaking, and white as a sheet. She couldn't even speak; she just looked at him, pleadingly. He broke discipline, held his arms out to her, and she went to him and held onto him, then burst out crying. Mason held her close, but not too tight, stroked her back, and let her get it all out. She held onto him, arms so tight around his waist, cried and cried for the longest time, until she regained control of herself. He looked at her, and softly said, "He'll be all right ma'am. Dr. Hassan will make him all right. He's going to be fine. Don't worry, now, he'll be okay, soon." She dried her eyes, and looked over at the table, at the shake cup.

Nurse Cohen sat down at the table, staring at the cup. Dr. Hassan walked over to her, and said, "He's come through the worst of it, I believe. He's asking for you."

She went over to the Captain, and he took her hand. This time, she did not pull away. Regulations be damned. She ran her fingers through his damp hair, and tried to smile, and not cry. He asked weakly, "You okay?"

Nodding her head, Nurse Cohen asked him, "How about you?"

"I've been better," he answered, and winced at the pain in his gut. "Where's Mason?"

"He's been here the whole time. Want to see him?" She asked, and Baines nodded.

She turned and motioned for Mason to come over, and he was there instantly. "You trying to take my lady from me, Marine?" The Captain asked, with a weak smile.

Mason smiled a little. "No, sir, she was just trying to keep me from throwing up, that's all."

The Captain almost laughed, but held his gut and grimaced. "Just don't get any ideas. I'll be out of here in a couple of minutes," he said.

"I don't think so, sir. Dr. Hassan doesn't look like he's letting you go anywhere for a while, sir," Mason said gently.

"Now, be still and rest, Captain. You've been through an ordeal today," Dr. Hassan said. "We still need to run more tests on you. If we had been much later, I'm afraid the outcome would have been very different, Captain Baines. Thank God Mason recognized you were ill. I have to notify Earth Command, you understand," Dr. Hassan said.

"Yes, I understand, Doctor. Talk to the Admiral directly, and not to anyone else. Tell him I'm okay," the Captain said, trying to sit up.

"You stay right there, Captain, and rest. The Tetrodotoxin must be eliminated from your system completely. We don't want any respiratory problems," Dr. Hassan said, very firmly.

"Tetro-what?" The Captain asked, feebly.

"Poison from the puffer fish, Tetrodotoxin. It is a very powerful neurotoxin, Captain. You are a very lucky man, very lucky indeed," Dr. Hassan stated. "Lucky they didn't give you the cocktail they gave Captain Kouras."

"Mason? Thank you. I..." the Captain held his gut in pain again.

"You're welcome, Captain," Mason replied, looking at his Captain, and then at Nurse Cohen. "I'll keep two guards posted both inside and outside the doors tonight. We have your quarters under guard now, Captain." He said 'G'night' to Nurse Cohen and the Captain, and walked back to the door. He called the Master Sergeant, and heard that the steward had been found, and was in the brig. He immediately went there.

The steward was in fear for his life, and should have been. He was terrified watching big Master Sergeant Alta watch him. The cell door was clear plex. There was no move the steward could make without being observed. When Mason came in, he nodded at the Master Sergeant, and took his place in front of the clear plex door. Every Prime Marine was trained in interrogation techniques. He removed his weapons belt. Mason said, "Open the cell door." He put his leather gloves on and went inside the cell, and stood directly in front of the steward.

"My name is Staff Sergeant John Mason, and I am a Prime Marine. Do you know what that means?" The steward shook his head. "Well, it means that you are going to tell me who put you up to this."

The young man shook his head 'no,' and said nothing.

"We have you in custody. You are accused of attempted murder of a Captain, the Commanding Officer of the ship Hesperia; not one Captain, but two, in one day. Quite a feat. You must really be proud of yourself. I am told your name is Stone, right?" Mason didn't move.

The man said nothing. Mason said, "Now, Stone, you better understand the ground rules here. You have an electronic collar around your neck, and electronic shackles on your ankles. You are chained to the wall in a cell in the brig. You can either decide to answer my questions, and play nice, or not. If you decide not to answer my questions, I will not play nice."

"You can't touch me. I want to talk to an attorney!" The man yelled.

"Well, Stone, I'm sure you do. But you see, the problem is, we are way the hell out in space, outside the solar system, and we forgot to bring along any attorneys this trip. So, you get to talk to me. In case you are too stupid to figure it out, I'm the good cop. For now," Mason said.

"Earth Command will get me an attorney! You can't touch me!"

"Stone, you just don't get it, do you? Earth Command doesn't know you're here, in this cell, in this brig, on the Hesperia. We might just forget to tell them that we found you alive. We might just let you stay chained up in here and rot. Our mission won't be finished for another five years. You're rotting carcass will just be a pile of shit by then," a smiling Mason threatened.

"You can't do that! I have rights, you know." He was feeling suddenly brave. "You have to treat me well, or you'll get into trouble."

Mason and Alta roared with laughter. Mason said, "You're such a dumb fuck; you don't even have the sense to know who's in trouble here. Well, let me spell it out for you, Stone. I haven't decided if the Master Sergeant here found you dead, or alive. Whether we report you dead or alive to Earth Command, believe me, they won't give a shit, after what you did. Now, Stone, you're only about one and a half meters, and about seventy kg, at best. I am over two meters and 120 kg, and I hold over twenty black belts in various martial arts. I can kill you with one blow, or give you a death of a thousand cuts."

Mason said, "I will ask you again; who put you up to this? Who do you work for?" Stone said nothing. "One more time. Who do you work for?" Stone was silent.

Mason smiled, and began his kung fu warm up. He stretched his muscular, long left arm right up to the prisoner's face, raised his hand, and formed a claw. He flexed his fingers so tightly that they cracked, and Stone flinched. Mason placed his left arm right next to his head, taught and tight, but not touching him. He drew up his right arm slowly, until his hand was even with his shoulder, and very slowly made his fist into a claw. He threw a jab with his right hand at Stone's head, stopping a centimeter from his eyes, as the man drew his head quickly back, hitting the cell wall.

Mason stepped back, and began to warm up his legs. Mason kicked with his left foot, stopping right in front of his mouth. He slowly pulled his leg back, twirled and jumped in the air, and kicked out at him with his right leg at his chest, again stopping short of touching him. Stone was sweating profusely. Mason stood still, and then reached behind Stone, grabbing his chains over his head. With one movement, Mason lifted Stone up in the air with one arm by his chains, his arms and legs pulled up behind him. "I will ask you once again. Who sent you to do this to my Captain?" Mason's face was contorted into the face of a madman. He held Stone aloft and drew him close to his own face, and asked again, "Who sent you to kill my Captain? Who do you work for? Who? Tell me NOW!" Mason shouted the word 'Now' so loudly that Stone started crying, and pissed his pants. "Who sent you to kill my Captain? Who do you work for?"

"She'll kill me if I tell you!" Stone cried.

"I'll kill you if you don't! Tell me who sent you to kill my Captain!"

Mason yelled. "Tell me now!"

"Miller. Lieutenant Miller. That's not her real name, but she goes by Lieutenant Miller. I don't know her real name. She works in the mess hall. Let me go, please, let me go!" Stone began sobbing incoherently. Mason lowered him slowly onto the floor, and let him cry a little while. Alta was gone. Lieutenant Miller would be here, soon.

"All right, Stone, you did good. Real good. Now, I'm going to help you sit down, just stand up, and sit down. Are you okay?" Mason used a soothing voice on him now, and helped Stone sit down, and straightened his uniform shirt. He gathered his chains, and hooked them onto the clip above Stone's head on the wall. "I'll tell them you were very cooperative, and tried to help us apprehend Lieutenant Miller. When and where did you meet her?"

"I met her on Moon Base, waiting for the shuttle to take me to the Hesperia. We got drunk, and had sex. She said she had two jobs, the Space Force, and some private job that paid her ten times more. She told me if I worked for her, and did what she asked, I would be a millionaire when this mission was over."

"Did she tell you what you would have to do to make this million? Did you know what she intended to do, Stone?" Mason asked him.

"No, I didn't. I really didn't, until I signed on with her on the Hesperia. She said she'd make it easy on me, and we could have sex every night. All I had to do was put a drop or two of a clear liquid into the Captain's coffee pot in the mornings. He never even tasted anything bad," he whined.

Mason asked, "How long did you do this?"

Stone stopped crying. "For about three days. Then I had to put several drops in his coffee, then drops in his food, too. He never looked sick, so I thought it was okay. Then two days ago, she told me to put an injection pen on his nightstand with a note."

"What did the note say, Stone?"

"It didn't say nothing. It just had DRH on it." Stone sighed and continued, "The next day, she gave me three injection pens for him, to go in his desk, next to that old fashioned pen he always used. This morning, she told me to put a whole spoonful into his coffee, and leave a big bunch of injection pens in his desk, and a purple one on his breakfast tray. So I did."

"Did you know Captain Kouras was in the hospital now?" Mason asked.

"Of course I did. She told me to serve the new Captain, Baines. She said it couldn't take as long as the first Captain, so she gave me a different dropper bottle. When he ordered a protein shake, I gave him the drops," Stone said.

"How many drops?" Mason asked.

"Four. She said to give him ten, but another officer came into the lift, and I didn't get the chance to put all the drops into the shake," he admitted.

Mason asked, "One more question, okay? Why was it she couldn't take as long with Captain Baines as with Captain Kouras?

"She said they wanted all the officers to run around like idiots, fighting over who would be in charge, and then they'd take over."

Mason got sterner with him. "They? They who? Who would take over?"

"I don't know who they are. But she works for them," he replied.

"Here on the ship?" Mason asked urgently.

"Of course. They gave her the drops, the injector pens, and the slices. They got to be on the ship, don't they? But I never met them. I don't know who they are." Stone sat back, and leaned on his chains. "I'm probably going to go to prison, right?"

"Probably, Stone, probably." Mason called out, "Open the cell door." He stepped out of the cell, picked up his weapons belt, and ran out.

Master Sergeant Alta took four Space Marines with him to Miller's quarters, and, after breaking the palm lock on her door, found her stabbed over a dozen times in her gut, and her throat cut from ear to ear. The corpsmen had to put a stationary brace on her to keep her head from falling off. The search of her room produced dozens of boxes of injection pens, and several assorted poisons. She obviously had more targets on her hit list. The next problem was to discover who the new assassins replacing her and Stone would be.

XV

Mason ran from the brig to the lift. He tapped his comm-link and said, "Staff Sergeant Mason to Lieutenant Davis."

"Lieutenant Davis here, Staff Sergeant. Good job with the prisoner." He was speaking almost in a whisper.

"Did you get everything recorded, sir?"

"Got the whole thing," Davis whispered. "Come to the bridge. Dr. Hassan is in with the XO. I'll tell them you're on your way."

"Thank you, Lieutenant Davis." Mason punched the 'Bridge' light on the lift's control panel. He stopped to salute Lieutenant Davis, sitting in the command chair, and went to the ready room. "Staff Sergeant Mason reporting, ma'am, Dr. Hassan."

"Come in and sit down, Staff Sergeant. Your timing is perfect," Westerly said.

"We were just discussing what to tell the Admiral when Lieutenant Davis advised we not contact him until we spoke with you," Dr. Hassan said, rather puzzled.

"Permission to speak, ma'am?" Mason asked.

"Speak freely and get to the point, Mason," she said.

Mason told them about the Captain's steward, Stone, and the interrogation. He handed his com-tablet to the XO to view. She put it onto the main monitor, and they all watched.

They watched the recording from Mason's hidden cameras, and saw only Stone, not Mason. The sound, however, captured everything. "Staff Sergeant, you deliberately confused and intimidated this prisoner. This recording tells it all," she said, frowning at Mason.

"The intimidation is about to start, ma'am." They both turned to look at him, then watched the interrogation from Mason's hidden camera angle.

Westerly's countenance changed completely when the gloved hand took the prisoner's chains and raised the man up, with one big arm. She looked at Mason, astonished at his feat and bravado. She and Dr. Hassan saw the prisoner crying, having wet himself, and being slowly lowered to the floor. They watched Mason help him up by his chains, and hang the chains up on the wall hook.

"Here's the only time I touched him," Mason said. They watched his gloved hands smooth Stone's uniform down and away from his neck. The gesture actually looked kind and sympathetic.

When Stone started talking, their eyes were glued to the recording. Dr. Hassan made notes of how many drops were used, and the frequency of the dosage. He gasped when Stone said the note had "DRH" on it. "The Captain thought I had given him the injection pens!" He furrowed his brow and continued to listen and take notes.

When the recording finished, Dr. Hassan and Lt. Commander Westerly stared at Mason.

"This is totally inadmissible in court, you, know, Staff Sergeant," the XO said. "The prisoner was not advised of his rights beforehand."

"Begging your pardon ma'am, but, since he attempted to kill two of our Captains in one day, I was not concerned about his rights. You were next in line, Lt. Commander Westerly." Mason sat still, and looked into her eyes, as she digested the validity of his words. Her comm-link beeped.

"Lt. Commander Westerly, this is Lieutenant Cheung."

"Westerly here," she said quietly.

"Master Sergeant Alta and his security team have found Lieutenant Miller. She's dead, ma'am. We're recording the scene now. With your permission, we will search her quarters."

"Granted. And do it by the book, Lieutenant," she ordered.

"Yes ma'am. Cheung out."

"Well, Staff Sergeant, I'm not sure whether to congratulate you, or put you in the cell next to Stone," Westerly commented.

"If it is your wish to incarcerate me, I surrender now, ma'am. If left free, I will endeavor to find out who the new assassins are, and apprehend them for you or the Captain to interview. It is your choice, Lt. Commander Westerly," Mason said calmly.

"New assassins?" She raised her eyebrows.

"Yes, ma'am. It is my opinion that whoever is behind the attempted murders of Captain Kouras and Captain Baines will not stop here. They want the Hesperia, at any cost, ma'am." Mason sat, and waited, but she did not speak.

"Lt. Commander Westerly, I'm afraid I must agree with our Staff Sergeant. We are all safer with him working to protect us from those who are attempting to take over the ship. Remember the Excelon, Lt. Commander Westerly. We do not want a repeat of that butchering here."

Dr. Hassan managed to convince her to let Mason go free, at least for now.

Lt. Commander Westerly called the brig Chief and ordered the recording of Stone's interview sent to her immediately. She played the brig recording for them to watch. The sound was not perfect, but the video was sharp and clear. The recording showed both Mason and Stone clearly. At no time did Mason touch the prisoner, except to smooth down his uniform, just as the Staff Sergeant said. His feet never came within ten centimeters of Stones' head or torso. Stone was never put in physical danger by Mason.

"Well, Staff Sergeant, it is clear from this brig recording that you indeed never touched the prisoner, until you touched his uniform. You were intimidating him, however, so it does not completely exonerate you. Your recording is not admissible; therefore I will delete it from your com tablet." She called to Lieutenant Davis, "Lieutenant Davis, you will delete the recording Staff Sergeant Mason made illegally, at once."

"It's gone ma'am. I must've deleted it accidentally," he responded.

She sat up and said, "Doctor Hassan, I believe it's time to place our call to Earth Command, and speak with Admiral Tomiko."

"Yes, it is," he agreed. They stood at attention.

She called for the Admiral, and updated him on the afternoon's events. She asked Dr. Hassan to provide the details on the health of Captain Kouras and Captain Baines. He finished by saying, "Captain Baines will be back on the bridge tomorrow, Admiral. But Captain Kouras will need to stay in the hospital for some time to come. His heart has been damaged, and there is most likely brain damage, as well."

The Admiral was stunned at the news of the attempted murder of two Captains in one day. He did not speak for several seconds. He turned to Mason, and asked, "How did you obtain the prisoner's confession, Staff Sergeant?"

"I used intimidation and coercion tactics, as we do with prisoners of war, Admiral. Lt. Commander Westerly has the interview recorded for you, sir." Mason never flinched standing at attention.

The Admiral began questioning Mason. "Did you beat him?"

"No, sir."

"Did you torture him in any way?"

"Sir, no sir."

"Did you touch him at all, Staff Sergeant?"

"I straightened his uniform shirt, sir," Mason replied.

"Let's view the recording, Lt. Commander Westerly." She played the recording for him, and he watched with intense interest and concentration. "Excellent interrogation, Staff Sergeant. Your control was exemplary. Many men would have used unacceptable methods with such a dangerous prisoner. Another commendation is in order, Prime Marine." The Admiral was obviously pleased.

"But, Admiral, the prisoner was not read his rights, and he was terrified. The Staff Sergeant…" The Lt. Commander protested.

"The prisoner was what, Lt. Commander? You must remember that there have been two murders of the URE's leading research scientists on the Hesperia, and attempted murders of two bridge Captains - in one day, mind you - and an attempted murder of Staff Sergeant Mason, too. I told you there was a much larger scheme at work here, and it is now a proven fact. Are you at red alert?"

"Yellow, sir," she answered.

"Go to red alert immediately, Lt. Commander!" Tomiko bellowed.

"Yes, sir, red alert." The computer announced the ship-wide status change.

"Dr. Hassan, I want Captain Baines in command of that ship as soon as possible, from his hospital bed, if necessary!" The Admiral demanded.

"Staff Sergeant Mason, you are hereby promoted to Gunnery Sergeant. I want all line command officers and you present at our next meeting, and you, as well, Dr. Hassan. Is that understood?" The Admiral was adamant, barely taking a breath in between orders.

"Yes, Admiral!" They all said.

"Our next meeting is in 12 hours. Good job, Dr. Hassan, reclaiming the lives of our two bridge Captains. Dr. Mohammed Hassan, you are hereby promoted to Captain of the Medical Corps, with all the rights and privileges thereof."

"Thank you, Admiral," the Doctor said, gratefully.

"Sir, thank you, sir!" Mason added.

"Dismissed!" The transmission ended.

Mason looked pleased with the outcome of the meeting, but Lt. Commander Westerly was perplexed. "Lt. Commander Westerly, may I be permitted to make one observation and one suggestion to the Executive Officer, ma'am?"

"Go ahead, Mason," she sighed, sitting down.

"Ma'am, my observation is that the bridge command has performed remarkably well, given the rapid succession of events occurring this day. No one panicked or acted in any way other than to reflect commendably on our Captain Baines. My suggestion is that the dinner with Mission Director Keene be cancelled, ma'am," he said.

"Dinner? I'd completely forgotten about it. And it's nearly 5:20. Thank you, Mason. You are dismissed."

"Aye aye, ma'am," he said, snapping a perfect salute. She stood and returned his salute, then plopped down in the chair.

Mason left, but Dr. Hassan did not. "Lt. Commander?" He asked. She looked up and realized he was still there.

"Yes, Dr. Hassan?"

"This is no doubt difficult for you. But I want to admonish you to not be too hard on yourself. You have been out of cryonic hibernation for just a few days, my dear. The events occurring on this vessel at first seemed unrelated, and almost nonsensical. What has been uncovered today is a diabolical plot involving sabotage and murder, directed at the very heart and head of the Hesperia. There will undoubtedly be more sinister attempts made in the future, so we must be vigilant. Mason was correct; you performed admirably at command, and kept the bridge calm and steady. You are doing a fine job, Lt. Commander Westerly." He spoke to her reassuringly, in his best "bedside manner."

"The Admiral doesn't think so," she commented.

"I doubt his report will reflect anything negative regarding your performance, Lt. Commander. It's very difficult to change gears from staff command to line command, as you have realized," the Doctor said, smiling gently at her.

"Thank you, Dr. Hassan. I hope you're right. And congratulations on your promotion, Captain." She stood and saluted him gingerly, and received a snappy salute right back.

"Thank you, Lt. Commander Westerly. I'll be sure to tell Captain Baines what a fine job you're doing at command," then he turned and left.

She went back to the command chair, and relieved Lieutenant Davis. She looked out the windows into space. The stars; she wanted to be among the stars all her life. Well, she was here, and no one was going to send her back, until she was ready to go. Westerly cancelled the dinner with Keene, and resumed running the ship.

Mason was sitting next to Nurse Cohen, who was sitting as closely as she could to Captain Baines. Dr. Hassan came in to check on both of his patients, and Nurse Cohen, too. She was in a more calm state than when he left to go to the bridge, but still quite anxious. "I'm going to check on Captain Kouras, and then I'll be right back," he quietly said to her.

Mason had not told Nurse Cohen about his interview with Stone yet. He stayed there with her, because he knew she would not leave Captain Baines. She was his best friend on the ship and he would be there for her, and their Captain. Mason remembered being in the observation lounge alone with her, more than a year ago, and how they relaxed with each other chatting and flirting. She stood to check a body scanner light that started blinking, and went around to the overhead scanner to check both sides. She entered something on her com tablet, and sat back down, looking at Mason.

"A hell of a day, ma'am," he said to her.

She nodded her head, and said, "A hell of a day, John. Thank you, for everything. And for being here with me, now."

"Sure, where else would I be, 'cept with you and the Captain? Friends help each other in times like these." He smiled a little at her. After a few minutes, he told her, "By the way, we got the steward. He's in the brig. Made a full confession." Mason smiled.

"He confessed voluntarily?" She asked, looking at him.

"Of course; eventually." She glimpsed Mason's potential at that moment, and knew no harm would befall Victor or her as long as John Mason was there. She took in a deep breath, and just nodded at him.

The Doctor walked up to the Captain's bed. He went around the scanner, checking all the indicator lights, and making notes on the com tablet. "He is responding well to the detoxification. His neural pathways are returning to acceptable patterns, and the swelling in his brain has subsided. We should both get some food to eat, Nurse Cohen." She didn't want to leave the Captain, but Dr. Hassan insisted.

"I'll stand watch over Captain Baines while you two get dinner. He's asleep now; it'll be okay," Mason said. "Go on now; I mean, please go on, Doctor, ma'am. I'm here." The Doctor took her arm and gently pulled her out of the hospital to the officers' mess hall.

Mason sat down in her chair for a brief moment, looking at Captain Baines. He liked him more now than when he first met him, when he was so obsessed with the orange cloud, and was impatient with everyone. Mason noted that every man was vulnerable. They had both been vulnerable to attempted murder. And they were both vulnerable to those gray-green eyes, dark red hair, and smile of Rachel Cohen. Mason came to terms with himself about her last year. He couldn't be with her; he accepted that fact. But Mason still loved her, and cared deeply for her, and how she felt. She was now in love with the Captain, which was plain to see. He determined to make every effort possible to protect them.

While he stood guard, Mason thought about his promotion. He laughed about how pissed off Master Sergeant Alta would be when he found out. It gave him a little comic relief. It was going to cost nearly a week's pay to change the insignia on all his uniforms, again.

When Dr. Hassan and Nurse Cohen returned, they looked a little better, with definitely more color in Nurse Cohen's face. The Doctor checked Captain Baines' scanner again, and made a few adjustments on both the scanner and the IV controller. Nurse Cohen walked around his bed, reading all the scanner information with the Doctor. She came over and sat down next to the Captain, and Mason sat next to her.

"Has he moved, Gunny?" She asked, smiling at Mason. So, the Doctor told her about his promotion. Mason smiled.

"No, ma'am, he's sleeping like a baby." Like a big baby; her big baby.

"Now, it's your turn to go and get something to eat," she said. "And be sure to pick up a new uniform for tomorrow. I'd love to see Master Sergeant Alta's face when he sees your new stripe, Gunnery Sergeant," and they both laughed softly.

"Did Dr. Hassan also tell you he's got to get new insignia as well?" Mason asked.

"As a matter of fact, no, he did not!" She got up, and went to the Doctor in Captain Kouras' room. He watched as Nurse Cohen called both nurses to attention in his room and saluted their new Medical Corps Captain Hassan. He blushed a little as he returned their salutes, and then they went back to their patients. "I'm so glad he got his promotion. He waited a long time for it, you know. Now, go get some dinner, Gunny!"

Mason stood, looked at her, and said only, "Yes ma'am!" He saluted her, and left the hospital. He stopped at the Base Exchange, and ordered a new one-piece uniform for 5am delivery. Then he went straight to the mess hall, and immediately got hungry when he smelled the hot food. He ordered a double portion of steak and a big bowl of beef stew. He sat at a nearby table and began to eat. As he was cutting into his rib eye steak, Chief Dawson came over and sat down to keep him company, and chat with him about the scuttlebutt.

"So, Lieutenant Miller was a spy? No wonder she didn't care about the schedules or menus. They came and totally stripped her office, you know. That steward, Stone, he was always hanging around her. The weasel. I hear he's the one who poisoned both the Captains." She really didn't expect him to say much about the gossip, probably couldn't.

"This rib eye is really good tonight," he said. He put another bite in his mouth and chewed while he smiled at her.

"Oh, I know you can't talk about it. But everyone else is! Thought you should know." She watched him eat, and finally he winked at her.

"The second steak's even better than the first one."

She wondered if his appetite for sex was as strong as his appetite for food. She hoped his bedroom personality was the same as the one she had come to know. She was close to finding out. Some guys change completely when they finally get what they want from you, she reminded herself.

He finally finished his man-sized meal, and chatted with her about anything but the hot scuttlebutt. He enjoyed her friendship, and her company. She was fun, and could carry on a good conversation. She was feeling more comfortable around him. It made him feel good.

"I want to ask you something, John," she said. "Would you mind if I wore street clothes on Friday? It'd feel good to dress differently for a change." For you, she thought, but was too shy to say it aloud.

"Sure. It'd be great, in fact," he answered, relieved she hadn't asked him anything really personal.

"How 'bout you, too?" She asked.

"Street clothes? Okay, I'll see what I can manage for you," he answered. Shit. Now he had to go shopping. He noticed the clock on the wall, and told her he had a special project to work on tonight. As he left the mess hall, he went up a few levels to the Esplanade. He hated shopping for himself, especially for clothes. Nothing special to him about a guy in street clothes. His uniform made him feel special.

Although the Hesperia was immense, there were few luxuries on board. The Esplanade had the 24 hour Base Exchange at one end, a gift shop, the spa, a great candy and nut shop, a sports bar, a couple of small restaurants, and one clothing store for both men and women. He went into the clothing store, looked around, and decided the best solution was to get help. All the shops were staffed by retired or off-duty crewmen and women, so at least he would not have a problem talking with the sales lady, like the regular shops back home.

"May I help you, Staff Sergeant?" A sales lady asked.

"I need clothes for a night out Friday, you know, the dinner and a show thing."

"Dressing to impress a lady, then? How about something comfortable, not too casual, but not a suit? Let's go over here and have a look." She led him to the men's side of the shop, and asked his size.

"I don't know, really. The Base Exchange has my sizes on file, and I just order what I need," he admitted.

"No problem, I'll call and get them for you right now." He wrote down his name and serial number and handed it to her on the card she gave him. She went back to her desk, made the call, and was back shortly. "Okay, Staff Sergeant, let's pick out a few shirts to try on."

Sherrie had better appreciate this, he thought. He finally found a shirt he was almost comfortable wearing, and trousers to match. The sales lady chose a few colored trousers, and he decided on "charcoal," and "pewter." How could a man tell anyone he bought "pewter" pants for himself? No wonder he hated shopping. He picked out another shirt that went well with both trousers. He'd stress over which combination to wear all the next day. He bought new black dress boots, ankle-cut, and fancy socks, as well. He handed her his charge crystal, and gave information for pick up tomorrow, after his trousers were hemmed and pressed.

Mason escaped the clothing store, and went to the sports bar for a couple of drinks. Thank God for beer, even if it was synthehol. He didn't want to think about how much he'd just spent. After he'd relaxed over a couple of drinks, he decided to go to the gift shop. This was a better experience. He enjoyed buying a wide silver bracelet for Sherrie, with a large stone from the Caribbean called "Larissa." It was a real pretty blue, like her eyes. He had it gift wrapped.

He hurried and went to the spa, and made reservations for the "couple's experience." Whatever that meant. He also bought a pedicure and manicure for Sherrie.

After a hard day shopping, he dropped off his packages in his locker, and trotted to the hospital. Nodding at the Space Marine sentries, he quietly went inside. Captain Baines was awake, and talking with Dr. Hassan. He went and sat down next to Nurse Cohen, who was listening to the Captain and the Doctor.

"But I feel much better, Doctor, and I'd really like to go to my quarters now. I want a shower and some clean clothes," the Captain said.

"I can't let you leave so soon, Captain," Dr. Hassan said, "We must be sure that all the Tetrodotoxin is completely out of your body. The first twenty-four hours are critical. You could feel fine, and then have respiratory failure. Or sudden paralysis in your extremities. It's simply not worth the risk."

The Captain was silenced by that remark. He looked at Nurse Cohen, and nodded in acquiescence. When he saw Mason sitting there, he smiled. "Mason!" He called out. He looked a ghostly pale, with sunken eyes, and gaunt.

Mason stood and said, "Hello, Captain. Good to see you in fighting form, sir."

"Fighting, but not winning," the Captain said, smiling a little. "They won't let me leave yet, Staff Sergeant."

"There's no Staff Sergeant here, Captain," Nurse Cohen said. "But there's a new Gunny." She smiled at Mason. The Captain congratulated him, and made him promise to tell him about the Admiral's decision to promote him. "There is also a third Captain on the Hesperia now," she added, looking at Dr. Hassan. Captain Baines offered his congratulations to Captain Hassan. He promised a party to celebrate their promotions in a few days.

Although the excitement was proving tiring for Captain Baines, Mason was glad he was awake, and talking. He looked a wreck, but he was clear-headed enough to converse with them. Better than poor Captain Kouras, who, by all that Mason could see and hear, was going through the DT's, full-blown. He truly felt sorry for him. He was a good man, and did not deserve this to happen to him.

When the Doctor suggested Nurse Cohen go get some rest, Mason offered to walk her to her quarters. He posted guards at her door, after his "interview" with Stone. The Doctor and Captain Baines insisted she get some rest, at least for a few hours, so she left with Mason.

When they reached her door, she saw the guards posted there. "Is it necessary to have the Space Marines here?"

"Yes, ma'am, it is," Mason said firmly. He sent her inside with both of the guards and checked to see that everything was okay, while he stood sentry at her open door. A few minutes later, the guards came out, and Nurse Cohen said everything was okay. Mason stepped inside the open door, and swept his scanner around the room. It detected no active cameras or other electronic bugs present. He went directly in front of her, and advised, "If anything seems disturbed, even something seemingly insignificant, like maybe a towel folded differently, or a sock out of place, tell the guards at once. Remember, ma'am, these people are capable of doing anything to anyone, and they will exploit any weakness and take advantage of any opportunity to advance their cause."

He moved a little closer, and lowered his voice. "You are the Captain's lady, and that makes you a target, too, ma'am. Please, please be careful." As he stepped back outside, he said in his regular voice, "If you need anything at all, just let us know, Nurse Cohen. We're here to help you, ma'am."

"Thank you, and good night, Mason," she said, and went into her quarters. She looked around more thoroughly this time, and nothing appeared out of order to her. She showered and lay down to rest for a while, trying not to think of how close she came to losing Victor forever. If not for John Mason.

XVI

The Hesperia slowed to nearly a full stop by 10:30pm, and Mason went to check the bridge once more before calling it a night. He went to the bridge, and the Space Marine guards gave him the "All clear" sign. Lieutenant Fuller was in the command chair and Lieutenant Urz at main communications. Mason saluted Lieutenant Fuller, and requested a few minutes to speak with him. They went to the ready room, and Mason introduced himself to Lieutenant Fuller using his "Special Chief of Security" title, and asked if everything was secure on the bridge.

Lieutenant Fuller replied, "Everything is quiet, and I hope it stays that way, Staff Sergeant Mason."

"Lieutenant Fuller, would you please check the Captain's doors from the ready room, and the Captain's Storeroom, making certain that they are locked and secure, while I am here, sir. I need to note their disposition for my log, sir."

The Lieutenant puffed his chest. "Okay, but let's be quick about it."

"Yes, sir." They tried to open the rear ready room door that led to the Captain's quarters, and it was locked. They left the bridge, and went to the Captain's Storeroom door. It was not showing the secure green light. The Lieutenant tried to open it by the door switch, without success. He tried keying in his code, and put his palm to the electronic pad, but it did not respond.

"Try to force it open," Lieutenant Fuller ordered. The Space Marine sentries tried to push it open, but it did not budge. The Lieutenant then ordered the lock to be opened or broken, whatever it took to get inside and ascertain the situation. Mason took his long knife out of its holster, and pried the lock cover off, hot-wiring the doors to open. "Be careful not to touch anything!" The Lieutenant ordered. The room was a disaster. Any cabinet with easy locks to pick open had been ransacked.

Mason went to the back of the room, carefully stepping over various boxes, tools, and electronics. He stopped in front of the last cabinet, which should have been locked, but was not. He saw the safe, apparently unopened. "Lieutenant Fuller, sir, the Captain's safe is here."

The Lieutenant climbed over the mess, and looked at the safe, "I didn't know the Captain had his own safe. Did you?"

"Yes, sir, and there are several valuable things in there, not the least of which is the evidence we collected the past eighteen months, investigating the deaths and attempted murders on board this ship, sir." Mason wanted Lieutenant Fuller to know the importance of the safe, beyond a doubt. "This was our evidence locker, sir."

"Is the safe opened? Please try it and see," he requested.

The safe was a tall rectangular steel cabinet, smooth on the front, without any apparent locks or handles. The white wooden cabinet was built around it as decorative housing. Mason ran his gloved hand down the smooth right side until he felt a tiny bump, and touched it. Nothing happened. "I saw Captain Kouras open this once. He placed his hands in various spots along the right side and the front to open it. From the marks along the top right and lower right, I'd say whoever broke in here could not open it either, sir. If they had opened the safe, they would most likely have taken what they wanted and left the safe looking like the rest of the room, Lieutenant. I'm positive they'll be back, now that the location of the safe is known, sir."

Lieutenant Fuller ordered a security team to record the room's condition, and secure the storeroom. He pulled out a small com tablet, and searched for an inventory list for the room. "The inventory list for this room is restricted to the CO and XO use only. We'll have to wait for Captain Baines." He stuffed the com tablet back into its belt pack, and looked around. "Is it procedure to check this room every night, Staff Sergeant?"

"No, sir," Mason answered.

"Then how did you know to check it?"

Mason said, "Because of the important evidence it contains, and because of today's events, Lieutenant. It seemed prudent to check, sir."

Lieutenant Fuller looked up at Mason. The tall Prime Marine had good instincts, he'd give him that. "Good call, Staff Sergeant. I've never been in this room before tonight."

"I've only been inside once with Captain Kouras, over a year ago, and tonight with Captain Baines, sir." Mason took a tiny vid cam out of his collar, and held it over the safe, moving over every centimeter of the exposed surface. He held the tiny vid cam next to his com tablet, and transferred the recorded data for storage.

Sergeant Lucas appeared at the door with four Space Marines and six security crewmen. Fuller ordered, "Sergeant Lucas, record everything, then secure this room as is. Touch nothing. I want everything scanned for prints, hair, DNA; everything. But touch nothing. Understood?"

"Sir, yes sir," Sergeant Lucas acknowledged.

"And get maintenance up here to fix that lock on the double. Let's go, Staff Sergeant Mason." The Lieutenant led Mason back to the bridge. He took back the command chair from Lieutenant St. Marten, and downloaded the recent events to the Captain's log. He dismissed Mason. He put his head on his fist, and leaned on the arm of the big chair with his brow furrowed in thought.

Welcome to the Hesperia, Lieutenant Fuller, Mason said to himself.

It was well after midnight by the time Mason got to the hospital, and all was mercifully quiet from the quarantine room, where Captain Kouras slept, still in restraints. Mason went to the bed where Captain Baines lie asleep.

"Doctor Hassan, please call me when he wakes up. It really is important, sir," Mason said, starting to leave.

"What is it, Mason?" The Captain asked, turning his head. Dr. Hassan glared at Mason, who shrugged his broad shoulders in response.

"Begging the Captain's pardon, sir, but the Captain's Storeroom was broken into tonight, sir." Mason watched the Captain's reaction.

"And the safe? Did they open the safe?" He tried to sit up, and only managed to rise on one elbow.

"The safe appears to remain closed. I recorded it for you, sir." Mason moved in closer to the Captain, and replayed the recording of the Storeroom, and, in great detail, the safe. "It doesn't look like they got in, sir." Mason added, "but we can't be sure until it's opened and the contents are checked, Captain."

"I didn't have time to grant access to Lt. Commander Westerly. I'll have to check it myself." The Captain tried to get up, but was stopped by the Doctor.

"That's okay, Captain Baines, Sergeant Lucas and a team of Space Marines are there now, recording and scanning the room for prints and DNA. Lieutenant Fuller is at the comm, sir. Nobody's going to get another try at the safe tonight, sir," Mason said reassuringly. The Captain gave up, and laid his head down in surrender. Mason walked away from the bed. The Doctor was right behind him. Mason was expecting a tongue-lashing from him.

"Mason, what's in the safe?" Dr. Hassan asked quietly.

"The octagonal tube, Dr. Hassan, and all the other evidence we collected over the past eighteen months," Mason said, and left.

At 5am, the knock on Mason's door interrupted him shaving his thick black beard. His new uniform arrived, all new and pressed, with his new insignia. He hung it up, and finished shaving, and combed his hair. He put it on, and stood back, looking at himself in the thin locker door mirror. Satisfied he was good to go, he left for the mess hall, to see if Sherrie was on duty.

The mess hall was crowded, and there was a waiting line. When it was finally his turn, he ordered his usual bacon and scrambled eggs, four of each. As he stood there holding his tray, Master Sergeant Alta called him over to join his table, and Mason headed there. Upon seeing his new arm insignia, Alta flipped, and ordered Mason to go back and dress in his proper uniform. "I am in proper uniform, Master Sergeant Alta."

"Mason, if you deserved that extra stripe, I would have known about it firsthand. Don't you tell me you're promoted. The Captain is still in the sick bay. How could he have promoted you?" Alta lashed out at him.

"The Captain did not promote me, Master Sergeant," Mason said, enjoying every second of his bantering.

"If the Captain did not promote you, then who did?" Alta bellowed.

"Admiral Tomiko, Master Sergeant." Mason sat down with his tray, grinning from ear to ear. Alta was red-faced, and having a rare attack of speechlessness. The Marines at the table all congratulated Mason, and he asked the Master Sergeant to sit back down with him. "What'll you do when I make Master Sergeant, Master Sergeant Alta?" Mason asked him, stuffing a slice of bacon into his grinning mouth.

"I will be long retired by that time, you son-of-a-bitch." Alta sat back down. "You'd better buy me a drink at your promotion party, or I'll kick your ass, Mason!" Everyone had a good laugh, and even Alta finally gave Mason a friendly punch in the arm, and laughed with them.

"Well, I figured this table was where the party was happening," Chief Dawson said, looking at the Space Marines. "What's all the commotion about, Marines?"

"Mason's got a new stripe," Corporal Johnson said.

"Yeah, and the Admiral forgot to call Master Sergeant Alta and get his permission first!" Corporal Milton said. They all roared again, having another laugh at Alta's expense.

"Well, congratulations, Gunny!" Chief Dawson said, smiling at Mason. "Let me know when the party happens, will you Marines?"

"Sure, Chief," they all said, eagerly anticipating the party. Now they all had something fun to look forward to.

Mason finished his breakfast with his fellow Marines, and went to the bridge for his 6am duty. He came in ten minutes early, and was told by Lieutenant Fuller to report to the hospital immediately. He ran to the entrance, and found Dr. Hassan there, waiting for him. "Ah, there's our new Gunny. Good morning. The Captain is waiting for you." He led Mason to the examination room, where Captain Baines was standing, rolling down the sleeve of his uniform.

"Mason, you're late. I want an escort to the bridge this morning, if you're not too busy partying to do your job." He was smiling at him.

"Sir, yes sir." Mason snapped to attention, and saluted his Captain.

"The Doctor has approved my leaving this establishment, so let's get out of here now, Gunny," the Captain said, walking more slowly than his usual quick gait. "Make sure I don't fall on my ass, will you, Mason? Just get me to the chair, and I'll be fine."

Mason walked behind Captain Baines, watching him carefully, and keeping up with his slow pace. When they reached the lift, the door opened as Commander Cohen started to get off. "Captain!" She exclaimed, startled and happy to see him up at last. "I over-slept. Why didn't you call me first?" She stayed in the elevator with them to ride up to the bridge. She smiled at him, and Mason stepped to the side to let her stand next to him.

"I was letting you get some rest, Commander. You obviously needed it. And, I wanted to surprise you," the Captain said.

"Well, that you did. At least you're all cleaned up, and looking much better, Captain Baines," she observed. Mason felt a little awkward with them in the small lift during the ride to the top, but it didn't last long.

The Captain walked onto the bridge, was welcomed by a traditional piping, and a "Captain on deck!" announcement, as all the officers stood and saluted him. He returned their salutes, stepping up to his chair, where Lieutenant Fuller released the comm, and steadied the chair for him to sit. Baines felt an overwhelming wave of emotion, so he turned his chair forward, and commanded, "As you were." Mason took his laser rifle from the storage bin, relieved the two Marine sentries, and took his post. It was a good day.

Mason watched the Captain try to get back into full form, but he was not one hundred percent. He performed the systems check well enough, but he saw him wince in pain if he tried to turn his chair to speak to one of the officers. After a few hours, the Captain called for Lt. Commander Westerly to take the comm, and she stood and held the chair as he got out of it. He took his time going into the ready room, and motioned for Mason to come.

"I need to eat something, Mason. And I'm sure as hell not calling for a steward!" They both had a little laugh at that comment. "I'd like to go to the Storeroom, and have you check out everything for me, after lunch. Think Chief Dawson would mind delivering my lunch up here? I don't want her to feel insulted, Mason."

"She won't, sir. I'll call her now, while you think about what you want, sir."

"Good. I'm starved!" The Captain sat back, and sighed. He looked around the room, and got up slowly to go over to look out of the window.

This was not the assignment he expected at all. It would most likely get more challenging as the mission progressed. He had to get back to full strength sooner rather than later. Baines ate what he could of his lunch, got up slowly, then went back to relieve Westerly.

Mason was still at guard when his two Space Marines came to relieve him, sent by Lt. Commander Westerly. He hurried through the chow line, ate half his lunch, and left to go to the hospital. He suddenly felt compelled to go, as if he was being called.

The hospital entrance was temporarily closed to all visitors when Mason arrived. The sentries did not know why, other than it was a direct order from Dr. Hassan. Mason called for Nurse Cohen on his comm-link, and she whispered, "Mason, thank God you're here. Tell the guards to let you in now."

"Are you secure, ma'am?" She did not answer him.

The doors opened to let him inside, and then closed immediately. He quickly went to the back, where everyone was gathered. Captain Kouras held a scalpel at Nurse Soo's throat, and Nurse Cohen was trying to talk him down. Dr. Hassan, Nurse Jones, and two corpsmen were in the viewing room, locked inside, with a chair wedging the door closed. They were beating on the door, trying to get it open, without success.

"Mason, can you help? He won't put the scalpel down," Nurse Cohen said, trying to remain calm. Nurse Soo was completely terrified, with tears running down both cheeks, and was sobbing. Captain Kouras appeared wild-eyed, shaking and sweating.

"Captain Kouras, I am your Prime Marine, Mason, sir. Do you remember me, Captain Kouras?" Mason asked softly.

"Prime Marine? Mason, yes, Mason, these people are trying to kill me!" The delirious man said, "They won't let me out!"

"Yes, sir, and that's why I've come to help you, Captain Kouras. I've come to take you back up to the bridge. Admiral Tomiko is on the vid screen, waiting to talk with you, sir." Mason motioned with a hand behind his back for Nurse Cohen to get behind him. "We can't keep the Admiral waiting, Captain Kouras." Mason was now about a meter from him.

"She tried to kill me! They're all trying to kill me, Mason!" He moved a little toward Mason, still holding the scalpel at Nurse Soo's throat.

"Captain Kouras, let's bring her with us to the bridge, and show her to the Admiral. He'll want to see who tried to kill you, sir."

"Yes, let's bring her!" His eyes opened even wider.

"Captain Kouras, I'll escort you and your prisoner to the bridge. I'll handcuff her so she won't get away from you." Mason slowly took his cuffs off his weapons belt, and showed them to the Captain. "The Admiral will be pleased to see your prisoner in hand cuffs, sir. May I put them on her now? Then we can go to the bridge, sir."

"Yes, we'll show her to the Admiral, so he can see who tried to kill me!" The delirious Captain moved close to Mason, still holding the scalpel to Nurse Soo's neck, and Mason slowly took one of the sobbing Nurse's hands.

"Let's cuff her behind her back, Captain. She is your prisoner of war," Mason suggested.

"Yes, she is my prisoner! Cuff her. Behind her back, yes." He lowered the scalpel, and Mason rushed him, pushing Nurse Soo away towards Nurse Cohen. Mason held Kouras' hand containing the scalpel in his left hand, bleeding. He was struggling with the Captain, who was knee-kicking and head-butting him, while Mason's blood was pouring down his arm. Finally, the sound of bones being broken in the Captain's wrist caused the man to scream in pain, and drop the scalpel. Mason subdued him in a headlock, and held him while Nurse Cohen hit his arm with an injection pen loaded with heavy tranquilizers. Kouras rolled his eyes back in his head, and collapsed onto Mason's body.

"Help me get him on the table, Mason," Nurse Cohen said. They lifted the Captain onto the messy bed, and put the restraints back on him: head, wrists, torso, and feet. She turned to Mason to help his bleeding hand. He was holding his bloody fist tightly, and he kicked the chair away from the door for Dr. Hassan to get out.

Nurse Cohen said, "I think the Captain's hand may be broken. I'll tend to Mason, Doctor." She quickly led Mason to a nearby basin to wash and sterilize his left hand, especially the thumb. "We'll have to scan your hand to check for tendon damage," she told Mason. She took a spray can from the shelf and sprayed antiseptic on the wound, and applied a compress. She tied a bandage around his hand, and led him to the wall scanner. Holding his lower arm, the machine scanned his entire left hand for damage. "You're lucky. The blade did not cut the tendons. The wound is deep, but should heal cleanly."

Nurse Cohen quickly scrubbed, donned gloves, and gathered her equipment onto a tray. Mason looked behind him at Kouras' room, and all four people were attending him. "What happened, ma'am?" Mason asked.

When she returned, she laid the tray on the exam table, administered a shot into Mason's thumb. "That will numb your hand for a few minutes, so I can work on it." She rolled up his sleeve, alcohol-swabbed a spot, and with a second injection pen, shot him again. "That one is for tetanus, and also contains antibiotics. Are you numb yet, Mason?"

"Only my brain, ma'am," he joked, trying to add a little levity to the situation. She looked at him and smiled very briefly, and returned to her work. She took her laser knife, and sliced his bandage off. She ran the laser knife's wide edge all over the wound, cauterizing it. When she finished, she sprayed the wound again with antiseptic, and gently pressed the cut sides together. Holding the closed wound with her left hand, she sealed the wound with the laser knife in her right hand. A new sterile thin bandage was wrapped over, under, and around his hand and thumb.

"You'll need to have the wrappings changed in four hours, and your wound inspected for infection, but you'll be good as new," she said, sitting down next to him.

Mason asked her, "Will you tell me what happened now, ma'am?"

"Strictly on the QT, John, understand?" She whispered. Mason nodded in agreement.

"Nurse Soo went to clean a wound on the Captain's leg, and failed to wait for the two corpsmen to help her. Somehow, the Captain managed to get one hand out of its restraint and released himself, but she did not realize he was free when she went to tend to him. He jumped out of bed and grabbed her. He got a scalpel from her tray, and, well, you saw the scene."

"How long had he held Nurse Soo like that before I came?" Mason asked.

"Only for a few seconds. He used it to force the others into the viewing room, and then wedged the door shut. I heard the commotion and went to see what was happening. I was afraid if he saw the guards, he might have killed Nurse Soo. I was trying to talk him out of the scalpel, when you buzzed my comm-link," she revealed.

"Will Captain Kouras be all right? I tried not to touch his internal organs, but I'm sure his hand is broken," Mason asked her.

"I think his hand will be fine. I'm more concerned about your hand, John," she said quietly. "You shouldn't go back to stand guard duty, holding that heavy rifle. Your wound needs these next few hours to heal properly." The Doctor checked his scans, and would not give him permission to return to bridge guard duty.

"You need to rest for a day or two, Gunny." The Doctor called Captain Baines and advised him that Mason could return to the bridge, but only on limited duty, as the Captain's escort. He sent Mason back to the bridge, and informed the Captain of their miraculous rescue.

Captain Baines threw his head back and laughed in disbelief. "Ah, Mason. What would we do without you? All right, let's go check the safe in the Storeroom, and then you'll be done for today." The Captain led them out through his quarters, and locked the door behind him.

The Storeroom was still a disaster, exactly as it was in Mason's recording last night. The two men tip-toed over the debris, and went to the safe at the back of the room. Captain Baines touched the smooth, keyless, handle-less safe in several places, then touched the right side of the big steel safe, and the door unlatched. Everything was there, as it was supposed to be. He started to close the door, when Mason asked for the octagonal tube. "Why? We have hundreds of recordings of it," the Captain asked.   Mason explained he wanted to study it.

"We can do that tomorrow, Mason, not now," Baines said.

"Beg your pardon, Captain, but tomorrow is my day off."

"Who said so?" Baines asked, stifling a smile.

"You did, sir," Mason replied quickly.

After locking the safe securely, Captain Baines asked, "Since when do you care about a day off, Mason? You took one day off in eighteen months." The Captain looked at him slyly, and carefully walked out of the room.

"Captain, I kind of made plans for my day off tomorrow, sir," Mason persisted.

"With a lady?" The Captain was enjoying giving Mason a hard time. "I thought you reported only to the Captain, Prime Marine," the Captain said, walking slowly back to the bridge. "Now, I find I have to share you with a lady." He turned to face him. "I suppose you'll want one day off every week, now that I have to share you, is that right, Gunny?"

"That'd be nice, Captain," Mason answered.

"As long as we can spare you. Have fun tomorrow. Dismissed, Gunny."

XVII

The quiet days of the Hesperia free-floating through deep space came to an end. The mining operations began in earnest Thursday night at eighteen hundred hours. The huge claws were reaching out for the easy pickings. The three rock crushers were grinding, crushing, and cracking, twenty-four hours a day, in Section Four. The huge bay doors were fully open.

The probes launched at 3pm would tell mining operations the properties of each asteroid, and the Mission Director would select which ones to pick. Quotas were set by Earth Command for iron, magnesium, zinc and copper. The last mining freighter in the area, the Excelon, secured and retrieved asteroids containing titanium, and even gold.

Rocks that were small to medium were easily picked up by the claws and baskets as they floated by. The real mining work involved flying teams to a large asteroid and drilling, using controlled blasting, or lasering off chunks to pick up.

The expertise of the mining operations came to bear in mining the larger asteroids. If the ship's quota of iron was already obtained, there would be the need to sheer off slices of an asteroid to get to its heart of more-desirable metals, like copper, or zinc. Great caution must be taken, however, to control the direction where the blasted or sheared debris was sent, so that the Hesperia was not hit. The ship's hull was fortified with thick sheets of corrugated iron over her even thicker-hulled steel frame. A direct, full hit from a large enough asteroid could push the Hesperia off-position, and precious fuel cells would have to be used to bring her back to the mining fields.

When the ship-wide general announcement was made about the beginning of mining operations, Mason was on the bridge. Then the great noises started up. Clunking, metal-on-metal grinding, and screeching; it was so loud that everyone on the bridge took notice. What a place for a bionic ear, he mumbled to himself. He was in real pain from the noise.

Mason went back to his quarters to get the books he'd taken from the library, and his larger com-tablet. He headed for the quietest place on the ship, the observation lounge. He chose an area that was farthest from the group of people watching the mining claws and arms work.

He borrowed a memory crystal with 200TB stored information in 5D. His big com tablet swallowed the crystal, allowing him to search the 18th, 19th and 20th century libraries for the symbols on the octagonal tube. He was surprised to find as little symbology in the reference material as he did.

In the mid-24th century symbology is very important. Although the URE is one world government, over 200 languages are spoken. The two most prevalent languages are English and Mandarin, with Spanish coming up third. Depending on which side of Earth you lived, one or the other is mandatory for government, corporate, or other employment. But most regions still had a preponderance of native languages and cultures that the people chose to keep alive. Uniform symbols were used all over Earth to provide easily understood directions, names of public places, money, and what have you. Symbols were everywhere in Mason's world.

Symbols had similar meanings for humankind in past centuries, but their usage was not always as wide-spread. In fact, Mason discovered that symbols were used to obfuscate true meanings from disapproving authoritarian eyes.

He read and searched until 1am. Mason checked his com tablet for any new search results, but nothing was new. He packed up to go back to his quarters. On his way out of the lounge, he thought of Da Vinci's Vitruvian man, and it hit him: Da Vinci wrote backwards to keep the church authorities from knowing what he was working on. What if the symbols on the octagonal tube were reversed? He had several new ideas to try when they all worked on solving the tube's mysteries Saturday.

When he awoke Friday morning, Mason headed straight for the hospital to get his dressing changed, hopefully by Nurse Cohen. She sat him on the exam table, cut the old dressing, scanned and inspected his healing wound. "You're doing fine. Just keep taking it easy, now. Don't do anything strenuous, and you'll heal properly."

"What about working out, ma'am?"

"You can run, and do anything using your legs, but no weight lifting, or martial arts. Just try not to strain the muscles in your left hand, particularly the thumb. Baby your left hand, if you can, John. You'll heal faster, and better." She looked at him, smiled, sprayed antiseptic on the wound, and began to bandage his hand.

Mason asked, "Captain Baines said we could try interpreting the symbols backwards, like Da Vinci's backwards writing. What do you think, Nurse Cohen?"

"I think it's a great idea, and you'd better make sure I'm there, John Mason! I'd love to get that tube open, wouldn't you?" She always got excited when discussing that tube.

"Yes, I would ma'am. I think whatever's inside it has a lot of bearing on this ship's events. I don't know if everything will tie together once it's opened, but we'll definitely have more information," he replied.

"So, John; I heard that you have a day off today. What's the plan?" She gave him that little saucy grin of hers, like she knew he had a date.

"Oh, just an outing, to do something different for a change," he answered coyly.

"Like what?" She had him, and was not going to give up without a good try. She was taking a very long time bandaging his hand.

"Well, you know they have that new musical Earth Command's bringing us this weekend, in the lounge," he told her.

She looked at him, and said, "I never thought of you as the Broadway show type. And?"

"You know, maybe the spa and some dinner on the Esplanade, that's all." He felt a little blush coming into his cheeks, talking with her about his plans with another woman.

"Sounds like fun. When do I get to meet her?" She was all over this conversation, and was enjoying every minute of it.

He chuckled. "Maybe after I find out if she likes me, first."

"Oh, I'm sure she will. What woman wouldn't want you, John?" She shook her shoulders a bit, and looked at him flirtatiously. Now, this was getting to be too much. He was positively blushing like a kid. "Will you wear your class A uniform for her?" Dammit, she did it again. More blushing.

Mason answered, "No. Street clothes." She stopped and looked at him.

"Really? Now that does sound intriguing. I've never seen you in street clothes, John. Why not meet up for a cocktail, all of us, before you head to the show?" She was smiling her upside down smile at him.

He was dying inside. "I really don't think it'd be a good way to start things off, Nurse Cohen."

"Why not? I'd love to meet her, John." The bandage was done, but she still had hold of his hand in both her hands. She was looking him right in the eyes, loving every minute of his anguish, her eyes twinkling.

He must *not* surrender. "Please, Nurse Cohen. Please, ma'am, I can't."

"Okay, John, I've had enough fun embarrassing you for one day; I won't ask anything more of you." She was grinning at him. "You're a gentleman to the end, John Mason. Have a good time."

"Thank you, ma'am." He slid off the table and headed for the door.

"And tell Sherrie I said 'Hi'!" She called to him. Good Lord, he is fun to tease, she thought to herself, giggling.

He barely escaped Nurse Cohen with his manly pride intact. Damn. What a woman. She had him wrapped around her little finger, and she knew it. She had too much fun with him. Oh, hell, he enjoyed the attention from her, if the truth be told. It was nearing noon, and Mason wanted to get something light to eat before going to the spa. He'd only been to a spa once before, but it was on a full stomach, and he didn't want the same nausea today at the "Couples Experience." He grabbed a quick sandwich and iced tea.

Running into the clothing shop on the Esplanade, he picked up his new street clothes, and they fit perfectly. He still hadn't decided which trousers to wear, "Charcoal," or "Pewter." His new boots were shined to a gleaming finish, just the way he liked them.

Thirteen hundred. He showered and shaved carefully, so as not to have a stupid cut on their first date. Come to think of it, he hadn't had a real date in years, not with this much planning and trouble. Getting girls was always easy for him with his physique and good looks. But, just maybe it was time to be with a lady that he had to work a little for, this time.

Thirteen thirty. Why was he so nervous? He saw Sherrie nearly every day in the mess hall. Suddenly remembering her gift, he ran back to his quarters and picked up the little box for her, then headed back to her deck.

Fourteen hundred. He knocked on her door. She answered promptly, and let him inside, staying behind the door. She had a little more room than he did inside her quarters, but not much. She closed the door, and he saw her, like seeing her for the first time. Sherrie was wearing a flowing blue, yellow and green dress that reminded him of summer. Her blonde hair was loose, and curled right above her neck. She wore a little make-up, and an inviting shade of lipstick he couldn't stop looking at. She was lovely. She looked like a fashion model. What a transformation!

He was trying to get any words out, and finally managed to say, "You look absolutely beautiful! I bought this for you."

She was looking at him, too, for the first time seeing him in something besides a uniform. He chose the "Pewter" trousers, and his shirt had khaki, black and gold colors in the pattern. She held the box, and he said, "Open it, Sherrie, it's for you."

Sherrie opened the box, and removed the wide silver bracelet with the big blue "Larissa" stone. "How did you know it would match my dress so well?" She asked, amazed.

"I didn't know what you'd be wearing. I bought it because it matches your eyes." She smiled at him as she put it on, and looked at herself in the mirror with it on her wrist.

"I love it, John. Thank you so much!" She went to kiss him, but decided a little hug was better. She'd spent a long time getting ready, and didn't want to smudge her lipstick.

"Ready to go? C'mon." He led her out the door, and then went up the lift to the Esplanade. They strolled around and window shopped, and finally landed in the little bistro off the main area. Mason kept to his bourbon, and Sherrie opted for a white wine.

"What do you want to do when we're back home, Sherrie?" He asked.

"I don't know. It's only been a few weeks to me, you know. I just got started. You've been awake the whole time, what, eighteen months? It'll be a much longer mission for you than me, John. What do you want to do when you get home?"

"See my family. My sister and her family live on Mars Colony III, and they're the only family I've got left. Earth is my home, but they are my family. I'd like to take her kids back to Earth for a while. They've only known life on Mars, under a dome. They need some fresh air, at least that's what I think of doing for them someday, when this is over. Do you have a family?"

"Oh yes. Two half-brothers and a younger sister. I'm the oldest." She swirled her wine.

"Would you try to go back to an Earth station?" He asked, being curious.

"I haven't really thought about it much. I like the service, and I like to cook for people. So, I guess I'll stay in. I don't know. A lot can happen over these next four years," she reminded him.

"A lot can happen anytime, anywhere, Sherrie. Look at all that happened in one day with the Hesperia. I've heard some guys say they were on missions for years, and nothing out of the ordinary happened. We are living history, now. Don't you just feel it?" He leaned in, closer to her, with a twinkle of excitement in his eyes. "We're lucky to be here, now, at this time, together." His brown eyes were shining, and it sure wasn't the synthehol. She could tell he really believed it, and was living it.

"Do you like being on the bridge so much?" He was so handsome, she realized.

Mason shrugged. "It's okay, why do you ask?"

"You know how most officers treat enlisted like we're real people, just like they are. But some officers, they treat us like we're their servants, and they don't show any respect at all," she said. "I've been around bridge officers who are pretty snooty. Do you get that from any of them?"

"No, not really, and it's probably because I'm not just a Space Marine. I'm a Prime Marine, and whether you're enlisted or officer, a Prime Marine is a rare entity." He paused, and thought for a few moments. "You and I have something very important in common in our careers, Sherrie."

"What? I'm just a cook," she said, timidly.

"No, you're not just a cook. Your provide quality fuel for us to live on. You and I both help keep others alive and well, the best we know how. You should be proud of what you do. All the officers I know think you're a genius, by the way."

"You're kidding me now, John," she said.

"No, I'm not. Dr. Hassan thinks you're cleverer than Merlin himself; he has said so on several occasions. And, I know Captain Baines doesn't trust anyone but you in that kitchen to serve him food to eat. You just don't know how special you are to everyone. Any man or woman who doesn't know and respect what you do for them is a fool, or a jerk. You should be proud. I'm proud of you." He looked at her, and she had a little red in her eyes.

"That's nice to hear, John. Really nice." She finished her drink, and they went to the spa.

"Mr. Mason, we're ready for you now." The hostess at the spa took them to the dressing areas, where they undressed, and put on thick robes, and waited together for their massages.

They were shown into a low-lighted room, with two massage platforms, side by side. Soft music was playing, and it almost drowned out the machine noise for them. She watched him take off his robe, and saw his back; broad, perfectly sculpted, and bearing the scars of his battles. She was nervous about taking off her robe, and then realized he had already seen her in a diaper, at her cryonic awakening.

They lay on firm beds, layered with foam and gel mattresses that made them feel like they were floating. The masseuse and masseur came in, introduced themselves, and began their massages. She was initially uncomfortable, but soon realized she was just another tense body to the masseuse. Mason's masseur was getting a workout. His back was so strong and tense that the masseur used his elbows on him. Sherrie enjoyed the foot massage the best, understandable for a woman on her feet twelve hours a day.

Sherrie had another surprise: the manicure and pedicure he bought for her. She had both of those services done, while he waited for her in the waiting room. She came out, looking even more relaxed, with nails prettier than she'd ever had. No man ever pampered her like this before.

They left, strolling down the Esplanade. Mason suggested they go to the observation lounge before going to the main lounge, to see where the ship was. He took her to the side where they had the view all to themselves. She saw the stars as she'd never seen them. They stood at the window, Mason holding her hand, and were totally happy. She looked up at him, and realized she was close to being completely defenseless. How did a man that nice, handsome, and that well-built, come to be with her? She never wanted the night to end.

He put his arm around her waist lightly, pointing out the various stars in Orion's belt, and nebulae. She found herself leaning on his chest, and looking into his eyes. She no longer cared about dinner or the new show from Earth. Mason lightly stroked the back of her neck. He asked if she was ready to go to the main lounge for the show, and she shook her head 'no.'

Sherrie turned to him, looking into his eyes. He took her hand, and led her to her quarters. He walked her to her door, and she unlocked it, and he held it for her to enter. Sherrie walked to the dresser, and inserted a music crystal into the player, and turned to him. She was trembling, nervous about what was to happen next.

Mason turned her around, stroking and kissing the back of her neck, and undid the back of her dress, taking it off, slowly. He teased her by running his big fingers lightly along the edge of her slip, lowering its straps. The slip fell to the floor, and he caressed her along the length of her body below her waist, and put his hand down the front of her bikini panties. She stopped his hand, and turned to face him, looking at him intently. He took off his shirt and let it fall behind him. She had never seen a man's chest so muscular; her heart was racing. He took her in his arms, and kissed her so tenderly that she nearly cried. Mason drew her even closer to him, kissing her deeply, while his hand began to explore the small area of her lower back, and down, caressing her derriere. He pressed her into himself, and she felt his desire, and his hardness. He picked her up in his arms, and kissed her from her neck, down the center of body to her pubic mound, until she swooned, and gave herself totally to him, body and soul.

XVIII

As with most things on the maiden Hesperia voyage, much happened in a few short months. The mining operations were going well. The ship's probes identified several asteroids worthy of harvesting, but none containing any rare or precious metals, and none with titanium. The Hesperia moved a few thousand kilometers closer, and to the west of their initial position. Probes were launched again, and the Mission Director was happier with the asteroids in this area than their initial hunting grounds. A few looked promising.

Shuttles were sent to the largest asteroid in the belt, RH-515. It was a large, elongated, spinning asteroid, rotating end over end at 112,800 kilometers per hour. It contained, according to the probes, not only magnesium, iron and zinc, but also titanium. Mission Director wanted this asteroid, and set about designing the plan how to harvest the beast.

Captain Baines had not received any unusual or overly-demanding request from Mission Director Keene, and they seemed to be working together well. That is, until RH-515 became Keene's target. He hounded Baines for a week to have Lieutenant Juarez, his science officer, develop a plan of attack that would not involve rock fragments either hitting the Hesperia, or being thrown off, into space. Since they had only been mining for six months, the URE quotas were far from being filled, and Captain Baines wanted to harvest the "normal" asteroids, before trying to harvest the silent monster.

Captain Baines was not excited about chasing an asteroid perhaps half a quadrant before they caught up to the spinning rock. Once it was caught, they would have to slow it down with intense short bursts of their lasers, hoping that their estimates of the rock's broken pieces continued their calculated trajectory, and not hit the Hesperia. In the Captain's mind, the escapade was too dangerous, too costly, and not worth the risk involved.

He wanted Earth Command to make the final decision on this one.

Several days passed while Earth Command was considering its decision on asteroid RH-515. The bridge was quiet, and the mining operations continued without any interruptions. There was even a little extra time for Mason and Commander Cohen to plot a birthday party for the Captain in secret.

Working with Chief Dawson, they planned a sumptuous buffet for the entire crew in the Captain's honor at dinner on his birthday, and he appreciated all their efforts. Everyone enjoyed a wonderful meal, and wished Captain Baines well. Commander Cohen had a few more surprises for the Captain, however.

Captain Kouras was asked by Nurse Cohen last month about giving up his quarters, and was surprised to discover that Captain Baines had not moved previously. "Absolutely. Please tell Captain Baines I expected him to take the suite the day he took command. The Captain should be living in the Captain's quarters. Period."

"I want to make this a birthday he'll remember for a long time, John." Commander Cohen went to the Captain's quarters with Mason. He helped her by moving the furniture so the Captain could take advantage of the incredible views the suite offered, being right off the bridge, the highest living quarters on the ship. Since moving into the Captain's quarters off the bridge last month, he was too busy to make many changes to the living environment. She was busying herself personalizing the suite for her private celebration with him, in honor of his birthday.

When Captain Baines left the bridge, more than one surprise was waiting for his coming home. She brought her favorite artwork from her quarters to add some beauty and color, and the blown glass sculpture Victor had in his old quarters, previously lost on a shelf of his bookcase, was prominently displayed. New silken bed sheets replaced the scratchy sheets that were on the bed when he moved in. She put a music crystal in the player and adjusted the lighting to heighten the ambience for him.

Although Captain Kouras could not leave his area in the hospital to celebrate with everyone at the surprise party, he gave Nurse Cohen his authorization to open his locker downstairs, and get two bottles of champagne, and a bottle of cognac for Captain Baines' birthday gift from him. She put one bottle of champagne on ice, and the other bottle on his coffee table with the cognac, for him to enjoy.

When the Captain opened the door, everything looked different, and much better. The suite was rearranged so that he could view the stars and space from both his desk and couch, and from the bed. There was soft music playing, and a bottle of real champagne in an ice bucket next to the bed, waiting for him. He looked around, and was very pleased. He tossed his com tablet down on the desk, and called, "Rachel?"

She came out of the separate bedroom in a long, flowing, completely transparent black negligee, and she was naked underneath the negligee. The enticing gown was held closed by a tied ribbon around her neckline. Her hair was down around her shoulders, the way he liked it.

"You are so beautiful," he whispered, taking her by her hand. "I can't believe you did all this today!"

"Happy birthday, Victor." She put her arms around his neck and kissed him deeply.

"Rachel…" and she led him to the bedroom for his private celebration.

Earth Command did not authorize pursuit of asteroid RH-515, which upset Mission Director as much as it pleased Captain Baines. Harvesting asteroids had taken precedence over many other issues on board, including the murder and attempted murder investigations, as well as the matter of the octagonal tube.

For Mason, however, the investigations and the tube were still preeminent, subordinate only to his primary duty to protect the bridge, engineering, and medical staff of the Hesperia. He was tenacious; like a pit bull, his teeth were deep in the meat of the investigations, and his jaws were locked. He would not forget about them. He never forgot about his "Persons of Interest" list, either. The list grew longer one day.

One year and six months into the mining operations, another unusual disturbance occurred; this time at the threshold between Sections 1 and 2. No miners could cross over from Section 2 into Section 1. The security team at the Section 1 threshold reported an attempted crossing by several dozen miners, and requested back-up. The ship went to red alert immediately. A second Space Marine team was dispatched to handle the incursion. That team requested back-up, and the Captain ordered sixteen Space Marines, fully armed, dispatched to the threshold. Mason donned full combat gear at the red alert, weapons armed and ready, in firing position at the doors. The bridge officers armed themselves, and went to their defensive stations.

Live vid cams were constantly feeding information to the bridge from all over the ship, all day, every day. The Section 1 live vid cams stopped recording or even registering as working at all. Mason felt a real concern about this event, and he shared it with the Captain.

"Captain Baines, sir, what if this is a diversion, and the real attack is taking place in another sector of the ship? We must be prepared, sir," Mason said aloud, in firing position on the bridge.

"Captain Baines to all sections. Secure all doors and entrances. This is no drill. Repeat: this is no drill. Engineering, report you situation."

"Powers to Captain Baines. We are on lockdown, all secure. Standing by for further instructions. Powers out."

Silence on the Hesperia was replaced months ago by machine sounds, yet, at this tense moment, the machine sounds were almost reassuring. The Captain softly requested, "Section 1, what is your status? Are you secure?"

"Bridge, we are under attack. Requesting back-up." Everyone on the bridge knew this was not the proper response.

"Captain Baines to Lieutenant Cheung. What is your status?" No response. The Captain repeated his call, and no response came.

"Engineering, this is the Captain. What is happening with the vid cams in Section 1?" Dead silence.

Mason hand-signaled to the Captain in the direction of the far communications station, where Lieutenant Urz was working.

"Captain to Engineering, Chief Engineer, report." No response. The Captain turned to Mason, and signaled him to guard the bridge doors. He hand-signaled Lt. Commander Westerly to take the comm, then approached the communications station, where Lieutenant Urz was turned to its computer, busy keying in instructions on the console. The Captain went behind Lieutenant Urz's chair, and spun it around.

"Lieutenant Urz, you are relieved. Get out of that chair, now." Lieutenant Urz was held by Lieutenant Fontenay, while the Captain quickly reconfigured the communications computer.

"Captain Baines to Engineering. What is your status?"

"Lt. Commander Powers, Captain. All secure in engineering, but all ship's communications are affected. We have just now been able to reach you. We are conducting tests to determine the source of communications failure."

"I think we found it, Powers. Stand by. Captain out."

"Lieutenant Davis, take over this communications console, and order Lieutenant Marston to the bridge immediately, red alert."

The Captain made enough changes to the communications computer to at least get bridge control back. By the time Lieutenant Marston came running onto the bridge and took over communications, the communications system was rebooting, and beginning to display reports from all of the Hesperia's departments, including Section 1.

"This is Captain Baines. Section 1, what is your situation?

"Captain, this is Lieutenant Cheung, sir. There was an attempted crossing by forty or so miners who were either drunk, or pretending to be drunk. We have them in custody now, sir. What shall we do with them, Captain?"

"Hold the miners for further orders from me. Captain out."

The Captain turned his chair quickly to look at a very nervous Lieutenant Urz. "Take that man to the brig, and place him in shackles, now, Lieutenant Fontenay."

The Captain went to yellow alert. Mason stood at guard again, more watchful than ever. Engineering sent Lieutenant Kim to test the communications computer console out fully, to determine how extensive the damage, if any, was to the console. Kim discovered the deception Lieutenant Urz implemented, making the vid cams shut off all over the ship, and destroying the bridge's ability to communicate with the main communications computer. Urz had just begun reprogramming the communications computer for alternate access, when he was discovered.

Captain Baines immediately reported the situation to Admiral Tomiko at Earth Command from his command chair, not the ready room. Baines wanted a recording made by Earth Command of the officers on the bridge, in case further sabotage took place. The Admiral said the job was well done, and signed out.

But Mason was not satisfied that all was over. Lieutenant Urz had been under observation by him and the Space Marines since Day 1; so, why compromise your position of trust on the ship by doing something this lame? Mason requested a meeting with the Captain at his earliest convenience. The meeting was set for tonight at eighteen hundred hours, in Engineering, and the Captain asked Lt. Commanders Powers and Westerly, and Lieutenant Davis, to attend.

"Lt. Commander Powers, I appreciate your holding this meeting for us in your conference room. The episode in Section 1 this afternoon was correctly identified by Gunnery Sergeant Mason as a deception. The bridge crew performed well, and I understand your engineering crew did, as well. The question is this: what was the purpose of this disturbance, and did it work well enough to try it again? This is not the first attempt at taking over the Hesperia, nor will it be the last, I'm afraid." Captain Baines waited a few moments to let his words be assimilated by all those in attendance.

Baines continued, "Lieutenant Urz is being held in shackles in our brig. We need to determine the full extent of the damage he caused, and ascertain whether or not any hidden viruses or malware has been planted. I want an analysis of both the communications system and main computer accomplished as soon as possible." The Captain looked at them for input.

Lieutenant Davis offered his contribution to the meeting. "Sir, since communications permeate every system, we cannot assume we are safe just analyzing communications and control systems. Lieutenant Urz could have reached into any system from the communications console, Captain."

"Very well. We will follow the initial systems check by the complete analysis of every system on the Hesperia," the Captain ordered. They discussed their procedures for the complete, detailed analysis of all systems on board the Hesperia. This would take some time to complete. When they appeared to have developed a plan, Mason asked permission to speak.

"Sir, I don't believe this was an isolated incident," Mason began. "Lieutenant Urz has been awake for almost three years with us. He has been at his station, doing his job for that period of time. I have had him under observation the entire time, from day one. Why would he compromise his position of trust today? What was it about today that caused him to disable the ship's communications? The episode with the supposedly drunken miners at Section 1 was just a ruse. This was pre-planned, Captain. What was his assignment? How far would and could he have gone, if you had not stopped him? What was their goal, Captain?"

"Those are valid questions, Gunny," the Captain admitted.

"The point is, Captain, that Lieutenant Urz was thwarted in his efforts from creating any further damage to the communications system," Westerly rebutted.

"Begging your pardon, ma'am," Mason added. "What I'm trying to say is, what if this was a practice run? What better way to test the Hesperia than this lame attempt today, just to see how we'd react?"

Powers asked, "You think this was a test?"

"Why not, sir? Now, whoever is really behind this sabotage knows exactly what we'll do, how long it took us to recognize the cause of the disturbance, and how long to correct it." Mason made his case.

"Gunny has a point, Captain. If there is someone else behind Urz's actions, he knows what he needs to correct, what adjustments he must make in his next attempt to take control of the ship," Powers said.

"I'm curious, Mason. Why did you have Lieutenant Urz under observation from day one?" Westerly asked.

"Well, ma'am, every officer on the bridge was in control of their station, competent and confident. Lieutenant Urz got flustered easily, and did not handle the comm console efficiently during high traffic situations. Also, he avoided any eye contact with Captain Kouras, or me."

"Perhaps he was intimidated by you," Westerly offered.

"In any case, we have much work to accomplish in a very short time, so let's get to the task at hand. Powers, I realize your crew is busy 24/7 running the ship. But I would like these tests conducted at the command console here in engineering, away from the main bridge crew. They have endured enough drama for one day. Westerly, conduct the tests we discussed immediately here in engineering, with the assistance of our Chief Engineer. Lieutenant Davis, you will coordinate with Lt. Commander Westerly from the main bridge, quietly, and notify me when the tests are complete for my review. Is that clear?" They all acknowledged. "Gunny, I think your assumptions have too much merit to not thoroughly research as soon as possible. You will assist me in scrutinizing all our available evidence this evening. You all have your orders." The Captain stood, and everyone went to work on their assigned tasks. Captain Baines left the engineering deck with Mason and Lieutenant Davis right behind him, back to the main bridge.

The first shift finished after many test results and their supporting data were entered into the log. Captain Baines reviewed all the test results and sent them on to Earth Command for documentation of the scope of their attack, and the corrective action taken by the bridge crew. Urz only managed to compromise communications with the main bridge. He was either too slow or lacked the skills needed to implement any further actionable damage to the ship's main computer, life support, or defensive systems.

The Captain arranged a meeting at nineteen hundred hours with Captain Kouras, his command staff, and Mason, to go over all available evidence. Since Dr. Hassan and Nurse Cohen were integral contributors during the first seventeen months of the mission, when Captain Kouras was in command, Baines felt it would be useful to gain their input now.

The meeting was held in the bridge conference room, with vid cam conferencing in Captain Kouras, from his hospital rooms. Mason sent them all his timeline for the events on the Hesperia, from his early awakening to today. His work even impressed Lt. Commander Westerly, who had formulated a negative opinion of Mason from his "interview" with Stone; she viewed him as a troublesome brute, undeserving of his position, and freedom.

"It appears at first glance that we have two separate avenues to pursue. One involves the murders of Dr. Reese and Dr. Wise, and the octagonal tube. The other involves the poisoning of Captain Kouras and Captain Baines, by the Captain's steward, Stone, and today's matter with Lieutenant Urz. Maybe I just don't have enough facts to examine, but it doesn't seem to me that these are all related, Captain." Lt. Westerly said, looking intently at the timeline.

"There are more facts to consider. The missing meat cleaver handle; what was that used for, if anything? Or was it another diversion? Then there are those unauthorized communication transmissions to consider. They were sent to Titan One, and Earth Command, in the headquarters complex. There are a lot of variables here to consider, Lt. Commander Westerly, many more than initially meet the eye. When you begin to ask why these events took place in such a sequence as they have occurred, the pattern of sabotage begins to emerge," Nurse Cohen summed.

"The Admiral himself alluded to a "greater scheme" at work. He has not shared with us the results of his investigations at Earth Command; perhaps he cannot. I fear we are left to rummage in the dark, waiting for another sinister event to occur, before we discover the truth, whatever that may be," Dr. Hassan said.

"If I may put my two cents into this discussion; it appears to me that we have failed to identify the chief purpose of the architect of this scheme, primarily because that is exactly what he intended. Too many clues here, too few there. Murders and attempted murders. Unauthorized communications transmissions to and from three points. We are confused because he wants us confused. Only our expertise has prevented him from taking control of the Hesperia earlier. I fear he will continue making efforts to take this ship until he's successful, Captain Baines." Captain Kouras was having great clarity in this situation.

"Yes, Captain Kouras, I agree with you, sir. I feel he will continue his attempt to gain control of this ship. But I would also like to mention a few more events that have me bothered, if I may. Why were the first deaths those of the URE research scientists? No one I've talked with has any idea what they are researching in their labs, or what they brought on board in their cargo containers on Titan One. Those containers were already sealed for the mission, supposedly checked and approved by the space patrol. We didn't even get a manifest for them." Mason pointed out more details.

"Where did Lieutenant Miller get the poisonous cocktail she gave to Stone to serve Captain Kouras, and the Tetrodotoxin for Captain Baines? The dozens of injection pens; where did they come from, and where were they stored, so as not to be discovered in our ship's searches? And the programming instructions Lieutenant Urz was using are not available in any training manual anywhere. I checked. The Space Forces does not train communications officers in hacking ship's systems, Captain Baines," Mason asked.

"No, they don't train communications officers to hack, but many others who work with communications and computer systems are trained to hack. If a computer malfunction occurred in deep space, for instance, it may require some form of skilled hacking to override the ship's computer to regain control of it," Lt. Commander Powers contributed.

"Systems developers and designers could also hack, as well as programmers, and many technicians I've known, Captain," Westerly stated.

"But we still don't know WHY, Captain, ma'am. What's his motive, his purpose? What does he intend to gain? I think if we could answer the question of why someone would want control of a mining freighter, we would begin to recognize his pattern, and anticipate his next move. Or, perhaps thwart him completely, and absolutely. Bring an end to this sabotage." Mason pulled them back to the core of the matter.

There was silence for several moments after Mason spoke. No one knew the answer to why; no one would speculate. "Well, I hope this meeting has accomplished something tonight," the Captain said. "We have hopefully shed some more light on the past events for Lt. Commander Westerly. And, perhaps we can take away something else, to paraphrase Captain Kouras: we are right where the architect of this sabotage wants us to be."

Captain Baines assigned two new tasks to Lt. Commander Westerly: she was to set up a dinner the next week with the URE scientists and lab techs; and she was to work with Mason and Nurse Cohen on the octagonal tube. The Captain went to prepare for his update meeting with Admiral Tomiko about the recent and past events on the Hesperia. He was determined to obtain what, if any, information the Admiral gathered and had not shared with him about their situation.

A few days later the private dining room was the location of the Captain's dinner party for the URE research scientists, their lab assistants, his command and medical command staff. Mason was in attendance, as well, the only enlisted man present. He was polite, as always, and only spoke in response to direct questions, mindful of his rank and station. But, beneath his crimson red class A uniform jacket was his hand weapon, just in case. The Captain had him seated directly to his right at the dinner table, in between himself and Commander Cohen. Mason showed the Captain his weapon privately before the guests arrived, and received his approval.

Dr. Bergen spoke to the Captain, "Captain Baines, this dinner was wonderful. One could almost forget he was in deep space with delicious food such as this. Thank you for inviting us."

"You're most welcome, Dr. Bergen. Our chef, Chief Dawson, has once again outdone herself. I'm glad you all could be our guests tonight." The Captain continued making friendly, polite conversation with them all for quite a while.

Dr. Honig had been placed in the center on the left side of the table, where he would not feel compelled, hopefully, to antagonize the Captain. But he could not hold his acid tongue all night. Honig looked at Mason, and asked, "So, Sergeant Mason, how is it that you come to be here with us? You are not an officer, or a doctor, but you are the best-dressed man here." He smirked, pleased with his remarks.

The Captain answered, "Mason is a Prime Marine, and a Gunnery Sergeant. He is here at my request. He has been an integral member of our team since we were awakened early by the ship's computer, when the anomaly first appeared. He is our criminal forensic specialist, holding a master's degree in that field. We are fortunate to have him on the Hesperia."

"I didn't know he had an advanced degree," Dr. Honig said, turning in his chair and reevaluating Mason. "My apology, Gunnery Sergeant Mason."

Dr. Hassan took advantage of Dr. Honig's poor remark, and said, "Dr. Honig, you gentlemen are not the only ones here with doctoral degrees. Each officer at this table holds at least one PhD in their field of discipline. Lt. Commander Westerly holds her PhD in Astrophysical Sciences, from Princeton, no less. Lt. Commander Powers' doctoral is in Astrophysical Engineering, of course. Our Captain Baines made quite a name for himself at Harvard with his doctoral studies in Mathematics, God help us all."

Everyone laughed politely.

Dr. Moore asked Commander Cohen, "And you are the Head Nurse; so your PhD is in nursing, Commander?"

"My master's is in nursing, Dr. Moore. My PhD is in Molecular Biology," Commander Cohen corrected.

"You didn't wish to become a medical doctor, then?" He asked her incredulously.

"No, Dr. Moore. I've spent my career in the Space Forces as a nurse, caring for those who serve. I will spend my time after this mission in research," she explained to him. Lt. Commander Westerly had a new appreciation for Commander Cohen after hearing of her doctoral degree. Molecular Biology was definitely no easy course of study.

"Well then, perhaps we will be colleagues at the URE Research Facility in the future, Commander," he offered.

"Perhaps, Dr. Moore. That step is several years away, as we all know." They all gave thought to her words, thinking how much time was left to be spent on the Hesperia.

"One thing we all have in common, despite our individual careers and scientific disciplines, is our on-going investigation, and the octagonal tube, of course," Captain Baines said, taking control of the conversation again. "Which of you two gentlemen is the project leader now?" Captain Baines asked. The two scientists just looked at each other in silence. "Who is in charge of your experiments, gentlemen?"

"We both are, I guess, Captain Baines," Dr. Moore admitted, looking at his colleague.

"That's odd. How often do you communicate with MM & E?" The Captain asked.

"We send in our reports weekly, as before, Captain. But we haven't spoken with anyone at MM & E since Titan One," Dr. Bergen explained.

"Haven't you spoken with anyone on Earth since we left? Not even your families?" Westerly asked in amazement.

"No. We were instructed to report weekly, and if the MM & E needed to speak with us, they would call us. We have no outside voice communications ability," Bergen admitted.

"Would you like to speak with your families, Dr. Bergen? I cannot permit frequent live communications transmissions of a personal nature, but I'm sure I could get permission for a quick call home for each of you," the Captain offered sincerely.

"I think we all would appreciate that courtesy, Captain Baines. And, I'll also ask for a call to MM & E, to discuss our sharing information regarding our experiments with you," Dr. Bergen said.

"Absolutely. Our staff meeting with Admiral Tomiko is in two days. I'll put your request for communications at the top of my agenda, doctors."

BARBARA J. ROBERTSON

The Captain successfully steered the conversation in the direction he originally intended. By offering live communications to the scientists to speak with their families, he hoped to gain their trust to discover the nature of their experiments.

Captain Baines and Commander Cohen went into his quarters, and he ordered the sentries to electronically sweep his suite again. Satisfied that all was secure, Baines locked the door for the night. When they were alone at last, Victor brought over his bottle of fine cognac from Captain Kouras, and two snifters. "Let's open this tonight, Rachel."

"I'd love it," she said, taking off her dress uniform jacket, tossing it lightly over the arm of the couch. He poured a generous amount into each glass. They toasted each other, and sipped the fabulous cognac. Rachel said, "This is really delicious, Victor. Must've cost a small fortune." He swirled the cognac in his glass, and took another sip. Then he sat his glass down.

Victor got up and went to the window, and held his hand out for her to join him. He turned her around so that they both were facing the windows, enjoying the view. He held her comfortably close, with Rachel resting her head against his chest, his arms around her waist. After a few minutes, he softly spoke in her ear. "One summer when I was in grad school, several of my fraternity brothers and I went to Denali, to climb the mountain. We could only get so far, though, because a series of summer storms forced us to return. On our descent, we took a different route than our ascent, and we came down the glacier." He paused for a brief moment.

"I remember walking around the glacier after we'd made camp. The sun had finally come out. I came to a crevasse in the glacier, and saw that it was deep, far deeper than I had initially imagined it to be, and it was full of light, as far down as I could see. Deep blue light. I was transfixed. It was the most beautiful thing I'd ever seen in my life. Until now."

She turned her head to look up at him, and he said, "When I met you, I was attracted to your physical beauty, not knowing anything about you. Now, I've seen a glimpse of how deep and wonderful you really are, and the light that shines within you." He gently touched her chin. "I want to spend the rest of my life with you, Rachel, learning more about you, and bathing in your light. Will you be with me forever, and marry me, Rachel?"

"Oh Victor..." was all she could say, and she kissed him passionately, as tears of happiness ran down her cheeks.

162

XIX

The asteroid mining continued for over two years, and the asteroid field itself looked none the worse. In fact, if one were to look at the field prior to the start of the mining operations and compare it with the field one year later, there was barely any difference. Yet they had not been able to find and harvest a platinum group asteroid.

The highly prized platinum group rocks could contain not only platinum, but also palladium, iridium, and other rare and precious metals, in much greater quantities than available on Earth. The Excelon found and successfully harvested a fifty meter asteroid containing platinum group metals, especially palladium. Since the Hesperia was working in fields adjacent to those mined by the Excelon, the URE had high hopes to locate and harvest another platinum group asteroid, or two.

The ship's foundries in Section 3 roared 24/7. The inferno belched smoke into the closed chimney systems continually, although great care was taken to capture all the smoke to prevent any pollution from being dumped into space. The furnaces needed to be continually fed the oxygen necessary to keep the fires hot enough to smelt the ores. There were the huge furnaces for iron, zinc, and magnesium, and smaller furnaces for more rare and precious metals. The smaller furnaces were quiet, so far.

The miners called Section 3 "Hell," appropriately. "Hell" was managed above the actual foundry floor by the mining technicians at their computer consoles on the Section 3 observation deck. The floor of Section 3, where the hot sparks flew and the poisonous smoke sometimes escaped was not the realm of men, as in the olden days of smelting. It was manned by robots, impervious to the smoke and sputtering sparks and slag. Any sparks landing on the 'bots just slid off their fireproof exterior onto the floor, without damaging the robotic machines.

The liquid contents of the huge buckets of molten iron, zinc, and magnesium were poured into big bar-shaped forms, traveling along a slow moving conveyor belt. After a dousing in precious water to cool and temper the metal bars, the forms continued to Section 2, for removal and storage. The entire process was a marvel of technology and automation, requiring much skill, precision and technological expertise from the mining operations personnel. As with any production line, any mishap or miscalculation along any point on the line caused disruptions further down, and could make for delays in processing at best, or damage to the equipment or personnel, at the worst. Sections 2 and 3 would, if all went as planned, be working full time during and after harvesting, all the way back to Moon Base.

Mission Director Keene requested that the ship's probes be launched again to scan two asteroids which were coming into range within the next two weeks. One was a medium sized round asteroid, the other elongated, containing two distinct halves, separated by a rock bridge. The "Big Peanut," as Keene referred to it, was smooth, and neither pock-marked or dimpled, and held great interest with Keene, Coordinator Garcia, and the supervisors. Plans were made for the probes' launching in two weeks.

Mason welcomed these boring times on the bridge, because they meant everyone was safe. He worked himself hard during his off-duty hours to stay ready by exercising, working out with other Space Marines, and his continual martial arts training. What was worrying him now was that he knew the men were bored, making them easy targets for anyone looking to do harm to them.

Captain Baines finally gave Mason permission for a space walk outside the Hesperia, to inspect the storage holds on the outside hull for a possible murder weapon with an octagonal end or handle. The walk was to be coordinated with several outer hull tasks, making the maximum use of personnel and breathing air. While Mason was inspecting the hull storage lockers, other crewmen would be carrying out their duties up above the top deck, maintaining the upper antennas, discs and other communications equipment. They would be supervised both on board in engineering and the bridge, and by a shuttle, hovering close, in case of any emergency.

Mason did not mind the uncomfortable space suit and the lengthy preparations for the walk. What he minded was having so many other tasks attached to his walk. He would only have taken ten minutes or so to go outside on the hull and carry out his inspections. But now, coupled with the maintenance work on the communications array, and his additional assignment, the walk would take three hours or more. The Captain was convinced by Lt. Commander Westerly that, since Mason was outside anyway, he might as well inspect the seals on the windows of the bridge and observation lounge. Lieutenant Roshkov from engineering would be accompanying Mason on his walk, as well.

Mason was concerned that the inspections would produce no other octagonal-handled objects that might be a possible murder weapon. He was still investigating the murders of Dr. Reese and Dr. Wise, and checked everywhere possible on the Hesperia for a murder weapon. If nothing was found outside, the octagonal tube must be the murder weapon.

Dr. Hassan, Nurse Cohen, and he tried to open that tube every way they could think of, but they were no closer now than before. It would not be cut open. It would not open under water. The symbols were, so far, incomprehensible to anyone who saw them. Over a year ago, Captain Baines assigned Lt. Commander Westerly to work with them on the octagonal tube; now she was as frustrated with the object as they were.

The space walks were set for 0-eight hundred hours, with Westerly monitoring all of their suits' controls for life functions. Mason reminded himself that she knew what she was doing, even if she did dislike him. The cargo bay was sealed off, and the internal atmosphere captured and stored for later use. He donned his space helmet at the signal, as had Lieutenant Roshkov and the other crewmen, and they each checked the other's suit and helmet for tight seals and green lights on the air tanks on their backs.

The men boarded the tram to the exit point, and waited. The cargo bay doors opened and the men got off the tram and lined up. The crewmen scheduled to work up top got into the shuttle. Mason hooked up his emergency tow line to the belt on his suit, and stepped outside the doors onto the hull ladder, with Lieutenant Roshkov. Mason theorized that someone trying to hide a murder weapon outside the ship would have had time only to access the storage lockers near the cargo bay doors when they were docked on Titan One, so that was where the two went to look. They reached the first storage locker, and got off the ladder, holding onto the hull hand-holds. They watched the shuttle launch, and slowly position itself and hover above the ship. The maintenance crew got out and took their positions, suspended in space, all tethered to the shuttle. They began working on the communications array at the very top of the ship.

Roshkov turned the round hatch cover lock to open the storage locker, and both men pulled opened the locker door. Everything was strapped in tightly, all the tools, huge wrenches and ratchets, and the grappling hooks, for emergency use. He checked inside the small panel inside the bottom of the locker and briefly looked into the smaller toolkit, and all was secure. Nothing here. They closed the locker door, secured the hatch cover lock, and moved on to the next locker. They checked out all four lockers surrounding the cargo bay, and found nothing out of the ordinary. They began the long climb to go up top to check the windows.

Roshkov called out to him to stop, and Mason turned around to see what he wanted. The Lieutenant was pointing to something Mason could barely believe: the orange cloud. "Gunnery Sergeant Mason to Captain

Baines. It's here, sir. It's here. Do you copy, Captain?"

"Affirmative, Gunny. Get back in here at once!" The Captain ordered all the men to return immediately, along with the shuttle. Their tow lines were retracted to pull them all in as fast as they could be towed, without damaging them. The shuttle beat them all back inside, of course, and held until the last man was safely in the bay. The cargo bay doors were closed, and the atmosphere was restored. The red alert was sounding ship-wide, as the men unsuited and reported back to their stations as soon as possible.

The Mission Director was holding for the Captain, who had informed Earth Command of their situation, when Mason made it back to the bridge. He was fully armed by the time he got to the bridge door, and took his laser rifle out of the storage closet, and stood guard. The Captain was receiving orders from Earth Command to hold position and maintain red alert. He informed the Mission Director of their status as briefly as possible, and ordered the claws and baskets retracted, and Section 4 doors closed.

"Lieutenant Marston, open a communications channel to broadcast to the orange cloud," the Captain ordered. "Davis, all defensive shields up and on full spectrum. Powers, stand ready." The men acknowledged his orders.

"Communications channel opened, sir."

"This is Captain Baines of the mining freighter Hesperia. What is your purpose?" No response came. "Lieutenant, resend." No response. The next move belonged to the orange cloud.

The minutes got tenser. The silence grew deafening. The only sound was the ship's crushers and foundries, grinding and firing. The cloud moved into full view, and held its position. The Captain sat still and rigid, waiting for any sign from the anomaly. He quietly asked Lieutenant Juarez for a status check and Lt. Commander Westerly for a systems check. All systems in good order; he waited.

It was a game of chess, each player staring the other down. The Hesperia was defense; but was the orange cloud going to be the offense? Mason was fixed on his duty. His martial arts training allowed him to be fully and completely centered, quiet and still, totally aware, one hundred percent ready. He waited.

The Captain hand signaled for his message to be resent, again. They all waited. And waited. The Captain was as immovable as a statue. Westerly was tense, but ready, at her station. Lieutenant Davis was fully focused, ready to activate weapons at the Captain's signal.

The orange cloud began to move forward slowly, directly towards the Hesperia. "This is Captain Baines of the mining freighter Hesperia. We demand to know your intentions. Your actions are proving hostile to this ship." No response. "Davis, charge the weapons array. Powers, stand ready."

"Weapons charged and ready, Captain," Davis said calmly.

"Ready down here, Captain," Lt. Commander Powers said.

"Unidentified orange cloud anomaly, this is Captain Baines of the Hesperia. You are to hold your position immediately."

The orange cloud stopped moving forward. It began to swirl, changing its cloud colors from orange to red, red to brownish blue, back to orange, and so on. The cloud started to spread out and get thinner, almost opaque, and the form of a massive ship shown behind it.

Suddenly, a high-pitched, shrieking, garbled announcement came over the ship's communications, in an undecipherable language, as the entire crew put their hands to their ears. Mason held his position, grimacing in agony from the terrible sounds tearing through his bionic ears. He felt blood starting to run down his left ear, but held.

"Lower the volume immediately, Marston!" The Captain yelled, holding his hands against his ears. He looked over at Mason for only a second, and saw him still in position, in pain. The sound finally stopped.

"Unidentified ship, we are unable to understand your communication. Please translate, if possible, or resend your message in binary code." The Captain wanted to talk with them, if he could, and was desperate to determine their purpose. He waited for a response.

Mason's ears were both bleeding slowly. He quickly got his earplugs from his weapons belt, removed his helmet, and inserted the plugs into his bloody ears. He put his helmet back on and reset his position. He calmed himself, and refocused, centering his being for the next move. Everyone on the bridge had been shocked by the very loud noise and the pain to their ears, but they regained control of their stations, as well.

"WE ARE ONE. YOU WILL SEND US ONE OF YOUR PERSONS FOR ANALYSIS." The words came over the communications as clearly as could be, in plain English. The Captain requested an immediate response from Earth Command to their demand.

Earth Command answered only, "Request denied to send a person to their ship for analysis." The Captain had that response sent to the strange ship. And so, they waited.

"WE ARE ONE. WE WILL SCAN YOUR SHIP FOR TEN SECONDS. DO NOT RESIST."

"Davis, monitor its scans, and if the slightest damage is inflicted, I want to know immediately!" The Captain sat still for the coming scan. They all braced themselves, for what, they could not know. A beam protruded from the underside of the unidentified ship, and dispersed into a wide angle, and it scanned the ship by its width. No ship's alarms went off, which would have indicated a threat to one of its systems. It was the longest ten seconds of their lives. Then the beam stopped, and went off.

"Damage reports, Westerly, Powers," the Captain ordered.

"Sir, no damage reported on all decks," Westerly said.

"No apparent damage in engineering, Captain. It appears to have been a low-energy scan, sir, but I can't be sure until we run a diagnosis," Powers reported.

"Copy, Powers. Run the diagnosis now, if you can." The Captain sat and waited. He asked without turning his chair around, "Everyone all right?"

They all said "Yes, Captain."

The ship began to spin its cloud cover back around itself, all the colors swirling, as the cloud began to get thicker. They watched as the cloud slowly pulled away from them, farther and farther back until it disappeared completely. The Captain ordered orange alert, and all systems to be checked. He looked around the bridge at everyone, and saw Mason's bloody neck.

"Get down to the sick bay at once, Gunny. No, I said at once!" The Captain ordered. Mason left the bridge, and ran down to the hospital to get treated. As he went into the hospital, Nurse Cohen and Dr. Hassan wanted all the details on their encounter from him. She cleaned his bloody ears, and the Doctor checked his bionic implants for damage. "Your implants were overloaded, Mason. They need replacing as soon as possible to prevent any damage to your own ears and hearing capability. At least they did their job, and did not implode or explode in your ear canals. They shut down, to protect your hearing. Good thing you wore your helmet to protect them."

"Do you have replacements here, Dr. Hassan?" Mason asked, uncertain if his implants could be replaced.

"Oh, yes, Gunny. When you were assigned to the Hesperia, we were sent a backup kit for your implants. But only one extra set of each. If these next ones blow, that's it, you understand," Dr. Hassan said. "In any case, we have to prepare you for surgery at once, Mason."

Mason spent the next few minutes trying to get out of having ear surgery, to no avail. Dr. Hassan held power over everyone on the ship when it came to their health and well-being. The Doctor notified Captain Baines of Mason's condition, and confirmed his intention to operate on him immediately.

"Tell Gunny to get his ears repaired at once, Doctor. Captain out."

Mason had no choice. He went to the surgical prep area with Nurse Jones, who told him to get undressed and into a gown. Now, he was dejected, and visibly flustered. He put the drafty gown on, but refused to fully strip. He left his boots on, and paced back and forth in the tiny room. Finally, they were ready for him, and he got on the table. Nurse Jones hooked up his IV, and made him take off his boots and get back on the table and lie down. Mason was wheeled into the Surgery room, where Dr. Hassan and Nurse Cohen were scrubbed and dressed for him.

"Are you going to knock me out, Doctor?"

"We'll see. If you feel any pain, we'll sedate you. But let's see what the extent of the damage is right now." Dr. Hassan lowered the body scanner over him, as Nurse Cohen injected something into his IV tube.

"This is to calm you down, John. The next shot will be in your neck, to anesthetize you for removal of your implants." Nurse Cohen told him everything she was doing, as usual, and her steady voice calmed him much more than any drug she gave him. He had complete faith and trust in her, and Dr. Hassan.

"There is a lot of damage to your left ear implant area, son, more than I originally thought. It's best that we sedate you from this point on." The Doctor went around to Mason's IV controller, programmed it, and a vile-looking green liquid oozed out of the box, into his IV line, and directly into his veins. "Prepare him for microsurgery, Nurse Cohen."

"Now count backwards from one hundred for me, John," Nurse Cohen gently said.

"Okay. One hundred, ninety-nine, ninety-eight, ninety-seven, ninety-six, ninety-five, ninety-four, ninety-three, nine…" Mason said, slowly going under sedation. At last, he went out, and Dr. Hassan lowered the microscopic surgery machine down to Mason's ear.

"That sedative took a long time. He sure is a big fella," Nurse Jones said to Nurse Soo, both watching the operation from the viewing room.

The operation took a long time, too. Mason's left ear, being so close to the wall of the bridge, received the brunt of the blow from the very loud transmission the unidentified ship sent. The sound reverberated from the wall into his left ear, inflicting more damage than was sustained by his right ear. Dr. Hassan utilized his tiniest instruments under magnification to remove the implants from Mason's ears, and not damage his ear canal or receptors. He took his time, and was extremely careful. When the left ear implant was removed, Nurse Cohen took over, cleaning his bloody ear and canal, while the Doctor rested a few minutes. When she finished, he examined his ear canal, and was satisfied the new implant could be inserted without inflicting any damage.

The right ear implant took significantly less time to remove and be replaced. When the Doctor finished, he sat down again to rest and relax his hands, and let Nurse Cohen finish for him. She would have made an excellent surgeon, he noted. She had the touch.

Mason awoke to the sound of Nurse Cohen's voice. "John, are you awake? Come back to me. Come back to me, John. Wake up and look at me."

He opened his eyes to see her beautiful face, smiling at him. He felt a sudden wave of emotion swell over him. He felt her hand on his arm, where she had been gently shaking him out of the drug's stupor. He looked at her, and all he could whisper was, "Too bad."

"Too bad for what?" Captain Baines asked, standing at the foot of his bed. He had come in to check on his Prime Marine.

"I really have no idea, Captain. Come on, Gunny, can you sit up a little?" Her voice changed, just enough to let him know she could not allow any more of that talk in this place. Nurse Jones helped her pull him up into a sitting position, so he could awaken more fully.

"Too bad for what, Mason?" The Captain asked again.

"I, I don't remember sir. I was dreaming, I guess." Mason looked at his Captain and asked, "Is everything secure on the bridge, sir?"

"Yes, it is, Gunny. All secure. How are you feeling?"

"A little fuzzy, Captain."

"I told Lt. Commander Westerly you needed your head examined," the Captain said, smiling. "She thoroughly agreed."

Mason laughed with him about that comment. "How soon do I get out of here, ma'am?" He looked at Nurse Cohen for an answer.

"Whenever you can stand up and get dressed, Mason. You've been under quite a while. The procedure took longer than we thought it would. But, you should be all right to leave, and go rest in your quarters. You will have to rest, and readjust to your new implants for a couple of days. Remember when you received the implants initially? You'll have to give yourself time to adjust to them, as you did before." She smiled at him and the Captain, and went to notify the Doctor that his patient was up.

"Did the orange cloud come back, Captain?" Mason asked him, feeling like he had abandoned his post.

"No, it did not. It just scanned us, and left. I gave the order for mining operations to resume about four hours ago," Captain Baines said.

"Four hours ago, sir? How long have I been down here?" Mason asked. He looked at Nurse Jones accusingly.

"Over six hours, Mason. You were the usual pain in the ass for my medical staff, Gunny," the Captain said, smiling at him. "Now, get dressed, when you feel you can, and go to your quarters and rest up. Be sure to have Dr. Hassan clear you before you return to duty."

"Rest a while longer, and then you can go to your quarters, Mason," Dr. Hassan said.

"Yes, Doctor." Mason watched Captain Baines and Dr. Hassan leave the room, and all was quiet. Mason realized how close he came to creating an awkward situation for Nurse Cohen when he came out from under the sedative. He thought those feelings for her were buried deeper than they actually were. They were still there, the love, the strong attraction to her, and his admiration for her. He knew they would never really go away, just be suppressed. She was the first woman he ever loved. But, that choice was made long ago by the both of them, and he would have to accept it. Her engagement to Captain Baines was announced last month, and he would never knowingly do anything to interfere. She had made her choice. He would have to bury those feelings deeper than before. She was his best friend, and so was their Captain.

Nurse Jones came over, and asked him if he felt good enough to get dressed. "I'm going to try in a minute, Nurse Jones," Mason answered.

He took off his gown, and got dressed. Mason put his weapons belt on, and made sure he took everything he carried in with him, and left for his quarters. When the door opened, he saw Sherrie sitting inside, waiting for him. "Nurse Cohen told me you would be coming to rest, so I waited for you. How are you feeling, John?" She looked very concerned, and held him.

"I'm okay. That thing blew out my bionic ears," he replied. He knew why Nurse Cohen called Sherrie, because of his waking whisper to her, heard by everyone. But that was all right. Sherrie was special to him. She was his friend, and his lover. He cared a great deal for her.

"How long do you have to wear those bandages over your ears, John?" She asked, looking at his ears, and back into his eyes.

"Just until Dr. Hassan okays me to take them off. He put new implants in for me, and they take a little getting used to. But I'll be better by tomorrow, maybe even back to work then."

Sherrie kissed him gently, and said, "We knew something happened when the red alert went off. Then, this loud noise came, and everyone held their ears until it stopped. I thought of you on the bridge, and hoped you were okay." She kissed him again, and Mason joined in, this time. But his ears began to throb.

"I was sedated for the surgery, honey, and I'm still a little woozy. I don't mean to ignore you, but I need to lie down now." She nodded, and helped him take off his belt and boots. She switched open his bunk-drawer, helped him take off his uniform, and put him to bed, alone.

"I'll come back in the morning to check on you, John. I left you some cookies and a sandwich in your fridge, in case you get hungry." She tucked him in, gave him a little kiss, and started to leave.

"Thanks for being here, Sherrie. Means a lot to me," Mason softly said to her. He held out his hand to her, and she took his hand and gave it a squeeze.

"You mean a lot to me, John," she said, crying. She closed his door behind her.

XX

Probes launched from the Hesperia scanned the two incoming asteroids, and analyzed their composition as common iron and magnesium for the smaller one; but the "Big Peanut" contained platinum grade metals, in both of its halves. Mission Director Keene was insistent in his requests to harvest those precious ores, as soon as possible. The Hesperia would have to go get the spinning rock first, and then Keene could work on the best method to harvest its metals. It would be in range in one week.

Captain Baines was appreciative of the Big Peanut's value to the mission, but he was obsessed with the orange cloud. The orange cloud ship was alien to Earth, yet understood his communications well enough to translate its message to them into plain English. Its occupants were obviously superior to the men and women on the Hesperia, yet made no overtly aggressive maneuvers. What did they want?

A meeting was set with Mission Director Keene, Coordinator Garcia, Chief Technician Takeda, and the Captain's planning officers. Baines elected to stay on the bridge, since two of the officers attending were in his command staff. He decided to have his dinner in the ready room, in case anything came up. He invited Mason to join him and Nurse Cohen for dinner.

Mason had been saving a question to ask the Captain, and this was the perfect opportunity. "Captain, may I ask you a question about the orange cloud, sir?"

"Please, Mason, go ahead," he said, fully attentive.

Mason began carefully. "Sir, do you remember colony GK-356, sir? The crazy lady scientist said that one of their members, a Dr. James, left the colony with the people from the red cloud, remember, Captain?"

"Yes, now that you mention it, I do. I didn't give it much thought at the time, because of her, well, her condition. All of their minds were affected by their starvation," Baines added, for Nurse Cohen's sake.

"What if she told the truth, and her red cloud was the same as our orange cloud?" Mason looked at his Captain. "That opens up a whole new set of questions for us, doesn't it, sir?"

"Yes, it does. I'll have to bring that up at our next status update with the Admiral. Put it on the agenda, Mason." The Captain frowned, and typed something onto his com tablet.

The knock on the door from the steward was a welcome break from the serious conversation about the orange cloud for Nurse Cohen. She looked at the men, eating in silence, and said, "There's a reason I asked to have dinner with the two of you tonight."

Captain Baines looked at her as if she just spoke in a foreign language; then he got on track with her. "Yes, there is. Nurse Cohen and I have something to ask you, Gunny."

Mason put his fork down. "Yes, Captain, ma'am?" Defenses up!

"You know that we are engaged to be married, Mason," the Captain started. Mason nodded his head. "We are to be married in four weeks, in a formal military wedding, with both of our families there via live vid cams. The Admiral will officiate, and marry us." The Captain looked lovingly at Nurse Cohen, who returned his gaze. She turned back to look at Mason.

"Since we are having a traditional military wedding, I require someone to walk me down the aisle. I'd be honored if you'd walk me down the aisle, John." Mason was stunned for a moment hearing those words. He not only had to see her marry another man, but he would be giving her away to him.

"I would be honored to walk you down the aisle, ma'am," he answered, and tried to smile. "I was just hoping for an invitation."

"Of course you are invited! Without you, there would most likely be no wedding! I probably wouldn't even be here, or I'd be split into two people, like our Captain Kouras," the Captain said.

"You were poisoned with a neurotoxin, Captain. You didn't receive the psychotropic drug cocktail like poor Captain Kouras. You don't have the brain damage he has," Nurse Cohen quietly corrected.

"No, you're right, Nurse Cohen, I'd be dead, or paralyzed." They looked at each other. "Nevertheless," the Captain continued, "of course you're invited, Mason. You'll be walking my future wife down the aisle." He smiled proudly, and looked again at her.

"I'm assuming mess dress, Nurse Cohen?" Mason asked.

"Of course. You have your mess dress with you, don't you, John?" She asked him.

"Yes ma'am. Just have to get the insignia changed, then I'm ready," he said quietly. His heart was in his throat. He still loved her so much.

"Mine too, Gunny," the Captain acknowledged, turning to type something into his com tablet again. Nurse Cohen shook her head.

Mason laughed, and so did the happy couple. Then the comm-link buzzed, bringing them back to business.

"Captain Baines, this is Davis. We have a question for you, sir."

"Go ahead, Davis."

"The asteroid will be in range in one week, Captain. We estimate that it will take approximately four days to intercept and match the asteroid's speed, and another three days' pursuit to catch it, sir."

Baines acknowledged. "Yes, I'm aware of that time schedule."

"Well, sir, it will take another two weeks to tow it back to the mining fields, Captain."

"Yes?" The Captain didn't catch his line of inquiry, but Mason and Nurse Cohen did, looking at each other after the Captain's response.

"Well, sir, will it interfere with your wedding plans?" Davis asked.

"I'll get back to you, Davis." Captain Baines switched off the comm-link. He looked at Nurse Cohen, whose countenance changed dramatically.

Mason was staying out of this one. He excused himself, and left the ready room.

After work, he went to the mess hall, and found Sherrie making next week's schedule. She fed him dinner, and he invited her out. "Let's go to the sports bar tonight, and grab a beer."

"All right. Meet you in the bar in about half an hour, okay?" She got up to leave.

"Make it twenty minutes, or I'll start drinking without you," he said, and left.

He waited more than an hour for her, but she made it worth his wait. She arrived wearing a lovely dress, with high heels on, hair and make-up done very nicely. The crewmen at the bar with Mason noticed her arrival immediately, and they all told her how great she looked. He was the proudest man in the whole place at that moment, and offered her his seat at the crowded bar. "You know, your secret's out, now, Sherrie," he commented, leaning close to her.

"What secret?" She immediately bristled.

"Now that the guys have seen how beautiful you really are, they'll all want you," he said, and she blushed.

"You're teasing me again," she said, lowering her head a little.

"Sherrie, every man here knows it. Look at them, drooling in their beers. I'll be lucky if I don't have to fight my way out of here with you tonight." He looked at her and smiled, and he could see she appreciated his comments to her. He was honest with her, and made it a point to always be that way. Mason generously shared Sherrie's attention with the other crewmen at the bar. When dance music played, he wanted to dance with her, but she refused. He was an accomplished dancer, although few on the ship knew.

They left the bar, strolling around the Esplanade. Mason always enjoyed showing her off, and tonight was no exception. A few women were dressed in street clothes, like Sherrie, but no one looked better than she did, and Mason knew it.

As they rounded the corner by the spa, they saw Lt. Commander Westerly with Lieutenant St. Marten, chatting with each other, standing a respectable distance from each other. Mason realized at that moment that his XO was probably gay. She wished Mason and Sherrie a good night, and continued her leisurely stroll with the Lieutenant.

They ended the evening at Sherrie's quarters. Mason showered and came out with a towel wrapped low around his waist. She sat at her table in her nightgown, waiting on him. She looked at him, at his torso and washboard abs, and leaned back, smiling. The body of Adonis, she thought, and he's mine tonight. She reached out to touch his chest, and let her finger slowly slide down to his waist, and put her fingers around his towel. She pulled him closer, and took off his towel very slowly. Without a word, she ran her hand up his thigh to his groin, taking his hard cock in her hand, and put her lips on him, teasing him and tantalizing him. When she placed her mouth around him, and began to give him a harder pleasure, he had to hold his hand against the wall for balance. He threw his head back as she slowly drove him to ecstasy. Mason went down on his knees and parted her long legs, kissing the inside of her thighs. He raised her legs over his shoulder, and nestled his mouth down on her to return the favor.

He drove her wild with his tongue. As she reached climax, she held onto the back of the chair, her body raised completely up in John's arms. After a short break, Sherrie stood up, sat him down on the chair, and mounted him, saying, "I'll do the hard work tonight, John." He loved every minute of her passion running wild all over him. They enjoyed their evening thoroughly.

The next morning, the incoming bridge crew found new orders waiting for them from the Captain. They were not going to wait for the "Big Peanut" to come to them, the Hesperia was going to go get it. Mason laughed silently to himself, remembering the look on Nurse Cohen's face. So, the wedding would not be postponed. The Hesperia's schedule would be changed, not Nurse Cohen's wedding to the Captain. Chalk up one for the ladies.

Lieutenant Davis had the plans all designed and ready to be entered into the ship's programs; all he needed was the final "Go" from Captain Baines. The Hesperia was put through all her system checks and tests, and passed them with flying colors. The mining operations were closed down in Section 4, the mighty claws and basket retracted for storage during the pursuit.

The chase was on. The Hesperia was on an intercept course with the Big Peanut. She would be in range within two more days, and plans for the actual intercept and capture of the asteroid were in place. Lieutenant Davis and Lt. Commander Westerly ran simulations testing sequences on the ship's computer for three days, preparing for all contingencies. They practiced their maneuvers with holographic models dozens of times, to be as prepared as possible to intercept and capture the flying rock.

Once the asteroid was in range, the Hesperia slowed to full standard speed to match speed and course with the Big Peanut. The ship stayed a safe distance ahead of the rock, and fired wide field, low-level plasma bursts head-on into the asteroid to slow its speed, without damaging it.

When the asteroid was slowed to one-quarter speed, Captain Baines aimed the plasma bursts at different points on the asteroid to not only slow its forward speed, but also slow its spinning. The Big Peanut was spinning end over end and wobbling at 25 degrees, plus or minus one, about its axis. When it came into sight of the bridge, it initially appeared to be a flying "X." Now its wobbling rotation was slowed significantly, and final preparations to catch the Big Peanut within the next twenty-four hours began in earnest.

A special metallic container specifically designed to capture an asteroid was utilized to catch the Big Peanut. The large metallic container, called the "glove," by the miners, was stored in its special compartment on the outer hull of Section 4, folded flat. Once its compartment doors opened, it would automatically open and unfold itself. The bottom of the container held small thruster engines on its underside, to maneuver the glove into position directly in front of the asteroid, once it was fully opened. The timing must be precise for a successful catch, else the asteroid and the glove might collide, and be lost in space.

Captain Baines ordered the launching of shuttles one and two at 0-nine-thirty for direct observation of the glove deployment, and the subsequent asteroid catch. Lt. Commander Westerly rode in shuttle 1 and Lieutenant Roshkov in shuttle 2.

Captain Baines gave a short countdown to begin glove deployment at precisely ten hundred hours. The giant hatch door seals were released, and the doors slowly began to open.

"Lt. Commander Westerly, Captain. The glove hatch doors are opening, sir, and the glove has begun to unfold," she reported. She reported the glove's opening progress at every thirty degree mark achieved by the hatch door. At one hundred eighty degrees, when the door completely opened and came to rest against the hull, it automatically locked itself down onto the hull. The glove continued its automatic unfolding for thirty minutes, until the massive container was fully restored to its bucket shape. It was much larger than Section 4 of the Hesperia. It was gigantic.

"Lieutenant Davis, assume control of the glove, and release it. Then move it into position," Captain said, watching closely on the front vid screens.

"I have control of the glove, Captain. I am moving the glove one thousand meters away from our hull," Davis said, "and now the glove is being rotated to position its opening directly in front of the Big Peanut."

The glove slowly closed in on the asteroid. "Lieutenant Davis, when the glove is in position, encapsulate the asteroid." The Captain was completely fixated on the glove and its target. Mason was watching the maneuvers, enjoying the full view from the bridge's front screen.

"Sir, the glove has reached the asteroid," Davis said.

"Steady now Davis, you're right on target," Captain Baines said, getting out of his chair to stand closer to the screens.

"Sir, the asteroid has entered the glove."

"Shuttles 1 and 2 at the ready for capture. Steady now, Davis," the Captain cautioned.

Everyone on the bridge and Mission Control was holding their breath at this point. "Captain, the asteroid is encapsulated inside the glove," Davis said a little louder. "Captain Baines, the glove is full."

"Shuttles 1 and 2, close in on your target, wait for my signal. Lieutenant Davis, close the glove," the Captain said calmly.

"The glove is closed, Captain," Davis said, relieved.

"Shuttles 1 and 2 launch tether lines at your target." Baines placed his hands on his hips.

All was silent as everyone watched the tether lines descend towards the container. This moment seemed even tenser than the encapsulating maneuver to Mason. The tether lines slowly came down along either side of the glove.

"Davis, release the gloves' tow rings," Baines ordered, and watched intently as giant rings on both sides of the container opened to a ninety degree angle.

"Catch your fish, shuttles 1 and 2." Captain Baines, as well as everyone else observing the procedure live, breathlessly watched as the shuttles advanced to attach their tethering lines' hooks to the container's giant rings.

"Shuttle 2 to Captain Baines, we've caught our sturgeon, sir!" Roshkov said proudly.

"Shuttle 1 to Captain, we have our fish, sir," Lt. Commander Westerly said, relieved.

The entire bridge and Mission Control erupted in cheers. The Captain said, "All right now, shuttles 1 and 2, bring your fish in," and he returned to his chair.

The two shuttles towed the glove and its asteroid captive closer to the

Section 4 aft doors. The Captain ordered the Hesperia to full stop. The last step to secure the glove for towing was to affix the heavier towing lines to the gloves' giant rings. The thick towing cables were released, one at a time, and let out slowly until they reached the giant rings. Lieutenant Davis maneuvered the two cables to the rings, opened the tow latches, and secured the cables to the rings.

"Towing lines attached and locked down, Captain. The glove is secure and ready for towing," Lieutenant Davis reported. The shuttles released their tethers, and the thinner lines floated freely behind the glove.

"Mission Director Keene, this is Captain Baines. We have your asteroid securely in tow, and are ready to change course back to your mining fields."

"A magnificent job, Captain. Your crews' performance was flawless. Send the Prime Marine down here to pick up my charge crystal. The drinks are on me tonight. Keene out." More cheering went up from the bridge crew.

"Shuttles 1 and 2 come home. Baines out."

After the shuttles were safely inside and locked down in their bay and the outer doors closed, the Captain sent Mason to Director Keene for his charge crystal.

Keene got up and went to his closet, returning with a big black box. He handed the box to Mason and said, "This is a private gift from me personally, to your Captain. He did one hell of a job. And this is for the crew and your shuttle pilots. Tell them to use it all up; I don't want it back." He handed Mason an expense account charge crystal with "URE" cut into it.

Mason thanked him and went back to the bridge, and delivered the black box and Keene's message. "Put the box in my ready room, Mason. Did he give you the charge crystal?"

"Yes, sir. He told me to keep it and buy drinks for the crew," Mason said.

"That's fine, Gunny. You can host everyone at the 6pm shift change," Baines said, returning to his log. Mason did as he was told, and placed the black box in the ready room.

"Marston, get Admiral Tomiko on my private vid screen. I'll take it in the ready room." Baines gave the chair to Lieutenant Davis and went to his ready room, locking the door.

"Admiral Tomiko here."

"Admiral, this is Captain Baines. We successfully captured the asteroid and have it in tow, and are proceeding at full standard speed back to the mining fields, sir."

"I know. Keene already notified me. Said your crew did a hell of a job, Captain."

"Yes, sir, they did," Baines said. "Was there something, else, Admiral?"

"Yes. Earth Command has no record of Dr. James being found, dead or alive, on GK-356. Perhaps the red cloud story is true. It could be one and the same as your orange cloud, Baines. Be extremely careful. Earth Command thinks that orange cloud ship might come back. You handled that situation well, Baines. But - be careful! Tomiko out."

The Captain read his "Approved for Promotions" list on the vid screen, along with a few more orders, when he noticed the black box from Keene. He peeked inside, and a smile came to his face. He held up a large bottle of 50 year-old Louis XIII cognac, in a gold-etched decanter, complete with two decorated snifters, etched in gold around their rims. He decided to save it for his wedding night, knowing Rachel would enjoy it just as much as he. He hid the box in his suite, on the highest shelf in his closet.

Baines had one more task to complete, an unpleasant one, to be completed tonight, per orders. He called for Mason to escort him, fully armed. The Captain told him, "We have unfinished business to attend to, Gunny, and Earth Command wants it done tonight."

Mason followed the Captain, who took Westerly with them. She glanced sideways at Mason, in full gear, helmeted, carrying his laser rifle. He led them to the brig. The Captain ordered the brig Chief to shut down all lights except Lieutenant Urz's cell, and put spotlights on him. He ordered his visit recorded. Lieutenant Urz was deep asleep. Mason announced loudly, "Captain on deck. All hands, attention!"

Lieutenant Urz jumped up and stood at attention.

The Captain ordered, "Jailer, chain the prisoner for interrogation." Urz was chained to the wall of his cell, not showing any emotion. He kept his eyes forward.

"Open the cell doors." The plex doors opened, and the three of them entered. They quarter-turned to face Lieutenant Urz.

"Lieutenant Urz, you have been held in this cell pending formal charges. Have you been treated well, with all respect and courtesy due an officer of your rank?" The Captain asked.

"Yes, sir."

"Have you been physically abused, hit, tortured, or received any acts of aggression, intimidation, coercion, or psychological abuse directed at your person?" Baines asked.

"No, sir." Urz stared straight ahead.

"Lieutenant Urz, have you received an offer to consult with an attorney?" Baines queried.

"Yes, sir. I declined legal representation, sir," Urz stated.

"Then, Lieutenant Urz, as Captain of the mining freighter Hesperia, it is my duty to formally charge you today." The Captain pulled out his com tablet, and read a list of twenty-three charges against Urz, first and foremost, sabotage against a Space Forces ship and her crew. "Do you

179

understand the formal charges brought against you by Earth Command?"

"Yes, sir," Urz replied.

"Then, how do you plead, Lieutenant Urz?" The Captain stared him squarely in the eye, as Urz looked straight ahead.

"Guilty as charged, on all counts sir." Urz never moved.

"Then by the authority vested in me by Earth Command, you are hereby stripped of all rank, privileges, and pay, and are now a prisoner of non-rank. Should you choose to provide substantial, meaningful information during the interrogation sessions that will follow, your actions may prove you worthy of a court-martial, and reinstatement of some privileges. Is that understood, Prisoner NR?" The Captain addressed him loudly and emphatically, and Urz never moved a muscle, or flinched.

"Yes, sir."

"Prisoner NR, do you have any information to volunteer at this time?" The Captain asked, staring at the young man.

"No, sir." Urz's eyes were beginning to get red.

"Then you will be subjected to interviews and interrogations at our will, in any manner we see fit to administer." The Captain turned to face Westerly, and said, "Interrogate Prisoner NR, Lt. Commander Westerly. Gunnery Sergeant Mason, you will stay and assist the Lt. Commander with her interrogation. Remove your helmet, rifle, and weapons belt, and give them to me." The Captain took Mason's gear, called for the cell door to be opened, and left the cell. Captain Baines gave Mason's gear to a crewman, who stood by him at guard.

Lt. Commander Westerly was not prepared for this task; Mason could read her eyes plainly. He asked, "Does the Lt. Commander wish me to interrogate the prisoner at this time?"

"Yes, Gunnery Sergeant, begin the interrogation. By the book," she added firmly.

"Prisoner NR, state your name for the records." Mason asked several questions to establish Urz' name, former rank, serial numbers, quarters location, and so on. Once the foundation was set, he began a new line of questioning.

"Mr. Urz, who approached you to commit sabotage against the Hesperia?" Silence.

"Mr. Urz, we know the extent of your actions, and probable outcomes of those actions if you succeeded. We also are aware of the distraction put into place that gave the opportunity for your sabotage to commence. You could not have accomplished this alone. So I ask you again, Mr. Urz, who approached you to commit sabotage against the ship?" Silence again; but Mason could see that the chains were beginning to irritate him.

"Since you have refused to answer any of my questions, I now ask Lt. Commander Westerly for permission to treat you as a non-cooperative prisoner of war." Urz quickly looked at Mason, and then resumed looking ahead.

Both Mason and Westerly caught the eye movement. Westerly walked in front of Urz, looked at him, and said evenly to him, "I ask you to tell me who put you up to this, Mr. Urz." But he remained silent. "I will have you systematically subjected to more physical methods of interrogation, in different environments. I will have you deprived of sleep, food, water, cleanliness, and light. I will keep you in shackles twenty-four hours a day, and forced to stand at attention or receive the shackles' intensive shocks." Still no reaction from Urz.

She stepped right in front of him, right in his face. Mason moved directly next to her. "I can and will do these things to you, Mr. Urz. I might even grow to enjoy doing things to you." He finally looked at her face, directly into her eyes.

Mason could see that Urz was about to lose his composure. He quickly stepped in front of Westerly and took the blow Urz intended for her. Mason subdued him in a head-lock and took him down to the floor, and held him.

"Now we have another charge against you, Mr. Urz: assaulting a command officer. You will never get out of here like this, Mr. Urz. Gunny, stand Prisoner NR up, and hold him by his chains." Mason did as commanded.

"Now, Mr. Urz, if you do not answer my questions, the next time I return I will not be nice to you. Once again; who recruited you to sabotage the Hesperia?" Urz was determined to hold his tongue.

"Very well, Mr. Urz. You are from this moment on to be treated as a self-admitted saboteur, a prisoner of war. You will be shackled, manacled, and chained to the wall of your cell in complete darkness twenty-four hours a day. You will be placed on half-rations and water until I decide differently. You will not be allowed any exercise or bathing privileges. From this moment forth, you have no name other than "Prisoner NR." You have no privileges other than what I give you. You have no rights. This is your only chance to speak in your own defense." She paused, and waited. Urz was silent. She began the final wrap-up of his initial interrogation.

"Do you willingly submit to my interrogations?"

"Yes, sir."

"Do you willingly sacrifice your rights and all privileges?"

"Yes, sir." He said that one forcefully, Mason noted.

"Very well then, Prisoner NR." She turned away from Urz towards the guards above. "Jailer, you will tighten his chains, restricting his movements. When I leave, he is to be placed in total darkness, 24/7. He is to receive half-rations and water, and make sure they're food pouches, served cold. His name is now "Prisoner NR." He has willingly sacrificed all his rights.

All privileges are hereby removed. He is to receive no exercise or bathing. He is now a prisoner of war." She stepped back one pace. They tightened Urz's chains, hanging the chains on the highest available hook in his cell.

"We will talk again, Prisoner NR," Westerly stated. "Open the cell door." With that command she and Mason left the cell. The brig lights came up, and Urz's cell went pitch black. Captain Baines handed Mason his gear, and the three of them went back to the bridge in silence. The Captain led them to the ready room, and sat down. "Please sit down. We will now discuss our interview with Prisoner NR, for the record." The Captain turned to his control console, and then said, "Full recording, begin now." He conducted their de-briefing very formally.

Mason and the Captain knew the routine well. But it was all new to Westerly. Mason knew all the line officers from Lieutenant and higher received interrogation procedural training, as had he, when he became a Prime Marine. This was another hard lesson in the realities of deep space military life for the Lt. Commander. Facing a real flesh and blood prisoner, especially a fellow officer, and conducting an interrogation complete with threats and other coercive tactics was no easy task.

"This concludes the interrogation de-briefing. Recording stop." The Captain sat back in his chair, and looked at them both. "I was ordered by Admiral Tomiko to formally charge Urz and interrogate him today. He surprised me by fully admitting guilt on all charges and waiving his right to an attorney. That took his interrogation down a completely different path."

Baines shifted in his seat. "In order to be considered for promotion to full Commander, an officer must have interrogation experience with a prisoner of war, field intelligence experience, combat experience, or all the above. The first interrogation is never quick or easy, especially with a fellow officer. Urz made it very difficult for you, Lt. Commander, and you were up to the challenge. Your only mistake was not reading his eyes and anticipating his attack, but Gunny did."

The Lt. Commander looked at Mason with more understanding. "You took that body blow for me, Gunnery Sergeant, and I thank you," she said quietly.

"Yes, ma'am. I am here to help you, ma'am," Mason responded.

"We will let Urz stand and suffer a little today and tomorrow. We will visit him in three days, Lt. Commander, so be prepared for an unpleasant session," Baines predicted.

"Unpleasant, how, sir?" She asked.

"Gunny, want to answer?" The Captain smiled a little.

"He'll stink worse than anything; no bath or toilet privileges for three days. He will have soiled himself royally. And I may puke, ma'am," Mason said.

The Captain laughed at Mason's last sentence. "Mason has bionic implants for heightened hearing, sight, and smell. So be prepared, Lt. Commander. But, that's three days from now, unless Urz wants to talk first. For tonight, I want you to go to your quarters and rest for an hour. Then meet me in the main lounge at seventeen forty-five. The URE is sponsoring a party for us, celebrating our successful capture of Mission Director Keene's Big Peanut. And I have a few more surprises up my sleeve, as well. Dismissed."

Captain Baines took advantage of the great party provided by the Mission Director to hand out crew and officer promotions, to everyone's delight. Davis, Powers, and Chief Dawson were among those promoted. The party lasted several hours before the crowd thinned out. Mason found Sr. Chief Dawson, and they left together, and went to Mason's quarters.

Sherrie was very quiet, and was not celebrating her promotion. "I've never kissed a Senior Chief before," Mason said, holding her and smiling. He kissed her until she warmed up to him. "Are you going to tell me what's wrong, Sherrie? You don't look like someone who just got a promotion. Why aren't you happy tonight?" She laid her head against his chest. "C'mon, Sherrie, what is it? Did somebody say something to upset you? You know you can tell me."

"Let's talk about it another time, okay?" She buried her face in his neck. He began to kiss her softly, until she kissed him in return. They made love until they fell asleep, satiated and spent. But Mason woke up early the next morning to see his door closing behind her.

XXI

The trip back to the mining fields was almost over, and the Big Peanut was securely in tow. Mission Director Keene advised Captain Baines that the miners would mine the asteroid while it remained encapsulated in its glove, so as to harvest as much of the precious metals as possible.

The prisoner Urz got frustrated from being bound in chains and shackles; he tried to get out of them, and was electronically shocked multiple times. The neck shackle was particularly effective with him. He struggled violently against it, and passed out from trying to tear it off his neck. He asked for the Captain.

Captain Baines took Mason with him to the brig immediately upon receiving the news about Urz, went to his cell, ordered a little light brought up, and confronted him.

"Prisoner NR, we are here at your request. What information do you wish to share?" The Captain began.

"I want these things off me now!" Urz screamed, trying again to pull himself out of the chains. He reeked of his own sweat. "Let me loose, and I'll tell you his name," Urz offered.

"It doesn't work that way. We control the chains, and whether they remain on you, or off. You tell us what we want to know," the Captain rebutted, and sat in a chair opposite Urz. "Who recruited you?"

"I never knew his name, just the Yellow Man," Urz said with a shake of his head.

Captain Baines asked, "When and where did he recruit you?"

"Moon Base. He had more slices in his pocket than I'd ever seen. He told me I could have them, and more, if I'd help him. He said I could be a millionaire," Urz revealed. "Now let me go!" Urz started twisting, and his neck shackle sent him another shock. "It hurts! Stop it!"

The Captain calmly spoke to Urz. "You actually control the mechanism.

Release his left leg from the chains, Mason." Mason released his leg, and stood back by the Captain. "Now, what did the Yellow Man look like, and what did he ask you to do?"

"He gave me ten thousand in slices, and gave me two things to do at first. Then he said I'd get ten thousand more every time I did something for him," he answered.

"What were the two things you did for him, Prisoner NR?" Baines asked.

"I copied the ship's manual and the communications keys for him," Urz said, smirking.

"The Hesperia manual of tech and computer specs?" The Captain sat forward. "What else did he ask you to do?"

"He said that, after I'd done everything for him, I'd have to escape in a shuttle. He had me program coordinates into a shuttle on board," Urz proudly reported.

"Jailer, bring up ambient lighting a little for Prisoner NR. Mason, release his other leg from the chains. Now, see how easy this is? You give me information, and I help you. Understand?" The Captain sat back, and watched Mason unchain his leg.

The dim lights showed a very different man than two days ago. His clothing was soaked with sweat, and his pants were soiled, front and back. His pride was gone.

"Now, Prisoner NR, what did this Yellow Man look like?" Baines asked.

"He was tall, I guess, and looked a little funny; you know, strange. With a pointy mouth. Bald. Pale yellow clothing. Hat, shoes, shirt, pants. All yellow."

"How did you meet him, Prisoner NR?" Baines sat back in his chair.

"I heard he was looking for officers boarding the Hesperia," Urz answered.

Captain Baines asked, "Did he say why the Hesperia?" Urz just shook his head. "Did you see any other crewmen or officers with him?" Another negative response.

"Did the Yellow Man ask you to kill anyone, either the scientists or one of the Captains?" Baines enquired.

"No. He just said there would be several deaths on board before the ship came home. Said I'd be safer working for him. Now let me go! I want to take a shower!" Urz started struggling again, and got another neck shock.

"How did he contact you?" Baines asked.

"You know. I modified the hand-held communicators on the shuttle. Data transmissions," Urz answered, smirking.

"When did he contact you to attack the ship's communications systems?" The Captain asked, sounding a bit more firm.

Urz was silent for a moment. He looked at Mason and the Captain, sighed heavily, and stated: "He sent the unauthorized communications transmission the day before. He sent me the programming instructions via data packets. Practically untraceable nowadays."

The Captain sat forward. "How many times did he communicate with you?"

"Only two transmissions, both the day before my attack," Urz replied.

The Captain was almost finished. "What stopped you from completing your sabotage, Prisoner NR?"

"I got the programming instructions too late to memorize them completely." Urz sounded disappointed with himself.

Captain Baines' mind was processing all the recent information that Urz had poured out to him. Mason leaned down and whispered, "Captain, may I?" Baines gave him the nod.

"Prisoner NR, it is my turn to ask questions. Raise the cell lighting a little higher, jailer." Mason stood right in front of Urz.

"Did the Yellow Man recruit anyone else from the Hesperia?" Mason asked firmly.

Urz became defensive. "Yes, two more that I saw. But I never met them."

Mason demanded, "What department? What color was their work shirt?"

"One wore green, like me. The other wore blue," he said.

"Prisoner NR, there are three separate crews who wear green: Communications; Engineering; and the shuttle pilots. Which section?" Mason asked. "Can you describe them?"

"I don't know, I'm sorry. I never saw them again, on the bridge, or anywhere else." Urz was getting tired.

"Prisoner NR, you've done real good. The Captain will let you have a shower and clean clothes tonight, and you may even get to lie down and sleep. Just one more question. How did you get paid the $10,000 while you were on the Hesperia, and where did you hide it?" Mason's voice was almost friendly.

"The slice was in an envelope, under my pillow." He looked down.

Mason saw the movement. "And where did you put it?" No response from Urz. "We need to test it for prints and DNA, you understand. You'll get it back," Mason lied.

Urz raised his foot and wiggled it at Mason. He laughed at him. "In your boots? You're a genius, Prisoner NR." Mason stepped back behind the Captain.

Baines asked, "Will you tell me why you agreed to do these things for the Yellow Man?"

"The money, at first. When I didn't want to do anything else, he said he'd kill me if I didn't reprogram the comm system, so I reprogrammed it; at least I started to." Urz was really tired now.

"Do you think there are others on board he recruited?" Baines asked.

Urz chuckled. "I'm sure. Ten thousand freedom dollars is a lot of money, Captain."

"Yes, it is, Prisoner NR. Did he tell you his future plans?" Baines asked.

"Only that we'd all be taken off the ship by New Years' Day, and wouldn't have to stay seven years." Urz began laughing. "Watch out, it's only three months' away! We were all leaving by New Years' Day."

"What code key should we use to decipher those transmissions?" The Captain asked.

Urz smiled. "The Hesperia tech manual. Start on page 357, odd pages, even paragraphs, letter skip sequence." He was proud of that key.

The Captain called for the cell doors to be opened, gave his authorization for Urz to get showered and receive clean clothes. He took Urz's nasty, piss-soaked boots, and left with Mason.

Several of the officers who were promoted were entitled to upgrade their quarters, as well as some of the enlisted crewmen. Mason knew Sherrie would get to move to a studio with a real bed, and leave the bunk drawer behind, for good. He went to the mess hall for lunch, hoping to see her and volunteer to help her move. She hadn't been with him in days, and was avoiding him.

When Mason got his food and sat down, the Senior Chief came over to him. "This is for you," Mason said, handing her his note. "I'd like to volunteer to help you move to your new quarters, when you're ready."

"I may stay. I don't know. Moving is such a hassle," she said, looking tired.

"You deserve it, Senior Chief. I'll get a couple of Space Marines to help, and we'll move you. You'll be all moved like that," Mason said, snapping his fingers. He smiled at her. "You just say when, and I'll be there for you," implying much more than just an offer to move her quarters. He stood up, and took his tray. "Will you call me? I'd love to talk with you."

"Maybe," she said, tucking his note inside her chest pocket. She turned and left.

Mason hoped she'd read his note, and not forget and toss it in the laundry with her jacket. He wrote to her: "I miss your smile. Whatever's wrong, we can make it right, together. You're my sunlight. You mean so much to me. John. XOXOXO."

He left for his new mission. Urz said one blue shirt, and one green. He took his com tablet and wore his weapons belt and side arm, for surprise inspections of the maintenance department and the engineering deck, utilizing his "Special Security Chief" title. He met the crewmen he had not met before, who worked the second shift. He notated meeting them and their names, and took brief physical descriptions of each man. Mason knew there had to be one or more assassins on board, called to readiness since Lieutenant Miller's death and Stone's capture. Urz said the Yellow Man promised several deaths, and that they'd all leave by New Years' Day. There remained very little time to locate probable suspects. He typed in a meeting request with Captain Baines for tomorrow, at his convenience. The Captain was target #1.

Mason was also concerned about the Captain's wedding to Nurse Cohen. What better time to kill officers than at a wedding, when they'd all be in one physical location together, distracted by a formal military wedding. It was common knowledge that the wedding was to be held in the general assembly hall. What a perfect place for a mass murder.

It was shortly before midnight when Mason got back to his quarters. His secret "tell" on his door was broken; someone had been in his room. He drew his sidearm and entered carefully, and found Sherrie asleep in his bed. He gently closed and locked his door, and put his sidearm and weapons belt away. He brushed his teeth as quietly as he could, undressed, and got into his bunk drawer next to her. She stirred a little, and asked, "John?"

"I'm right here. Go back to sleep." She turned on her side, and they lay like two spoons in a drawer, and went to sleep. In a few hours, her alarm went off, and they got up. They only had time for a few kisses and the promise to get together tonight, before she had to leave. But something was wrong, and it was something important; Mason could feel it. Did he do something wrong? Did he not do something he should have? He showered and shaved, and got dressed. Since he was up earlier than usual, he decided to make up for his light fare the day before. He went to the mess hall and ordered a big breakfast, double bacon, juice and coffee. He picked a middle table, and sat down to feast.

"I figured you'd come in early, Gunny," Sr. Chief Dawson said, coming up to his table. He immediately stood and went around the table to hold a chair for her to sit, and she obliged. "Where were you last night?" She asked softly.

"Conducting surprise inspections in maintenance and engineering. I have to do inspections periodically as Special Security Chief. I wouldn't have gone, if I knew you were coming to visit me," he answered.

"I read your note," she said. "It was nice, John," she told him, looking down.

"When can we talk about it, Sherrie?" Mason asked. She looked at him, noticing that he never touched his breakfast. "I know this isn't the right time or place," he added.

"Tonight, if you want to. I'm not trying to put you off, John, it's just ..." she began to get red-eyed. A few more crewmen entered the mess hall, and she looked down again.

"Tonight it is. How about I come by around nineteen hundred? Maybe help you move, too? I'll make sure your new quarters are ready for you tonight, okay?" He waited for her answer.

"Well, I guess so, if you know where it is," she answered apprehensively.

"Great! We'll get you all moved into a nicer, bigger place. A suite, actually. You can stretch out both arms and not touch the walls," he said, smiling at her.

Sherrie looked at him, at his handsome face and wide smile. She smiled a little in return, all she could muster for the time being. She thanked him, and went straight to her office, closed the door, and turned the lock. Facing away from the window, she picked up her com tablet, pretending to read something, as tears ran down her face onto the tablet's screen and down to the floor. She was hopelessly in love with John Mason. But could she talk with him about this?

The Captain ran the engineering systems check, and evaluated the status of the ship and the mining operations. Around ten hundred, he gave Westerly command, and took Mason into the ready room. Mason updated him with his surprise inspections, and showed him his cross-referenced personnel list. "Captain, may I ask you a question, sir?" Mason asked.

"Of course. What is it?" The Captain replied.

"Captain, please assume for a few minutes that you are the new assassin working for the Yellow Man." Mason was getting better asking hypothetical questions.

"Okay, go on," the Captain said, suddenly interested.

"Sir, I'd like you to consider a certain scenario. You're the assassin, and your primary target is the ship's captain. Your secondary targets are probably the line command officers. You identify a time and place when they will all be together and away from their primary stations." The Captain nodded, and Mason continued. "Your job is to kill officers and cause as much panic and pandemonium as possible, so that the Yellow Man can take the ship, and you will escape with a lot of money during the chaos." Baines nodded, so Mason continued.

"Captain, the general assembly hall is wide open, accessible from eight sets of doors, through three corridors, the main mess hall, and the main lounge." Mason saw the Captain's face change. "Not to put a damper on your plans, sir, but after interrogating Urz, frankly, I'm concerned, sir," Mason said in all seriousness.

"My fiancé is not going to want to hear this, Gunny," the Captain said, disappointedly.

"Please, sir, let me make arrangements to hold the ceremony in a small room, and the walk-through and your reception in the main lounge. I can observe the situation and control the crowd better. You'll be an open target. And, Nurse Cohen will be, too, sir," Mason warned.

"What do you recommend, Mason?"

"Sir, I recommend the actual ceremony take place in the observation lounge. It's smaller, and only open on one side. The wedding party could then move down the lifts to the short end of the main lounge, and hold while the room fills up. The officers would line up with crossed swords, and you enter through the main doors, for the reception. Instead of being seated in the center, you should choose a location away from the doors, like here, Captain." Mason showed him the floor layout with his suggestion.

"She's worked so hard making the arrangements," he sighed. "I'll let you know," he said.

Mason made his case, and it was up to the Captain and Nurse Cohen to decide now.

XXII

Full mining operations resumed on the Hesperia. All concentration and effort was focused on the Big Peanut asteroid for drilling and excavation of its rare and precious metals. If the Chief Technician Takeda was correct in his initial estimates, the asteroid contained more platinum and platinum-group metals than the total amount mined on Earth in its entire history. The estimate on the platinum content alone was in the hundreds of trillions of freedom dollars.

The iron, magnesium, and zinc ores initially taken in the first year's asteroid harvest were nearly finished being smelted, so Mission Director Keene notified Captain Baines that they would be initializing the smaller furnaces for the platinum-group metals, and shutting down the big furnaces. Since the furnaces all required oxygen for their fires, this decision would save a huge amount of oxygen for later use, either as a furnace fire component, or breathing air.

In Section 2, where the smelted metals were stored, there were several compartments designed for precious metals storage. They were all capable of being locked and electronically sealed, to prevent theft. One twenty kilogram bar of pure platinum would easily fit in a miner's duffle bag, and it was worth two years' pay. The problem facing Director Keene was not enough secure storage was available. The decision was made to move several emptied cargo containers to Section 2 for platinum storage. The miners were tasked with welding the cargo containers to the floor and walls, for additional security.

The Captain did not wait for Mason's assistance in discussing changing the location of the ceremony with his fiancé Nurse Cohen. He should have waited, he decided in retrospect. Then she would have blown up at Mason for suggesting the change of locale instead of him. Baines understood both Mason's concerns and Nurse Cohen's resistance to the recommendation.

191

But the wedding and reception would take place in the general assembly, as planned.

Captain Baines gave Mason the news of their final decision, and he accepted it without further discussion. But Mason was not about to let their wedding and reception take place without additional security measures. He met with 1st Lieutenant Cheung, Sergeant Lucas, and Master Sergeant Alta to design their own security plan. Mason was fully briefed on the ship's security team's plans, so it would be easy to weave more security in and around it, to protect the Captain and future Mrs. Baines, and the officers of the Hesperia.

Mason took Corporals Garcia and Johnson with him to move Sherrie at exactly nineteen hundred hours, and she let them into her quarters nervously. They took her clothes and uniforms, music player, and everything she owned, carefully transporting everything to the lift and up two levels to her new quarters on the anti-gravity cart they brought with them. When the moving party arrived at her new suite, Mason had her program her palm print and retinal scan into the electronic lock. He opened the door for her, and her eyes opened wide. It really was a suite, with a real bed, a desk, a table, and twice the room she had before.

On the table sat a beautiful silk flower arrangement and a box of chocolates, both from Mason, of course. The bed was already made up with silky sheets and a duvet cover, a thank-you gift from Nurse Cohen, for all her help planning the wedding. "I made sure they set you up with a new mattress and new pillows, Senior Chief," Mason told her. Sherrie was speechless.

Mason and the two Corporals brought in her things, hung up her clothes and uniforms, and placed her storage boxes like they were arranged in her former quarters, while Sherrie sat and supervised. The last thing they brought in was a bottle of genuine California chardonnay for her. The two Corporals left, and Mason quietly slipped each man a few slices for his help.

"Sherrie? Do you like it?" Mason asked her. "I tried to get you the best suite available. It's all new; no one's lived in it before," he added.

"Of course I like it, John. How did you arrange this?" She looked at him suspiciously.

"I've got to have a few secrets from you, now don't I?" He answered, smiling at her. "Do you want me to help you unpack?" Mason was all smiles for her. Sherrie was still sitting at her new table, watching him.

"I'll unpack myself, John, but thanks for the offer. You, and the Corporals did most of the work for me already," she said. "This chardonnay is cold!" She just realized.

"You've got a bigger fridge here, see?" Mason went and opened it for her to see, and it was full of wines. He smiled at her broadly. "I'd like to say they're from me, but they are actually from Captain Kouras. He wanted to give you a gift for your promotion to Senior Chief."

"Really?" She got up at last, to inspect her wine treasure. "Do you think I could tell him thanks in person sometime?" Sherrie asked. "Wow! Champagne, too!"

"I'm sure he'd like that. We'd have to get Dr. Hassan's permission first," Mason told her. "We all wanted to make you happy, Sherrie," he said. "Especially me."

Sherrie found a corkscrew, conveniently placed on top of the fridge. She opened the cabinet directly above, and found two wine glasses, just as she expected. She opened the wine quickly and poured them each a glass, and asked Mason to close her door and sit down with her. She felt the time had come to tell him.

"Why did you take this seven year billet, John? A Prime Marine, from what I'm told, can go anywhere they want, even a star cruiser," she asked him, swirling her wine to aerate it.

"This was the first mining mission to go out since the Excelon; you know, the mutinied freighter?" Sherrie nodded. "They had a Prime Marine billet, with an automatic step up for me, to Staff Sergeant. Major Hawkins suggested I take it, to accelerate moving up, and use the time to get another master's degree. So, I guess it was for career enhancement," Mason answered. "I was worried about being bored," he added, and laughed sarcastically. "How about you?"

"I've always been on an Earth base, cooking for thousands every day. I was also asked by my Company Commander to volunteer for it, but that wasn't the reason I took the billet." She sipped her wine. "Most of our mess billets are two or three years. I doubled up and spent four years at Earth Command, in Houston. But you already read that in my file," she added dryly.

"I haven't read your file, Sherrie. I've read only the personnel files for those I'm assigned to protect; bridge and command officers, mainly." He was surprised at her comment.

"I thought you'd read everyone's file. Then you don't know," she realized. She looked at him, surprised and stunned. She took another sip. Sherrie took a deep breath. "I've been engaged three times, but never married. My last engagement was, let's just say, damaging to me. My file says I'm "Non-committal.""

"So? Were you abused or hurt?" He sat up and listened intently.

"He was a Master Chief. Ran the whole mess hall on the base. I met him my last year in Houston. Whirlwind romance, that's all I'll say. We got engaged, and he changed. Boy, did he change!" She took a longer drink of her wine. "The first time, I thought it was my fault for working a party off base; you know, a catering gig, for some extra money. The second time, he was drunk. The third time, I ended up in the hospital for two weeks."

Mason was upset at this man he'd never met. He hoped to never meet him. He'd better never meet him. "What else, Sherrie?" He asked quietly.

"I broke off the engagement, and he spent the next four months ruining my reputation, and nearly got me kicked out. Fortunately, I went to the base counselor after the second beating, and kept going, so everything was documented. They transferred him out, and I took this billet, to get away from him. Get away from Houston. To get away from everything." She stood up, and poured more wine for them.

"I was running away," she summed. "I sold everything in my apartment I could, packed up what was left, and ended up on the Hesperia. Four weeks later, I'm in cryo-sleep. The next day, I'm awakened early by you and Commander Baines."

Mason waited for her to continue. He reminded himself that he had been up and awake on this tub for fifteen months while she was in cryonic hibernation, so she never felt any time differential between her being put into cryo-sleep and the day she was awakened. It was just the next day, to her.

"When I told you "no strings," that's why. And all this time I thought you knew, at least knew some of the facts. But you didn't. You must think I'm a real bitch, John." She drank a little more wine. "I'm such an idiot." She slapped the table.

Mason got up and went to her, holding his hand out to her. She stood and let him hold her. "I think it's this wedding for Nurse Cohen that first bothered me. She and I have been meeting nearly every day planning the reception. And this came in last week." She picked up her com tablet, and found the transmission to show him. "My little sister, who is twelve years younger than me, told me she's getting married next month. She also inferred I'm gay, and told my parents," she said, and took another drink of wine. "How's that for family support?"

"Not much support at all," John said, and read the bitchy transmission. "Everything's come down all around you now, Sherrie."

"Yes, it has. My sister told my parents I'm gay. Nurse Cohen, who is four years older than me, is getting married, and is happy as a teen-age bride. And all I want to do is keep running away." She plopped down in her chair, and looked straight at him. "I keep waiting for you to change. To be rude, or be a jerk, or hit me. And all you do is treat me better that anyone's ever treated me in my life, John." She saw him pause before he spoke to her.

"Everyone's got several personas, as do I. You've never seen me in combat, Sherrie. I'm a very different person then. I am a warrior." He wondered if he'd frighten her, if she saw him in battle. "But I am the same man whose been bugging you since the day you woke up," he said, smiling at her. "I'm the guy who won't leave you be. I'm the guy who thinks you're special, Sherrie. I'm the guy you can share your secrets with, and they'll be safe with me. I'm the man who loves you. Even if you are gay." He smiled, and made her laugh out loud.

"I'm not gay, John Mason. Crazy, maybe. Scared, definitely. And relieved that I told you almost everything." She stopped briefly. "Did you just say what I think you said?" She put her arms around his waist. "Did you?"

"Who, me? Naw, must've been some other guy," he said, "not me." He kissed her at last, and she responded passionately.

"Yes, you did. I heard you say you loved me, John Mason," she said, kissing him. "It's okay if you say it again."

"Huh-unh, no way. You won't get me to say it again," he said, kissing her, and moving her to her bed. "No matter how hard you try," he said, taking her blouse off. They both laughed and took each other's clothes off, and tested out her new silky sheets all night long, until the alarm went off, announcing that they survived the storm, and emerged as one.

XXIII

Tonight was the rehearsal for the Captain's wedding to Nurse Cohen, and everyone participating in the wedding needed to be present. Mason came down to the general assembly hall directly after his bridge shift, still wearing his combat vest. Mason, Master Sergeant Alta, and Sergeant Lucas surveyed the general assembly hall for an hour, finding the best places to hide weapons during the wedding. It was imperative the weapons not be noticeable, but be accessible in case of emergency. They decided underneath the buffet tables would be the best places to conceal the weapons, and hastily rigged holding anchors and pins, but placed nothing inside them. The tables were not set up with tablecloths yet, and Mason was concerned that, if their riggings were obvious beforehand, they could be dismantled by a liaison of the Yellow Man.

The wedding party participants gathered for the rehearsal near the front of the hall. They were all shown their places for the procession, and lined up. A large vid screen was hung at the place where Mason would walk Nurse Cohen to meet the Captain. They would face the screen together, for the ceremony to be officiated via vid comm by Admiral Tomiko. Following the ceremony, the happy couple would turn and go through the crossed swords of the ship's officers, take their seats at the head table, and the reception would follow. Mason kept looking around the huge hall at all the places an assassin could hide, and effectively murder a dozen or more officers in seconds.

"Gunny. Gunny. GUNNY!" The Captain interrupted his thoughts, wanting him to take his place with Nurse Cohen for the initial walk down the aisle. "Please pay attention, or we'll be here all night."

"Yes, sir," Mason said, jogging over to Nurse Cohen.

The music started, and the rehearsal began. Mason did his part, handed the bride-to-be over to the groom, and stepped back one pace. He was watching the practice movements of the participants, when his bionic hearing picked up something. He couldn't identify the sound, but it came from above. Looking quickly up at the ceiling, he saw a ceiling tile part ever so slightly. He leaped at the bride and groom, rushing them off the stage and down on the floor, covering them with his body, yelling, "Get down!" The laser blasts were heard throughout the big hall, and return fire from the Space Marines and ship's security teams followed. The entire stage was ripped apart by the blasts.

Chaos ensued, as officers and crewmen alike ran for cover while the laser fire battle continued. Mason saved the Captain and Nurse Cohen from certain death. He asked them if they were all right, and they nodded, and held onto each other. Mason pulled a nearby table over to cover them, drew his side arm, and fired into the ceiling. The mess hall crewmen had been watching the rehearsal from the near side of the room and, unfortunately, a few of them were hit. Mason went to look for Sherrie, and was relieved to find her just coming out of her office, having heard the commotion. "Stay in your office, Senior Chief. Go back now," Mason bellowed, and she did as he ordered. The attack lasted only a few minutes, but much damage was done to the psyche of the wedding party members, and the assembly hall. The Space Marines killed the assassin, who fell to the floor about ten meters from the stage where the happy couple stood only minutes ago.

As he went back to the demolished stage area, four corpsmen came running into the hall with anti-gravity gurneys, having been summoned by Dr. Hassan. Mason sent them directly to the mess crewmen. He went back to the Captain and Nurse Cohen, who were now standing, but still holding onto each other, and looked up at the ceiling again. The tiles were damaged or missing in one large section.

"Mason, are you feeling all right?" Captain Baines asked, looking at him.

"Yes, sir," Mason answered, looking pale.

"Corpsman! Corpsman! Over here! He's been hit!" Nurse Cohen said, suddenly coming out of her terrified state, and becoming a nurse again. She went to Mason, touched his head where the blood was pouring down, and looked at his back. His uniform was quickly getting soaked with his own blood from the laser fire bursts. She put her hand to his temple to stop the blood from flowing as the corpsmen reached him, just in time to catch his fall.

"Take him immediately to the hospital," she ordered, and went with them, holding Mason's bleeding head with her hand, and calling Nurse Jones to ready the surgery room for several incoming wounded. The corpsmen and Nurse Cohen ran to the lifts with their full gurneys and headed up. Several ambulatory wounded, mostly mess crewmen, were helped to the lifts by officers and security teams. The two dead mess hall crewmen were taken away a few minutes later.

Dr. Hassan met the corpsmen and Nurse Cohen in the hospital shortly after their arrival, and they quickly triaged the wounded. Having a head wound that was bleeding profusely, Mason was selected for surgery first. He was set up with an IV, and his wounds cleaned as much as possible, while the Doctor and Head Nurse scrubbed and donned their surgical garb. He was wheeled in, and his surgery began. Out of the other injured crewmen, only one mess hall crewman required any surgery. Other wounded were taken care of outside the surgery theatre by Nurse Jones and Nurse Soo, who came quickly to assist, foregoing her sleep to help, and also the nurse droids, activated for the emergency.

Mason was in recovery. The Captain and Nurse Cohen quietly talked with Dr. Hassan about halting their wedding plans for tomorrow, and moving the wedding out another few months' time. "I don't feel comfortable having the wedding now, with all these terrible things having happened. I think it would be best to wait a few more months, when everything's settled down, don't you?" The Captain asked, looking at Nurse Cohen.

"Don't even think about canceling, sir," Mason said from his bed. "That's exactly what the Yellow Man wants." Mason tried to sit up, but it was little too soon for that.

"Now, lie down, Mason," Dr. Hassan said, coming over to his patient. "You need to rest now. Your new musculature needs time to adhere and bond to your own, you know. You were hit on your head and your side, young man. Your uniform saved you from being killed, but you didn't wear your helmet," the Doctor said to Mason. His one-piece uniform of nano-fibers and vest repelled most of the body blast, but the direct hits he took were high-intensity laser fire, and it fried the topmost fibers under his arms and down along his right side, where the uniform fibers were worn through from frequent wear. His right side along his ribs was scorched; part of his side musculature damaged or missing, and several ribs were bruised or cracked. His lymph nodes under his right arm were destroyed, along with several sections of skin. His head bore the scars of a straight line of laser fire over his ear, burning a path through his thick hair.

"The bastard used a mounted laser rifle, full intensity. We only brought one on board the Hesperia, and ours is still in the armory, Mason. We're trying to discover where he got it as we speak," the Captain said. "How did he get it up there?"

"He had help, Captain. No one could carry a mounted laser rifle up to the ceiling by himself, sir. It weighs one hundred twenty kilos, sir," Mason offered. "Were the vid cams' feed checked nightly, Captain? I installed them last month inside the entire ceiling for observation."

"I will certainly find out the answer to that question, Mason. That bastard nearly killed Rachel. It's a good thing he's dead," the Captain said bitterly. "Thank God you were there."

"What color was his shirt, sir?" Mason asked.

"I don't know. I didn't see him. The Space Marines took him to the morgue for autopsy. I'll find out, Mason." The Captain showed a look on his face Mason had never seen on him before; the look of revenge. Mason knew it well. Everyone who had ever seen a buddy fall in combat felt it one time or another. Mason had seen it before on his own face. It was a dangerous sign, especially for a ship's Captain.

"Is Nurse Cohen all right, sir? She wasn't hurt when I took you both down, was she? I'd never forgive myself if I hurt her, sir." Mason didn't see her in the back of his room.

"I'm fine, Gunny. You moved so fast I didn't have time to think. One minute we're going over the ceremonial vows, the next second we're flying across the stage, down to the floor, covered by your body. Thanks to you, we're both alive and here with you." She came over to him, still in her stained surgical gown, and took his hand. "You saved my life, John." She smiled at him, and held his hand tenderly. "I should have listened to your advice, and moved the ceremony somewhere else. You were right, John."

"Please don't postpone your wedding, ma'am. That's just what he wants, everyone running scared. You and the Captain need to get married, just like you planned. That'll show him," Mason said, trying to smile for her.

"We'll see, John. Tomorrow would be too soon, after all that's happened. Right now, you should rest. I cut your uniform off you with my laser knife. Some of the fibers were burned into your skin by that big laser rifle he used, so you'll be sore for a while. You took the brunt of his attack upon us."

Mason raised his sheet and looked at his body and the bandage. He noticed he only wore a gown, and no uniform or underwear. He looked up at her, and blushed, quickly putting his sheet back down over his body. *She finally gets me naked, and the room's full of people,* Mason thought, and laughed out loud.

"What's so funny, Mason?" The Captain asked.

"Nothing, sir. I just felt a draft," Mason said. They all laughed with him.

"Let's let the man rest, now, shall we?" Dr. Hassan said, ushering them all out of Mason's room. Mason lay there, coming awake, and wondered how the assassin got that big rifle up there. That particular rifle was used primarily on mounts, it could not have been held; it was over two meters long. It couldn't be held by one man and fired more than once; the recoil would knock a man down. It was standard issue for armored land vehicles, space shuttles, and the small interceptor craft used by the Space Forces on patrol. The Yellow Man did not intend for anyone to survive the night. Thank God for his bionic hearing. Nurse Cohen was all right, and Sherrie was safe.

He closed his eyes, and tried to sleep. All he could think about was how close the Yellow Man came to carrying out his plans. Strike 2. How many strikes would the Yellow Man get before he was out?

The wedding, originally set for the next day, was postponed for two weeks. It would take several days to investigate and analyze the situation in the general assembly anyway, and then clean it up. More time for the Yellow Man to get another assassin ready, in Mason's view.

Sherrie came to visit him the next morning, and brought him clean underwear and a uniform. Dr. Hassan agreed to let him leave, and put him on restricted duty. That would give him time to investigate on his own. He dressed after Sherrie left for work and was about to leave, when Nurse Cohen came in to see him. She sat next to him on the bed to talk.

"You were really remarkable, John. I've never seen anyone move as fast as you did, holding the Captain and me in your arms. I had no idea what was happening. You just flew us off the stage onto the floor, and held us down, taking the blasts intended for the Captain. And me, as well. I was up all night in my quarters, thinking about it, about you. I wouldn't be here now without you, John. Thank you." She looked at him, and lowered her head. "The blasts that wounded you were on your right side, where I was standing."

"Yes, I know, Nurse Cohen. I'm just happy you weren't hurt. I was afraid I hurt you, taking you to the floor like that. I'm a heavy guy," Mason said, shyly. He felt her emotions swell.

"You did not hurt me, John. You saved my life! No one's ever done that for me before. No one's ever stood between me and death," she said, her voice trailing off. "I just don't know what to say to you, except thank you. Thank you for saving my life, John." She looked up at him, and began to cry. "There's so much we haven't said to each other, John. We couldn't. So much…" She looked at him, and opened her mouth slightly, as if to say something else. "I have always…" Then she went to her office, concealing her tears. She glanced at him, hiding her face.

Mason slowly walked out. He wished he could talk with Nurse Cohen privately in her quarters; but they both knew better. Bury those feelings deep, he told himself; let it go. He was unsteady, and his head was pounding. The bandage was a little too tight, but maybe it was supposed to be that way. His right side ached like a son-of-a-bitch. Nurse Cohen was right; the blasts he took were aimed directly at her. Maybe the shooter was a lousy shot. Maybe he aimed at the Captain and missed because he flew them down off the stage so quickly. And, maybe his aim was spot on, and he was trying to kill her, intentionally. But why? He had to find out.

Mason went to the mess hall. Sherrie made him a bacon sandwich, gave him hot tea and orange juice, and sat with him. "I was really scared, John. The rehearsal was happening, the music was playing, and then all the laser fire exploded. If you hadn't been there to tell me to go back, I might have been hurt, too. They said you saved both the Captain and Nurse Cohen, in one move. I can't believe this happened."

"Believe it, Sherrie. Someone's out to take the ship. They've tried before, and they'll try again. Promise me you won't come out to see what's happening if you ever hear laser fire. Stay in your office, lock the door, and get down, away from the window. Just promise me you'll stay down, please." He held her hand, and squeezed it gently.

She looked at his hand, scarred from scraping the floor with Nurse Cohen and the Captain in his arms. "You probably will have more scars, John." She looked at his bandaged head, but couldn't see his bandaged right side.

"No doubt. The Doctor said the scar on my head took out all my hair on one side. Maybe the barber will cut me a deal next time." He laughed, trying to lighten the conversation. She looked at his head bandage again, and tried to smile at his joke. Four Space Marines came in for breakfast, and saw them. They came over, and congratulated Mason for saving the Captain and Nurse Cohen.

"You should've seen him, Senior Chief. This big horse just up and flew off the stage with the Captain and Nurse Cohen in his arms, and held them down under protection until we got the shooter. I didn't think you could move your big ass that fast, Mason," Sergeant Lucas said. "He flew like an eagle diving." He used his hand to illustrate Mason's flying maneuver. "Never seen anything like him," Sergeant Lucas said.

Sherrie smiled and asked, "Are you going to the bridge? Shouldn't you go rest, John?"

"Dr. Hassan assigned me restricted duty for a couple of days. I have to report to the Captain," Mason answered. "I'd better get up there. Thanks for breakfast, Sherrie. See you tonight, okay?" She nodded, and Mason left for the bridge.

The bridge was abuzz with talk about last night's attack. They all got quiet when Mason came on the bridge, and their sudden silence made him uneasy. He told Lieutenant Fuller he needed to report to the Captain for restricted duty, so he waited next to the Space Marines. Captain Baines entered the bridge from the main doors, and walked past Mason, not seeing him. Lieutenant Fuller nodded in Mason's direction, and the Captain took him into his ready room.

"Why are you here, Gunny? Shouldn't you be in the hospital?" The Captain asked with a concerned voice, and looked at Mason's head.

"Dr. Hassan released me with restricted duty, Captain. I need to know what you want me to do for you, sir." Mason waited for his response, and the Captain motioned for him to sit.

"Mason, if I knew you were being released, I would have come to see you. I honestly thought you'd still be there most of today, anyway. You know, I told the Admiral what you did. How you heard the noise in the ceiling, and rushed Nurse Cohen and me off the stage in the nick of time, and saved both our lives. You took the laser blasts intended for me, and Rachel. How can I possibly thank you enough? I'm here because of you, again." The Captain stood up, and looked out of the window. "There's a reason we've all been saved from death, Mason. We just have to find out what that reason is, and fulfill our destinies."

"Yes, sir. My reason is to serve you, Captain. I took an oath to protect you, sir. And Nurse Cohen, as well."

"Yes, you did. But there must be a greater reason, for all of us. I know it, Mason. It's not an accident, your being on this ship. Earth Command was afraid of another mutiny. One may happen, once they get that platinum smelted. Who knows? But this situation with the orange cloud, the Yellow Man, the deaths, and that bloody octagonal tube; there's something tying all this together, don't you see, Mason? We have to find out what it is, before anything else happens." Baines stared out the window.

"Do you want me to continue my investigation while I'm on restricted duty, Captain? Or, I can stay here as your escort. Which would you prefer, Captain Baines?" Mason asked calmly. The Captain looked at him, sitting there with a bandaged head, a blood stain showing.

"I want you to continue your work in the library, and I'll send someone down there to assist you today. When you get that bandage off your head, and Dr. Hassan releases you, then you can come back on duty here on the bridge. If anything urgent happens, I'll call you. Otherwise, continue your investigation. And Mason," the Captain paused, "Thank you for saving her life. She means everything to me. I nearly went crazy after the attack. Thank you."

Mason stood and saluted him, and received a very crisp salute in return. He left the ready room, and went to his favorite table in the ship's library to study. He spread out his books, papers, and his com tablet, looking for the place where he left off reading. He referenced his timeline, and had the com tablet bring up a 3D holographic model. Everything happened in clusters, nothing was evenly spaced. Using his hands in the air, he spread out the holographic timeline to better read certain time periods where events happened all at once, or at least felt that way while they were happening. He was looking for a pattern, a pattern of disruption. He narrowed his eyes, and cleared his mind to meditate on the holograph, ignoring his pain.

Mason was completely absorbed in his meditation and did not notice he was about to have company, until they were nearly behind his chair. He jumped up and turned, immediately assuming a defensive kung fu posture, ready to fight, his hands held outward, stiff as boards.

"Whoa, there, Gunny. It's just Nurse Cohen and me, come to check on you," Dr. Hassan said. "You'll give an old man a heart attack like that."

"I'm so sorry, Doctor, ma'am. Usually I hear people come in, but I didn't hear you. I'm sorry if I scared you, Nurse Cohen." Mason held out a chair for her, and they sat down with him.

"We can safely assume your reflexes are fine, Mason," she said, smiling. "What were you doing that had you so fixated?" She asked, looking at his holographic timeline, spread in the air along the length of the table.

Mason explained what he was doing. "It's blatantly obvious that there are periods of time where nothing out of the ordinary happens to us, and then, we get these groupings of events. I'm trying a meditation technique to attempt identification of a pattern; I call it a pattern of disruption. If there is such a pattern, and I can recognize it, perhaps I can predict when something is getting ready to happen again. Does that make sense?"

"Yes. I see what you're trying to do now," Nurse Cohen said. She leaned forward to read the occurrences of events near the beginning of the timeline, and followed the timeline to its end point. "We have to add yesterday's attack," she mentioned.

"The only problem with what you're doing, Mason, there is probably missing information that should be on the timeline for the pattern to emerge. What criteria did you use to qualify and quantify events you added to the timeline, and which ones were excluded?" The Doctor asked, looking at his work. "It looks comprehensive; can we be certain that everything is here?"

"I did use my judgment in deciding what to take out of the timeline, and what to leave in. Maybe I could copy this timeline, and add all out-of-the-ordinary events to a new one, and a pattern would emerge then. Let me just cross-reference the log," Mason said, and in a minute he had a new timeline constructed, with more events added along the timeline. The clusters of time grew bigger for them to look at, and he spread the timeline out with his hands, in the air.

Then Mason stood up, looking at his slightly different timeline, and said, "You know, I've used only the main log from the ship, the bridge log. What if I added the engineering log?" Mason keyed some strokes on his com tablet. The timeline showed more data points, and more groupings.

"And now, I'll add your medical log," and the groupings got bigger, and more clumped. "I'll overlay the shuttle logs, as well," he mumbled, watching the clumps grow even bigger.

"Remember to add the timing of the unauthorized transmission communications," Nurse Cohen reminded him. The timeline beginning filled up significantly more.

"I'll extend the timeline beginning to include a one-week waiting period, when the Yellow Man was recruiting at the Moon Base." When the timeline beginning extended, more groupings of events popped onto the new section. They all stared at Mason's new creation in wonder.

The Captain walked into the library with Lt. Commander Westerly, watching his three investigators staring at a long, 3D holograph that now ran the full length of their table, and beyond. "Captain, look what Mason's got," Nurse Cohen said, excitedly. She quickly explained what had been done with Mason's original timeline, which now included a new time period before any of the crew boarded the Hesperia.

"I still don't see a pattern, Gunny," the Doctor said.

"Neither do I," said the Captain.

Westerly walked along the timeline, studying it, then said, "You know, we humans all think that time is linear, when it really is another dimension, and definitely not linear. What if we apply a little Einstein and Hawking to this timeline? May I, Gunny?" She sat down next to him, and he nodded. She took her hands to the holographic timeline, and converted it with several strokes of her arms and hands into a four dimensional, layered, yet somewhat spherical shape. She typed several keystrokes into Mason's com tablet, and the timeline began to come alive, undulating, expanding until it was about two meters high. Westerly then typed more instructions into his com tablet, and points of small lights lit up, where events had taken place on his linear timeline. Then points of light connected, and a web was formed. "It's a grid," she said.

"That's fascinating," Nurse Cohen said, the sphere having surrounded and encompassed her, the Doctor, and Mason.

"Lt. Commander, how do I remove some points? For instance, any minor maintenance conducted in engineering. Anything routine," Mason said, looking at the sphere surrounding them. "These are all ship's log entries," he clarified for her.

Westerly sat down, and typed for several minutes on his com tablet, hit the last keystroke, and sat back to watch. "I adjusted the algorithms," she said. The sphere rotated and undulated again, and the points of light disconnected, reconnected, and repeated that sequence for three times, until a new spherical shape emerged, slightly smaller than the first sphere. Upon the last connection of light points, a new web emerged. She got up to look inside the grid, as did Mason.

Captain Baines stood silent while all this was occurring, watching with extreme interest. He suddenly cried out, "There it is! The next one!" He moved inside the sphere, talking quickly with Westerly, pointing and talking way over Mason's head.

Nurse Cohen and the Doctor may have been following their conversation, but Mason could not. But he did see an empty area in the web that did not contain any lighted points at all, connected or unconnected, where the Captain pointed with his finger, while talking excitedly with Westerly. The Captain was going on about combinatory equations, whatever that was. Mason knew a little about probability analysis, but that level of calculus was way above his head. He backed away from the sphere, looking at the grid, or web, whichever it was, and saw a hole.

He isolated the area of the "hole" on his com tablet, and said politely, "If you'll excuse me just one moment, Captain, I need to see this." He copied the sphere, and saved it, just the way the Lt. Commander made it, and then opened another holographic linear timeline, spread it out along the table as before, reached into the sphere with his hand and popped in the "hole." It all became clear as the hole fit right in. The probable time for an event to occur was eight days' time from today. They all looked at the two holographs, one sphere, and one linear timeline.

"I'm no math genius or astrophysicist, sir. But I think we'd all better be ready in eight days for something to happen." Mason sat back down, now leaning on the back of the chair. He looked up at both of the holographs. "Yep, something big."

"How do you know it will be big, Mason?" The Doctor asked.

"Because of the size of the hole. See?" Mason pointed to the sphere, and then back to his more familiar linear 3D holograph. "It will either be a cluster of events in a short space of time, or a big event. We should be ready for either to happen, Captain."

"You are the genius here, Mason. None of us thought to construct a timeline of ship's log events, except you, at the very beginning. Looking for a pattern among the myriad, terrible events that have happened on the Hesperia was your idea, Gunny," the Captain said, still transfixed, standing inside the sphere.

"Anyone with advanced mathematics could have constructed the sphere for you," Lt. Westerly said. "But the original idea was yours, Gunnery Sergeant." She looked at Mason, and smiled at him. That was a first.

"Now that we know the pattern predicts something in eight days, what do we do?" Nurse Cohen asked. She looked up, and Mason saw she was worried, her brow wrinkled. He didn't like her to be worried.

"Nurse Cohen, I wonder if it would be too much to ask you to check my rib bandages, ma'am. Nurse Jones nearly cut off my breathing this morning when he put these on," Mason said, smiling at her.

"I'll be happy to, Mason. In fact, let's go now, before Commander Powers comes in here, and the conversation ratchets up another level," she said. "We'll be in the hospital, Captain." They got up and left the room.

Mason went to the hospital with Nurse Cohen, sat on an exam bed, and she removed his rib bandages. She was quiet, too quiet. "What's got you bothered, ma'am?" Mason asked, already knowing the answer. He liked her reaching her arms around him to remove his bandages.

"I'm worried about what could happen in eight days, Gunny, you know that," she said, stopping her work and looking at him. She finished removing his bandages from his ribs and side. "The plasti-skin is adhering nicely, faster than it usually does. Must be your enriched blood accelerating the adherence process. You might not have too much scarring down your side, after all. Let me scan the area to make sure there's no infection." Nurse Cohen used her hand scanner, as Mason held his right arm up. "Looks clean, no infection. That's interesting," she said, resetting her scanner, and scanned him again. "It should be several weeks before muscles begin to grow back after being burned as badly as yours were, but there's new tissue forming already. Remarkable." She picked up her com tablet and made several notes, and then put it back into her jacket pocket. "We gave you one and a half pints of plasma-enriched blood during your surgery to replace what was lost from your open wounds. It's helping you heal faster, John, and that's good." She managed a little smile. Mason could still see the concern in her eyes.

"You know, ma'am, nothing may happen in eight days. Maybe I'm just blowing smoke, trying to make sense out of all that's been going on. Maybe something will happen, but we can't know the future, not really. I'm trying to predict the pattern of disruption in order to heighten our efforts to be ready for any occurrence. We may not have any control over what an outside force tries to do, Nurse Cohen," Mason said. "But we can make sure we're prepared for most contingencies." He was glad she was still close to him, listening to his words. She needed reassurance from him.

"Admiral Ashford at Bethesda said I would be going stir crazy on a mining freighter for seven years," she said. "Wait until I see him the next time." She turned to get some can of spray out of her cabinet, and sprayed his entire burn area.

"Kick his butt, ma'am," Mason said, smiling at her. She laughed with him.

"This mission will definitely be one of the academy's case studies. I can read the title now: 'The Strange Case of the Mining Freighter Hesperia,'" she said cynically. "I just hope we all get off this ship alive, and in one piece, Gunny." Nurse Cohen placed the self-adhering pre-medicated big bandage around his side wound where his muscles were burned away. She started wrapping a new wide bandage around his midsection.

"Me too, ma'am. In fact, it's my duty to see that very thing happens, Nurse Cohen. OW!" A sharp pain stabbed him on his right side.

"Sorry, John. That rib is surely cracked, and not just bruised. Let's scan you and make sure. Come over here." She led him to the wall scanner, told him to hold up his right arm, and scanned his right side. "Oh yes, it's cracked, all right. Lucky for you the crack runs around the bone, and not along its length. No deep breathing for a while, now."

"I can't promise that, ma'am," he said in her ear with a low voice, smiling at her broadly.

She laughed out loud at him, and made him sit on the table. After she finished wrapping up his right side and ribs, she said, "Now, let me look at your head wound, before I kick you out of here." She unwrapped the bandages carefully, and used the hand scanner on the wound site. "It's a mess. Let's get that cleaned up." She gathered her equipment in a tray, scrubbed, and came back to him. She had him cleaned in a jiffy, with fresh antibacterial gel on the wound, and new bandages in place. "There you go, John."

"Thank you, ma'am. That feels better already," Mason said, sliding off the exam table. She hadn't backed up, and he was very close to her. He could feel her breathing accelerate. They were dangerously close. They just smiled at each other tenderly for a few moments, and said not a word, and yet said everything. The romance that never was.

"Now get out of here, John. I've got work to do." She turned and walked away towards the front of the hospital.

Mason walked out silently.

XXIV

The Big Peanut produced a thick vein of solid platinum and smaller areas of rhodium, palladium, and plutonium. Mission Director Keene told Captain Baines at a meeting in his conference room that same afternoon that the platinum alone would pay for the construction of the Hesperia, twice over. What worried Keene was whether or not increasing their shares would be enough to satisfy the miners. He was worried about a mutiny attempt, once the precious metals were smelted. The Captain acknowledged his concern was justified, and recommended additional security vid cams be placed in Section 2, where the smelted metals all were stored. Neither man had extra security crews to add for more protection.

"I can request more security details as your crews are placed back into cryonic hibernation. But, for now, we have to keep our crews aligned as they are. You have been briefed on the two sabotage attempts already made on the Hesperia. Someone wants this ship, Director Keene. They attempted to take control even before your platinum-group asteroid was discovered. We cannot reduce our security numbers now. I cannot even spare a security droid for you at this time." The Captain felt it was necessary to lay his cards on the table with Keene. The two men worked together well during this mission because of each other's honesty and candor.

"I understand. But you see my point, don't you? Six hundred miners could over-run my security pretty quickly, Captain Baines. Then, they'd be your problem. I'd like to make it back to Moon Base alive, and not in a body bag," Keene said.

"As would I. How much longer do you expect to mine the Big Peanut?" Baines asked.

Keene answered, "We're down to the smaller half, Captain. That's where the deepest platinum vein was found. Should take us another six to eight months to drill, mine, and harvest. Then you can empty the remaining slag rock in the glove, and fold it up for storage again. We'll pick up a few more iron chunks, and be done."

"Sounds like a good plan, Director," the Captain said.

"Thanks for the update. See you again in a couple of weeks." Director Keene got up and went back to his control console as the Captain and his security detail left.

The general assembly hall was still a mess from the attack last week. All of the Senior Chief's hard work building and decorating a stage for the Captain and Nurse Cohen's wedding was for naught. Security personnel were still sweeping and analyzing the area and the ceiling for prints and DNA. Mason updated his security log with their results.

The assassin in the ceiling was from maintenance, a quiet man named Thomas, according to the Maintenance Chief. He and an unidentified accomplice used a small grappling hook and pulley apparatus to get the two meter, 120 kilo laser gun and mount in the ceiling. The vid cams didn't pick up anything at all. One of them had to have training in vid communications or engineering to accomplish that feat without setting off an alarm. The Yellow Man's web of deceit was more intricate and far-reaching than they previously realized. Mason suspected one or more people at Earth Command were paid accomplices of the Yellow Man.

Too many contraband items were brought on board the Hesperia: mini gas canisters of opiated sleep inducers used on him and the late Dr. Wise; the infamous octagonal tube; hundreds of injection pens, containing both prescription tranquilizers and stimulants, and illegal psychotropic drugs; dozens of vials of various poisons; and a mounted, two meter long laser rifle. What else was smuggled on board, waiting to be used in an attack against them?

Captain Baines checked over Mason's log of the days' discoveries, and his itemized list of contraband. Too much time left for this mission. Plenty of time for more sabotage and attacks. He asked Mason for his recommendations regarding the expected trouble in eight days.

"Captain, I think we should focus instead on several other matters: one, conduct inspections of all cargo containers remaining that have not been unsealed and opened; two, conduct random, spontaneous inspections of all work areas and crews, including maintenance, mess halls, cargo bays, engineering, and the bridge; three, test all active vid cams for operational effectiveness; four, re-inventory all authorized weapons on board, whether hand, concealed, or carried; and five, secretly alter emergency procedures for command staff evacuations." Mason waited while the Captain considered his recommendations.

"If all these steps are executed, it will take at least eight days' time, Mason. If there was one step you would deem most important, which would it be? The first one listed here?" The Captain had learned he should pay attention to his Prime Marine's recommendations.

"Number five, sir. The evacuation procedures for the entire crew are well documented in the procedural manual. I recommend they be altered secretly, as soon as possible, for the command staff's protection. There is one other item I did not list, sir. More of a personal nature, sir, if I may?"

"What is it?" The Captain crossed his arms across his chest, defensively.

"Nurse Cohen has kept her Commander's quarters, and will surrender them only after the wedding, is that correct, Captain?"

"Yes, of course. It is not appropriate that she do otherwise."

"Sir, with all due respect, I suggest she keep those quarters as hers, even after the wedding. They are located deep inside Section 1, with no outside windows. The only access is one door, which is more easily guarded. In case of attack or other emergency those quarters are much safer than your own quarters, Captain Baines."

"I see your point, Gunny. But they are not easily reached from my quarters in an emergency," the Captain stated.

"They are from the maintenance shaft, sir. We could seal off the shaft below her floor, and put a one-way hatch cover on the seal. You could enter from the far end of the bridge conference room supply cabinet; install a hidden trap door into the maintenance shaft, and climb down to her level in less than two minutes, Captain. Make a right on the hospital level, and two access panels later, another hidden door could let you or Nurse Cohen inside, Captain." Mason showed him the route on his com tablet.

"That's brilliant, Mason! Think the Space Marines could do that in secret?"

"In a few hours, Captain Baines," Mason volunteered.

"Then, make it so. I want you to notify me directly when you're through, Gunny. I'll have Lt. Commander Davis lead the security teams on their inspections at once. I'll notify Admiral Tomiko of four courses of our action, and your warning. We'll keep silent on the new evacuation routes. He'll probably want you to attend the staff update meetings on Friday morning again, Gunny, if you're available," the Captain said with a smile. Mason had reserved his Fridays for Sherrie for over two years.

"No problem, sir. It's coming down to the last leg of the mission, sir. We must all be vigilant, Captain Baines," Mason agreed. Then he was dismissed.

Mason called his favorite Corporals, Johnson and Milton, and Master Sergeant Alta, to meet him quietly at the cargo bay command room. They met in secret, and Mason told them of his plan to create two hidden doors and a one-way hatch cover for a maintenance shaft. He would not even tell them where they would be installed, just gave them instructions to gather the necessary materials and tools, and meet him at 0-four hundred tomorrow morning near the maintenance shaft entrance in the main lounge, two floors below the hospital deck. They were happy to get moving again. They had all been on guard duty too much for comfort lately.

Mason left the cargo bay and went to the gym to shower. He stuffed the plastic wrap into his thigh pocket Nurse Jones gave him to protect his head, rib and right side bandages from getting wet. He showered with some amount of difficulty, but finally got clean enough to see Sherrie. He went to his quarters to shave and change uniforms.

Sherrie was walking to his room as Mason got off the lift, and he welcomed her inside. She was worried about his head wound, and put her arms around his waist to hold him. Mason grimaced in pain, and backed away from her. "I'm sorry. I don't you think know about these," he said, and unzipped his uniform top, and took it off, revealing his rib and side bandages.

"Oh my God, John! I'm so sorry! I didn't know you were hurt anywhere besides your head. Did I hurt you? Of course I did, or you wouldn't have yelled," she cried out.

"It's okay; you just hit my cracked rib. I got hit with some laser fire. I wore an old uniform, and it was worn through under my arms, and the shooter got me along my side. It's healing up just fine, though. I'm okay now, Sherrie." He came back to her, and said, "I'm getting better every minute I'm with you," and kissed her gently.

She was afraid to touch him. She let him kiss her, but refused to hold him, or get too close to him. "Let's just sit down for a while, okay, John? How long before you're healed?" She was very concerned. "You don't look like you have any muscles along your side, John."

"Dr. Hassan said it could take several days for my new muscles to grow back. I'm on restricted duty now. I can catch up on my special project," he said, sitting at his tiny table.

"I'm scared, John. I've never dealt with anything like this before, real laser fire, deaths of my crewmen, and all. Is it over?" she asked, looking at him for answers.

"No one knows. We are taking every precaution possible to prevent any other occurrence of violence from happening, Sherrie. But I won't lie to you, honey. We have to be prepared, and be very careful. That's why I told you to stay inside your office if you should ever hear those shots being fired again. I don't want you getting hurt," he said, and kissed her hand.

"But what about you, John? You go everywhere the Captain goes, and they're after him. You'll be in the thick of it, if he's attacked again," she asked.

"That's my duty, Sherrie. I am a Prime Marine. I took an oath to protect the Captain and the command officers." Mason tried to console her.

"I never realized exactly what all that meant until yesterday. I just cook, John, and serve meals. You, you go out and trouble finds you. You could have been killed yesterday. I thought your head wound was bad enough, but you're all bandaged up." She was trying to stop crying, but could not. "Just hold me, John," and she buried her face in his neck until her tears stopped.

He felt her fear, and tried to comfort her. He tried to tell her of his duty to the Captain, and that it was his honor to protect him, and the Hesperia. But all Sherrie could think about was that her man was hurt, and would probably get hurt again, maybe more seriously next time.

The Space Marines met with Mason at 0-four hundred the next morning near the maintenance shaft entrance in the main lounge with their equipment, as planned. Mason led them up the maintenance shafts until they reached the hospital level. They installed a one-way hatch cover in the shaft that could not be opened from below, effectively sealing off the shaft. It would take a blow torch and several hours work to get through the shaft now.

Mason told the Space Marines to take the maintenance shaft up to the bridge conference room. He hustled up the shaft ahead of them, trying his best not to reopen any of his wounds. He used an access panel to exit the shaft, and went to the Captain's quarters, where Captain Baines was already up and waiting for him. Mason updated him on their progress, and informed him that they were ready to install the bridge conference room's hidden door, and save Nurse Cohen's quarters for the last.

Captain Baines tried to keep the work in the conference room as secret as possible; he led Mason through the back of the bridge while Lieutenant Fuller had the comm. He closed and locked the conference room door, and they went to work. The built-in storage cabinet was emptied and the back removed, and a panel cut out of the wall. Mason showed the Captain the shaft ladder access, and the motion-sensitive lights installed above the door opening. The Marines finished the door, and rebuilt the cabinet around it, with the new hidden door concealed as the back of the cabinet.

The Marines climbed down the shaft to wait for the signal to begin cutting the door in Nurse Cohen's quarters. Captain Baines led Mason out of the conference room right after the 6am shift change. They went to her quarters, and the Captain said, "She's at the hospital now. We can go inside."

Mason reached his hand up to the palm recognition pad and the door opened. Captain Baines said, "I didn't know you could enter her room!"

Mason replied, "As your Special Security Chief, sir, I have access to all doors and locking mechanisms on board, Captain Baines, except for your private safe in your storeroom, and your private locker in the cargo bay." Mason ignored the Captain's disapproving looks, and held the door open for him to go inside ahead of him. They walked over to the selected wall where the built-in bookcases were, and scanned the wall. Mason and the Captain removed all of her books and things from the lower shelves of the bookcase cabinet. "The maintenance shaft runs right along this wall. Would you like a small or large access door behind the cabinet doors, Captain?"

"What are you doing in my quarters, gentlemen?" Nurse Cohen asked, standing inside her doorway with her hands on her hips.

"Good morning, ma'am," Mason said, and smiled at her. "Captain Baines said you were at the hospital already."

"I was. Now please answer my question. Captain?" She was not pleased with them, seeing her scattered books and things lying on the floor.

"Please come in and lock the door behind you, Nurse Cohen. I'll explain," the Captain replied. She did as he ordered, and sat down at her desk, facing them.

"Full or half, sir?" Mason asked.

"Full or half what?" An impatient and irritated Nurse Cohen asked.

"Full is fine, Mason." The Captain went over to his fiancé and explained what was happening to her bookcase wall. Mason tapped with his knuckles on the wall, and the cutting noise began, as his Marines started making the hidden door.

"You could have told me about this first, Captain," she said, perturbed.

"It was a secret, Nurse Cohen, as I said. We are secretly changing evacuation routes for my command and senior officers' protection. No one was to know but myself and Mason, unless we came under attack."

They made quick work installing her hidden door. Mason called her and the Captain over to show them the maintenance shaft ladder, and the new motion sensitive light. "You can make it from the bridge conference room to your quarters in less than two minutes, ma'am. The access to your level has been cut off by a one-way hatch that cannot be opened from below. You'll be safer in your quarters than anywhere else on the ship, Nurse Cohen," Mason told her confidently.

She put everything back the way she wanted them, and closed her cabinet doors "Will you be doing this in all the officers' quarters, Mason?"

"No, ma'am, this is special for you and Captain Baines, for your safety," he replied. Although she was not happy about being left out of the loop in the decision to make this escape door, she admitted it was a clever idea.

She thanked him, and he started to leave. "Just a minute, Gunny. Let me see your rib bandages." She came over to him and he unzipped the top of his uniform, and removed it for her to look. He felt uncomfortable with the Captain watching him partially undress to show her his bandages. There was blood covering his side and rib bandages. "Just as I thought, you tore open your wound. Let's go to the hospital, that is, if you're finished altering my quarters, Captain?"

"Yes, we are finished," he replied, looking for the first time at Mason without his shirt on. "You have a splendid physique, Mason. Now get dressed and go to the hospital. I'll expect you back on the bridge in short order," the Captain quipped, walking quickly out of her room.

Nurse Cohen detected a twinge of jealousy in the Captain's voice. "Let's go," she said. They went down the hall a short distance to the hospital, where Mason again took off the top of his uniform for her to unwrap his bandages. She scrubbed and gathered her equipment, and came back to him. She unwrapped his rib bandages, and scanned his wounds on his right side. "You've torn away part of the plasti-skin, Mason. I'll have to reseal it. Lie down and I'll be right back."

He watched her moving back and forth from cabinet to shelf, gathering exactly what she needed to help him, wondering how many men she patched up in her career. "I'm sorry we took you unaware this morning, ma'am," he said. "You weren't supposed to be there."

"I know. I'm just perturbed that the Captain didn't take me into his confidence about this. He could've said something to me about it," she said. "Or you," she added, looking at him.

"It was a secret, ma'am. That way, you would have plausible denial ability," he revealed.

She stopped and looked up at him. "Plausible denial ability about what?"

"Altering the evacuation routes of the senior officers. We haven't even told the Admiral about it, ma'am," he added. He pressed his lips together.

"You're thinking someone at Earth Command is part of this sabotage, aren't you, Mason? My God, that's it." She stared at him for a moment, and picked up an injection pen. "I don't like this, John, not one bit…. This will numb your side, so I can reseal the plasti-skin for you." She continued her work, silent for a while. "You really must be more careful. If you tear it again, we'll have to remove the plasti-skin and put a new one on your wound. Then it will take longer to heal."

"I probably did it climbing the maintenance shafts today. Sorry, ma'am, I didn't mean to make more work for you," he said apologetically.

"It's all right, just be more careful. Now, I'll need to seal it again. Hold your arm up as straight as you can." She used her laser knife again. Mason noticed she was pretty good with that little knife, a real pro. She went across the entire sheet of plasti-skin with a wide band of light, and used a more concentrated, narrower band around the edges. He couldn't feel anything except warmth, but he could smell the plasti-skin burning into his own flesh. He turned his head, and did modified deep breathing and slow exhale to calm his nauseas stomach. "I'm almost finished, just a little more over here," she said, noticing his queasiness. "I can help you. Just a minute." She went back to the cabinet, picked up another injection pen, and gave him the shot. "There, that'll settle your stomach. Feel better, John?" She asked. Nurse Cohen wrapped his new bandages around him, and smiled. He smiled and nodded, and left.

Mason hurriedly went to continue his task of secretly altering emergency procedures for command staff evacuations for the bridge officers, Commander Powers, and Dr. Hassan. No changes would be made to their living quarters, but they would have new escape routes planned for them, different than those in the Hesperia manual, known so well by the Yellow Man.

XXV

Eight days came and went and nothing out of the ordinary happened. Mason was the only one not relieved about it. He figured the Yellow Man knew about their newer defensive preparations and was figuring out how to catch them unaware. Even Nurse Cohen was more relaxed, and concentrating on her upcoming wedding to the Captain. The general assembly hall would be used only for the reception. It would be under armed guard and constant surveillance, to prevent another attack. The actual wedding would be held in the observation lounge, as Mason originally suggested. The happy couple would enter the general assembly hall under the officers' crossed swords. What decorations could be salvaged from the demolished wedding stage in the hall were re-worked into a trellis in the observation lounge, or used as table decorations.

The head wound on Mason's right temple ran over his ear. It healed, but his hair had not grown back enough to cover the bright red scar. He cut his hair "Gunny short" on the sides to try to look less obvious, and his hair even. His right side was still in the healing process, but at least that did not show. Mason had a special nano-fabric undergarment constructed of the same material his one-piece uniform was made from to shield him from laser blasts, knife wounds, and so on. He urged Nurse Cohen and the Captain to wear the same type of undergarments, but they refused.

Master Sergeant Alta and Mason hid laser rifles in several spots in the general assembly hall for extra protection. Mason would be in his formal mess dress, being a member of the wedding party. He could not carry a laser gun, but he would have several blades hidden in his clothing, including his martial arts round blades for throwing. He was very accurate; in fact, he spent hours practicing the week before the wedding.

The day before the wedding, everything on the bridge ran as smooth as silk. That was not the case in the mess hall, however. Of the three refrigeration units, the one that broke down was the unit with the hors d-oeuvres, made painstakingly by the Senior Chief herself. They were all spoiled, and there was not enough time to remake the hundreds of individual items all over again. Anyone who ever planned a wedding knew that anything could go wrong, but an anxious bride was always a nervous wreck beforehand, especially Commander Cohen.

Commander Cohen, Head Nurse, was a highly organized career military officer; meticulous, dedicated, and detail-oriented, all perfect qualities for a Head Surgical Nurse and a command medical officer. But she had become more than a nervous bride, due to the attack on her and Captain Baines two weeks ago at their wedding rehearsal. And now, her hors d'oeuvres were ruined. To top it all off, her hairdresser from the Esplanade salon developed influenza, and called in sick for work. Her nerves were fraying quickly.

Overhearing the Captain remark twice about his "nervous bride" made Mason sympathetic towards Nurse Cohen. When his sister Sarah got married, she was so frazzled the day before her wedding that she actually ran away. Mason had to go find her, and bring her back. He asked for the afternoon off, and decided to bring lunch to Nurse Cohen to make sure she was all right. He knocked on her door, and heard a stern "Go away!" in response. So, he called her on his comm-link, and said he'd brought lunch for her. She let him in.

"I thought you could use a little lunch and some company, ma'am," he said nicely.

"Lunch, maybe. Company, no." He brought the tray inside, and sat it on her dining table.

"I have to make sure you eat something, ma'am, to keep your strength up," Mason said.

She replied, "Adrenalin is keeping my strength up, Mason."

"I can see that, but the crash will leave you weak without some food in your system." He saw she was so nervous she could not sit down. "If you'd like, ma'am, I can see about getting you a massage," he offered, in his nicest voice.

"I don't want a massage, Mason." He knew she needed one. "I was supposed to get my hair done today, but the only hairstylist on this bloody tub is out sick. TODAY! Of all days, she's out today." She was pacing, and visibly distraught.

"Nurse Cohen, you're too tense now, ma'am. You've got to relax. If you were a man, I'd offer to spar with you to help you calm down," he said.

"If I were a man, I'd be calm, because by bride would be worrying about the final preparations, and I'd be sitting on my ass!" An emphatic arm gesture accompanied that comment.

"Nurse Cohen, the time has come, ma'am," he said, facing her.

"The time has come for what, Mason?" She asked impatiently.

"For strong medicine, ma'am. You've been taking care of me for over five years, and today, I'm taking care of you." He reached into his thigh pocket and pulled out the bottle of bourbon Captain Kouras gave him four years ago. "I've been saving this for a special day, ma'am, and that day is today. Now, please get us a couple of glasses with ice, ma'am."

"I don't like bourbon. Never have," she said belligerently.

"You will today, ma'am. This is twenty year old Woodford Reserve, and we're going to enjoy it today. How about those glasses, ma'am?" Mason asked.

"Will you please leave me alone?" She implored.

"No, ma'am. Not today." She grunted loudly at him.

"Oh, all right. I'm out of everything else." She got the two glasses and put some ice cubes into them, brought them over, and held them while he poured four fingers' worth in each glass.

"That's too much for me," she protested.

"We'll see about that. Here's to you, ma'am," and they drank it down. "Good, isn't it, Nurse Cohen?"

"I prefer cognac. This is too rough." She shuttered.

"Rough is better than nothing, ma'am." She shot him a look after that remark. "Now here, let's have another. What shall we toast?"

"How about men? Damn you all!" She exclaimed.

"To all of us damn men!" They clinked glasses and downed another double. She threw her drink down her throat with a vengeance, took off her lab coat, and unbuttoned the top button of her uniform blouse. She untied her tie, ripped it off her neck, and threw it onto the floor. "Are you out to get me drunk, Mason?" She asked accusingly.

"I'm going to drive out the demons who are trying to take you over today, ma'am. To driving out your demons!" They belted it down again. She didn't even make a face this round.

"It tasted better that time. We'd better have one more, just to make sure," she said.

"One more it is, ma'am." And another glass was downed. "Maybe you'd like to sit down now, ma'am?" He asked, beginning to feel the liquor.

"I'm fine. I need to stand up." She began telling him all the myriad details that had her anxious. Mason listened like a good friend to all of her ranting and raving about hors d'oeuvres, decorations, hairdressers, the ruined rehearsal, the destroyed wedding stage. She was depressed about the poor dead, young mess hall crewmen, too. She paced back and forth while talking, getting more pissed off by the minute. When she said, "Damn that Yellow Man," Mason jumped up with another bourbon for her. The big bottle was now half empty.

Mason was being a good friend. The Captain was busy running the ship.

The Senior Chief was busy running the mess hall. Mason was busy getting drunk with Nurse Cohen.

"Will I be hung over at my wedding, John?" She asked, taking her hair down, shaking it loose. He finally got to see her thick, dark red hair falling all around her. Good God, please help me, Mason thought; she was beautiful when she was pissed off!

"What time is your wedding, ma'am?"

"Three o'clock. Fifteen hundred hours to you, Gunnery Sergeant," she giggled. The bourbon was finally starting to work on her.

"You'll be fresh and sweet as a daisy, ma'am." He poured them another, shorter drink.

"To fresh sweet daisies!" She toasted, drinking the bourbon down. She looked at her glass, and asked, "Did you ration my bourbon, John?"

"No, ma'am. I just need more ice." She trotted to the fridge, kicking off her shoes, and came back with two more glasses, filled with ice. He refilled their glasses once more. After that double, she sat down and took a deep breath.

"That's better. Definitely better, John." The second button of her blouse was unbuttoned. "It's hot in here."

They talked and talked, and drank the afternoon away. She decided she could fix her own hair after all. They toasted that decision. Suddenly, the comm-link on Mason's wrist beeped. "Mason here." She giggled in the background.

It was the Senior Chief. "I've tried for hours to reach Nurse Cohen. Have you seen her?"

"About what?" Mason asked.

"About her hors d'oeuvres." She heard giggling in the background.

"What about them, Senior Chief?" He asked her, trying to speak normally, and slurring.

"Does she want spinach or chicken breast?" She asked impatiently.

"Do you want spinach or breasts?" Well, that did it. Nurse Cohen burst out laughing so hard she doubled over, and Mason joined her. Two drunks on her couch, in hysterical laughter.

"Are you all right, Gunny?" The Senior Chief asked.

"No, I'm perfect. You'd better bring a sample of the spinach and the breasts to Nurse Cohen, right away," he said, laughing like a fool.

"And tell her to bring more bourbon!" Nurse Cohen added. They laughed so hard Mason slipped off the couch, and landed on his ass on the floor. She was laughing hysterically at him.

"I'll see what I can do, Gunny." She sounded different.

"I think the Senior Chief's perturbed at me, ma'am." He removed his comm link.

"She just needs bourbon. Do we have any left for her, John?"

"Enough for one drink." They decided to save it for the Senior Chief. The conversation continued in the vein of the ridiculous, until the both of them were in tears. Nurse Cohen lay on the couch next to Mason, sitting on the floor facing her, and put her arm on his shoulder.

Neither Nurse Cohen nor Mason could hear the knock on her door above their laughter, so the Senior Chief was let in by the guard. She came over to the couch, and saw Mason sitting crossed-legged on the floor, the top of his uniform unzipped, with Nurse Cohen lying on the couch facing him, both of them laughing so hard they were in tears.

"Ma'am, you wanted to try your hors d'oeuvres?" The Senior Chief asked, smiling at them. At least they were dressed, she thought.

"Hi, Senior Chief! Nurse Cohen will try the spinach, and I'll take those breasts!" They got hysterical again, while the Senior Chief laughed, too.

"Sit down, Senior Chief. We saved this for you. I'll get you a glass." Nurse Cohen tried to stand, but fell back on the couch. More laughter.

"I think I'll get the glass, ma'am. Are they over here?" All she got in response was a finger pointing at the cabinet.

She poured herself the last of the bourbon, and asked, "What are we toasting?"

"To men. Damn them all!" Mason said, and Nurse Cohen laughed all the more.

"I'll drink to that," the Senior Chief said, looking at Mason.

"Did you bring any more bourbon?" Mason asked, trying in vain to stand, and falling back down. Nurse Cohen doubled over laughing at him.

"No. But he brought the cognac," she said, as the Captain walked in.

"Hi, Captain Baines, sir!" Mason tried again to stand, and fell. Nurse Cohen laughed out loud and lay down on the couch again, nearly in hysteria. She finally noticed her Captain standing next to the couch, holding a bottle of cognac.

Nurse Cohen started giggling at him. "Hi, Captain. We started without you," she said.

"I can see that, my dear," the Captain said, smiling. "Senior Chief, I believe there are snifters next to the glasses in the cabinet - do you mind?"

The Captain poured them all cognac. He innocently asked, "What are we toasting?" He sat on the arm of the couch.

They answered, "To men. Damn them all!" Everyone laughed; the two drunks belted the cognac, as the Captain and Senior Chief sipped their drinks.

"Please sit here, Senior Chief," and the Captain patted the cushion next to him. She sat down, and they looked at Mason and Nurse Cohen, their two happy drunks, and toasted each other. "You are in a much better mood than this morning, Commander," the Captain said. "I have you to thank for that, Mason." He raised his glass to him, sipping his cognac.

"He brought me lunch. I tried to throw him out, but he wouldn't leave. He made me drink bourbon with him," she said, smiling at her Captain.

"I thought you didn't like bourbon," Captain Baines commented.

"I don't. But it's better toasted!" She said, and they were off laughing hysterically again.

"We're going to have to get some food into them, Senior Chief. Why don't we have dinner brought here? Maybe you and I can catch up!" The Captain said to his friend, his eyes twinkling.

They all enjoyed dinner together in Nurse Cohen's quarters. Mason was somehow able to stand before the food arrived, with great effort from all four of them. After their meal, Nurse Cohen thanked Mason again, and told the Senior Chief how much she appreciated all her hard work, and whatever she did for the wedding reception would be fine.

Mason and the Senior Chief thanked their hosts and left. Captain Baines asked his fiancé, "Would you like another cognac?"

She saw her door close, and went to lock it. He came up to her, and she told him, "I'd much rather have dessert, Victor."

He picked her up in his arms. "You are the dessert, my love," and took her to bed.

The next morning, a small package was delivered to Nurse Cohen, from "A Friend." It contained a bottle of aspirin, and a note which read: "Best Bachelorette Party Ever."

XXVI

The wedding day was finally here. Mason decided to sweat off his hangover on the treadmill, and then a sauna. It was working well. He was still hung over in the sauna, but happy. Sherrie wasn't mad at him for getting Nurse Cohen drunk. In fact, it enabled her to get her work done for the wedding faster, with less interference from the nervous bride. He met Master Sergeant Alta in the observation lounge at noon, to secret laser guns away as best they could. Mason went up into the ceiling to make double sure no one nested there for another attack. Satisfied they had done all they could, Alta said, "Better go get prettied up, Gunny. Wear that uniform proud, or I'll kick your ass."

Mason cleaned up and shaved, and put his special nano-fiber undergarment on. The garment ran from his neck all the way down to his thighs. It reminded him of the ancient coats of mail that knights wore in King Arthur times.

His formal mess dress uniform was similar to his class A; the same boots and trousers. His coat featured tapering lapels, worn open over a white shirt with a thin black tie. The coat had an inverted cutaway "V" on the front; a cutaway coat with tails, crimson red, with a single gold button at his waist. He wore a golden sash diagonally, over his right shoulder, down his front and back, and tied in the front directly below his jacket. Full tails in the back, waist-length in front. His hat was black, trimmed in gold braid on the sides. And, of course, the white gloves.

Mason went to his weapons belt, and took all his martial arts throwing blades, concealing them in his uniform. He carefully slid his unsheathed long knife down inside his right boot and a thinner blade inside his left. He put another folding knife in his pocket, along with a hand energy shield, and checked his look in the mirror. He donned his hat and white gloves, ate breath mints, and went to the observation lounge.

All the male officers' mess dress uniforms were worn with their traditional swords tonight. Captain Baines came up to Mason and asked how he felt. "Like a million bucks, Captain." The Captain said he looked like a million bucks, and they shared a laugh.

Fifteen minutes to show time. Lt. Commander Westerly called Mason over to admire his uniform, especially his gold sash. She looked great in her mess dress, very feminine, in fact, and he complimented her. Ensign Campbell joined them, and told the Lt. Commander that the Captain looked "tall, handsome, and blonde, like a Norse god." Those gold braids did a lot for the Captain's uniform. He filled it out perfectly, tall, wide shoulders, thin hips and long legs. He wore his Captain's sword, with the gold scabbard. Mason had never seen a Norse god, but knew the Captain was feeling like one tonight.

Dr. Hassan, also a Captain now, wore the same braids on his shoulders and sleeves. He looked very dapper, with a touch of gray hair on his temples. He showed Mason his Captain's sword, a custom-made one previously owned by his father, much more decorative than the swords of the junior officers, or even Captain Baines. He had waited long enough to attain the rank to wear it, Mason noted. The hilt was very ornate, much like the old French Colonel's cavalry swords. It was magnificent.

Five minutes. The Space Marine guard detail marched into the lounge. They were armed with laser rifles, all that their class A uniforms allowed. They saluted Captain Baines, and took their positions. Ship's security was positioned outside the lounge, both men and the red security droids. Mason took his place.

The soft music started. Mason waited for Commander Cohen. She emerged, the perfect picture of a formally-attired senior military officer. Her hair was flawless, and her make-up was delicate and perfect. She came to him and softly asked, "Ready to give me away, John?"

Mason took off his hat, smiled sweetly at her, and whispered in her ear, "*Never!*" She returned his smile, her eyes twinkling, and a little blush came to her cheeks. He told her she was the most beautiful bride he'd ever seen, as she took his arm. The processional began and he slowly walked her down the carpeted aisle, to her Norse god Captain. She was beautiful, poised and elegant, with a faint blush still on her cheeks. He handed her over to an enraptured Captain Baines, and stepped back.

The ceremony was brief, and perfect. Admiral Tomiko married them, and the Captain kissed his bride, while both of their families watched live, via vid cam feeds. Mason watched them kiss, filled with so many mixed emotions, and applauded dutifully with everyone else as the happy couple walked out of the lounge. He scurried downstairs for their crossed swords entrance.

They came off the lift, the swords were drawn, and "Captain and Mrs.

Baines" were announced. The walkthrough went perfectly, starting the reception. When it was time to cut the cake, Mason noticed a late change take place with the mess crew woman who was to serve them. With so much distraction, almost no one saw her switch the knife on the table for one from under her napkin, but Mason noticed. They cut the first piece and Mrs. Baines was handed a fork by the new crew woman from her apron. Mason made it just in time before Mrs. Baines put the fork and bite of cake in the Captain's mouth. He stopped her hand, saying, "Let's have the new crew member taste it for him, first." The Captain began to object, and the crew woman took the cake knife and lunged at the Captain. Mason stopped the knife, tightly held her arm, and called Corporal Johnson over to take her away. The entire episode lasted only a couple of seconds, and few witnessed the event, having taken place behind the huge wedding cake. Mrs. Baines put down the fork with the cake and held her new husband.

Mason said, "Time to cut the cake," when the white jacketed Senior Chief gave Mrs. Baines the cake on a fork, and began serving everyone. Mason stepped back, like nothing happened, and the reception continued. But Captain Baines and his new wife knew what almost happened. They danced the first dance, looking at one another anew, savoring the moment.

The reception eventually thinned out in a couple of hours, with everyone wishing the happy couple well. Mason sat right beside Captain Baines the entire night, drinking water and coffee. "Captain, I know it's early, but perhaps you and Mrs. Baines would like to retire, sir?"

"Nonsense, Mason. There are still many people here, having a good time," he said.

"Yes, sir," Mason said, and stood up. His hair was standing straight up on the back of his neck. He softly called to Alta on his wrist comm-link, "Be ready. Something's up." His bionic ears picked up a fast whine, and he looked in the direction of the sound in time to see the mini seeker missile coming right at the Captain. He stepped in between the Captain and Mrs. Baines, yelling "Get down!" and pushed them down to the floor. The missile hit the wall behind them and exploded. Another was right behind that one. It exploded against the wall. He pulled out his hand energy shield, and gave it to Captain Baines.

Panic took hold of the crowd immediately, with people running for the doors or hiding under tables. Master Sergeant Alta ran up to Mason and tossed him a laser rifle, and they stood over the newlyweds, protecting them. Laser fire was heard coming from outside the hall, as three dozen or so uniformed men burst into the hall, firing their weapons towards the bride and groom, hiding behind Mason's plasma energy hand shield. The Space Marines engaged the shooters, and a laser battle erupted in the hall, with shots streaking everywhere.

Three attackers broke out and headed right for the Captain. Master

Sergeant Alta was hit, but managed to toss his rifle to Mason, who stood on their table and fired both rifles at the attackers, stopping them cold. He ran out of laser ammo in both rifles; and no more chargers. The Space Marines took down most of the attackers, but their rifles were also empty. The Marines engaged the remaining attackers in hand to hand fighting, as two men in officers' uniforms came out from under a table and rushed Mason, brandishing their swords. Mason leaped up in the air, spinning, and launched his martial arts round blades at them and kicked them, taking them both out. Three more officers charged at the Captain, now standing, with drawn sword. One attacker also drew his sword, and engaged the Captain in an old-fashioned sword fight. Mason fought the two officers in hand to hand combat, until he heard his name called by Dr. Hassan, as the Doctor's sword flew towards him in the air. He unsheathed it the moment he caught it, and charged the two attackers, samurai-style, beheading one, and skewering the other.

The only remaining sound was Captain Baines, fighting with the first swordfighter, who was one of his junior engineering officers. Mrs. Baines was watching in horror. The younger man sliced across the Captain's right arm, causing Baines to drop his sword, and Mason took over. He stopped the man's next thrust, aimed at Baines' neck, with his sword, and picked up the Captain's own sword. He fought the young traitor down to the death knell, with Mason holding crossed swords at his neck. Mason called out, "Marines!!" and held him, until the Space Marines came to take him away. The entire attack took less than ten minutes. Why did their rifles go dry?

"These attackers came from our own ranks, Mason," the Captain said, holding his bleeding right arm. "How many were there?"

"At least forty, Captain Baines. Is Mrs. Baines all right, sir?" She was looking at her husband's bleeding arm. "Please take her to her quarters, Captain," Mason requested, and the Captain did as Mason asked, escorted by Space Marines.

Mason looked for Sherrie everywhere, and finally found her under a table, unconscious and wounded. He carried her in his arms to the hospital, and laid her gently on the only available table. Dr. Hassan was already in surgery, with Nurse Jones assisting, and Nurse Soo had her hands full with wounded crew and officers. The nurse droids were in full service, working quickly at their tables, as the humans worked nearly as fast. Mason took Sherrie's white coat off to look at her wound. He held his hand over the wound, stopping the bleeding. He lifted her eyelids; she was in shock. She was very white and her skin was sticky and cold.

"I'll take her from here, John," Head Nurse Baines spoke, and scanned her head to toe. She was still in her formal mess dress and high heels, with her white lab coat over it. "Help me get her undressed. I'll start an IV." She whipped Sherrie's pants off in a flash, and Mason saw blood; a lot of blood.

Why so much blood from a flesh wound? Then he noticed the blood did not come from her flesh wound, it came from underneath her.

Her wound did not look too deep to him, but she required surgery, according to Nurse Baines. She stabilized her heart with some drug she injected into her IV line and temporarily bandaged her wound. Sherrie was taken in for surgery, with Dr. Hassan and Nurse Baines. Mason watched her in awe. This is her wedding night, he reminded himself.

The Captain notified Mission Director Keene of their situation, and the URE doctor and nurses crossed over into Section 1 to help them out. Mason spoke with Captain Baines while he waited. Nearly the entire maintenance crew attacked the wedding party, along with several junior officers from engineering. The Yellow Man was an excellent recruiter. The situation was now under control, and they would deal with the traitors later. Captain told Mason to stay with the Senior Chief, and they would analyze the attack tomorrow.

Sherrie's surgery was just under two hours, and then she was brought out to recover. Mason stayed at her side. The new Mrs. Baines came over after another surgery to check on Sherrie, as she took off her surgical garb and tossed it away.

"She'll be fine, Mason. She had a lot of internal bleeding, however. I'm afraid she lost the baby. I'm sorry, John." She gently placed her hand on his arm, to console him.

"Baby?" He asked, disbelieving.

"You didn't know?" She asked him quietly. He shook his head.

"I'm truly sorry, John." She took his hand, and gave it a squeeze. "I'll be back later this morning," she said, and left the hospital.

Mason was now the one traumatized. Sherrie lost her baby. Why didn't she tell me? He sat up the entire night with her, watching her sleep. Sherrie lost her baby. Sherrie lost *his* baby.

Sometime later, Sherrie stirred, and Mason held her hand. She eventually opened her blue eyes, and saw him standing by her. "I'm right here, Sherrie. You're all right. Dr. Hassan said you'll be fine," Mason said to reassure her. She said, "I love you," and closed her eyes, falling back to sleep. Later, she woke up, and reached for Mason. He held her close, bending over her so she wouldn't pull any wounds out of repair. He comforted her, whispering soft words of reassurance.

She asked to sit up a little, and Mason went around to the other side of her bed, and gently pulled her up a bit, and put a pillow behind her back. She blinked until she came out from the sedative, and looked at him. "I'm sorry; I don't know what happened to me. Everything was so fast. I saw the men come in and shoot their lasers, and I looked for you. I saw you jump so high, and spin in the air, throwing something at the shooters. You were standing on the table, shooting two guns at the same time. Why did you throw your guns away, and fight with them?"

"Our rifles ran dry. All the charges were empty. No ammo, honey. I had to fight with my hands and knives; at least until Dr. Hassan threw me his sword," he answered.

"I saw you kill those men, John." She paused, and looked in his eyes. "I saw his head roll off his body," she said, turning her head away from him. "I saw the Captain fighting with his sword, and get hurt. Then you took the Captain's sword, too, and brought that officer down on his knees, with your swords crossed at his neck to kill him. Then I went out."

"I didn't kill him, honey. I wanted to, but I called the Space Marines to come get him, Sherrie," he said. Mason could tell she was still terrified over what she witnessed firsthand. "A battle is a horrible thing to witness, especially the first time."

"It was the most horrible thing I've ever seen. You killed so many men, John." She looked at him with fear in her eyes.

"I protected the Captain and his bride. I saved their lives, and the lives of most of the officers and crew in the hall. If I hadn't done my job, they would be dead now," Mason explained.

"I see our Senior Chief is awake. How are you, my dear?" Dr. Hassan asked, and gently smiled. "I'll need to scan you for a moment." Mason stepped out of the way as the Doctor lowered the body scanner down over her. He walked around the bed, making adjustments.

"Ah, yes. You'll be fine in a few days, Senior Chief. But you will need several days of complete rest, just staying in bed. You need time to recover from your trauma, and to heal inside." Dr. Hassan looked at her, and Mason. "I'm afraid you lost the baby, Senior Chief. You had a great deal of internal bleeding, and miscarried while in surgery. We did everything we could to try and save the baby, but it was not possible. You need to heal inside your reproductive organs before I can allow you to resume your work."

She turned her head away from Mason, and started crying. The Doctor went to the IV controller, and programmed it. "I've given you a sedative to allow you to sleep, Senior Chief. You'll sleep for a few more hours, and then we'll talk again." He was so gentle with her, and kind.

Mason was going crazy inside. He wanted to ask her why; why didn't she tell him she was pregnant? But there would be time for that later. Dr. Hassan told him to go get some sleep, but Mason knew that would not happen. He could feel his adrenaline start flowing again. He watched Sherrie fall back asleep. He covered her, and kissed her. Then he left to go to his quarters, showered and changed. His mess dress uniform was ruined, soaked with the blood of the dead, and shredded from laser blasts. His nano-fabric undergarment saved his life, for which he was thankful. He went down to the armory.

Sergeant Lucas was on duty, checking out the laser rifles and the extra charger packs. "Have you found out why we all ran dry, Sergeant Lucas?"

"Gunny, it seems that the rifle cradles were all set to discharge," he said, looking at his scanning computer. "While the rifles were sitting here, waiting for use, their charge was being dispersed. It's a miracle we had even half charged rifles to use last night. The indicator lights all showed full charge, but, in reality, they were all being slowly drained. If you and Master Sergeant Alta hadn't taken a couple of dozen out to hide in the observation lounge and the general assembly hall, we would have had no ammo at all."

Thank God he brought his blades with him last night. Thank God the Space Marines knew how to fight without rifles, too. In fact, they specialized in hand to hand combat, as have Marines throughout the centuries. "Did you scan for prints and DNA, Sergeant Lucas?"

"Yes, that was all done last night. Corporal Johnson is on the other side of the charging array, reconfiguring the computer to begin charging again. We should be back in business in a couple of hours, Gunny," he said.

Mason went to the engineering deck, and found Commander Powers, his head and shoulder bandaged up, but in control. They talked about the last night's events briefly. The Commander was deeply troubled that several of his junior officers from the second shift attacked them. He had never dealt with traitors from his own ranks before. Neither had Mason, and both men were unsettled because of it. Everyone was now under suspicion, regardless of his or her station or rank.

Mason went to the maintenance offices, and found the few surviving ship's security officers there, conducting their investigations. The loyal Maintenance Chief was killed before the wedding. It was appalling to him; nearly the entire department turned traitor. How could those men turn on their own? He would never understand. He would never forgive the surviving traitors.

When Mason came back up top, he was ordered to the Captain's ready room. "We will be joined this morning by Admiral Tomiko, Gunny. Also, my command staff and medical command officers will be present. Please arm yourself, and be in attendance."

"Aye aye, Captain." Mason went to his bridge locker, donned his helmet and vest, and took his laser rifle, which was fully charged, thankfully. One charger station missed by the traitors. He went back into the ready room, and stood guard by his Captain.

The officers came in, one by one. They all stood very stiffly at attention, waiting for the transmission to begin. "Please hold for Admiral Tomiko," the Earth Command operator began.

"Admiral Tomiko here. Is your command staff present, Captain Baines?"

"Yes, they are, Admiral Tomiko. We are all present and accounted for, sir." Captain Baines activated the vid cam so the Admiral could see those in attendance.

"There is nothing worse than a traitor, in my eyes, and in the opinion of Earth Command. Those officers who struck out against their own comrades will be severely dealt with upon return to Moon Base, Captain Baines. Do you know the final tally?"

"Yes, Admiral. Thirty-seven officers and crew from the Maintenance Deck, eight officers and crew from Engineering Deck, and one crewman from the mess hall; all were traitors, and all fought against their fellow officers in an attempt to disable the Hesperia."

"I understand the mess hall crew woman tried to poison you and Commander Baines, is that correct?" Tomiko asked.

"Yes, Admiral, and when the attempt at poisoning us did not succeed, she lunged at us with a knife, but she was stopped and apprehended," Baines replied.

"I didn't hear about that, Captain. How did you stop her?"

"Gunnery Sergeant Mason stopped her. He stopped us from eating the poisoned cake, and then stopped her knife," the Captain responded.

"How many faithful officers and crew did you lose, Captain Baines?"

He went through the roster of dead officers and crewmen, and their numbers totaled twenty-three. "All in all, forty-six dead traitors, and twenty-three dead loyal officers and crewmen. A very devastating night, Admiral."

"Not the way you wanted to remember your wedding day, I'm certain, Captain Baines. My condolences to you and Mrs. Baines," the Admiral said reverently. He paused, obviously considering the impact of the lost men on the crew of the Hesperia. "I understand that there was sabotage inflicted on your armory, Captain," the Admiral resumed.

Baines said, "Yes, sir. The entire charging array for our laser rifles was disabled, and the monitoring computer system was reprogrammed; hence, we did not know until it was too late. Most of our laser rifles were discharged. We had less than ten percent charge in them, except for those rifles taken earlier by the Space Marines and hidden in secret in the observation lounge and general assembly hall. Those arms had about a forty to fifty percent charge in them."

"Are the surviving traitors in custody now?" Tomiko asked.

"Yes, Admiral, although the brig is quite full, now. I ask your permission to put the former brig occupants in cryonic hibernation to allow more room for the new prisoners, sir," he requested.

"Permission granted. All traitors are to be treated as prisoners of war, Captain Baines. Interrogate them, and put them under as soon as possible." Tomiko looked very angry. "We don't want them spreading the word, to gain sympathizers. Earth Command considers this a mutinous rebellion. This rebellion needs to be crushed as soon as possible, Captain. Do you understand? Crushed, without mercy."

"Yes, sir, we all understand." Captain Baines was thrust in the role of a tyrant, Mason noted, and it would be his job to assist him.

Admiral Tomiko asked, "What about the mining operations? Have they been affected by this rebellion?"

"No, Admiral. The mining operations have continued as planned. And Mission Director Keene sent over his own medical team to assist us last night. They proved invaluable to our triage efforts, Admiral," Baines added.

Tomiko nodded. "They will receive word from URE that, upon completion of the platinum mining, all operations will cease, and the Hesperia will return to Moon Base early. I believe the Director is receiving those instructions as we speak."

"Very good, Admiral. Sir, the Director suggested that his miners be placed in cryonic hibernation as soon as possible, to prevent any…altercations, sir," Baines related.

"Agreed. Get as many of them put under as quickly as possible, lock and seal the compartments, Captain Baines. Now, regarding your own crew, Captain. It is the usual practice to place all non-essential officers and crew under cryonic hibernation at the termination of mining operations. But, in this case, I am giving you full autonomy to put any member of your crew under at any time, or keep them awake the entire length of the journey back to Moon Base, is that clear, Captain Baines?" Tomiko asked.

"Yes, Admiral Tomiko. Full autonomy, I understand." To Mason, that meant he was damned if he put them under and a mutiny was attempted, and damned if he did not, and no attempt was made.

"My congratulations to you and Mrs. Baines." They thanked him. "Gunnery Sergeant Mason, in recognition of your selfless bravery protecting the lives of your Captain and Commander Baines at both their rehearsal and wedding reception, and saving the lives of many other officers and crewman, you are hereby awarded the Bronze Star." Mason quietly thanked him. The fallen officers and crewmen were also awarded medals, posthumously, including a Bronze Star for Master Sergeant Alta. Admiral Tomiko took a deep breath.

"And, Captain Baines, you have permission to implement the Omicron Protocol, at your discretion. Were you briefed on that procedure?" Mason wondered if he heard that right.

"Yes, Admiral Tomiko, I was briefed," he confirmed.

"Then be prepared to implement the procedure. Admiral Tomiko out."

The Captain said to his command staff, "At ease. Please, everyone be seated." They all sat down, the officers still stiff and trying not to show emotion. "I will be reassigning officers to fill new vacancies as soon as possible. Our eyes must be on the remaining crewmen, in case there are any unrevealed traitors in our midst. None of us enjoy this situation, I know.

But we must remain vigilant, and defensive. The Hesperia is less guarded than before. We cannot afford to relax, or take our duties lightly. All time off is hereby cancelled. We are all considered on duty twenty-four hours a day, every day. All efforts will be taken to provide regular rest for the officers and crew, but the needs of the ship must take precedence over our own, for now." The Captain let his words sink in. "It is my primary goal to have as many miners and traitors in cryonic hibernation as possible within the next few days. We need to start at once."

"Captain, if I may ask, what is the Omicron Protocol?" Commander Powers asked.

Captain Baines hesitated. "I cannot say. If implemented, those with a need to know will be informed of their duties, and not until then."

"Is it a self-destruction procedure, Captain?" Dr. Hassan asked.

Baines shook his head. "No, quite the opposite; and that's all I can say on the subject."

No one left the ready room. The news was too heavy, and its impact so bold, that they all needed a few moments to absorb it. Mason stood guard, while the Captain talked with his staff, trying to relax and enjoy their camaraderie. At last, the Captain said, "We will meet again this evening at eighteen hundred hours, in the conference room. Hopefully, we will have something to eat, as well. Dismissed." Everyone felt anxious, but blessed to be alive.

XXVII

The Hesperia was a very different place after the mutinous rebellion. All the stores on the Esplanade closed, one by one, even everyone's favorite, the sports bar. The civilians who ran the shops, bar and restaurant were all placed into cryonic hibernation for their protection. It was all work from now on for the entire crew. Once anyone got some time off duty, they generally went to the gym for exercise, then straight back to their quarters. Camaraderie took the back seat for the remainder of the voyage.

Mission Director Keene authorized several crews of his miners for early cryo-sleep. The big iron ore furnaces would not be re-lit. Only the smaller furnaces for platinum-group metals would stay lit, leaving one hundred forty miners as surplus hands. They were all put into hibernation in one day. Keene was very concerned about his lack of security teams available.

Mason took Sherrie back to her quarters after several days in the hospital, and helped her settle in for complete bed rest. She barely spoke to him for days. He tried his best to comfort her, and he was as gentle with her as any man could be, yet she was still terrified of him.

Nurse Baines came to visit her the third day, and brought her a tray of hot soup and a sandwich. Sherrie let her inside, glad for some female company. Nurse Baines scanned her abdomen, and assured her she was healing properly. They chatted about how poor the food selections had gotten in the officers' mess hall, and that made Sherrie feel appreciated. "No one cooks like you, with the care and concern you always showed. It's still better than food pouches, mind you, but by a very slim margin." They enjoyed a good laugh after her comment. "I have to ask you a question for my log, and you have my word your answer is confidential. Did you know you were over two months pregnant?"

Sherrie looked at Nurse Baines. "I know you are familiar with my medical history, and my hospital stay six months before I came on board the Hesperia," the Senior Chief said.

Nurse Baines nodded. "We reviewed your medical files after you were injured."

"I was beaten badly, and kicked repeatedly in my abdomen. I was told by the doctors that I would never be able to have children after that beating." She started to tear up, but continued. "I just assumed the doctors were right, and didn't use any birth control. Why would I need it? Then two weeks ago, I realized I missed my cycle. I thought it was just the stress I was under, you know. I didn't pay any attention until about two days before your wedding, when I got sick in the morning. I planned to visit Dr. Hassan in a few days, ma'am."

Nurse Baines said, "There is the matter of the birthing license from Earth Command. Dr. Hassan put in his report that you were unaware of your pregnancy. He'll be happy to know it was true." She smiled at the Senior Chief. "He listed Mason as the father."

Sherrie began to cry. "I was going to tell him after your wedding. I couldn't believe it. It was a miracle! I didn't even consider we'd need a birthing license," she said, trying to calm herself.

Nurse Baines asked, "Have you talked with him?"

"No. I...I'm afraid of him, Nurse Baines." She cried harder, and Nurse Baines held her hand, and stroked her head.

"Has Mason ever hurt you, Sherrie, abused you in any way, or hit you?" She asked.

"No, he has only been gentle and kind to me. But I saw him kill those men. I'd never seen anyone killed before. I knew he was a Marine; but he was ruthless. He frightens me. I'm terrified he'll kill me." She burst out in tears, sobbing incoherently.

Nurse Baines put her com tablet down, and held Sherrie while she cried and cried. What could she say to her? She was right; Mason was a ruthless killer. Fast, efficient; a master of killing. "I was horrified at the attack myself, Sherrie. I was sitting next to the Captain, and everyone was having a good time. The next second, Mason pushed us down off our chairs on the floor, and saved us from two missiles. Did you see those hit the wall and explode?"

"No, but I heard the explosions, and turned to see what was happening. That's when I saw him, holding two rifles and killing those men running at you and the Captain. Then he leaped in the air and spun around so fast, kicking and fighting. When he got that sword and cut that man's head off, I...I couldn't believe it. Then he stopped the other officer from killing the Captain, and had two swords at his neck to kill him. Then I passed out." She looked at Nurse Baines, and said, "I know he saved you and the Captain, and probably other people, too. But he scares me to death now. How can I know he won't do that to me?"

"Because he loves you, Sherrie. He carried you up to the hospital in his arms when he found you, hurt and bleeding. He stayed by you all night, so worried and concerned about you. He never left your side until you woke up, and you both were told you would be all right. Has he come to see you lately?" She asked quietly.

"Yes, every day. But I can't face him, Nurse Baines. I'm afraid of him." She cried again. "What can I do? I love him so much, but he scares me."

"I'm sure you'll work it out, if you love each other," she said, trying to console her. "Mason's a good man. He's my best friend. I know he'd never hurt me, or you either, Sherrie." She patted her hand, and helped her back to bed, tucking her in. "I'll let myself out. You try to rest, and sleep as much as you can. I'll come back to see you, if you'd like."

"I'd like that, Nurse Baines. Thank you," she said, rolling over.

The bridge officers wore their side arms now. Mason knew the Captain was expecting another attack any day, from anyone. He wore his full combat gear at all times, plus or minus the helmet. The Space Marines were the only ones on board he would eat his meals with. They were all ready for action. They took turns sparring with each other, to sharpen their reflexes. There were few times of laughter, all of them fully aware that the next attack could again come from the officers they guarded daily. Keenly aware of their loss of Master Sergeant Alta, and two other Marines killed during the wedding attack, the Space Marines closed their ranks to all outsiders. It was the way of the warriors.

The loneliest man on board was John Mason. His lover, Sherrie, now feared him, and would barely talk to him. He knew if they couldn't get past this, it was over for good. He had tried to be good to her, and treat her with kindness and respect since the first day he met her. Maybe when she healed, she would get close to him, and love him again. It was tearing him up inside. They had been together three years on the Hesperia, and Mason never considered a future without her. He could not give her up without trying everything to show her how much he loved her.

At his lunch break, Mason went to see her. He knocked on her door, and she let him inside. She sat at her table, in the corner chair, and pulled the table close to her to block him. She had done this every day to him since she was ordered complete rest. He sat down at the opposite chair, and asked her if she felt any better. She just shrugged her shoulders, and said, "Some, but my belly still hurts. My wound is healing okay."

"Would you like me to bring you something to eat? I'll go get whatever you'd like, Sherrie." Her eyes were very red from crying.

"No, that's okay. Nurse Baines brought me some soup and a sandwich earlier. We talked for a while, and she scanned me." At least she was talking with someone, Mason thought. Nurse Baines could get almost anyone to talk with her.

"Sherrie, you know you can talk to me. I'm here for you, and I want to help you. Please talk to me." He held his hands out to her. "Please let me hold your hand, Sherrie. I need to feel your touch." She put out her right hand to him tenuously, not looking at him. Mason took her hand in both of his, and gently held it. "I miss us, the way we were. I want us to be that way again. I want to be next to you, always." She started to cry, tears rolling down her face. He gently touched a tear as it fell, and stood up. He pulled the table away from her, and took her hand again, standing her up. She was trembling. He kissed her hand, and gently took her in his arms, holding her tenderly. She broke down and cried, her head on his shoulder.

He held Sherrie until she stopped crying, stroking her back gently. He led her to her bed and helped her lie down, and covered her. After he removed his weapons belt, he laid on the edge of her bed, spoke to her softly, and caressed her. At long last, she opened her arms, and held him close to her. She said, "I love you, John," and kissed his cheek. He felt such a wave of emotion come over him that he could hardly bear it. She embraced him tighter, and they both lay in each other's arms and cried softly for several minutes.

"Can I come back tonight and stay with you? I know we can't make love, but we can be together." She nodded, and he kissed her again, and got up to leave. He came back to her after his duty on the bridge, brought her dinner, and stayed the night in her bed.

By the month's end, most of the traitors were interrogated by one or more of the command bridge officers, and a security officer, or Mason. Lt. Commander Westerly now realized how much self-control Mason exhibited with Stone when he interviewed him. She was without pity or mercy with the traitors, yet was even with her voice. She wanted to throttle one of the engineering junior officers in particular, who was rude and verbally abusive to her. Mason knew she was ready to hit him, which would have made her the attacker, and him the victim. He stepped in front of the shackled and chained Lieutenant, and intimidated him until he shut up, and the tense moment was resolved. Westerly later thanked him, and apologized to him for thinking he was being a bully to Stone all those years ago.

Most of the traitors would not provide any information. There was not enough space in the brig to separate the men, who were bonding together in solidarity, and refusing to cooperate. The Captain decided to put all prisoners in cryonic hibernation, to maximize his command officers' energy, and their food and water resources. They would be interrogated to Earth Command's satisfaction on Moon Base.

Director Keene approved another two hundred miners for cryonic hibernation, and the next two days was spent putting them in cryo-sleep. When a room's racks became full of hibernation containers, the room was locked and electronically sealed, and fully alarmed. Mutineers would hardly be above awakening their comrades to assist in an attack.

Dead traitors were body bagged, and irreverently stacked one on top of the other in an empty walk-in freezer. The killed loyal officers were also bagged, but stored in the other empty freezer, laid out respectfully. Those makeshift morgues were locked for safety. There were two more freezers left, containing the crews' food for the remainder of the voyage.

The Big Peanut was down to chips and big chunks in a few weeks. Only one crew was still drilling and mining platinum and palladium on it now, while the precious metals furnaces ran 24/7. The take from the Big Peanut was even more than Coordinator Garcia originally estimated.

XXVIII

The Hesperia was set to depart the mining fields in three to five weeks, and all mining activity was focused on harvesting the final chunks of the Big Peanut for its platinum and palladium. Shuttle activity was 24/7, transporting the miners into the massive container - the "glove"- and back to the ship. Drilling was completed, and the huge claws and baskets would not be used again.

The cargo bays were getting emptier by the hour. All available cargo containers had their goods consolidated into as few containers as possible. As many empty cargo containers as could be salvaged were provided to Mission Director Keene for precious metals storage. The Hesperia was bringing in the largest harvest of platinum and platinum-group metals in history.

Earth Command ordered a battle cruiser group escort for the Hesperia, and they were to intercept and continue together near Titan One. Captain Baines and crew were focused on getting to Titan One with no further bloodshed or loss of life. Mason knew doing so may be their goal, but achieving it would be impossible.

No Space Forces crew member alive, officer or enlisted, had dealt with a mutinous rebellion. A mutiny, as defined by Earth Command, was a successful take-over of a ship. A mutinous rebellion was an unsuccessful attempted mutiny that resulted in loss of life. There were few infractions an officer could commit that, if found guilty, resulted in the death penalty; mutiny and mutinous rebellion convictions resulted in a public death sentence. Those convicted Hesperia officers would be publicly hanged in the Main Yard at Earth Command Central in Houston. Convicted enlisted were also put to death, but without the public spectacle.

There were only two remaining traitors still in the brig, both officers from Engineering. They remained silent during their initial interrogations, standing in solidarity with the other traitors and held with them in the brig. But now, each Lieutenant was alone in his own cell, in electronic shackles. They were still receiving treatment as officers, with respect and courtesy. Today, unless they cooperated, they would become prisoners of war, and lose their rank and personal rights. They received their initial interrogations from Commander Powers, and expected him to return for the second interrogations today, but they were in for a surprise.

Lt. Commander Westerly and Mason had become an effective interrogation team. She was cool and efficient, and learned to suppress her emotions in the interrogations. Mason played the "Bad Cop," like a killer guard dog whose leash Westerly held loosely. He was very good in his role. Admiral Tomiko ordered the Lieutenants' interrogations to be conducted as prisoners of war, "with all expediency," meaning Westerly and Mason could go beyond words with the prisoners.

Since both Lieutenants surrendered their rights for legal representation in the initial interrogations, Captain Baines gave free reign to Westerly to proceed at will, according to the manual. She and Mason both knew exactly how far they could go as the interrogation proceeded deeper. Mason promised the Captain to do what was necessary to extract a confession and information. The Lt. Commander decided to save the interrogation of Lieutenant Prentiss for later. It was Prentiss who sword fought the Captain, subdued by Mason's crossed swords at his neck.

Lt. Commander Westerly and Mason entered the brig with Commander Powers, acting as their observer. They ordered spotlights on Lieutenant Kolski, and lights out for the cell holding Prentiss. They entered Kolski's cell with all formality; he stated his name and rank for the record. Westerly read the charges against him, and asked again if wanted legal representation. Kolski pleaded guilty to all 48 charges of murder and attempted murder, sabotage, and mutinous rebellion, and waved legal representation. She proceeded with him as was done with Lieutenant Urz, then they began their alternate path of interrogation as ordered by Admiral Tomiko.

Westerly summed their progress: "Lieutenant Junior Grade Kolski, you have waived your right to legal representation, and plead guilty to all 48 charges, including murder, attempted murder, and mutinous rebellion. You have waived your rights as a Lieutenant Junior Grade, and are now to be known as "Prisoner NR." Do you wish to volunteer any information to us that could possibly help our investigation, and restore some of your rights?" Westerly asked.

"No, sir." Mason saw Kolski smile; he expected to be taken away for cryonic hibernation now, as the enlisted men had been.

"Very well, Prisoner NR. We have received orders from Admiral Tomiko to proceed with your interrogation "with all expediency." Do you know what that means, Prisoner NR?"

"No, sir," he said, smirking.

"It means we can and will do whatever is necessary to gain a confession and other pertinent information to our investigation. The penalty for mutinous rebellion is public execution by hanging. We can do what we will to you, as you are sentenced to die anyway." Westerly was as cool as ice.

"You can't do that. I have to have a court martial first!" Kolski yelled.

"Wrong, Prisoner NR. We are authorized to do what we will to you. In pleading guilty and waiving your rights, you also waived the right to a court martial." Westerly stared at him.

"I want to talk with an attorney!" Kolski cried out.

"Too late for that, Prisoner NR." Westerly stared him down.

Kolski yelled, "You queer bitch, you can't do this to me!"

"We have another two charges against you now, Prisoner NR, being insubordinate and verbally abusive to a command officer. How do you plead, Prisoner NR?" Westerly asked.

"This is bogus. You can't do this to me!" Kolski screamed.

"I am doing this to you now, Prisoner NR," Westerly stated. This line of badgering continued for several minutes, and Westerly ordered Kolski's chains tightened. He protested, and was verbally abusive to her, while she remained like an iceberg.

"Prisoner NR, do you wish to make a confession?" She asked.

"No, sir dyke." He laughed.

"Prisoner NR, I am bored with you." Westerly stepped back and stood at parade rest. It was Mason's turn. He stood in front of Kolski, who was shorter than Mason.

"Prisoner NR, do you know who I am?" Mason asked.

"Yes, her robot." He laughed at his own joke.

"No, Prisoner NR. I am Gunnery Sergeant John Mason, Prime Marine. I report directly to Captain Baines, who has given me free reign to extract a confession from you. I hold over twenty black belts in all forms of martial arts. Do you know what that means, Prisoner NR?"

"It means nothing. You can't hurt me," he said flippantly.

"Oh yes I can, Prisoner NR." Mason removed his helmet, protective vest, and weapons belt and laid them down in the corner of his cell.

"Are you going to take off your uniform, too, you pompous ass?" Kolski asked, sounding a bit effeminate.

"Not yet. Only if I get excited and decide to sodomize you, Prisoner NR." The Prisoner was suddenly silent. Mason had uncovered the key to break him.

Mason put on his gloves, and began his kung fu warm-ups as the Lt. Commander stepped back. He proceeded as he had done with Stone, throwing punches close to Kolski's head. Mason unzipped the top half of his uniform and removed his arms, and continued his warm ups. He began to stretch his long muscular legs, and said, "Would you like to make a confession, Prisoner NR?" Silence. Mason asked, "Prisoner NR, will you tell me who hired you?" Nothing. "Prisoner NR, you are now my new sparring partner." Mason kicked his thigh, and Kolski yelled in pain.

"You can't do this to me! Stop it!"

"I can and I will, Prisoner NR. Who hired you?" Silence. Mason jumped and threw a flat kick into his upper back, and Kolski yelled again. Mason stopped, went directly in front of Kolski, and said, "I can and will make you talk. I have hit you with easy kicks in your heavy muscle areas, to not deeply injure you."

"You can't do this this to me, you big fag," Kolski cried.

"You don't get it, do you, Prisoner NR? How'd you ever get to be an officer? You dumb piece of shit. I get to come in here every day and have fun with you. We'll play every day, the entire eighteen months back to Moon Base. Then, if there's anything left of you, they'll drag your over-fucked ass to the gallows at Earth Command Center, and hang you, while everyone watches on public video. The Lt. Commander will make sure your entire family watches their son be hanged as a traitor." Mason hit him open-handed on his chest.

"Stop it! Stop it! You fag!" Kolski was crying.

"Prisoner NR, we all know who the fag is here. Did the man who recruited you promise you his big dick every night?" Another flat handed hit, in his mid-section.

Kolski cried, "No, he didn't."

"Tell me who he is, or I'll make you cry like a girl," Mason warned.

"No, don't hit me again. Don't hit me anymore," Kolski said, teary eyed.

Mason patted him on the head. "Now, now, Prisoner NR. Don't cry. All you gotta do is answer my questions and I'll stop. Who recruited you?" Silence again. "Okay, you sweet little queer. Here it comes." Mason kicked at Kolski's groin, stopping short of touching him. Kolski screamed anyway. Mason shouted, "Tell me who recruited you!" Silence.

"Oh, great. I get to really have fun now." Mason kick both thighs, and spun around to give him a big kick on his ass. After Kolski yelled in pain, Mason went around behind him, picking him up by his chains. He leaned in to Kolski's ear and whispered, "She likes to watch me, you know. Look at her. It makes her hot. I fucked that other guy for over an hour until he screamed and bawled like a baby. I tore a gash in his anus. He bled like a stuck pig all over me."

"No! Don't do that, please, no. Stop!" Kolski broke down sobbing.

"Okay, Prisoner NR, I won't hurt you anymore. Just be a nice little boy and tell me: who recruited you?" Mason asked nicely.

"The Yellow Man. He asked me to help him." Kolski was sobbing incoherently.

Mason faced him. "Where did you meet the Yellow Man?"

"Moon Base. He had a party for us." Kolski was beginning to speak normally. "He paid me $10,000 every time I helped him and $10,000 in gold coins to start. He said the ship would not be coming back, and a lot of people would die. He promised to get us off the ship if we helped him," Kolski confessed. "He sent the signal."

"What was the signal, Prisoner NR?" Silence. Mason asked again, but no answer. Mason pulled on his neck shackle and sent electronic shocks into Kolski. "What was the signal?"

Kolski cried out, "An envelope with $10,000 was put under my pillow, with a note telling us to attack during the reception."

Mason asked, "How does the Yellow Man know everything that happens on the ship?"

"Through the mining ops computer. A monitoring program was installed for surveillance of the engineering deck from the mining ops computer. They know everything we do!" Kolski shouted at his former boss, Powers, silently observing. "We installed it during our stop on Titan One," he admitted.

"Who helped you install it?" Mason asked forcefully.

"Urz and Prentiss and…"

"And who else?" Silence. Mason was determined to get the other traitor's name.

"Now, Prisoner NR, You're pissing me off. You were doing so good, too." Mason karate chopped him in the abdomen. Kolski spat out a little blood. "Tell me who else, or you'll get more." No response. Mason reached down and grabbed him by his balls. Kolski screamed.

"Now tell me who helped you!" Mason squeezed Kolski's balls again.

"Juarez! Lieutenant Juarez! Stop it! It hurts!" He was crying again.

Mason let go of his genitalia. Commander Powers' chair was empty. "Now you did good, Prisoner NR. Just tell me who else is working for the Yellow Man we don't know about, and I'll go. Tell me." Mason put his hand on Kolski's neck shackle again. "Tell me, or I'll shock you for five minutes, and you'll piss your pants."

No response. Mason knew there was someone else, someone Kolski feared as much as him. "Tell me.TELL ME!" Nothing. Mason grabbed the electronic neck shackle and sent the current to Kolski, the man crying and grimacing in pain. When he pissed his pants, Mason let go.

"You're letting me have all kinds of fun today, Prisoner NR. You know, I think I'll come back tonight, and…" Mason whispered obscenities in his ear, promising to sodomize him all night.

"No, I can't. He said he'd kill us if we told." He sobbed like a baby.

"Who did? Who threatened you? WHO!" Mason screamed in his ear.

"Takeda, the Chief Tech. He's the boss. He's the one." Westerly quickly left his cell.

Mason spoke softly now. "Do you meet with him on the ship?"

"Yes, Section 2, near the platinum stacks. There are more, many more, but I don't know their names. They're miners. I don't know their names, I swear it," he whimpered.

"One last question and I'll leave. Who drained the laser rifles?" Mason was very nice.

"Juarez did. He rigged a control switch in engineering at his station. He drained them all before the Captain's wedding, and reprogrammed their control computers to not register properly." Kolski said, and smiled. "He even drained the main lasers on the ship."

Mason grabbed his gear and left, calling Captain Baines with the new info. So, something happened on the eighth day, after all. They had been rendered defenseless. Mason's timeline projection had been correct.

Captain Baines ordered Juarez arrested pending investigation. Admiral Tomiko was immediately informed of the new information gathered by Westerly and Mason. The URE quickly authorized the arrest of Chief Technician Takeda, but since he was a civilian, he was held in the miners' brig in Section 3. A plan was devised by Director Keene and the Captain to uncover the plotting miners in Section 2 when they stored the bars of platinum tonight.

Commander Powers discovered the rigged electronic switch by Juarez, and ascertained that he had indeed drained the ship's defensive laser weapons. The Hesperia's engines were engaged to power the main guns back up to full power, but it would take over an hour to get back to one hundred percent charge.

The surveillance program installed on the mining operations computer system was now embedded with the general mining operations, and had been running in tandem with it for years. The Director did not know if it would be safe to disengage it. Earth Command had no direct control over the URE mining mission computers. It became a logistical nightmare. While the URE and Earth Command duked it out in Houston, Mason and the Captain devised their own plans.

There was no question that another, or perhaps several, attacks would be made on the Hesperia, until the Yellow Man gained control over the ship. Baines thought of the ship captains in ancient times, with their precious cargos of gold and silver from the New World, facing dangerous seas fraught with pirates. There was little difference now. Only the technology had changed. The greed and treachery of some men had not changed over the centuries. Their own technology was used against them, with Urz's attempted sabotage of the ship's communications systems, and this newly-discovered surveillance program in the URE's mission operation's computers. He remembered what Kolski said, "They know everything we do." Since Urz gave the Yellow Man the ship's manual, he also knew everything that could be done. Almost.

The Captain called an emergency meeting with Commander Powers, Lt. Commanders Westerly and Davis, Captain Kouras, and Mason, and held the meeting in the hospital, inside Captain Kouras' suite. "If he knows everything we do, what I want to know is, does he know everything we *can* do?" Captain Baines asked Kouras.

"There are still a few tricks up our sleeves, Captain Baines. As you know, not all information is stored in the ship's computers, for times such as these. The real test will be implementing the procedures without the Yellow Man detecting our intentions, and attempting to thwart our efforts."

Mason asked for permission to speak and received it. "Captain, not telling anyone what you were about to do until you were actually doing it is the best way to maintain secrecy. I don't think you should consider sharing any plans with anyone, sir. We don't know what other surveillance programs the Yellow Man may have in place. He has played all of us like marionettes, Captain. We just today found out how he managed to do that. What if we could beat him at his own game, sir? He has used decoys, subterfuge, information, and misinformation to his advantage, because everything we do is straightforward, by the manual, and upfront. That's how the service operates. Captain, perhaps the time has come for counterespionage tactics, sir," Mason suggested.

Baines eyes suddenly lit up. "Yes, Mason. We will balance the equation!" He assigned a special task to each of the officers present to be completed in total secrecy in four hours. He dismissed the officers, but kept Mason behind to speak with his old Captain.

"Captain Kouras, I fear the Yellow Man has more than one helping hand at Earth Command. I don't want to infer anything of that nature to the Admiral during one of our communiqués, but I think he fears the same thing. Do you know how many at Earth Command are aware of the Omicron Protocol?" Baines asked.

Kouras thought for a minute, and then answered. "The protocol has only been available on this ship. The systems designers would have to know the protocol, as well as programmers and builders during the assembly process of the ship. It's safe to assume that the Yellow Man, if he does indeed have liaisons at Earth Command, will be able to recognize the protocol when it commences, Captain Baines."

Captain Kouras looked at Baines, and added, "I can think of no other person I would want in command of this vessel right now, Captain Baines. If anyone in the Space Forces can outthink the Yellow Man, it surely is you." He smiled, and saluted his former executive officer. Baines returned his salute, and left with Mason.

Mason was sick to his stomach after interrogating Kolski. He stopped the lift from going down to the mess hall, and selected another option. He went inside the chapel, and it was empty. It was all-denominational, meaning that it was just an empty, quiet room, where you could sit and talk with the Man Upstairs. No crucifix, statues, tiles with Koranic verse, alters, or artifacts. Mason bowed his head and tried to remember some of his childhood prayers, but could not. How could a child be prepared for what he had to do in his career? He had done many terrible things in his career, and many wonderful things. It all depended on who read the report.

Today's interrogation made him sick to his stomach, and now he was sick to his soul. He had no tolerance for traitors, so he did what was necessary. He identified latent homosexual tendencies in a young officer, and amplified the man's fear of them to his advantage to break down his defenses. Mason knew he obtained information that might help save the ship and all of their lives; that's how he could do the things he did. But it reviled him to recall what he said to Kolski. He could only imagine what actually happened to Kolski as a little boy that allowed his fear to overcome his senses. The prisoner was right; even if someone interrogating him wanted to sodomize him for torture or to induce pain, it would not be allowed. Only the threat of committing those acts was allowed, even when dealing with traitors. You could threaten to do almost anything.

Mason asked God for forgiveness for what he said to Kolski. He asked for them all to make it back home alive. He prayed for strength and wisdom. Then, he left.

In the mess hall, Mason picked up a turkey sandwich and a soda, hoping to settle his stomach. He hoped Westerly hadn't heard what he whispered in Kolski's ear, but she probably did. Now, she must think I'm a sodomizing brute, Mason thought. Wonderful. He was so disgusted with himself, he threw down the other half of his sandwich and left.

He went back to see Captain Kouras, who was riding his Exercycle again, pedaling so fast, going nowhere. The Captain welcomed him back, and sat down with him for a few minutes. "I had a feeling you'd be coming back around today, Mason. What's bothering you?"

Mason told him about his interrogation today, leaving out the really disgusting parts, but covering the low points. "I've interrogated more prisoners in the last three days than in my last eight years, Captain. And today, particularly important information was gathered. But I feel sick about it. That young officer had obviously been violated or somehow damaged as a child, and I saw it, and used it to my advantage. Maybe I'm getting soft. I know I'm supposed to separate myself from the role I have to play in those interrogations, but I crossed over today, and felt sorry for him. I hate him for being a traitor, but maybe he would not have become one, if someone had not violated him as a boy."

"You are to be commended for feeling compassion for him, yet understanding what brought about expedient results with the prisoner, Mason. I would be more concerned if you did not feel sick after what you did today. Few men are capable of separating themselves completely each and every time we are called to perform an unpleasant duty. If it did not bother you, think of the man you would be turning into. The Space Forces have people who actually enjoy that type of thing. They are specialists at it. The ones I've met are the sickest people one can imagine. It only proves to me what good qualities you possess in your ability to reject your own performance in that interrogation room today. It will bother you for quite some time, I fear, but know this. Do you think that Captain Baines would have sent a specialist in there with the traitor? No, for the specialist would have enjoyed prolonging the interrogation, making the prisoner suffer. Baines knew you would discover the prisoner's weakness, use it to uncover important information, and then leave. You did not hurt him too much with your easy kicks and jabs, or torture him. A specialist would still be in there with him, enjoying his pain and anguish, making the poor fool writhe in agony. You actually treated him with kindness in leaving immediately when you got what you needed, don't you see?" Kouras explained.

"Yes, sir. But it's still a little too fresh for me, Captain Kouras," Mason said.

"That's exactly what makes you a good Marine, Mason." He thanked the Captain for his time, and took to heart his advice.

After the second shift came on duty, Captain Baines asked Mason and his four hand-picked Space Marines to meet with him in the Captain's storeroom. Corporals Johnson, Milton, Garcia and Sergeant Lucas sat with Mason as the Captain unfolded his plan. "We need to discover what the miners are planning. I want you to go to Section 2 precious metals storage area and record as much information as possible, without being discovered. This will require you all to be virtually invisible to the naked eye, and to their scanners. You'll have to wear plasma cloaks. Have any of you worn a plasma cloak before?" Only Mason raised his hand. "They are unwieldy, and difficult to use. They are nearly frictionless, meaning they will not lie next to their own fabric. They slip and slide over themselves, yet closure of their seams is required for full invisibility. Once they are on, you must remain motionless. The slightest movement will give you away, and we'll have a laser battle on our hands, with too much explanation to the URE as to why we were in their precious metals storage area in the first place."

He continued. "It is imperative that we uncover their plans, and discover who the liaison for the Yellow Man is, the one delivering his money and messages to them. He is the kingpin on the ship. If it was Chief Takeda, then the Yellow Man will have to select someone else to deliver his money and threats. Since Takeda was arrested tonight, I'm hoping there will be new and important information passed to the miners in Section 2. I want maximum stealth, and no confrontation. We do not want them to know we are on to them and their meeting place. Are we in full understanding with one another?" The Captain waited for their responses.

"Will there be any back-up if something goes wrong, Captain?" Corporal Garcia asked.

"No. In fact, I will not admit any knowledge of your activities, to protect the ship and Earth Command. You will be on your own. This is strictly voluntary," Baines stated. "Are you men up for this tonight?" The Captain looked at the five of them, one by one.

"Yes, sir," they all answered.

"Good men. Now, the precious metals are stored after smelting is completed, around midnight. That will give you a few hours to get familiar with these plasma cloaks." Captain Baines opened a box, and handed each man his plasma cloak. Only Mason held on to his cloak without dropping it, due to its slipperiness. "Gunny will train each of you to hold, transport, and wear your cloaks in total stealth. If any man fails tonight, you all fail. Are we clear?" The Captain looked at each man for understanding and confirmation of the risk they were taking. "There can be no mistakes, gentlemen. Understood?"

They all acknowledged him, and saluted him as he left them in his storeroom. Mason deftly swirled his cloak up, over and around him, and it was on him in a flash; he disappeared completely. Although the Marines laughed at his maneuvers, they knew he had much more practice with the tricky cloak than they would have time for tonight. Each man practiced swirling the cloak, with Mason assisting their hand and wrist movements. The cloak had no buttons, Velcro, or closures. It must lie perfectly on itself to provide total invisibility to the wearer. Mason had them all practice their martial arts breathing techniques for relaxation, and they tried the swirling maneuvers again.

"We will stand next to the precious metals storage lockers and cargo containers, and blend into them. The miners will see no difference between a locker, container, or wall, and us. We must become the thing we stand in front of, or next to. We must listen and observe undetected. If you stand in front of the wall, you are the wall. The wall does not breathe or move. If you stand beside a locker, you are the locker. The locker does not move. Understand? The most effective method for using the cloak is meditation." They practiced for over two hours, until each man was confident in his ability to don the cloak correctly, and stand silently. They folded their cloaks, tucked them into their uniforms, and casually strolled to the Section 1 crossing area.

"We are here to ascertain the accuracy of the vid cams installed along the crossover corridor," Mason said. Since he was the Special Security Chief, he moved with impunity anywhere on the Hesperia. The ship's security crewman let his group pass into Section 2. They made their way slowly down the long corridor, listening for the midnight shift change. When they heard the ship's security change the guard, they hurried towards the precious metals storage area. Each man chose his spot, trying to hide in a crevice or on top of a cargo container welded to the wall, for maximum stealth and protection. When Mason heard footsteps approaching, he signaled them to swirl their cloaks around and over them, and be silent.

"Hurry up with that anti-grav cart, idiot. We can't be gone too long," the leader said. "Just put it here for a minute, and close the door. All right, now you heard Takeda was busted tonight, right?" Grumbled agreements were heard.

"Keene won't get anything out of him, and the military can't touch him. So we have nothing to worry about," the leader said.

"Yeah, but what about our money? I haven't seen any money the last three weeks, and it's getting near time." More grumbling about the absence of their pay-offs.

"Just shut-up, Pearson. He's always given us our money. Now, we have to make sure no more of us get canned in cryo-sleep, you get me? Enough of us are gone already. It'll take an entire day to get everyone awake now, as it is. We have to be ready when he gives us the signal. This platinum smelting is nearly finished, and we need to take over the ship the minute he gives us the signal, you got me?"

"What if the Space Forces crew is on to us, Max? They've got the heavy firepower in there. I don't want to get blasted, or spend the rest of my life in prison, like the Excelon guys."

"The Excelon guys didn't have the Yellow Man, and we do. He knows exactly what they're going to do even before they do. He's called every step they took before they knew what to do. There's enough of his men left inside Section 1 to take over the ship. When they do, we just blast the rest of them, and it's a free ride to Titan One." He laughed. "Those guys will all be standing there with their dicks hanging out when we come through that bridge door. It'll be beautiful."

"Are you sure that he got us enough blast packs to blow the doors?"

"You just worry about your assignment, and he'll worry about his. Now let's get this stuff loaded into the cargo container, and seal it up."

Mason had to wait until the miners loaded up the new platinum bars into the cargo containers, locked and sealed them, and left the room. His Marines waited until Mason gave the "all clear," before leaving Section 2. They jogged down the corridor until they got close to the security guard, then casually told him all was well, and walked down the hall. When they were out of the guard's sight, they ran to the lift for the bridge, while Mason signaled Captain Baines they were coming.

The Captain met with them in his conference room, listened to their recordings, and got very silent. Mason collected their cloaks, and the Captain swore them to secrecy. The Space Marines left to get a little shut-eye, leaving Mason sitting with Captain Baines.

"Captain, will you be advising Admiral Tomiko of our new findings, sir?" Mason asked.

"I don't know, Mason. I don't know. Our transmissions are surely being monitored by someone, I'm sure." The Captain's brow was furrowed deeply.

"Sir, it's safe to assume that he's listening right now," Mason said, and the Captain looked at him with all seriousness and scrutiny. Mason stood and went to the storage cabinet, removed some paper, and sat back down. He wrote on it, "We are swimming with the sharks." He handed the paper to Captain Baines, and received a slow nod of his head in response. He further wrote, "Recommend you request Keene inventory all weapons and blast packs immediately, and report any missing or "defective" items." The Captain nodded in agreement, and typed a memo to Mission Director Keene.

XXIX

On the bridge, everyone seemed preoccupied with their work stations, so Mason quietly relieved the Space Marines on guard, and took over his guard position. He knew he would be awake for the full nineteen or so months to get back to Moon Base, but he wondered if Sherrie would be allowed to stay awake, or be deemed as non-essential and put into cryo-sleep. He knew she'd be safer in a cryonic container than in the mess hall, but he also wanted her to be with him. He would just have to wait and find out the Captain's decision.

In his bridge observations, Mason overheard someone talking with Lt. Commander Davis about cargo containers, and he had a revelation. The only place the contraband could have been smuggled on board was in the MM & E cargo containers loaded on board on Titan One. He suspected as much over the last few years, but there was no way to prove anything. Maybe someone was in too much of a hurry to hide something. What if Dr. Reese was one of the conspirators, and wanted out? What if he was the one who brought the octagonal tube on board in the first place, and was only trying to find out what was inside the thing when someone tried to stop him, using the tube to kill him? Perhaps they would find something now, when the containers were being consolidated.

The Captain met his command staff in Captain Kouras' room, and received input from them on their assigned tasks. Westerly formulated the plan to refold the big container that the remnants of the Big Peanut were presently being harvested from, and Davis was tasked with inspecting all the cargo bay containers, and consolidating their contents even further to give Director Keene as much holding space as possible.

Powers was given the task of plotting six alternate courses to Titan One, other than the one already programmed into the ship's computer. He felt he was treated like a junior navigator with that assignment. The Captain had not permitted any of them to utilize the ship's computer in completion of their tasks, make notes in their com tablets, or even reference an entry in the computer. They had to do all the calculations manually, on paper. "I only got three alternate courses plotted, Captain. These calculations take forever to complete. That's why we use the computer in the first place."

Captain Baines took his paper notes from Powers, and plotted the other three courses in less than five minutes, as his staff watched in awe. "All right, did anyone else have any difficulties with their assignments?" No one dare raise an objection after his impressive performance with astro-navigational problem solving. "Very well, then. You will all retain this information at your work stations, available only to yourselves, and only while you are present at your station. If you go to the officers' mess hall, or the toilet, take them with you. You are to say nothing to no one about these, understood?" They all nodded.

"Now, Davis, you are to commence your inspections early tomorrow morning. You've planned for all four cargo bays, correct? Good. Mason, have four of your most trusted men in cargo bay 1 at o-five hundred hours tomorrow to assist Lt. Commander Davis. Your task must be completed before eighteen hundred hours tomorrow night."

"Yes, Captain," Davis and Mason answered.

"Now, Westerly; Director Keene thinks he needs another four or five weeks to get the chunks of platinum out of the glove. What did your study conclude?"

"He could empty the container into the main floor of Section 4 in less than two hours, with the assistance of the shuttles, and pick up the chunks from there. Then, we could close the Section 4 bay doors. We could refold the glove in another hour, and have it re-stored in its locked hold in one more hour, Captain."

"Did anyone see any of you working on these contingencies?" The Captain asked.

They all said "no."

"Very good. You are to make sure no one sees them, knows about them, or has any inkling what I have asked you to do today. Is that clear?"

They all said, "Yes, Captain."

"Westerly, do nothing until I order you to begin. Powers, be ready to implement any of those six courses, but do not, I repeat, do not load them into the computer. Understood?" They all said they understood, and the Captain dismissed the meeting.

Mason had been listening with a high degree of interest to Captain Baines' meeting. The Captain looked at him after his command officers left, and asked him what he discerned from the meeting. "We're planning to book five weeks early, Captain Baines, and not tell anyone about it until the Hesperia is at hyper-speed."

"Good man, Mason. Now, if you have any unfinished work in the ship's library, wrap things up tonight. The library won't be available for a few days." The Captain gave him the night off, and left.

"Well, that was an interesting turn of events, eh, Gunny? I know he has more than one option up his sleeve, however. Best to be prepared for anything. By the way, I had this brought up for you and your lady, Mason. Captain Baines and I are consolidating our things." Captain Kouras pointed to his other room, where stood one case of wine, and another case of bourbon. Mason thanked him, and left with his gifts before he changed his mind.

The ship's library was Mason's primary study location about the octagonal tube. It had been the bane of his existence since he found it. Mason was certain it held an important, if not crucial bearing on his investigations, and the current state of affairs the Hesperia was in today. Since this was probably his last day to study the tube, he wanted to give it his last best shot.

The octagonal tube would not open, no matter how or what they tried. It was the most likely weapon used to murder Dr. Richard Reese, yet the proof was not 100%. Soon, the other members of his "tube group" would join him for an hour or so, in one final attempt to make sense of it: Nurse Baines, Dr. Hassan, and Lt. Commander Westerly. They were bringing the octagonal tube with them from the Captain's safe for one last discussion.

Per Mason's recommendation, Lt. Commander Davis asked the Captain for permission to inspect Dr. Reese's and Dr. Wise's private lockers. The Captain gave his approval, so long as either Dr. Moore or Dr. Bergen would approve and observe the locker's opening and inspection. Davis placed the request with Dr. Moore, and they were waiting for his answer.

Mason got up to look out the library window to clear his mind. He needed clarity and focus, if his hunch proved true. It might only be a few days before the Hesperia would be heading back to Moon Base, or a month, at the latest. Not much time left for investigation; too much time for treachery and sabotage.

His comm-link beeped. "Gunny, this is Lt. Commander Davis. Dr. Moore is with us. The live feed begins now." Davis began narrating his breaking of the seal on Dr. Wise's locker. He watched them open the locker, scan it, and quickly search its contents. It contained clothes, shoes, books, and a case of brandy; the same contents when he sealed that locker so long ago. Davis repacked the locker and affixed the ship's electronic seal on the door, which would shriek if removed or tampered with.

They moved down to Dr. Reese's locker. They found clothes, shoes, books, photos, scotch, a cane and a walking stick.

"Lt. Commander Davis, please ask Dr. Moore if Dr. Reese used a cane," Mason requested, his neck hairs beginning to twitch.

"Gunny, Dr. Moore said Dr. Reese was very fit and ran the treadmill daily. Why would he have a walking stick?" Davis asked Dr. Moore.

"Lt. Commander, bring the cane and walking stick to the bridge at once," Mason heard the Captain say. "Mason, in my ready room immediately." Mason ran out the door, carrying his com tablet and bundle of papers into the lift.

The lift stopped and Dr. Hassan and Nurse Baines got in with him. "Mason, the Captain ordered us to the bridge immediately. Do you know why?"

"Yes, Dr. Hassan, I do. Would it be possible to get Captain Kouras a live vid cam feed, if you and Captain Baines approve it, sir?" Mason was trying not to show his excitement.

"I'll arrange it now, Gunny." While the Doctor made his call to Nurse Jones to set up the live feed, Nurse Baines was watching Mason, holding his com tablet and papers, and not saying a word. Mason raised his eyebrow and nodded his head at her.

"What took you so long, Gunny? Davis and Dr. Moore will be here any second," the Captain said anxiously. Mason asked if Captain Kouras could join in, and he said, "Of course." They all stood in the ready room, waiting.

"Captain Baines, these are the two items of question found in Dr. Reese's locker," Davis said, laying the cane and walking stick down carefully, with his gloved hands.

"Please, everyone be seated." Captain Baines asked Dr. Moore to repeat what he told Davis about Dr. Reese's excellent physical conditioning. "Captain Kouras, did you inventory Dr. Reese's personal things in his locker prior to having it sealed, sir?"

"Absolutely. There's a log entry and a recording available detailing the contents," Kouras said.

Captain Baines searched his log and found the entry. "I'll play the recording for all of us now." It showed the locker being opened, containing clothing, shoes, a few books, photos, and two cases of scotch whiskey.

"Then where did that cane come from, Captain?" Dr. Moore asked. "And that stick? How did they come to be inside his locker, if it was sealed?"

"Now, that is what we are all here to discover, Dr. Moore. Davis, have Lt. Commander Westerly join us, and bring her scanner. This meeting is now being recorded, ladies and gentlemen." He tossed a vid cam in the air to record everyone present. The Captain ordered Westerly and Nurse Baines to scan the stick and cane. "Now, both of you download your results to the Gunnery Sergeant's com tablet, and my own computer. They held up their scanners and projected their downloads. "Mason, please tell us what you see." The Captain turned to listen.

"Captain, both items are of identical composition. They appear to be wood, but they are metallic. Sir, they are tubes, not solid, both with octagonal ends. The stick is etched or carved with symbols in a pattern, and the cane has raised symbols on it. Neither scanner could penetrate the cane or stick to identify the contents. There are two partial prints on the big stick, Captain. I am accessing the computer to check them against the ship's database now for positive identification. One print has been partially identified, Captain Baines. Do you wish me to read the name, sir?" Mason asked calmly.

"No, show it to me, Mason." He showed the com table to the Captain. Baines called Admiral Tomiko on a secure channel, Code Red. He also ordered a security detail to be readied. Baines stood up with everyone else, and waited for the Admiral.

"Admiral Tomiko here. What is your Code Red, Captain Baines?" The Captain turned the vid screen around to show the Admiral everyone present in the room. He brought him up to speed on the meeting, the cane and the stick, and the yet-to-be-announced owner of the fingerprint.

"Do we have a positive ID on the second fingerprint, Gunny?" The Captain asked calmly.

"Yes, Captain Baines. The second name is the same, sir," Mason answered quietly.

"Admiral Tomiko, I am sending you the results of the fingerprint ID, sir." The Captain took Mason's com tablet, and sent over the fingerprint ID results to the Admiral.

"Make your arrest, Captain Baines. Tomiko out."

"Dr. Moore, please accompany Lt. Commander Westerly and the security team to your research labs. We are going to arrest Dr. Honig, sir." He did as instructed.

"Gunny, do you have any more information for us from the scans?" Captain Baines asked, sitting down again.

"Sir, Lt. Commander Westerly's scan read "non-Earth metallic compounds" on both items, while Nurse Baines' read "non-Earth DNA" on the cane's curved end, Captain Baines. We should not touch either item bare-handed, Captain," Mason said.

"I have here the infamous octagonal tube. I am placing it next to the two new items of evidence now." The Captain removed the tube from its container with tongs, and laid it on the table. There were identical, matching symbols on the cane and on the octagonal tube. Dr. Hassan quickly put gloves on, as did Nurse Baines, and they stood, each taking one of the items. Dr. Hassan placed the cane with the raised symbols adjacent to the octagonal tube held by Nurse Baines, and the octagonal tube and the cane began to vibrate, and the symbols began to glow.

"Doctor, ma'am, shouldn't this be done in a sealed lab? We don't know what's inside there, except it's not from Earth," Mason said cautiously.

"He's right," Nurse Baines said, pulling the octagonal tube away from the cane. The symbols went dim and inactive.

"I'll get a bio sealed container for all three of these things at once," Dr. Hassan said, and ran out of the room.

"This is very exciting, yet highly dangerous. As I held the octagonal tube, I felt compelled to touch it to the cane, Captain. Like a magnetic force. The raised symbols must be the key to opening them, sir," Nurse Baines said, sitting down.

"Male and female, He created them both," Captain Kouras said. "That's Bible scripture, friends. I think the tubes are male and female DNA. I would not want either tube opened anywhere near me, Captain Baines."

"Captain, I believe we may have reason to be very concerned, sir. What if these are intended to be used for a colony? You know, to seed their DNA? We may be looking at the first wave of an invasion, sir. If so, we now know why they wanted the Hesperia, sir. It's genius," Mason said, concerned.

"That's pretty far-fetched, Mason," the Captain said.

"Not really, Captain. We send men and women in space ships all over the solar system, and beyond. We carry seeds for blue-green algae, and simple food crops, our intent being to colonize other planets and asteroids. This is much more efficient, really. Just transport the DNA to the Hesperia, a ship of eight hundred plus men and women. See if they are curious and intelligent enough to open the tubes and voila! Your colony is accomplished," Nurse Baines said, looking at Mason. Her PhD was in Molecular Biology, after all.

"Captain Baines, this is Westerly. Dr. Honig is dead. Dr. Jenkins is missing, and so is Dr. Bergen, Captain," Westerly reported.

"Davis, check shuttle 4," Baines ordered. Only three shuttles were in use today.

The Captain went to take over the command, leaving Nurse Baines and Mason in the ready room, fully able to hear everything transpiring.

"Westerly, leave the forensics to the Space Marines. See that 1st Lieutenant Cheung gets down there to oversee the investigation. Then get back here at once." The three bio containers were stored in the morgue, locked and sealed.

"Captain to security. Escort Dr. Moore to his quarters. Search and scan before he enters. Then keep him under protective custody. Baines out."

Lt. Commander Westerly returned. "Captain, we found Dr. Honig murdered, sir. It did not look like it happened quickly or easily, sir." She returned to her bridge station.

"Captain, shuttle 4 did not respond. I sent Lieutenant Fontenay down to check on it sir, and it's gone," Davis reported.

Captain Baines asked, "Lieutenant Fuller, is shuttle 4 in communications range? Order it back here at once, or we will fire on it." He did so.

"No response, Captain," Fuller reported.

"Fire on that shuttle to disable the ship, Davis. Do not destroy it," Baines ordered.

"Aye aye, sir. Fire away." They all waited.

Davis said, "Direct hit, sir. Their engines are inoperative now, Captain."

"Davis, order shuttles 1 and 2 to tow shuttle 4 back here at once. Notify me of completion," Baines ordered, and turned to the vid screen.

While Mason and Nurse Baines waited in the ready room for the report on the shuttle's return, a loud explosion was heard, violently rocking the Hesperia. Mason reached out to her, holding her to calm her. Shuttle 4 had exploded. Shuttles 1 and 2 were sent careening towards the Hesperia from the force of the blast.

"Red alert. Powers, all shields up and on full. Prepare for impact," the Captain ordered urgently. The shuttles were blown with an intense force; shuttle 1 was sent spinning into the asteroid mining fields and exploded upon impacting floating asteroids. Shuttle 2 hit the Hesperia dead on in Section 3, exploding upon impact, again rocking the ship. The ship alarms went off.

"Damage reports, now," Captain Baines, said.

Westerly started reading the reports of damage, mostly coming from Section 3 mining personnel. The Hesperia took the full force of the shuttle 2 impact, yet her hull was not breached. The extra layer of solid iron protected the interior walls, and the furnaces and machinery inside. The miners operating the furnace conveyor belts were seriously injured, however. No atmosphere was lost, and mining operations were not compromised.

"Davis, I want to know how that shuttle exploded," the Captain barked.

After a minute, Davis spoke, "It was exploded from inside, Captain. Our lasers only knocked out her engines. The computer says it was a bomb detonated from inside the shuttle. They self-destructed, Captain Baines."

"Westerly, you have the comm." The Captain went back into his ready room, and ordered Mason to escort Mrs. Baines to her quarters on the hospital level, and stay there with her until called by him directly. Mason did as ordered. She was obviously shaken, now apprehensive about their situation.

Now the Hesperia was down to only one shuttle, and Westerly's plan to dump the remaining chunks of the Big Peanut onto the floor of Section 4 would not work. It would definitely take another month to complete harvesting the platinum and palladium.

XXX

It was the last Tuesday in November, and Mason sat in his quarters, reading his personal transmissions from home. His sister Sarah and her family were all looking forward to their Thanksgiving Day feast, and a few days off work. Since the advent of the United Republics of Earth, everyone celebrated that Thursday as a national holiday. Unless you were on a mining freighter in deep frigging space, Mason thought. They were too busy suppressing mutinous rebellions; storing alien DNA; and maintaining a constant state of readiness, prepared as best they could be for any nefarious enemy, from within or without.

Mason reminisced about spending holidays with his family. Looking at the embedded photos of his beautiful niece and young nephew, he grew sad, knowing he missed most of their childhood. He decided to ask Sherrie to join him during his call home in December, the one live call everyone got each year. He hadn't spent much time with her lately because of his duties.

Interrogating the other traitor, Lieutenant Prentiss, was a snap. Lt. Commanders Westerly and Davis managed to break him in less than half an hour. When he realized he was going to hang for his crimes, he became very remorseful, blaming Lieutenant Urz for talking him into sabotaging the Hesperia, and killing his former shipmates. He begged for mercy and forgiveness. Westerly and Davis offered their sympathies and condolences. But only Earth Command could decide whether or not they would grant him mercy and let him live.

Prentiss sang like a bird. He repeated the story of being recruited on Moon Base by the Yellow Man; paid $10,000 in gold coins to start, and $10,000 each time he carried out an order from him. He admitted his guilt freely, but unlike Kolski, he was ashamed. He confessed and told them everything in an attempt to clear his conscience and to right the wrongs he committed. He tried to back out of the deal, he said, and wanted to give all the money back, but he never discovered who the Yellow Man's liaison was. No one knew who kept putting the envelopes with $10,000 under their pillows. An interesting item of information he added was the Yellow Man knew the Hesperia would never leave the mining fields. Prentiss believed over half of the original crew worked for him, leaving many undiscovered traitors in their midst. He said the time was very near for the Yellow Man to take over the ship, probably in a day or two.

Lt. Commander Davis asked Prentiss an interesting question that no one asked any of the traitors before: why did the Yellow Man wait so long into the mission to take over the ship? The only answer Prentiss could think of was that the ship was fortified to a greater degree than the tech manual read, and he needed more men and time to circumvent the heightened security measures. It meant the recruiting was still taking place, even as the Hesperia floated in the mining fields, harvesting its asteroids.

Upon hearing the information obtained from Lieutenant Prentiss, Mason and Captain Baines agreed to try to smoke out a few of the undetected traitors in their midst as soon as possible. It would be better to defend the ship with one hundred or fewer loyal officers and crewmen than risk having the man or woman next to you suddenly turn on you in battle. Captain Baines and Mason worked together well on this scheme, both intent on undermining the Yellow Man's plans as soon as possible. They worked on different aspects of the plan in total secret, never using their com tablets or the computer, only the old-fashioned pen and paper method. Mason also worked alone in the middle of the night, in total darkness, utilizing his bionic eyes, installing another level of defense for engineering and the bridge.

The "smoke-out" plan consisted of a relatively simple system of contacting the night crew in single points of contact, and giving a code signal to begin the next wave of attack. Although the Captain was not about to put an envelope with $10,000 under anyone's pillow, he was determined to incarcerate anyone who took action on the false signal.

Using an old-fashioned music crystal recorder that Dr. Hassan had brought with him, Mason recorded several modified voices of the false signal, in order that his voice not be recognized by anyone. The Captain and Mason developed the plan and designed the time table. It would have to be accomplished all in one night, with the most trusted officers and crewmen available to apprehend the guilty parties, and incarcerate them in the brig for interrogation, and early cryonic hibernation. The message played: "The time is now. Cargo bay 1 in one quarter hour. Your reward is waiting. The ship is ours."

The most trusted Space Marines were Corporals Johnson and Milton, Sergeant Lucas and 1st Lieutenant Cheung, who had been working with Mason the longest time. The Captain decided the first private, individual calls would be made to the remaining twenty-six Marines, hoping all would pass the test. The mechanized calls went out to all twenty-six Marines, most of whom were asleep in their quarters. Mason was disappointed that two Marines did show up in cargo bay 1 in fifteen minutes, one of whom was Corporal Gomez. They were arrested, taken to the brig and shackled. Of the remaining twenty-four Marines, half of them were called to duty immediately to help Mason with the arrests and apprehensions.

The next calls went out to the two maintenance crew men on duty; both came to the cargo bay, and were arrested and taken away. The two largest areas manned on the ship were engineering and the mess hall, but only engineering was busy this time of night. The Captain signaled for the calls to go out to the engineering officers on duty, Lieutenant Roshkov and Fontenay; neither man showed up. Then the private calls went out to the engineering night crew of twelve crew men and women. Five strolled into the cargo bay, looking around for their comrades, and were arrested and taken away.

The next private calls went out to the brig crew; Baines was flabbergasted that all three crewmen came into the cargo bay looking for their money. The jailers stood by and watched their fellow traitors be interrogated time and again, and said or did nothing; or did they? Mason was certain the Yellow Man knew what they knew, who confessed, and how many they nabbed that night. Captain Baines and Mason decided to act more quickly. The remaining Space Marines were called to duty, four of whom were sent in to replace the jailers.

The next series of private calls went to the ship's security teams; two men came in, and were arrested. Since over twenty of the ship's security crewmen and both officers had been killed in the wedding reception attack, only a handful were left to defend the ship; now there remained only three. Mason and Captain Baines kept the calls going all the next hour to the various crews, and they nabbed seven more.

When the time came for the call to the bridge, Mason and Captain Baines held their breaths. Lieutenant Fuller had command, and his call was sent out first. He responded with, "Who is this? What's this about? Who is this?" Captain Baines was relieved. The private calls went out to the remaining bridge crew members immediately afterwards. When the three officers came in to the cargo bay, the Captain was very discouraged: Lieutenant Rabic, the navigator; Lieutenant Hilton, the life support expert; and most disappointing was Lieutenant Sukesh, the full grade Lieutenant on defensive systems.

The next private calls went out to the mess hall after 3:30am, when the morning crew was reporting to work. Two crew members came in, one man and one woman, both dishwashers. Mason was relieved to not see anyone he knew well show up. All in all, nineteen officers and crewmen working for the Yellow Man were caught and taken away. There was one last area to call, the hospital.

Mason was not surprised at the one hospital officer who showed up, since she had been held by a scalpel at her throat by a Captain she barely knew before he became criminally psychotic, but he was nevertheless disappointed to see Nurse Soo enter the cargo bay. He dreaded giving Dr. Hassan the news.

Twenty officers and crewmen were apprehended in their sting operation. It would be up to Admiral Tomiko and Earth Command as to what the appropriate punishment would be for them, if any. Since this was an unsanctioned action, the Captain was not certain the arrests would hold up in a court-martial. But he recorded the entire operation, the private calls made and the responses to those calls, and those persons entering the cargo bay, looking for their money.

There was only one hour before the shift change at o-six hundred hours. The Admiral must be notified of their nocturnal sting operation and netted results. Captain Baines took Mason into his quarters, and made the secure call to the Admiral on his private vid screen. The Captain put in a Code Red, and a red-eyed, robed Admiral Tomiko answered his call. The Captain was succinct, telling the Admiral of the new information obtained from Prentiss and Kolski, which underscored the need to rid the Hesperia of untrustworthy officers and crewmen before they became full-fledged traitors.

"You're on a very slippery slope, Captain Baines. When these officers and crewmen get their attorneys into the picture, you might very well be ordered to release every one of them, and be accused of entrapment yourself. I hope you are prepared for this to happen. Since your actions were not sanctioned beforehand, you stand alone. What has been done with your prisoners?" Tomiko asked.

Captain Baines explained they were being held in the brig, and that the jailers themselves showed up for their money. "Now we know the Yellow Man is aware of what we know from our interrogations, Admiral. We have already been told he is planning to act quickly, which I believe justified our extraordinary actions this evening."

Tomiko said, "I don't blame you, Captain, but I'm not an attorney. Will you keep them in the brig, or put them in cryo-sleep now?"

"I think we'd all feel better if they were put to sleep, Admiral. Then let the chips fall where they may, sir. No man wants to worry about a fellow officer's knife in his back when he is facing an enemy," Baines said.

"Yes, Captain Baines, but remember, they did not take any actions yet, and that's where you will have difficulty. Be very careful, and treat the officers especially with courtesy. Do not interrogate any of them. Only ask for information and their cooperation. You may yet be surprised what someone may offer to get out of the brig."

"Yes, Admiral. There's one other matter, sir." Captain Baines gave a very brief synopsis of their subterfuge in Section 2, and what was overheard from the miners' conversation.

Tomiko was very disturbed by this turn of events. "Has the Mission Director been informed of this meeting?"

"No, Admiral. I wanted to inform you first, sir," Baines said.

"Keene needs to know this at once, although it can be interpreted as hearsay, Captain Baines. Has he inventoried all his blaster packs?"

The Captain answered, "Yes, Admiral, and several cases are indeed missing. He just wants to pack up and go as soon as possible, and put the miners back in cryo-sleep with maximum expediency. He was shocked at losing Chief Technician Takeda, sir."

"What actions have you taken as a result of this information, Captain Baines?"

"We have double-checked all hatches, doors and seals on the rooms storing the miners' cryonic containers, and doubled their alarm mechanisms, sir," Baines reported. "We have also taken several more intensive measures for defense of the engineering and the bridge main doors."

"Excellent, Captain. I believe that this will all die down when the miners are in cryo-sleep and you're in hyper-space, Captain Baines."

Baines sighed. "I hope you're correct, Admiral Tomiko."

"Why not question a few of the officers you have in the brig now, and try to gain their confidence and cooperation. They may be willing to share more information than you think if..."

"Red Alert! Red Alert! Section 1 has been breached! Red Alert!" The computer announcement cut off the Admiral's advice just then, and Mason and Captain Baines went into action. Mason geared up for the worst, while the Captain took back the command chair. He ordered battle stations for everyone, and for the engineering deck and the command bridge to have live vid cams feeds online to Earth Command. All non-essential corridors, halls, lifts and rooms were forced closed, and locked. The Space Marines and ship's security teams went inside their assigned areas, out of the halls and corridors. The halls and corridors must be kept clear for the Captain and Mason's new plan of defense to work.

Lt. Commanders Westerly and Davis reported for duty, as did the other day shift bridge officers, all wearing their side arms, and carrying extra belts of ammo chargers across their chests. This was the real thing.

Baines ordered, "Lieutenant Marston, contact Earth Command and advise them of our situation. All stations, report." The reports came in rapidly, no action yet. Davis' vid cams showed no movements anywhere, and the Space Marines at the access crossing point showed no entry, yet the alert was still going on, indicating a breach. Mason handed out laser rifles to all officers on the bridge from the new stash he and the Captain installed last week, then returned to his post. He wondered where Nurse Baines was; was she next door in the Captain's quarters, or in her old quarters, safe and sound? Was Sherrie at work?

"Red Alert! Red Alert! Breach in engineering deck! Red Alert!" They were attempting to take over engineering from either the shafts or the main hall. Commander Powers reported, "No sign of them yet, Captain. All the vid cams are steady, sir, no movement."

"Red Alert! Red Alert! Section 1 crossover is breached. Red Alert!" Suddenly, an incredible blast was heard and felt all throughout the ship, as the miners blasted the main door at the Section 1 crossover. The vid cam feeds showed the hole, big enough for only one man at a time to crawl through. Damage reports came from all over the ship, and although most were minor, the voices of the crewmen reporting were tense.

"Battle stations, all hands, battle stations. This is not a drill. Repeat: this is not a drill. All hands, battle stations," the Captain said calmly in his comm-link. He watched the vid cam feed on the front screen, and it showed the hall filling up with dozens of men, man after man entering through the blast hole, armed with laser rifles, hand lasers, twenty-five centimeter wrenches, crowbars, anything they could use as a weapon. "Engineering, report. Powers, do you have the live feed?"

"Yes, Captain, I see them coming. They'll be here in less than one minute. We will hold as long as possible, sir," Powers advised. A short silence occurred.

"Powers, this is the Captain. We are implementing the Omicron Protocol. You will release your engines control to me on my mark; three, two, one. I now have control." The Captain inserted a crystal from his boot into the command chair, and now controlled the entire ship from his chair, engines and all. "Powers, do you copy?"

"Yes, Captain, you have engine control. We will hold this deck, sir. Good luck, Captain."

"All bridge hands, prepare to secure the bridge. I have the comm, the nav, and the helm. Westerly, Davis, Marston, stay at your stations, and follow my commands. Everyone else, form defensive security perimeters in the conference rooms, ready room, and the main bridge door. Keep them out of here for five minutes." He buckled into his command chair.

The Captain's fingers flew over his command keys and screens, as he concentrated every bit of mental energy into his maneuvers. The ship began to screech, a metal-on-metal sound magnified one hundred times over. Mason quickly got his earplugs out and plugged his bionic ears, never letting go of his rifle. The computer said, "The Omicron Protocol has been engaged. Captain Baines, you are in control. The Omicron Protocol has been engaged. Two minutes until completion." The computer continued its countdown, as the Captain's fingers flew, manually working the computer controls and vid screens with both hands.

The Hesperia shook suddenly like an old wet dog shaking the rain off his back, throwing everyone against the walls and each other, and the grating metallic sound came again, louder this time. The live vid screens on the front showed the first wave of attackers firing on the engineering emergency hatch door, the second and thickest door in front of their main door. It would take more than laser rifle fire to get through that modification, Mason thought. The computer continued its countdown: "Forty five seconds to completion. The Omicron Protocol is engaged. Thirty seconds to completion…"

The ship lurched, throwing the bridge crew against the walls, as an incredibly loud blast pounded against the main door. "Hold your fire!" The Captain yelled, hands and fingers still flying over his controls. "The Omicron Protocol is engaged. Ten seconds to completion. The Omicron Protocol is engaged in five-four-three-two-one. The Omicron Protocol is complete." The Hesperia bolted forward like a bucking bronco out of the chute. Everyone but the Captain was hurled backwards. He was still in his chair, holding onto the arms of his command chair, bracing himself against the forward motion. Mason was thrown backwards, as was everyone else.

"Lieutenant Marston, open a ship wide hailing," Baines ordered.

"Opened, Captain," Marston said, crawling back into his chair.

"This is Captain Baines. You will lay down your weapons at once and surrender. This is an order. You will lay down your weapons and surrender." The only reply was more laser fire against the bridge door.

"Westerly, Davis, watch the front monitors closely and report." They began to report, first starting with reports of live laser fire against the engineering emergency hatch and bridge emergency hatch, then they reported gas in the halls.

"Mason, distribute gas masks; Powers, distribute your gas masks," the Captain ordered, and Mason quickly distributed the cigar-shaped gas masks to all officers on the bridge.

"You will lay down your weapons and surrender at once. This is your final chance. Lay down your weapons at once and surrender." But the fools in the hall continued firing, as the gas poured down on them in thick white streams, the gas blown on them from large outlets all around their heads. The sounds of laser fire were replaced with coughing and choking and sputtering gasps to breathe. The views on the live monitors became gruesome, as the attackers grabbed their throats and eyes, and eventually collapsed onto the floors.

The Captain calmly said, "You must surrender. Raise your hand to surrender or forfeit your life." No hands went up. All grew quiet.

From engineering and the bridge, a chorus of cheering erupted. The Captain said, "Front monitors off." He sat back, and watched, his face and uniform blouse covered in sweat.

As the front vid screens faded out, and the full viewing windows cleared, everyone realized what the Omicron Protocol was: Section 1 and 2 of the Hesperia was separated from Sections 3 and 4. The bridge was looking straight into the other half of the Hesperia, perpendicularly. The side vid screens showed the new aft area. Men were floating off the Section 2 opening by the dozens, flailing their arms in a futile attempt to get back to the pressurized ship. Laser rifles, big wrenches, torches, and whatever weapons the miners brought with them to kill the Space Forces officers controlling the ship were free floating away in space along with the bodies of dead attackers. It was a macabre scene.

"Gas masks off," the Captain ordered. "Engineering, report."

"We're all safe here, Captain Baines. Nice work, sir. Would you like us to take back control of her engines now, Captain?" Powers asked.

"Yes, Powers, take over engine control," the Captain said calmly. He turned his chair around. "Davis, systems check. Marston, any word from Mission Director Keene?"

"No response from anyone in Mining Mission Control, sir," Marston said quietly.

"All systems are good, sir," Davis reported.

Baines asked, "Westerly, damage reports."

"Sir, damage to Section 2 and Section 3 access doors. They were blasted away by the miners, sir, not by the Protocol. They are showing large holes in their main doors and fire doors. All their atmosphere in Section 3 has been lost inside the main bays. Atmosphere lost completely in Section 4, sir. No damage to the cargo and precious metals storage, sir."

"What about their Mission Control? Any information?" He asked with a concerned voice.

"The computer is reading full atmosphere in Mission Control, Captain, but no life signs." Everyone was silent.

"Marston, get me the hospital. Are you secure down there, Dr. Hassan?" He asked.

"We're all topsy turvy down here. It's a mess. Captain Kouras and I are a little bruised, sir," Dr. Hassan reported.

"Anyone else down there injured, Doctor?" The Captain asked, and everyone knew of whom he was speaking.

"Only Captain Kouras and I are here, Captain Baines," Dr. Hassan reported.

"Thank you, Dr. Hassan. I'd get ready for some incoming injured soon, Baines out."

"Any injuries reported, Westerly? Is everyone all right?" He quietly

263

asked.

"None, yet, Captain. It's pretty quiet. Seems everyone is still sealed up." She was correct, as the Omicron Protocol forced all entry and exit doors in the first two sections of the ship to close and lockdown, protecting the crew.

Captain Baines stood up, looked around at his bridge crew, and said, "As you were. Lt. Commander Westerly, you have the comm. Mason, come with me." He went into the ready room, with Mason on his heels, into his private quarters. Mrs. Baines was not there. He called for her: "Nurse Baines, report," but there was no answer forthcoming. The two men came back on the bridge, and opened the main bridge doors. Bodies of dead attackers were piled against the door knee-high in the hall.

Mason stepped in front of Captain Baines, saying, "Follow me, Captain," and closed the door manually, leading him into the conference room instead. Mason shut and locked the door, and went to the hidden door panel, raising it for the Captain. Both men went down the maintenance shaft to the hospital level, and across two access panels to the other hidden door for Nurse Baines' quarters, and entered. The Captain pushed out her books, and climbed into her quarters. She was not there, either. Baines called her again, and did not receive a response. Mason called for Senior Chief, and did not receive a response. The two men left her quarters for the hospital down the hall.

No attackers made it to this level, thankfully, allowing injured officers and crewmen access to the hospital. Inside were Nurse Jones, Dr. Hassan, and Captain Kouras. The Captain was getting frantic. Mason asked, "Maybe she went for an early breakfast, Captain?" The Captain ran down to the lift with Mason, and they got inside, quickly pushing the light for the mess hall corridors.

"Corporal Johnson, release Nurse Soo on her own recognizance to assist Dr. Hassan in the hospital," Baines ordered as the lift moved up the few decks to the mess hall. There were several dead attackers in the hall, lying with their laser rifles strewn about. They stepped over them, and entered the officers' mess. It was empty. Captain Baines was very red in the face now, looking about everywhere.

Mason got in front of him again, and took the Captain through the kitchen to the big mess hall. Several tables were overturned, probably from the lunging of the Hesperia as she broke away in the last maneuver of the Protocol. Mason led the Captain towards the back, where the mess office was. He tried to open the door, but it was blocked by the big desk. Mason looked through the cracked window, and saw the Senior Chief and Nurse Baines on the floor, unconscious. He called for the corpsmen, broke through the window with his rifle, and climbed inside, the Captain right behind him. Captain Baines called Dr. Hassan with the information, and was told the corpsmen were coming as soon as possible. Mason was not going to wait. He picked up Nurse Baines, handed her to the Captain, and picked up his Senior Chief, and they carried them into the hospital. They laid them together on the only open table in the room. Both women were in shock, out cold. Neither showed any open wound, but that didn't mean they were okay. Nurse Jones came over to triage them, and called out for Dr. Hassan to come at once.

Nurse Baines had indeed gone down to the officers' mess for an early breakfast, but when the red alerts sounded, the Senior Chief came and took her to her office. They locked the door, and waited, sitting on the floor, out of sight. They were knocked unconscious by the Omicron Protocol movements, neither of them remembering whether it was the first shaking or the final lunge of the ship that knocked the desk into them. They both received minor concussions in the back of their heads. Nurse Baines wanted to get up right away and help, but was not permitted by the Doctor. The two women lay together on the table, glad to be alive, and happy their men found them. Captain Baines kissed his wife's hand, and said, "You just lie here for a while, my dear. I still have a couple of things to do up top." She nodded, and smiled at him, not having any idea what had transpired in the last half hour. The Captain quickly left, telling Mason to come back up top in a few minutes.

The women were still shaken, with cold compresses around their heads, and fluids given to them via their IV lines; the color was returning to their faces as Mason watched them both lying on the table together. "What'd you say I just roll you both out of here, and we'll go have a little bourbon, ladies?" Mason asked, smiling at them. He got a little laugh out of them. He held one hand from each of them in his hands, softly telling them the worst was over. "We did the Omicron Protocol. You should have seen the Captain, ma'am. He took over the entire ship from his command chair, his hands and fingers flying all over the monitors and keyboards. He separated the Hesperia into two ships by himself. When you get to your room, you'll see the other half of the ship. He was really amazing. We all got thrown down and banged around like you two did. Except I didn't have a desk attack me," he added, and smiled again.

"Did the miners attack us, Gunny?" The Senior Chief asked.

"Yep. Sorry ass bastards," Mason said. "Two beautiful ladies laying here together, and I got to go back to work. Just my luck. I'll be back as soon as I can, okay?" He picked up both of their hands, and kissed each one. They reached up to him, and he hugged them both, and left. It was a good day.

XXXI

When Mason returned to the bridge, the drama and activity dissipated, and things sounded fairly normal, if you didn't think about the hall being full of dead miners above your knees. Lt. Commander Westerly was at the comm, and she threw her arm towards the ready room, indicating Mason to report there at once. As he entered, Captain Baines was on a live secure channel to Admiral Tomiko, and the four-star Admiral Worthington. Mason snapped to attention.

"When the Omicron Protocol was fully engaged, the poison gas was released, and the miners all succumbed in one minute or less, Admiral. Our attack was over, sir." Captain Baines looked at Mason, both men standing at attention.

"There must have been missing footage in the live vid cam feed, Captain Baines. Your Chief Engineer was not controlling the engines in sync with your command maneuvers," Admiral Worthington said.

"There was no missing footage, Admiral. The second by second feed was provided live to Earth Command as it happened, sir. Chief Engineer Commander Powers was ordered to release engine control by myself, sir, during the engagement of the Omicron Protocol."

Worthington yelled, "That's ridiculous, Baines. No man could control the engines, separation procedures, maneuvering the helm and navigation computers, and command functions. It is impossible. How was this accomplished?"

"Permission to speak, Admiral?" Mason asked, with all confidence.

"Who is this man?" Admiral Worthington asked abruptly.

"He is my Prime Marine, Gunnery Sergeant John Mason, Admiral. He has attended all our staff reporting meetings with Admiral Tomiko during this mission, sir."

"Very well, speak, Gunny." The Admiral was very impatient.

Mason stepped forward and gave an articulate report of the Captain's efforts during the implementation of the Omicron Protocol, how he had total control of the ship and all of her computers and engines for the duration of the actual two-minute implementation process. "It had been decided well in advance of those measures taken by Captain Baines that he would keep the procedures to himself, to prevent anyone knowing what eventuality the procedures would accomplish. That was the only way to maintain total secrecy, Admiral Worthington. No one else could know but Captain Baines, sir." Mason stood silent.

"Impossible! No man could perform so many programming instructions in that short of time and successfully implement the Protocol alone," Worthington said.

"Captain Baines did it, Admiral. I watched him, and Earth Command had full view of his every keystroke and programming instructions. He did it, sir, and we all watched him, Admiral Worthington. Believe it, sir. It is now history, with all due respect, Admirals Worthington and Tomiko." Mason stepped back, knowing he was going to be reduced in rank any second. But he would not let that four-star demean his Captain. Baines and Mason waited in silence.

"Hold transmission for one moment, Captain Baines," Admiral Tomiko said. Mason looked at his Captain, as both men stood stiffly at attention, neither saying another word. They were kept waiting several minutes. Mason knew they were replaying the actual Omicron Protocol implementation by Captain Baines, to either confirm or deny his testimony.

"Describe the step by step procedures of the Omicron Protocol, Captain Baines," Worthington ordered. And Captain Baines did. Every keystroke, every navigational adjustment; every helm maneuver, every engine adjustment; every step in the final separation was described in full detail by Baines, looking straight ahead, never looking down at his com tablet, or any notes.

At the end of the more than ten minute process, he finished by saying, "Of course, the actual procedures had to be completed within the two minute window, else the Protocol would have aborted, and everything reverted back as it was before. I completed the procedure, and the Omicron Protocol was successfully implemented. Sir!" Baines stood like a rock, never flinching.

"How long did it take you, Captain Baines?" Worthington asked, less accusingly now.

Baines answered, "One minute fifty eight seconds, sir."

The two Admirals were silent. Finally, Admiral Tomiko spoke. "Could you do this again, Captain Baines, if asked to?"

"I could do it right now, or at any time in the future, Admiral. Once I commit something to memorization, I never forget it, sir," Baines answered self-assuredly, looking ahead.

"Then, you have indeed accomplished the impossible, Captain Baines. Forgive me for doubting your ability. The Omicron Protocol was designed specifically to be implemented by the Ship's Captain, the Chief Engineer, and the Executive Officer, all working in tandem with one another; all this to be completed within two minutes' time, else the Protocol would be aborted, as you have said. You may be called upon to demonstrate the Protocol before our systems designers at a future date, Captain Baines. My apologies to you," Admiral Worthington spoke, much less full of himself now. The Earth Command camera swept beyond Admiral Worthington and Admiral Tomiko, revealing the entire Joint Chiefs of Staff present. Baines stood there, at attention like Mason, waiting for the next move, which belonged to the Joint Chiefs.

"Captain Baines, we are retroactively authorizing you to implement any necessary procedure to remove any officer or crew member suspected of involvement in the attempts to sabotage the Hesperia. You have our sanction." Admiral Worthington announced.

"Captain Victor Baines, in recognition of your exemplary performance under duress and threat to your ship, your crew, and your person, your battlefield promotion to Captain is now conferred as a permanent promotion to Ship's Captain, effective immediately, and Captain of the mining freighter Hesperia. With our gratitude, congratulations, Captain Victor Baines," another four-star Admiral announced. The camera moved to the other side of the big table of officers.

"Prime Marine Gunnery Sergeant John Mason, in recognition of your exemplary performance in the line of duty, and saving the life of your ship's Captain, his command and medical command officers, and crew of the Hesperia, you are hereby promoted to Master Sergeant, effective immediately, with a promotional path recommendation to Officer Candidate School, immediately upon return to Earth Command. Congratulations, Master Sergeant Mason," the Commandant of the Space Marines announced.

"Thank you, sir," they both said. The transmission ceased.

Both men now breathed easier, and Captain Baines motioned for Mason to sit down. "Well now, Master Sergeant Mason, you're officially out of uniform, and the Base Exchange will not reopen. What will you do about this situation?" The Captain said, smiling at him.

"Open a bottle of bourbon with you and Mrs. Baines, sir," Mason answered confidently, and both men laughed in relief.

"I think cognac is more in line with this night, Mason, don't you? Let's see if my wife and the Senior Chief are still in the hospital, and we'll plan from there," the Captain said, making the call to Dr. Hassan. Both women were still on the bed, resting, so Captain Baines and Mason left for the hospital. As they carefully stepped over the dead bodies now being removed by the ship's security droids and Marines, Captain Baines said, "I wish I could know if this was truly over, Mason, but I don't think it is."

"Neither do I, Captain, but at least we took him by surprise this time, sir." Both men finally reached the lift, and took it down to the hospital.

Captain Baines reached the exam table where his wife and the Senior Chief were lying side by side, resting comfortably. He smiled, and went to Mrs. Baines, gently touching her arm. "How are you feeling now?" He asked her softly, smiling at her.

"I have a bad headache, Captain," she answered softly, so as not to waken her partner, the Senior Chief. "What's going on up there?" She reached for his hand.

"Everything's under control. It's actually pretty boring now, my dear." He smiled at her, and leaned down to kiss her on her forehead. "Nothing to worry about, Mrs. Baines," he said confidently. She looked at the foot of her bed, and saw Mason standing there, watching her and the Senior Chief.

"Why is that man smiling, Captain? Doesn't he know we're in the middle of a battle, Captain Baines?" She asked, and looked back at her husband, trying to smile with him.

"Mason's merely filled with delusions of grandeur, my love. Pay him no attention whatsoever, or he'll be impossible all night!" The Captain said to her, stroking her hand, and watching her. They both managed a little laugh, as the Senior Chief stirred, and realized she was still next to Nurse Baines, with the Captain and Mason both watching. "And how are you, Senior Chief? Do you have a headache, as well?" The Captain asked, with concern in his voice.

"Yes, sir, I have a headache. Can we leave now?" She asked him.

Dr. Hassan walked up to their bed. The Captain asked, "We were wondering when your guests would be allowed to leave your hospitality, Doctor."

"They should be able to leave soon, Captain. Just let me have a look at them." Dr. Hassan pulled down the full body scanner over both of the women. "Nasty bump on your head, Nurse Baines. You'll have to rest for a day or two before I let you back to full duty."

"And you have a concussion as well, Senior Chief, but in a different locale. Still, you should rest for another two days before going back to duty. I'm afraid we'll all lose another kg or two," Dr. Hassan said, smiling at her.

He pulled two injection pens out of his jacket, and gave each of his patients a separate shot into their IV lines. "Now this will take care of your headaches. Just make sure you eat something soon. Gunny can take you back to your quarters."

Captain Baines said, "We don't have a Gunny with us anymore, Dr. Hassan. Just this out of uniform Master Sergeant, with a free pass to OCS from his Commandant of the Space Marines, no less."

"Master Sergeant? Promoted by the Commandant himself? Why, Mason, that's very impressive! And a pass to OCS, as well. What did you do to deserve that distinction?" Dr. Hassan asked, his eyes wide open in admiration.

"I told off Admiral Worthington, Dr. Hassan," Mason said, and Captain Baines laughed.

"Admiral Worthington? Mason, do you know who he is?" Nurse Baines asked, shocked.

"He's the four-star who doubted Captain Baines, ma'am," Mason said. "I thought he was going to bust me back down, but I said what I saw anyway. I watched Captain Baines do it, ma'am. He's a genius, and he saved us all." Mason looked at his Captain with all seriousness.

"We'll all have to hear the details of this at a later time, I'm afraid. Now, get these IV's out, and go rest and relax for the remainder of the evening. I have sick patients to attend to." Dr. Hassan left Nurse Baines to remove the IV's from her and the Senior Chief, and stand up slowly.

"I suggest we all meet in our quarters in two hours for dinner. As a matter of fact, Mason, Senior Chief, I order it! Let's take it easy now, my dear," the Captain said, helping Nurse Baines down off the table. She took his arm, and they slowly walked out of the area.

The hall in front of the engineering deck was still being cleared of the dead miner's bodies when Mason arrived. If the Hesperia's designers had not added the extra blast-proof emergency hatches at the main doors of engineering and the bridge, the outcome may have been much different. Captain Baines may not have had the two minutes he needed to implement the Omicron Protocol, and save the ship and her crew.

Commander Powers gave Mason the full scoop on the damage and injuries from his engineering deck, and Mason notated them for his security log. The Commander was relieved things turned out well, even though he was very vocal about not being included in the secret plans Mason and Captain Baines enacted to protect the ship. Maybe now he'd understand their need to keep things secret, like the poison gas system installed in the corridors.

Mason and Corporal Johnson installed the poison gas system in the engineering deck corridor ceiling first, then the bridge corridor. Mason made a mental note to tell Captain Baines that either the Yellow Man did not know what they were doing up there, or considered the gas dispersal system less of a threat to his plans than it actually turned out to be.

One thing Mason knew for certain was that the Yellow Man would try again. Somehow, somewhere, he would get more recruits, and try again. Mason determined to find out how many miners were left awake, and what had happened to Mission Director Keene. Lt. Commander Westerly had command, and informed Mason there was no response from Mining Mission Control. They would have to go and check the other half of the Hesperia to find out for themselves. The atmosphere in Section 3 was totally gone, and the platinum furnaces were out. Section 4 atmosphere was still present in Mining Mission Control and the adjacent quarters of the Director and Coordinator Garcia, but nowhere else. Westerly told him they were planning to send a security team to the other half of the Hesperia later to find out.

But the smelted platinum and palladium were in safe storage, and that was all Earth Command cared about. The miners in cryo-sleep were in locked and sealed rooms and, according to the ship's computers, their occupants were safe in hibernation.

Captain Baines acknowledged Mason's latest reports on his findings, and reminded him to be in his quarters for dinner. Mason hurried to his own quarters to clean up and dress. His tall boots were scuffed and scraped from the wedding reception, but he shined them up as best he could. With the Base Exchange closed, he had no choice but to wear them. He made it to the Senior Chief's quarters with only a few minutes before they had to go to the Captain's quarters.

"I brought two bottles of wine for dinner. What do you think?" Mason asked his resident wine expert. She looked at the bottles and checked the labels; both were very good red wines. She wrapped them in white tissue, and tied red ribbon around the top. "It's always better to present the wine like a gift, John." Mason was saved from another faux pas by the Senior Chief.

They timed their arrival perfectly at the Captain's quarters. Also in attendance were Lt. Commanders Westerly and Davis, Dr. Hassan, and Commander Powers. Commander Baines answered the door and welcomed them inside, and Mason gave her the two bottles of wine. She was elated to not have to serve synthehol wine for this special dinner. She was such a gracious hostess, Mason thought. The perfect wife for a Ship's Captain.

Captain Baines called Mason over, and formally announced he was out of uniform. All heads turned to watch. Mason stood at attention, as the Captain pinned Mason in front of his command officers, saying, "I know they aren't Prime Marine insignia, but they are Space Marine, Master Sergeant. They will have to do for now," he said, and they all saluted Mason. Mason returned their salutes very crisply, and thanked the Captain. He was happy Captain Baines never mentioned the endorsement to OCS, which would have made the Senior Chief uncomfortable.

After dinner was over and everything was cleared away, the guests all left, but Mason and the Senior Chief were asked to stay. Captain Baines went into his bedroom and emerged with the black box. "I received this from Mission Director Keene, and put it away for a different night. But I think tonight is the right time to share this with the four of us together." He proudly showed Commander Baines and his guests his prized bottle of 50-yr old Louis XIII cognac. The Senior Chief brought over four snifters, and the Captain poured a generous measure into each snifter, handed one first to Commander Baines, the Senior Chief, Mason, and took the last one for himself.

"To the best friends any man could have: my wife, Ms. Dawson, and Mason, our protector and best friend." They all toasted, and slowly enjoyed the fine cognac. Mason's bionic sense of smell was fully engaged in the snifter. Regular cognac had a very nice smell, but this was in another league altogether. It was the perfect nightcap.

He held the snifter in his hands to warm it, as they all did, and enjoyed the delicate scent for as long as he could. He and the Senior Chief tastefully declined a second snifter of the precious cognac, and Mason congratulated the Captain. The Commander had not been told the news of his permanent promotion, and was elated for her husband. Mason and the Senior Chief gave their thanks for dinner and the private celebration, and left the Captain's quarters.

"Why didn't you tell me the Admiral made your promotion permanent, Victor? You certainly deserve it," she commented.

"I knew Mason would tell you when we were alone, just the four of us. He's got a talent for knowing when to say something, that's for sure. You know, he really did stand up for me to Admiral Worthington, Rachel. I was afraid he would lose a stripe over it, but he defended me staunchly, with tact and aplomb. He was superb," he said, smiling, and sitting next to her on the couch. "He was promoted by his Commandant of the Space Marines, you know. And he got the endorsement from Admiral Worthington and the Chiefs of Staff for OCS."

"I wonder if he'll actually use that endorsement. He'd still be a Prime Marine, wouldn't he, Victor?" She asked.

"Of course, unless he wanted to give it up. He'd get promoted faster as a Space Marine officer, but I can't imagine Mason giving up his Prime Marine status. That's a very significant, coveted achievement," Baines acknowledged.

"They will be very hard on him, if he and the Senior Chief decide to marry," she said, knowing how the majority of officers still treated an officer with an enlisted spouse as a second-rate officer, an ages-old prejudice. It was often referred to as a "contamination of the officer gene pool." She silently thought about her own decision to not get involved with Mason at the beginning of the mission because of that prejudice, despite her deep feelings for him. It was bad enough for a male officer to take an enlisted woman as a spouse. But it was a career-ending decision if a female officer took an enlisted man as her husband, or even a steady boyfriend.

She was deemed from then on as unworthy of her rank, and she could forget about any further promotions, or decent assignments. Mrs. Baines sipped her cognac, absorbed in reflection.

In her quarters, Sherrie took off her uniform jacket and hung it up as Mason watched her. Seeing her on that table in the hospital after the miners' attack, so soon after her bad internal injuries at the wedding reception, brought the realization their time together was precious. Sherrie was a special gift from the Man Upstairs, and he wanted to love and cherish her all of his days. Mason decided now was the best time for the Big Question. "You know we will get our live communication transmission home in the next couple of weeks. I'd really like it if you would meet my sister Sarah and her family, and they could meet you, Sherrie," Mason said sincerely. "Would you join me on my call home?"

She looked at him, and said, "They'll wonder who I am, John."

"No, we'll tell them you're Mrs. Mason and it's time they met you," he said nonchalantly, unbuttoning his crimson red tunic, leaning against the wall. She asked what he just said.

"You heard me. I'd like you to meet my sister Sarah and her family when we make our live call in a couple of weeks."

"I heard that much," she said, coming over to him. "What was the last part, John?" She looked in his eyes, and he reached for her. He drew her close to him, spoke softly to her, looking directly into her eyes.

"I don't want to get engaged to you. I want to be married to you, and introduce you to my family as my wife, Sherrie, as soon as the Captain will marry us. Our love is so very special and precious. We've been together for long enough to know we can make it work out. Will you marry me, Sherrie Dawson?" He stared into her eyes, with that smile of his she could not refuse. While she was still in shock, he kissed her, and stroked the back of her neck. "Will you?" He kissed her again, with more passion and intensity.

"John, I ..." she began, and he kissed her again.

"Just say yes, woman," he said, still holding her close and kissing her, pulling her blouse out from her skirt. He put his hand under the back of her blouse, and in one swift movement of his thumb and two fingers undid her bra. She gasped for breath as he gently squeezed her bare breast. "Say yes, Sherrie," he said softly.

He moved his hand to raise her skirt, caressing her thigh, and teasing her with his fingers on her labia. As he inserted his middle finger inside her, she moaned and kissed him deeply. "Say yes, Sherrie," he said.

"Oh, yes, John, yes," she said breathlessly, and he drew her legs around him, laid her on the bed, penetrating her, slowly and rhythmically bringing them both to a powerful orgasm. As they lay there later, catching their breath, Sherrie asked him with a smile, "Why not take off your boots and your uniform, and stay a while, groom?" They both laughed with each other, still in their disheveled uniforms. After finally taking off their uniforms, they made love again and again, with Sherrie deciding she was no longer "Non-committal."

XXXII

Mason and four Space Marines were flown over to the other half of the Hesperia to investigate the whereabouts of Mission Director Keene and ascertain the situation there at 3am the next morning. They donned their space suits and carried as much firepower as they could. Without any atmosphere or pressurized environment, they would be easy, clumsy targets for anyone with a laser rifle. They must stay together and be very careful. The shuttle landed inside Section 4, whose big bay doors were still open and facing the huge glove container, nearly emptied of the Big Peanut asteroid fragments now. The men were left there while the pilot flew back to the Hesperia for another security team.

All was pitch black. They tethered themselves together, with Mason at the lead. His bionic eyes could see 75% in total darkness; better than illuminating their position with their helmet lights. They cautiously and quietly went to the middle of the section, and found Mining Mission Control in Section 3 under the foundry areas. The observation room windows were all blown out from loss of pressure. They went directly to Mission Control. Their helmets had vid cams for live feed of their movements and all their communications. To maintain as much stealth as possible, the Marines used battle hand signals, and rarely spoke above a whisper. As they came to the Mission Control door at the opposite side of Section 3, they saw several pieces of bodies free floating inside the room, some still holding a weapon. Mason led them to the main entrance, programming the pressurized air lock.

Mason led the Marines into the airlock, sealed the door to Section 3 bay, and hit the switches for pressurization and atmosphere. In seconds they were able to lift their gold visors and breathe naturally. The second door opened automatically, but the Marines did not enter; all was total blackness. Mason looked inside first, and stopped to listen before proceeding further.

There were some breathing sounds coming directly ahead of them, so he quickly motioned the team to get down. A barrage of laser fire came at them, hitting one of the Marines. They returned the fire, and Mason tossed stun grenades into the darkness; they lowered their visors while the grenades exploded, their flashes exposing several armed men now holding their heads in agony. Laser fire came from across the room, and was returned in kind by the Marines, silencing the shooter.

"Lay down your arms and surrender now," Corporal Johnson boomed in his big voice.

"Surrender, my ass," was the response, accompanied by more laser fire.

Sergeant Lucas unpacked his gas canisters, handed them to each team member, and they lowered their helmet visors again. On his signal they were hurled into the room. After the choking and coughing stopped, the Marines crawled on the floor until they reached the computer console desk. One man stood at the control desk, busy pushing buttons for some sabotage or other event to happen. Corporal Johnson took him down from behind with one head twist, and killed him. Sergeant Lucas rolled a flasher flare set towards the center of the room, and hit his remote control switch. The room instantly lit up like high noon, exposing three more shooters wearing gas masks who got temporarily blinded by the flash, and were easily taken out by the Marines. Mason stood and went to the computer console.

The bridge crew could see the computer console through Mason's vid cam. Westerly gave Mason instructions on what to program into the computer for a quick analysis, and she determined that the computer was being rigged for a total systems crash. Mason followed her step by step instructions and effectively rebooted the computer to initialize a clean-up of its recent memory, and full restoration to original programming. The Marines lie in wait, ready to fire on anyone else in the room. At the final keystroke, the room lights came up and illuminated the large room for them. There were many more dead bodies lying about the room than the Marines killed. The earlier deaths must have been from last night. The Space Marines got up, looking for Director Keene or Coordinator Garcia.

Coordinator Garcia was sitting in a chair, his hands bound behind him, and his mouth gagged. He was dead and cold; a victim of the earlier firefight last evening. The Marines fanned out along the room walls, while Mason opened the door to one of the suites to check the adjacent apartments. Blackness again greeted them.

Mason got down and went into the room, motioning for another Marine to go along the opposite wall. He raised his hand for the Marine to stop, and listened. After a few seconds, someone was heard inhaling slowly. Mason followed the sound around to the left, and stopped again. The man tried not to breathe, but could not hold his breath any longer. As the man exhaled, Mason was on him, disarming him and taking him to the floor.

The remaining Marines switched the lights on, and the horrible remnants of a torture session were displayed. Director Keene was beaten to a pulp, cut with knives all over his chest and face, and his left hand was lying on the floor. A hand ax on his desk was bloodied and covered with skin fragments.

The Space Marines went across the hall quickly to Coordinator Garcia's rooms. Labored breathing could be heard by all the Marines. Sergeant Lucas took the initiative, tossing in his last flasher grenade, and rushed the room with the other Marines. The shooter was taken out in short order. Tied across the bed was an unfortunate woman, used for sex by the miners while they waited. She was gagged, beaten and bloodied, barely alive, and was clearly terrified of the Marines in their space suits. Sergeant Lucas called for corpsmen. He went over to her and covered her naked and abused body, and told her she would be taken to the hospital shortly. None of the Space Marines had an ounce of pity for the miners after seeing those two rooms. Sergeant Lucas confirmed acknowledgement from Lt. Commander Davis that the crimes were recorded, and that help was on its way for the raped and beaten woman. The second security team landed, and made contact with Mason's team. They closed the door to the room with the terrified woman, and went further into Section 3.

There were unarmed, dead miners strewn about in every hall and room they checked. Evidently, many miners were loyal to Director Keene and the URE, and refused to participate in the mutiny. But Mason knew there were far too many miners unaccounted for; the numbers didn't add up. There should be over two hundred sixty miners left after the last round of cryonic hibernations. Mason called Captain Baines.

"Captain, I think they're in Section 2, hiding out, sir. We've searched both Sections 3 and 4, and covered the entire length and breadth of the sections. They must be in our half of the ship, Captain, lying in wait to try again. Are the hibernation rooms still secure, Captain? We should be getting back to you now, Captain Baines." The urgency in Mason's voice made the Captain go to red alert, and send the shuttle back for them at once. The last team to arrive back on the Hesperia was Mason's team. The Marines stripped off their space suits, grabbed their full combat gear, and headed to the bridge.

The blast fire hatches sealed off the bridge and engineering main doors, and corridor passage hatches were sealing automatically. Mason could not access the bridge from the corridors; they would have to climb up the crawl shafts and emergency escape passageways to reach the bridge. Mason called the Captain on his comm-link and was told all was secure. He notified the Captain they were taking the long way home, and Baines knew what he meant. He told Mason to stop off for some burgers and fries on his way home; that meant to check the mess halls and hospital areas first.

Mason decided to make a quick stop at the armory. It would be one of the best decisions of his life. His team of four filled their pockets with everything they could carry, and switched out their used laser rifles for fresh ones, and four belts of charger ammo packs each for back up. They each took a helmet, hand shields, and a small back pack, which they loaded with stun gas canisters, flasher grenades, and incendiaries. Mason and Sergeant Lucas took the two meter rifle and mounts, and Corporal Johnson grabbed the suitcase of that monster's extra charger ammo packs. Mason closed, locked and sealed the armory door.

The men jogged down the short corridor to the access door for the crawl shafts, and they climbed up one level to the mess halls. Everything was quiet, far too quiet. There was no noise of dishes or tables full of crewmen eating; it was deadly still. Mason called the Captain in a whispered voice, and got the go-ahead to enter the mess halls. They crouched down below the viewing windows of the main doors to the dark officers' mess, and Sergeant Lucas gently opened the door with the barrel of his laser rifle. No sound was heard. They knew what was coming; all four of the men had been in battle before, and could feel it before the first shot was fired.

Corporal Milton, the smallest man, crawled inside the darkened room and positioned himself behind the longest counter. Corporal Johnson followed suit, taking the counter on the opposite side. Sergeant Lucas crawled gingerly along the floor to the ninety-degree angled intersection of the two counters and took his position. Mason removed three canisters of stun gas from his back pack, pulled their plugs and threw them behind the counters into the kitchen. Laser fire then came from every conceivable angle at the Marines from behind stoves, sinks, and prep counters inside the kitchen. Sergeant Lucas lobbed four flasher sets into the fracas, and switched them on to illuminate the kitchen. There were at least a dozen men holed up there, hiding behind protective steel of the kitchen appliances. With the instant lighting of their kitchen positions, the miners fired into the officers' mess indiscriminately, blasting everything they could. They wasted their laser fire on destroying the entrance to the kitchen, where they thought the Marines would be entering upright. But they were not entering upright. They crawled under the laser fire into the first kitchen prep counters, and took out several of the shooters.

Mason crawled around to the front of the prep counter on his belly, rolled and took out three shooters, as Sergeant Lucas threw four flasher sets into the middle of the kitchen. When he switched them on and the room illuminated, they killed most of the shooters instantly. Trained battle-hardened Marines against armed miners; no doubt who would win this one. They advanced slowly, making certain to completely clear the path towards the big mess hall. They let the miners use up their ammo, and waited for the click-click-click of the charger packs being reloaded.

At the first sound of reloading, the Space Marines rushed the remaining shooters, killing them quickly and efficiently. They checked the entire kitchen, and were pleasantly surprised to discover that most of the crewmen hid inside their steel pantries, refrigerators, and walk-in freezers. Mason ran to the mess hall office, where he found the Senior Chief and Sammie hiding with three other crewmen inside her locked office. Mason gave them the thumbs up, but told her to stay until she heard the "all clear" from the Captain.

The Marines advanced into the big mess hall and were greeted with more laser fire, but from fewer men. Corporal Johnson tossed two stun grenades into the hall, and the miners stood up, firing at anything and everything. Those easy targets were taken out. Mason reported to Captain Baines they cleaned up the kitchen, and moved on to "get some antacid." The bridge and engineering were still secure, so the Marines moved up to the hospital floor.

The Marines ran into the hall, down to the hospital, and found Dr. Hassan and all three nurses huddled with Captain Kouras in the back room. "Mason, what's the situation?" Kouras asked. He was given the very short and sweet answer to that question, then Mason checked with the bridge again. "We have begun to exchange fire with them, Mason. We need you up here," Captain Baines said.

Mason looked at Nurse Baines, and said, "I think it's time we went to your old quarters, ma'am, except for Nurse Soo and Captain Kouras. They'll be safe here." She understood immediately. She led the Marines, Nurse Jones, and a confused Dr. Hassan to her old quarters. The Marines emptied her bookcase and helped Mason with the big rifle up the maintenance shaft to the conference room hidden door. They entered the conference room, to the astonishment of everyone on the bridge except Captain Baines. Mason set up the big rifle on its mount at the main door, while the Marines took their positions.

Mason said in a whisper to the CO, "Captain Baines, Nurse Baines and the Doctor are safe with Nurse Jones in the Commander's old quarters. Please join them, Captain." The Captain protested at first. But when engineering reported their door was being fired upon, the Captain realized he could be more help to his Marines by being inaccessible to the attacking miners. Mason had installed a secondary computer control console in Commander Baines' old quarters, for such an occasion. The Captain could monitor and control all their efforts safely from there. The Captain left down the hidden door to be with his medical command staff, and his new control console.

All bridge officers were at their stations, armed with side arms and laser rifles, waiting for the main door breach. The miners brought blowtorches this time, and were making good progress cutting through the hardened steel blast hatch. They would be through in a few minutes. Commander

Powers reported they were holding, but the miners were using blowtorches on their door, as well. Mason checked with the Space Marines holding up in engineering, and they were ready for the onslaught.

The main door to the bridge started turning a soft green, then glowed, and turned into red. "Prepare for a breach of the bridge," Westerly yelled, as the officers took cover behind their stations, laser rifles at the ready for the oncoming miners. The interior screen shields activated to protect the bridge viewing windows. There was no gas in the ceiling lines to use this time. It had all been used in a one-time dispersal yesterday. They would have to fight their way out of this one.

As the main door panel turned from red to a black, the miners began firing into the door panel, accelerating the door's destruction. "Hold your fire," Sergeant Lucas ordered. Suddenly, the center of the door came flying apart, and laser fire came through. "Fire cannon!" Sergeant Lucas yelled, and Mason let them have it. It only took one blast to not only kill a man, but to send him into the back of the corridor. Man after man tried to come through, and Mason took each one out, with carefully aimed shot after shot at them. The miners finally got smart, and stuck laser rifles through the hole in the door, firing in all directions. The Marines held their fire, and Corporal Milton tossed an incendiary bomb perfectly through the center of the hole in the door. The explosion rocked the bridge, but the laser fire stopped momentarily.

The pause gave the Space Marines time to reposition to attack from different angles, not just be on the defensive. Mason moved his big gun up on the center bridge deck, next to Lt. Commander Davis' station. When the laser fire erupted again, he fired not only through the hole in the door, but also along a line adjacent to the door, taking out more jammed up miners waiting to try their hand at taking the bridge. Sergeant Lucas tossed a handful of gas canisters through the hole, in several directions, for maximum effect. The choking and coughing also caused the laser fire to stop for a few seconds. But the miners would not give up, they kept coming up to the door, firing their rifles at no one in particular, blasting through the hole in the door. Mason continued to pick off the miners one by one.

The Space Marines in engineering were close to having their door breached. Mason called Corporal Milton over to the big laser rifle, and went over to the Sergeant. They spoke secretly, and Mason left for the ready room, carrying two laser rifles in hand. Mason emerged from the Captain's quarters, firing both laser rifles behind the miners' line of attack, and took out over a dozen miners before they realized where the fire was coming from. He continued to fire at them, bringing down the entire line of attack. Satisfied he got them all, he went back inside the bridge. Westerly agreed with Mason they should assist engineering, and the Space Marines left through the hidden door in the conference room, and climbed down to engineering. They burst through the access panel after Sergeant Lucas called to the other team of Space Marines on his comm-link. Mason took the big rifle, and positioned it directly in front of the main engineering door, as he had done on the bridge. They waited, while the engineers took cover behind their stations.

The impatient miners started blasting their laser rifles much sooner than they had on the bridge, and were nearly empty when they broke the hole through the door. Mason picked them off one by one, as the Marines cross-fired at angles through the hole. Sergeant Lucas held up his hand to cease fire, and hurled two incendiaries at opposite ends of the outer corridor. That all but cleared their way. They thought their problems were over, until they heard Westerly say, "The door to the ninth deck has been breached. We will have more incoming. Get ready." Someone awakened more miners, and they were headed their way. Indeed, the miners hiding out in Section 2 spent the night awakening their fellow mutineers.

Mason got an idea. He called Captain Kouras in the hospital. "Captain, what did you do with your one-man ship, sir? We may need to use it." Kouras had stored it in the cargo bay, held aloft by pulleys at the top ridge near the observation deck for the bay. Mason called Captain Baines, and informed him that upwards of another two hundred miners would be attacking as soon as they could be awakened. Mason told him his plan. The Captain was skeptical, but decided to trust Mason and Captain Kouras, and agreed. Mason took four laser rifles and four bands of charger ammo packs, and all the incendiaries Sergeant Lucas had left. Corporal Milton was right at home on the big rifle, and the officers were at the ready. Mason left for the access door.

He entered the hospital and went to Captain Kouras, and told him his plan. "It has all the elements of a successful stealth attack but one, Mason," the Captain said. "That little one-man ship will not get off the ground with you and two laser rifles, period. I flew it just fine, but I weigh only 80 kg. I will pilot the craft, surprise them, and lead them to you." Mason needed to get Captain Baines' approval for this change of events.

"I cannot approve of his leaving the hospital, Captain," Dr. Hassan said in the background. "We don't know what he will do under duress."

"Captain Baines, I am lucid and alert. I know how to pilot my little ship. Mason will never get off the ground in it. He's too big. I have served the Space Forces for over two decades, in battle and in times of peace. I know my duty, Captain Baines, to my ship, to my crew, and to you, who have followed in my footsteps. I willingly lay down my life for you all. It is better to die in battle fighting the enemy, than to live out my life in a hospital for the criminally insane, is it not, Captain Baines?" What argument could Captain Baines have against him? It was worth trying, in any case.

The plan was in motion. Mason and Kouras slipped easily down the crawl shafts, with their feet on the outside of the ladders, sliding down quickly to the cargo bay observation deck. The little ship still had eighty percent charge in her batteries, more than enough for a trip to deck nine.

Mason helped Captain Kouras into the tight seat, and realized there would have been no way he would have fit inside it, with or without rifles. He handed two laser rifles to his old Captain, who took one belt of extra charger ammo, and put it over his head. He started the engine, and she purred like a kitten. Kouras smiled. "It will take me three minutes to fly to the miners' quarters where their hibernation containers are stored. I can hover for a minute while you take your position at the end of the corridor, and we can run them into the gauntlet. What shall our signal be, Mason?"

"When I get into position, I'll hurl gas canisters down the hall. You'll hear them start to fire, and that will be your signal, sir." Mason said, knowing that Captain Kouras was not planning to return. "It has been my greatest honor to serve you, Captain Kouras," Mason said, saluting his old Captain and friend. The Captain returned his salute, his eyes tearing up. "And it will be my greatest honor to serve you, Master Sergeant Mason. Let's get to work!" With that, Kouras uncoupled the little ship from its moorings, and she flew up, and away.

Mason ran down the cargo bay to the crawl shaft, climbed up to the ninth floor, and looked out the access panel. All clear. They did not know he would be there, waiting for them, ready to rip them to shreds. He removed the access panel door off the wall. It wasn't much protection, but it would help some. His only defense against their fire was his energy hand shield and that access panel, but it was his only hope. If another two hundred miners were awakened and able to attack, the Hesperia would be lost. Mason resigned himself to his fate. He asked God for clean shots and protection for Sherrie and Mrs. Baines. He committed himself to the warrior's way fully. He took his position and began his centering process, when he heard footsteps in the shaft. He saw Captain Baines' head pop out, smiling. "I can't let you have all the fun and glory, Mason. This is my ship, and I will not hide like a coward while she is in her hour of need. Two Captains and a Master Sergeant should be able to make quick work of a couple hundred miners, don't you think?"

"Yes sir, Captain Baines. It is my honor to serve you, my Captain." They exchanged salutes. The Captain brought a laser rifle, his side arm, a combat vest, helmet, another hand shield, and his sword. He took his position next to Mason, behind the access panel.

"How did Mrs. Baines take this news, sir?" Mason asked, getting his gas canisters ready.

"She got completely hysterical, so Dr. Hassan sedated her," he said, laughing. "There's Kouras now!" He said, and they watched the little ship hover, and dipped its nose in acknowledgement of them. Kouras flew around the corner of the corridor, turned and waited.

Mason handed Captain Baines two gas canisters, and they threw them together down the corridor. They got on one knee in firing position, activated their hand energy shields, and waited. Soon they heard sounds of choking and coughing, and miners yelling. They heard sounds of many feet running towards them. As the miners rounded the far aft end of the corridor, Mason and the Captain were seen, and fired upon. Wave after wave of attacking miners came directly at them, but they had the advantage. After emptying half a belt of charger packs, Mason reached inside his pack and pulled out two incendiaries, hurled them at the fresh onslaught of miners, picked up his rifle, and continued firing. Every shot must count.

The deafening sounds of laser rifle fire kept on for what seemed an eternity to Mason and Captain Baines. They emptied all but the last four charger packs, and the bodies were stacked high; but miners continued to charge at them, firing their rifles. Mason loaded his last pack into his rifle, and said, "I saved the last pack for you, Captain Baines," and Baines picked it up and reloaded. Mason threw everything remaining in his pack at the miners, now climbing over their dead comrades, stepping irreverently on and over them, and firing at the two men holding them off at the end of the hall. Their energy shields were almost drained, offering a much narrower field of protection. Baines was wounded in the leg, but continued firing from a prone position. Mason received several flesh wounds; the one on his exposed neck narrowly missed his jugular.

Suddenly, the miners came in double, screaming and yelling, with looks of terror on their faces. Some even threw down their rifles, as the little ship mowed them down from behind. Kouras was standing, holding and firing both rifles at once, and screaming at the top of his lungs. The miners never saw him around the far forward corner as he picked them off individually, at first. But when Kouras saw the last wave leave the storage room, he got behind them and forced them into Mason and Baines, into the gauntlet. They finally stopped coming when the pile of dead bodies was half way to the top of the hall. Kouras waved at Mason victoriously. One last miner raised his head up from the pile of bodies and fired into the little ship, hitting Captain Kouras, forcing him to sit down in the cockpit. Kouras turned the ship around, headed towards the hibernation room, and a loud explosion was heard. Kouras took as many with him as he could. The vid cam analysis showed Kouras saved his last ammo pack, fired upon it, and exploded in midair above the last awakening miners, sending them to hell.

XXXIII

All was quiet on the Hesperia for the next few months. Each Space Marine was promoted, and every crew member received at least one medal for their battle efforts. Captain Kouras was honored with a Bronze Star, posthumously. Captain Baines and Mason each received Bronze Stars, as well, each man wounded in his stand in the hall, victorious against over two hundred miners. No attacking miner ever set foot on the bridge or the engineering deck of the Hesperia.

Earth Command learned its lesson; all future mining expeditions utilized new robotic mining drillers. Fewer than fifty miners would be assigned to any one mining freighter again. The robots never rebelled or mutinied, unlike their human predecessors. The dead bodies of the Hesperia miners numbered over four hundred. The Hesperia could not take them back without fear of contamination or disease, so Earth Command ordered their bodies taken to the big Section 3 furnaces, and cremated. Only the bodies of Mission Director Keene, Coordinator Garcia, and their slaughtered medical staff were brought back for proper burial.

Captain Baines' leg wound took some time healing, as his outer knee ligaments were all but destroyed. His name would be remembered in the Space Forces' Academy for many generations, with plaques honoring him in the Academy's halls. The Omicron Protocol was formally renamed the Baines' Protocol, in his honor.

Nurse Baines survived the attacks well, overcoming her fear to help heal the injured, including her Captain and Mason. No men every received better care. Baines and Mason received her healing skills for weeks. She spoiled them both immensely, and they loved her attention. Captain Baines and Mason became even closer; their friendship lasted the rest of their lives.

Mason and the Senior Chief were married as soon as Captain Baines could stand and perform the ceremony. Their ceremony was small and intimate, with only Captain and Commander Baines, Dr. Hassan, and Sergeant Lucas attending. They celebrated together with dinner in the Captain's quarters, with Mason's bourbon.

Sr. Chief Sherrie Mason and her husband placed their call with his family at the holidays. She loved meeting her new in-laws, and Mason's niece and nephew. She introduced him to her parents, and they were elated to meet their oldest daughter's husband.

The Hesperia was re-coupled, and the glove was emptied and refolded in its hold on the side of the Hesperia. Mason supervised the retraction of the container's tow cables from inside Section 4, dressed in his space suit. He stayed on the deck as the massive room was pressurized, and the atmosphere replenished. As Mason walked the long way back to the crossover into Section 3, he noticed several clumps along the wall. They were black and shiny, and he didn't know what they were. He put them in his space suit pockets, and took them with him. Captain Baines said he could keep them as souvenirs. They would become his greatest treasure.

The officers and crewmen who allied themselves with the Yellow Man were put into cryonic hibernation immediately following the final battle with the miners. Nurse Soo was the exception. She admitted being recruited by the Yellow Man, but she was never called upon to do anything for him, and never received any compensation. Everyone knew she had been approached right after Kouras attacked her, at the weakest moment of her life. She worked unselfishly after her discovery to aid the officers and crew of the Hesperia when they needed her healing skills. She was allowed to remain out of cryonic hibernation for the entire journey home. She received a favorable ruling later at her court-martial. Captain Baines and Dr. Hassan spoke highly of her, and she was given a second chance to redeem herself. She served in high distinction for a forty-year career.

Mason and Sherrie moved into a married unit. The Senior Chief was kept from being put into cryonic hibernation, to the delight of everyone. She loved to cook for them all, and they were ecstatic to not have to eat food pouches for a year and a half, the original plan. They were doing their best to make their wine stash from Captain Kouras last until Titan One.

In the twelfth month of their journey home at hyper-space 3, Mason was on the bridge at his post, when he felt his hair on the back of his neck stand up. The Captain was occupied reading his reports, and all bridge officers had their heads down, busy doing something or other. Mason looked at the main windows, and saw it first. "Captain Baines!" He called, and the Captain looked up, and saw the orange cloud coming closer to them.

The computer announced "Red Alert! Red Alert!" Captain Baines watched the orange cloud come closer and closer to them, as if the Hesperia was free floating in space, and not speeding along at hyper-space

3.

"This is Captain Baines of the mining freighter Hesperia. Please identify yourself, and state your intentions." No response. The Captain ordered his announcement repeated once, twice, and a third time. He waited.

"WE ARE ONE. YOU WILL GIVE US ONE OF YOUR SPECIES FOR STUDY IMMEDIATELY."

Captain Baines ordered Lieutenant Marston to hail Earth Command for a response, as he had done before with the orange cloud. Earth Command refused to give them a human for study; request denied. The entire bridge crew held their breath. They thought they were nearly home free, and now this orange cloud was back.

"WE ARE ONE. YOU WILL GIVE US ONE OF YOUR SPECIES FOR STUDY. WE WILL GIVE YOU ONE OF OURS IN TRADE." Now, that was a very different matter. Earth Command was thinking about it. Were they actually considering handing over someone for the orange cloud species to study, probe, and do who knows what to?

"WE ARE ONE. YOU WILL GIVE US ONE OF YOUR SPECIES FOR STUDY. WE WILL GIVE YOU ONE OF OURS IN TRADE." The same message, repeated. Still no response from Earth Command.

Captain Baines sat up, and commanded, "The ONE, show yourselves to us. You can see us; we want to see you." Silence.

The orange cloud began changing colors again, swirling and undulating, turning colors in front of them. The huge ship appeared, the full view this time. It was the size of an Earth city, massive, black and gleaming, with thousands of lighted areas. The ship's forward windows began to get a scrambled digital projection, and everyone was transfixed, watching the image gradually emerge. When the image was finished assembling on the Hesperia's front screens, it showed a very large seated lizard, which must have been their captain, or whatever he or she was called. Standing beside the large lizard was a smaller, nearly human man, dressed all in yellow.

"WE ARE ONE. WE HAVE SHOWN YOU OURSELVES. YOU WILL GIVE US ONE OF YOUR SPECIES FOR STUDY. WE WILL GIVE YOU ONE OF OURS IN TRADE."

Mason walked up to Captain Baines, and they both instantly recognized the figure in yellow as their Yellow Man, who was the cause of the Hesperia's troubles from day one.

Mason asked, "May I speak to them, Captain Baines?" The Captain merely nodded, as captivated with the images on the screens as anyone else. Earth Command had not responded.

"Hello, Dr. James. It is good to meet you, at last." Mason said calmly. Baines looked at Mason as if he were insane. "My name is Mason. How long have you been with the ONE, sir?"

The Yellow Man screwed up his strange face into something resembling a smile. He answered, "I have been with the ONE since my rebirth. I am one with them, Mason. We have been searching for the Perfect Man. We will create in him the seed for the advancement of our combined species. We want one of your species for study. We will give you one of ours in trade." His face was not the exact face of the picture of Dr. James who embarked on the colonization of GK-356, but it was obvious the creature before them had once been Dr. James.

"We cannot do that, Dr. James. We are sentient beings, and have the right to exist on our own. Why did you try to take over this ship, Dr. James?" Mason was very non-threatening in his line of questioning.

"We are looking for the Perfect Man. The odds were greater with so many to study that we would find the Perfect Man." The Yellow Man kept looking around the bridge, sizing up everyone.

"We are denying your request to send over someone for you to study. We have no desire to study one of your kind. We wish to be left in peace. You have caused us enough grief, Dr. James. Please let us pass," Baines said firmly. Dr. James pointed a finger at Captain Baines.

Mason stepped in front of the Captain, saying firmly, "You may not take our Captain. You may not take anyone. We do not want anyone from your ship. We want to be left alone in peace."

"Your species is a vast collection of individuals, egotistical and ego-centric, only interested in their individual gratification. We are ONE. We are interested in advancement of our species and wish to align with you. You will give us one of your species to study. We will give you one of ours in trade," Dr. James said.

"We will not give you one of our species. We do not want one of your species to study. We want to be left alone in peace. You will let us leave in peace now," Captain Baines said. The huge ship began to gather its clouds around it, swirling and changing colors, then disappearing altogether. The Captain waited several minutes more, then got up and gave the comm to Westerly. He motioned for Mason to accompany him to his ready room.

"How did you know the Yellow Man was Dr. James, Mason? How did you piece that together?" He sat down and motioned for Mason to sit.

"It was the only thing that made sense, Captain Baines. How did the Yellow Man know to be at Moon Base one week before the Hesperia left? How did he know which bar to hang out, waiting to recruit the youngest, least experienced crew and officers? How did he know to tempt them with large amounts of money, drugs, and casual sex partners? It only makes sense if the Yellow Man previously experienced having to report one week prior to departure for a deep space mission; if he went to that bar to hang out, waiting for departure, seeing all the young people respond to money, casual sex and drugs. He knew too much about us. He even knew to ask Urz for our technical manuals and communications manuals," Mason answered. "It always bothered me about the starving woman on GK-356 saying Dr. James left with the red cloud people, and more of them wanted to go, but they only had room for one. Dr. James was the most perfect man the ONE could find in their colony. So they took him and changed him, hence, the "rebirth" Dr. James mentioned, sir."

"Your intuition told you it was Dr. James, too, isn't that right, Mason?" The Captain asked.

"Yes, sir. But I wasn't sure until they showed themselves to us. He was still human enough; it had to be Dr. James, Captain Baines."

"Remarkable, Mason. I would not have assumed that at all. And the fact that you were correct in your assumption pleased him a great deal, did you notice that?"

"Yes, sir. But when he raised his finger and pointed directly at you, I had to let him know he could not take you from us, sir."

"That was very unsettling. I trust you won't say anything to Mrs. Baines about it, Mason."

"No, Captain Baines, I won't." Mason looked at his Captain, who became the "Perfect Man" for the ONE to want to study. Well, he at least agreed with the aliens on that count. Captain Baines was the most perfect, definitely most intelligent man on board the Hesperia. But they still couldn't have him to study, and turn into a human-reptilian hybrid, like Dr. James.

As the weeks rolled by, the crew became more relaxed. It seemed only Mason was concerned about more trouble finding them. He never assumed for one minute that the Yellow Man had given up on his attempts to take over the Hesperia. Mason was so troubled by this singular thought that he began to have nightmares about it. The technology of the ONE was obviously superior; why had they not boarded the Hesperia when the ship was floating in the mining fields, for four years? Why entrust the colonization plans of the ONE to greedy miners and traitorous Hesperian crew members alone? Mason felt there might still be another traitor on board, lying in wait, to sabotage the Hesperia before her battleship escort could take them to Moon Base.

During one particularly violent nightmare, he awoke with the fear that the waiting battleship had been taken over by the ONE, and the Hesperia was flying at hyper-speed right into a trap. Sherrie put up with his nightmares for months, and insisted Mason go talk with Dr. Hassan about them. Reluctantly, he went in for a private consultation with the Doctor.

"I don't know how to explain my nightmares, or whether my fears are justified, Dr. Hassan. But I feel we are making a terrible mistake in relaxing our defenses against the ONE. They are still following us. I don't know how, but I do feel them, and know they will make another attempt. I think there is at least one more traitor on board, in the service of the Yellow Man," Mason confessed.

"Perhaps you're just overworked, Master Sergeant, or you just need a few days off from bridge guard duty," Dr. Hassan offered. "We're almost home."

"That's just the thing he wants us to think, Dr. Hassan, that we're home free, and everything's all right. We're not home. We have another four months of hyper-speed 3, and then we meet up with the battleship group to escort us to Moon Base. Too much time for another attack." Mason said, holding his head in his hands.

"Let's just make sure you're okay physically, Mason," the Doctor said, and took him to lie down under the full body scanner. "You are definitely suffering from sleep deprivation and slightly higher blood pressure than normal. Your brain wave patterns seem a little off, too," he commented, moving around the scanner making adjustments. "This is significant. I'd better call the Captain." He was looking at Mason's brain at work on the imager, becoming concerned. "You'll stay here for a few hours, Mason."

Captain Baines came to the hospital first thing that morning. Dr. Hassan told him of Mason's brain wave pattern alterations, and his frequent nightmares. "He has not complained of any symptoms such as these the entire voyage, Captain. Something is going on with him."

"Could it be he's overworked, or too worried? I must admit I haven't given his warnings much credence lately with everything going so smoothly," Captain Baines admitted. "His intuition is usually reliable, but I felt he was just being overly concerned."

Mason looked at them both, feeling like an amoeba under a microscope. "I'm not being paranoid, Captain Baines. I am certain of another episode occurring, sir. We have let our guard down, and that's just what he wanted us to do, Captain. We are vulnerable now, sir," Mason said with all seriousness in his voice.

"The brain area showing the highest activity is the region normally associated with intuition, and extra sensory perception. It was active, even when he slept for a couple of hours, Captain," Dr. Hassan said, showing Mason's scans to the Captain.

"Is he fit for duty, Dr. Hassan?" The Captain asked, now concerned.

"Oh yes, he's fit. But he needs to get some quality sleep soon. And a good hot meal. Your weight's down several kg, Mason," the Doctor said. "When was the last time you ate?"

Mason could not remember when he ate last. "I feel like I'm running on pure energy, Doctor," Mason said with an unusual tone of voice. "Something is definitely about to happen, and soon." Mason pushed the scanner away from his body, and sat up. "We should be on the bridge, Captain Baines."

"Yes, well let's be off, and get some breakfast first, Master Sergeant. Neither you nor I have eaten yet today. Thank you, Dr. Hassan," the

Captain said, as they left the hospital.

They went into the officers' mess and ordered big breakfasts, juice and coffee. The Captain took a table in the back and motioned for Mason to sit. "They'll bring everything over to us, Mason. Now, tell me everything you've dreamt about lately." The Captain sat across from him, and leaned in to hear.

Mason told him about his nightmares, all of them. They contained terrifying images of death and destruction of the Hesperia. He related his concerns about the Yellow Man already having taken over the battleship supposedly waiting for them, to escort them to Moon Base. He also shared his most fearful dream: Earth Command in Houston being fed misinformation about them, and believing it, causing them to give orders to the battleship to destroy the Hesperia after taking her platinum and palladium metals on board.

The Captain did not know what to think. He had relied upon his Prime Marine for over six years, and Mason had never steered him wrong. But these dreams were the stuff of fantasy. Was Mason suffering from deep space sickness? "When did these nightmares begin?" He asked quietly.

"About three weeks after our last encounter with the orange cloud, Captain. I know I sound nuts. There's no physical evidence for my nightmares. But, sir, remember when you said you could feel the orange cloud was following us? That's the feeling I have now. I'm afraid we're being set up, that the battleship is under the Yellow Man's control, and no one at Earth Command is aware of that fact. It's the perfect ending, don't you see, Captain? He's tried everything he could to take over the Hesperia, and failed. He knows everything we do, sir. He knows we're heading for the battleship at Titan One, and he's made certain he either takes our ship there, or takes the battleship, in our place. He wants his colony, Captain Baines."

The wonderful feelings of relief and calm that permeated Captain Baines' psyche for the last few weeks disappeared. "Mason, if you're correct, we are heading into a trap at hyper-speed 3. This is not the homecoming we think it is, if what you say is even half right. Or, you could be delusional and suffering from deep space sickness," the Captain said. "How is it you have these dreams, or nightmares? Have you done anything out of the norm, or hit your head?"

"No, Captain. I haven't hit my head or anything," Mason said, dejected that the Captain did not trust his intuition. Suddenly Mason thought of a possible solution. "Captain, what if we were to arrive at Titan One a week early, sir?"

"The battle group wouldn't even arrive there by then, and we'd have no escort to take us to Moon Base." Captain Baines realized what Mason asked. "If they didn't know we'd be coming in early, they could not prepare…" he said to himself.

"And we might have the upper hand, Captain Baines. We could even circumvent Titan One altogether, and head directly for Moon Base. We could utilize one of your alternate navigational routes, Captain, and reach Moon Base via the dark side of the moon, unnoticed until our arrival."

"We'd be taking an awful risk, Mason. If the Hesperia was attacked by pirate ships between Titan One and Moon Base, we'd be defenseless, or at least severely hampered in our efforts to defend ourselves."

"Not if we didn't go by Titan One, Captain Baines. They'd still be waiting for us, and we'd be docking at Moon Base, sir." Mason suggested.

"I'd have to get clearance for this diversion from Earth Command first, Mason. This is not something I could do on a whim," the Captain said, looking at him for suggestions.

"But if someone at Earth Command was under the Yellow Man's influence, he would not allow for such a diversion, sir. At the very least, if you specifically requested such a diversion, and told Earth Command what you wanted to do, the Yellow Man would know, and could prepare for it," Mason suggested.

"I have to think about this." The Captain was relieved the conversation had ended. He and Mason finished their breakfasts, and they left for the bridge.

Mason took up his guard post as usual, and wondered if Captain Baines would pay heed to his warnings. There was little time to make course adjustments to circumvent Titan One.

XXXIV

One week later, the Hesperia was still on the same course to Titan One. Mason resigned himself to the fact that no one believed his nightmares as forewarnings of events to come; maybe they were right to do so. Dr. Hassan gave him sleeping tablets and they seemed to help. At least Sherrie was getting some sleep, Mason thought. The tablets calmed him enough that he would fall asleep, but he did not stay asleep. He decided to ask Commander Powers if any suborbital transmissions were being received, before heading up top to report for duty one morning.

"No, Mason, we haven't received any suborbital transmissions, or transmissions of any kind, other than the usual communiques from Earth Command. Why do you ask?" The Commander was in his usual gruff mood.

"I was curious if any unusual transmissions had been received or sent during the past few months, sir. No particular reason, Commander," Mason answered.

Mason was about to leave engineering when a junior grade Lieutenant offered, "Would that include the tachyon pulses, too, Commander?"

"What tachyon pulses, Lieutenant?" Powers asked sharply.

"Those pulses I put in my report last month, sir. You know, they start and stop within a four hour window each night; random distribution, intermittent, pattern dispersion within a ten thousand kilometer grid, Commander Powers?"

"Have they continued every night for the last two months, Lieutenant?" Mason asked, already knowing the answer.

"Yes, they have. How did you know?" The Lieutenant was then subjected to a barrage from the Chief Engineer about not reporting the tachyon pulses to him directly, as Mason left.

He called Captain Baines about the "new" information he discovered, and was ordered into the ready room. Powers was asked to provide complete information on the tachyon pulses immediately, while Mason stood at attention in front of Captain Baines. Soon Dr. Hassan entered the room, and snapped to attention, seeing the Captain's countenance.

"Lieutenant Marston, get me Admiral Tomiko at once, orange alert."

The Admiral was brought up to speed about the tachyon pulses, as well as Mason's nightmares and intuition. Dr. Hassan sent Earth Command copies of Mason's brain wave patterns, which coincided with the exact time of the tachyon pulses, at least the nights the patterns were recorded. "I fear we may be followed by the ONE, Admiral. In fact, I am concerned we may be heading into a trap," the Captain said. He stared directly into the vid cam at the Admiral, and silence between the two men transpired. Mason wondered if the Captain said something to Admiral Tomiko earlier about their conversation, and had not received the authorization to take an alternate course.

"How is it you received these visions or nightmares, Master Sergeant? Are you now psychic, too?" The Admiral asked.

"I honestly don't know, Admiral. I know others thought I was having deep space sickness. I cannot explain, Admiral. But I know the ONE are out there, following us, waiting. How would we know if the Yellow Man had successfully taken over another ship, if he managed to do so without violence, Admiral? Would the Captain of that ship even know he was now following the Yellow Man's orders, instead of Earth Command's directions, sir?" Mason's questions were very disturbing to everyone present, and to the Admiral.

"Very well, Captain Baines. Your earlier request is now granted. I am giving you autonomy to take your ship to whatever base you desire, via your own navigational coordinates. But know this: it will not reflect well on your judgment if that load of platinum does not reach Moon Base, is that clear? I am taking a big risk here, Captain Baines, and doing so not on your Prime Marine's intuition, but on credible evidence. The approved course is to rendezvous with the battleship and its group at Titan One. You have autonomy to divert from this route, as you see fit. But you'd better be right on target, Captain. Do we understand one another?" Tomiko asked.

"Yes, Admiral Tomiko. I understand." Captain Baines was at attention, not flinching. "Does the Admiral wish to know in advance if a new navigational course is chosen?" The transmission ended.

Captain Baines, Dr. Hassan, and Mason stood at attention for another few seconds, in case the transmission would be reconnected. But it soon became clear to them all: stay on course, and possibly get taken over by a fully loaded battleship controlled by the Yellow Man; or divert from the approved course, and run the risk of encountering pirates with no battleship to protect the Hesperia and its precious cargo.

"Thank you, Dr. Hassan, you are dismissed." The Captain then looked at Mason, saying merely "Sit."

Mason pulled out his scanner, showed it to the Captain, and got his nod to sweep the ready room; all clear. He pulled out his papers, and wrote, "What if the Hesperia could enter the solar system on course to Titan One, divert behind Saturn, and slingshot to Mars? From there, it's an easy run to Moon Base, and the slingshot effect could possibly enable us to outrun any pirate vessels, Captain."

"That is much more difficult than it sounds, Mason. If we were a star cruiser, I'd say, 'No problem,' but we are a huge mining freighter, ill-suited for these types of maneuvers, and a slingshot would propel us at hyper-speed 5 to 7. I'm not sure she could take it," Baines replied.

"Then, we'd have to move the platinum into Section 1, just to be safe, Captain Baines," Mason responded, "and do the Omicron Protocol again."

Captain Baines looked at Mason. It might work. "Dismissed," was all the Captain said.

1st Lieutenant Cheung was ordered to conduct an emergency inspection of the cargo bay in Section 1. With three of her four shuttles missing, there was ample room to load up the platinum and palladium from Section 2 in there, but there were no sealed precious metals lockers. Their only choice was to fuse-weld cargo containers to the walls, as was done in Section 2 three years ago for protected storage of the precious metal. The security droids were trusted to move the precious metals, not any remaining miners or the ship's own security forces.

Captain Baines ordered the platinum moved "for safekeeping" in the cargo bay, along the walls of Section 1. The cargo containers holding the platinum bars in the locked vault of Section 2 were moved into Section 1, and welded closed by the Space Marines. The containers were welded shut with their front openings up against the walls of the cargo bay. No one was getting inside them until their welds were removed, period. It took three days' work to move out all the precious metals on Section 2 into safe and secure cargo containers on Section 1.

The Captain closed the cargo bay doors, and sealed them shut. The shuttle was moved into launch position on the opposite side of the cargo bay, where it could be launched in an emergency from the open bay door during or after the Omicron Protocol, if it was implemented. All observation and bridge windows were resealed from the inside, as a precaution, in case any had cracked from six years' use. The Hesperia would enter the solar system tomorrow, still on course for Titan One. She passed through the Kuiper belt the last day and a half.

Pirate ships were not uncommon in the outer solar system, where space patrols were few and far between. They used small ships, customized with fast engines stolen from much larger vessels, and loaded with awesome firepower. The Hesperia could withstand any direct firing on Sections 2 through 4, but Section 1 was vulnerable. Her defensive weapons were greater than any pirate ship, but she was not very maneuverable in an emergency. The Hesperia was an easy target.

The word was out that the Hesperia was bringing in the greatest load of platinum in the history of mankind. Many news broadcasts talked of her vast stores of platinum, palladium, and gold, of which there was none. But the broadcast media kept talking about gold cargo like it was true. Gold or not, the Hesperia entered the solar system with a giant target on her back.

The ship slowed to hyper-speed 1 upon entering the solar system, ordered by Earth Command. The tachyon particle bursts grew more frequent and pervasive. Mason felt the Yellow Man had grown confident enough not to hide them. As the Hesperia continued on the approved course, Mason watched closely. The Captain must commit to a new course by tomorrow, or stay the course onto Titan One.

The dinner menu for that night was ham, turkey and stuffing; Mason realized it was a holiday meal. He was so preoccupied with their situation that he forgot it was Christmas Day. He had been working more than sixteen hours a day, on the bridge during his regular duty hours, and accompanying Captain Baines wherever he went whenever he wanted him, which was every day and most every night during the last two weeks. He stopped taking his sleeping tablets, in case he was needed in an emergency. He could not afford to be groggy on the bridge. As he stood in line for dinner, Mason was deep in thought, when a familiar voice said, "Hello, Master Sergeant Mason. Would you like to join me at a table for dinner?"

Mason looked up to see the lovely face of his wife. "Of course I would, Senior Chief." He knew he was distant the past couple of weeks, completely absorbed in his duty to the Captain, and it had been at her expense. She led him to a pre-set table at the back of the mess hall, where two plates of hot turkey dinner were already waiting for them, along with a half carafe of synthehol chardonnay. She smiled as he pulled out the chair for her, and sat down, as Sergeants Johnson and Milton razzed him about getting preferential treatment in the mess hall.

"I'm not sure if you remember me, but I'm your wife," she whispered, taking a sip of white wine. "I'm the one who sleeps in the bed next to you every night," she finished, doing an excellent job of making her point.

"I'm sorry, Sherrie. But I can't always share with you what's going on, you know. I promise to do better, I swear." She could tell he was sincere, and dropped the matter. They enjoyed their meal, and talked with each other as if everything was normal. He even managed a smile for her, the first one in several days. She had gone upstairs to clean up and change to have dinner with him. Mason realized he had not taken care of his wife's needs – as well as his own – for weeks, and was obsessed with the Captain's pending decision.

"I haven't seen you eating more than once every day or two, and it's really got me worried, John. Dr. Hassan said you're losing too much weight," she said, obviously concerned about him. "I never thought I'd have to worry about your appetites, John," she said, looking at him, and how thin his face appeared. He noticed she said appetites; plural, not singular.

"I haven't been anywhere else to get my appetites satisfied, if that's what you're concerned about, Sherrie." He smiled at her, and she blushed. "Let's finish up here and go to our quarters before I get called again," he suggested.

To his amazement, she stood up and said, "Let's go now." He followed her to their quarters. She went to her fridge and got out a bottle of real white wine, opened it quickly, and poured two glasses for them. Mason took off his boots, stripped off his uniform and went into the shower. He came out with a towel wrapped around his hips, and saw her sitting at the table, watching him.

She had the look of a stalking tigress in her eyes, focused on her prey and his every move. A force to be reckoned with. Her glass of wine was nearly empty, so he filled her glass for her. "You've started with the nightmares again, John. Can you at least tell me what those are all about?" She was slowly twirling the glass stem in her fingers.

He tried to explain the tachyon pulses and particles to her, how a ship with hyper-space drive always emits those particles. She asked quietly, "So, our ship is being followed, and you're dreaming about it?"

"Sort of. My heightened bionic implants are picking up its frequency whenever it gets too close to us, or sends out any signals. That's what Dr. Hassan thinks is happening. My brain does the rest. I can't say any more about what the Captain's doing, Sherrie, and how I'm assisting him."

She had heard enough. She slapped the table with her hand, jumped up and said, "What the hell are all these officers for? Can't someone else do something around here? Why do you have to do everything for him? You need a break, John." She was really upset with him and his lack of attention to her, and got next to him, saying, "And I need you. I need you like crazy." She planted a killer kiss on him, throwing her arms around him so passionately that he nearly fell backwards. No foreplay necessary tonight. The tigress had pounced, and he was her willing prey, enjoying her violent frontal assault, offering no resistance. He ripped her uniform blouse off her, responding in kind to her strong desire. Sherrie pushed him to her bed, pulling the towel off him. Mason ripped her trousers off her as she kneeled. He forcefully held her against him and drove her body down, and penetrated her. Her long legs wrapped around him, heels digging in to his ass. She set the frenzied intensity, and he the powerful thrusts she craved.

He held off until she reached orgasm, and then some, to begin to satisfy and calm her. They lay next to each other, panting, their bodies glistening with the sweet sweat of lovemaking. She started to laugh, and turned to him to see his beautiful smile. "I hope I didn't hurt you, John," she said.

Sherrie threw her head back as he took her again and again. Their lovemaking eventually relaxed into their usual slow, deep rhythm, with tender passion and shared orgasms. When he looked back on this night, he would always remember the look in her eyes; her pure, unadulterated desire for him, and the strength of her love.

Captain Baines spent the majority of that night in engineering with Lt. Commander Westerly and Commander Powers, communicating with each other via pen and paper. They were devising their plan for sudden and swift course corrections, the timing of the slingshot move that would propel the Hesperia towards Mars, at a greater speed than her ship's designers originally intended. Whether or not all four sections held together was the question, and they made several attempts at contingency simulations, without the ship's computers. They could be certain only that, once they commenced a course correction, the Yellow Man would know their plans. Baines was positive Dr. James planned for several contingencies of his own, using their technologically advanced computers to run simulations.

Baines was also keenly aware that the price for making a mistake would be the end of his career. If they continued on course and were taken over by a Yellow Man-controlled battleship, Earth Command would judge him as incapable of assessing risk, putting his ship and its treasure in peril. If they changed course, and were attacked by pirates, Earth Command would say it was his fault for not staying on his prescribed course towards the escort group. He endeavored to make the best decision possible at the right time, having thought through all possible scenarios; he strove to have as few floating variables as possible, to balance the equation. Satisfied they thought of every possible contingency, their meeting broke up by 4am.

Mrs. Baines was not happy to be awakened at 4am, especially with her husband falling off to sleep the moment he got into bed. She had been all but ignored for the last three weeks, without being told any reasons why her husband had become so obsessed, and what he was trying to accomplish. Like most of the crew, she believed that the worst of the Hesperia's troubles were over, and they would be home in a couple of months, safe and sound. Tomorrow, she decided, she would stay in her old quarters, and see if he noticed she was not there in his bed.

XXXV

The Senior Chief was in a much better mood this morning. She served Mason his breakfast the moment she saw him enter the mess hall. They talked about their tentative plans when they arrived at Moon Base. "Do we have to request our next billet now, or can we relax for a couple of weeks on Earth first?" He knew she wanted to visit her parents in Wisconsin, and that sounded all right to him. "How does it work when the ship lands? Do we have to immediately take a transport, or do we stay for a few days somewhere?"

"Usually, the main crew disembarks within two days of landing. I'll get a room at one of the hotels for us. We'll be able to take any leave we have coming to us up to two weeks with Captain Baines' approval. The rest of our leave will have to be staggered, according to transport schedules, the new billets, and so on. I may have to stay on board the ship for a few days longer than you, Sherrie, so be prepared. You could go home to see your folks, or you could wait on Moon Base, and we'll take the transport together." Mason knew the drill.

"I'll stay and wait for you. I don't want us to get separated, John," she said.

"There'll be stuff you can do on Moon Base if you have to wait for me, remember? Shopping, and restaurants. You can even get a real salad with fresh vegetables." They continued their conversation until he had to leave. She reached across the table for his hand, and squeezed it. "I love you, Sherrie," he said, kissing her hand, and standing.

"I love you more," she responded. He blew her a kiss, and left.

The Hesperia was still on her way to Titan One at hyper-space 1, and Mason could begin to see the faintest outline of Saturn and its rings. Captain Baines must make a commitment soon, one way or another.

The Captain hailed the battleship group confirming their rendezvous in ten days' time at Titan One. He asked if anything unusual had been encountered on their journey, and was told all was in order. He told the battleship captain he would be happy to reach Moon Base, and head for home. The conversation sounded like a normal exchange between two courteous command officers, Mason noted. Captain Baines signed off, and ordered Lt. Commander Davis to sweep the quadrant with both long and short range scans. There were a few merchant vessels in the far quadrant opposite them on a heading for SS10. No Space Patrols within four days of the Hesperia. All was quiet. Another hour passed.

"Lt. Commander Westerly, Commander Powers, make ready Delta David 11," the Captain said in a normal voice. The officers responded they were ready. Here we go, Mason thought.

"Helm, release your control to engineering now. Powers, take the helm. Navigation, release your control to the XO. Westerly, take navigation. Engage Delta David 11 on my signal; 3-2-1, engage!" Captain Baines' voice increased in volume slightly, but enough that Mason knew exactly what was happening. He was using his authorization, redirecting the Hesperia's course and speed; they were now making hyper-space 4, and a hard 30 degree banking turn to the port side.

Mason's bionic ears heard some creaking from the massive ship, but nothing indicating she would not hold together. A few calls came over Marston's communications console about the turn, and he responded all was normal. At their present speed their trajectory would take them away from the outer planets entirely, missing several space stations, including Titan One. The Captain committed the Hesperia, its crew and cargo to an unprecedented course through our solar system, heading straight for Mars at the earliest, with Moon Base as her target. There was little room for error or for further course modifications. He had also added another six weeks to their mission, if the slingshot effect could not be correctly executed.

The bridge crew was the first to realize the Hesperia's course had been altered, as well as her speed increased. Nothing was said, and no one questioned the Captain, at least while on bridge duty. But off the bridge, and in all other areas of the ship, scuttlebutt was running rampant. Captain Baines held a command-level meeting in the bridge conference room at fourteen hundred hours to answer the many questions he knew would be circulating the ship after the Delta David 11 maneuver. He was smart to do so, nipping any questioning of his authority to make such changes in the bud. He invited Admiral Tomiko to join in the meeting with them via live vid cam feed. When his command officers were all assembled, he nodded for Mason to call them all to attention, for hailing the Admiral.

"Admiral Tomiko here. You may proceed, Captain Baines."

The Captain thanked the Admiral for his attendance, and proceeded to give them brief information for their course alteration. He hoped to have them at Mars Colony in two and one half months, and at Moon Base another two weeks after that, totaling a full month ahead of their previously scheduled arrival.

The Admiral repeated his authorization for this action by the Captain, and signed off, wishing them luck on their new course. Mason stood guard and listened, as Baines patiently answered every one of their questions. One question from Davis was particularly unsettling to members of his command staff:

"Captain, I understand why you have made these changes. But, aren't we expecting the Hesperia to maneuver more like a star cruiser than a mining freighter? I mean, sir, no one has ever successfully executed a large planet slingshot with a mining freighter before; not even a small planet slingshot, to my knowledge, sir."

Baines calmly answered, "We will attempt the slingshot with all four sections of the Hesperia together. If she is not responding satisfactorily, we will implement the Omicron Protocol, and proceed with her Sections 1 and 2 to Mars Colony."

"That's going to require perfect precision and timing, Captain Baines," Davis said, tapping his fingers lightly on the table. "You have my utmost respect, sir, and my full cooperation in those maneuvers, Captain." Mason could hear the sincerity in his voice, but the man was not confident it could be accomplished. Westerly and Powers were noticeably silent; they previously voiced their doubts and concerns about this course of action over the last three weeks.

Commander Baines was poised and reserved as she listened very closely to all that was being discussed at their meeting. Her composure belied her heightened state of anxiety; Mason tuned in to her emotions. After the Captain dismissed the meeting, she stayed behind, still sitting at the table, hands neatly folded. Mason looked at her, and asked to be dismissed; but the Captain refused. "Sit down, Mason. Commander Baines has a few questions for us now."

She began, "You said the Yellow Man knows everything we do on the ship. Then he will know of this course modification, as well, isn't this correct, Captain?"

"Yes, I must assume that he already knows what we have done, Commander."

"Will the battleship, if he has indeed gained influence and some control over its movements, be able to intercept our present course?" She asked carefully.

"If we execute the slingshot, no. If we have to travel the entire course without the slingshot, then another six weeks will be added to our course, and then it could intercept us after Mars, but not before." The Captain was being as open and truthful as possible with her, after having kept all his plans secret from her for weeks.

"You are the mathematician, Captain. What are our odds of successfully concluding this mission on Moon Base without any further interference, external confrontation, or outright attacks?" She looked him right in the eye for that one.

"Given your parameters of no further interference, confrontation, or attacks, I'd give us a zero point four-two-five chance of success, much greater than our chance of success by our original course, Commander Baines," he replied flatly.

That information did nothing to reassure her. But she asked, and he answered honestly. "Thank you for your time and frank answers. I'd like to go to my quarters, Captain Baines."

"Of course, Commander Baines," he said quietly. Mason stood with her, and held open the door for her as she left, quickly walking off the bridge.

Saturn was coming into full view as they made their way towards the giant gas planet. They would have to approach Saturn at full speed head on, then utilize the planet's gravitational forces to slingshot the Hesperia around the planet, accelerating to more than three times their engines' maximum speed, and down through the center of the solar system on yet another new course. The maneuver would take place in two days, and the Captain made everyone practice their roles in the maneuver over and over with holographic models, until they could execute them without error or hesitation. By the end of their shift, they were more than familiar with their parts to play in the slingshot; by tomorrow, they would be able to do them in their sleep.

At his shift's end, Mason went to Commander Baines' old quarters, and found her sitting on the couch in the dark, looking forlorn and doomed. She told him not to bother with any bourbon, it would not work tonight, and he agreed with her. "It's good to cheer you up sometimes, ma'am, but it would only make you feel worse at times like this. Has Captain Baines invited you to have dinner with him, ma'am?"

"No. He's still ignoring me. Why don't you?" She said in a melancholy voice, not even looking at him.

Mason stood in front of her. "Well, I can't ignore you, ma'am. I never could ignore you, and I can't now. You're my best friend, and I won't leave you alone like this. Not for the whole world. I'm going to order us some dinner and wine, and we're going to enjoy ourselves, all right, ma'am?" He would do anything for her.

"Whatever. I won't eat anything," she warned him. She was still in her full uniform. Mason called the Senior Chief and ordered dinner for them, and asked her to bring wine.

"Is this another bourbon party, Master Sergeant?" She asked her husband.

"Not this time, Senior Chief." She noticed the seriousness in his voice.

Mason turned the lighting up a little, and found a music crystal to play. He asked for her jacket. She took it off without so much as a word, and handed it to him. He hung it over the opposite arm of her couch, like he had seen her do several times before.

Mason went in back of her, massaging her neck gently. Commander Baines liked that, and responded well to his touch. She removed her tie, and unbuttoned the top button of her blouse, giving him more room to work. His fingers worked the base of her neck, and her throat, gently stroking away her anxieties. He worked his way up to the back of her head, massaging the base of her skull, and over her ears. Gently he brought his hands around her forehead, and back to her temples, and massaged them in circular motion, until he saw her tense face relax in his hands. She brought her hands up, took his hands and crossed them around her neck and shoulders, still holding them. "That was very nice, John. I needed it. And don't you dare come any closer to me now, just stay right where you are," she said to him in a deeper, more relaxed voice, finally looking up at him. She was breathing more deeply, and just a little faster.

Mason kneeled down behind the couch, and continued to let her hold his hands. He laid his head down next to her head, saying nothing, feeling all her anguish and fear, and loneliness. She put her head next to his, and they stayed that way until her doorbell rang, disturbing the peace of their togetherness. She gave him a little kiss as he got up to let the Senior Chief bring dinner inside.

"I found this lost man in the hall, and thought you wouldn't mind if he joined you for dinner, ma'am." She did it again; she managed to round up the Captain to take care of his wife.

"How is it you can get him here when I can't, Senior Chief?" Mrs. Baines asked, trying to smile. She received no answer.

"Let's get some food into you, Mrs. Baines," the Captain said. He helped her off the couch to the table, as the Senior Chief sat their places, dinner for two.

"I brought this for you to enjoy, instead of the synthehol tonight," the Senior Chief said, opening a bottle of California cabernet franc for them. She poured them each a glass, sat the bottle down, and held out a chair for Mrs. Baines. She lit the candle between them, smiled, and wished them a good evening. Mason was waiting for her at the door, and they left.

The next day, everyone on the bridge was quiet and in full concentration of what tomorrow's activities would require from them. Mason wanted to be at his best for the slingshot maneuver. They all knew by now that their mission on the Hesperia would be in the history archives; they merely wanted to live to tell the story to their children and friends someday. Another quadrant sweep produced nothing out of the ordinary, while the mining freighter streaked towards Saturn. Tomorrow they would execute the slingshot, and be on their way to Mars at star cruiser speeds; or not. No one openly talked about failure, but they all acknowledged its possibility.

Captain Baines seemed in good spirits all day, not nearly as stressed as the day before. Mason tried not to think about how he was the one to relax Mrs. Baines' neck and head areas, and the Captain took care of everything else.

Mason and Sherrie enjoyed each other's company and bodies before going to sleep. He awoke around three, and could not go back to sleep. He lay watching Sherrie sleep, quiet as a baby. She stirred, saw him watching her, and reached out for him. They made love again, until she was late for work. "Let someone else make breakfast for everyone today, and stay a little while longer with me, Sherrie," he pleaded with her. Later, he would wish he had never let her out of his arms.

Everyone was early for their shift this morning. Captain Baines was relaxed and confident, and he permeated those feelings to everyone on deck. The maneuver would begin in one hour, and they would have a two hour window for execution. After that time, their best opportunity would diminish. No second chance.

"This is the Captain. Prepare for slingshot. Brace yourselves for maneuvers in ten minutes." His announcement went ship-wide. Baines made sure they were all ready, on his bridge and in engineering, and had Davis count down in increments of fifteen seconds for them. At the precise moment, Mason could feel the ship enter the gravitational pull of the large gas planet, and accelerate. They would let Saturn pull them in closer, until the optimum speed and angle was achieved, and execute the maneuver.

"One minute to optimum speed. Helm, release your control to me. Navigation, release your control to the XO. Westerly, you have navigation. Davis, you have ship control and stabilizers. Shields on maximum. On my mark, in three-two-one, commence the maneuver." The Captain was cool and calm.

Mason felt the Hesperia accelerate at a very rapid rate, and he could hear her great bulk start to creak and moan. As the ship flew towards Saturn, she accelerated even faster, and he bent his knees for better support. He watched them hurling downwards towards the gas giant; would they be able to pull away and slingshot in time? The ship was shaking, and her metal hull began to strain. He heard every nuance in the hull, every sealed door stress against its frame, every hatch stress against its vacuum-seal.

"Slingshot on my mark in five-four-three-two-one-engage!" The Captain held on to his command chair for dear life as the mammoth ship shot forward as if from a cannon. Everyone on the bridge was hurled backwards, fast and hard into walls and each other; the officers crawled back to their stations, the force was so great against their movements.

Mason felt as if he were as powerless as a gnat in a hurricane. He could crawl, but not stand. He helped Westerly back to her station; she had been thrown directly into the third tier rail. He held her by her waist and arms.

"All stations, report now!" Baines ordered, and they all reported their situations. All engines were on override, dangerously close to overheating. Shutting them down was no longer an option. The ship's computer was performing calculations at such a great rate that it could not report the results in increments longer than one millisecond, rendering its reports useless to its human masters. Powers still maintained engine control, but the man sounded like he was in pain. Westerly kept up with the navigational adjustments, her hands and fingers flying over her console. Marston was in control at communications, calmly advising everyone to report their situation and remain calm. Davis was in his zone, controlling three consoles, his years at tactical making swift work of the many spilt-second adjustments required.

Mason felt the ship begin to slow a little, and her shaking lessen in intensity, but her metal components were still screaming in his ears. He heard the start of a great ripping begin, as the Section 4 portside aft bay door buckled and tore off, leaving the biggest section of the ship open to space. With the strain of its port door having been torn off, the starboard bay door ripped off its hinges, as well. The huge ship began shuddering. The long-armed basket for harvesting asteroids unfolded, and fluttered outside the open aft door like a handkerchief in the wind, until it broke apart and flew out of the door.

The ship was slowing down, but she was not done ridding herself of Section 4 components. The giant claw came unhinged, beating against the huge hull, and flew out, spinning like a child's toy. The Section 4 tram tracks flew out next, along with several tram cars. The shaking began to subside.

"Captain, I've lost aft stabilizer controls, attempting to rebalance now," Davis said. "Unable to stabilize the aft controls, Captain."

"Engineering, we have slowed to hyper-speed six, and slowing. Hold her steady, Chief Engineer, we're almost there," the Captain said. "Hyper-speed five and holding. Hyper-speed four. Locking engine control at hyper-speed four. Chief Engineer?"

"She's holding steady, Captain, but her rear stabilizers are imbalanced, due to losing so much weight in her ass, sir. Compensating for stabilizer imbalance now, Captain. She is stabilized, and the helm is steady. We did it, Captain Baines!" Powers yelled into the comm.

"Stand down from slingshot, all stations, report," the Captain said, his voice calming down. The reports came in fast; minor damage to the port air lock hatches; one of the communications components in the top array flew off; and so on. But they all survived the maneuver, and the precious platinum was still on board.

There were more than a few broken bones and bruises from crew and officers being thrown about. Dr. Hassan utilized his nurse-droids for bone-setting, the only thing he thought they were good for. The droids would inject the area of the bone break to numb it, set the broken bone, and run a healing laser along the path of the break, speeding up the patient's recovery time ten-fold. The hospital was a very busy place that afternoon, for the Doctor, his nurses, and the droids.

Captain Baines reported their success to Earth Command, without waiting for a response. He was now busying himself with their next task of getting to Mars via an uncharted course taking them near the asteroid belt in a few days. He would make certain they flew well above the belt, to keep any stray asteroids from colliding with his ship. All seemed calm again.

Two hours after the slingshot stand-down, the computer sounded the alarm: "Red alert! Intruder alert! Red Alert! Intruder Alert!" The Hesperia came into range of two pirate vessels, closing in on her flanks quickly. They were coming in at hyper-speed six plus, and armed to the teeth with laser cannons. No torpedoes were detected, but they armed missile launchers. Baines called engineering.

"All shields on maximum. Commander Powers, is engine four back on line yet?"

"Not yet, Captain. We are working on it still, sir," Powers reported.

"All available power to the defensive weapons array. Davis, be at the ready," Baines ordered.

"We're all powered up and ready, Captain Baines. The ships have us in their missile range in ten seconds, sir. Incoming missiles expected, sir," Davis calmly reported.

"All hands, battle stations. This is no drill. Red alert, battle stations everyone, repeat, this is not a drill." Captain Baines commanded, his voice steady and in control.

Davis said, "Their missiles are underway, Captain. They are targeting our engines, sir."

"More power to lower shields to protect the engines, now, Davis," the Captain ordered.

"Shields increased on her belly, Captain. Expect hit in three seconds, sir."

As the first of the missiles exploded against the shields, the Hesperia rocked from the force of the explosion, but was not hit directly. Her shields were holding.

"Captain, the second wave of missiles are cluster-seekers, sir! Impact in five seconds, sir." Davis' voice ratcheted up noticeably. Those cluster-seekers were nasty things, Mason reminded himself. He had seen them used against a battleship, and they took out the entire starboard side of that heavily armed vessel. They consisted of dozens of smaller bombs encased in a missile, and would explode their load of small bombs near their target. The smaller bombs would adhere to any surface, and detonate after impact. Whatever they would stick to would be blown to shreds.

"Lower shields and fire on cluster-seeker missiles now, Davis. Take them out NOW!" Captain Baines raised his voice for the first time. "Westerly, fire laser cannon at those cluster-seekers. Do not let them explode near my ship!" They fired at the wave of incoming cluster-seekers, and exploded all but one away from the Hesperia, but the one they missed was going to hit. "All shields at maximum, Davis. All hands, prepare for impact."

The cluster-seekers blew apart, heading all over the ship. Most were repelled by the shields, but a few stuck and blew up on her hull.

"Damage reports, now," Baines called out. "Davis, when those ships are in range, take them out of my sight!"

"Aye aye, Captain. They are in range in three-two-one, firing plasma torpedoes on both ships." Mason saw two large explosions in the front screens, as both ships blew apart.

The damage reports kept anyone from celebrating. The hull was breached on Decks 9, 8 and 5, where the bombs adhered and blew apart. Gaping holes were shown on the vid cams on the outer hull. As the Captain was assessing the damage, Westerly called out, "Captain we have reported gas leaks on Deck 5 at the sight of the explosion, and we..." BOOM!

The very large explosion rocked the Hesperia. Her main gas line had taken a direct hit, and exploded into Deck 5, taking out a large interior section of the ship. The atmosphere was lost on the port side of Deck 5, and all adjacent compartments sealed off by the computer instantly. Mason was in sudden shock; Deck 5 was where the mess halls and kitchens were located, the primary users of gas lines, for cooking, baking, and broiling foods. He tried to focus and remain calm.

"All engines full stop. Damage reports now! Corpsmen to Deck 5!" Captain Baines was still in control of the situation, coordinating all efforts to assess damage and render assistance to crew on Deck 5. Decks 9 and 8 were used for cryonic hibernation, but most capsules would be on the starboard side, away from the blast.

"Go to yellow alert. All hands, stand down. Render assistance to crew on Deck 5 at once. Westerly, get me those damage reports for Decks 5, 8 and 9 NOW!" Baines commanded.

Mason made it through the confusion by using his martial arts meditation techniques, but he already knew what was to be discovered. He no longer felt Sherrie; he knew with all certainty she was gone. He centered himself, and remained at his guard post, protecting the bridge and his Captain, trying to decipher the melee of incoming damage reports flooding

Marston's console. Davis went to the second communications station to assist. Captain Baines turned to Mason, and got down from his command chair. "Westerly, take the comm. Mason, come with me."

Captain Baines and Mason took the lift as far down as it would go, and then went the rest of the way using the stairs, down to Deck 5. The implosion of the main and auxiliary gas lines shredded most of the portside Deck, and noxious smoke was everywhere. Mason handed the Captain a cigar-shaped temporary gas mask, and both men unrolled them and put them completely over their heads, sealing them at their necks. Fire retardants were being sprayed towards the blasted sections as corpsmen went in for more bodies. The officers' mess hall was closest to the hull, and was blown outwards by the cluster-seeker bomb. The kitchen, in the middle between the main and officers' mess hall, was a grisly scene, fires and smoke everywhere. The only chance of anyone's surviving would have been in the very back of the main mess hall, but that area was filled with noxious smoke and fire retardants being sprayed down from the ceiling.

They assisted the corpsmen with the anti-gravity gurneys, carrying the injured up two flights of stairs before the lift could be used. Both men knew what news awaited them about Senior Chief Mason. After more than an hour, everyone who could be found was evacuated to the hospital, and Captain Baines took Mason there. They removed their gas masks, and threw them away. The Captain motioned for Mason to wait outside the hospital as he went inside. Full triage efforts were underway. Even the nurse droids were being used, so many were the injuries. Captain Baines asked about the Senior Chief. Mason saw Nurse Jones just shake his head, and his heart sank. He had no feelings in his body suddenly, and leaned against the wall. Captain Baines came out, and took Mason by the arm, leading him to his own quarters up top.

Mason slumped down on the chair while Baines poured him a large cognac and another for himself. Mason took off his helmet, and the Captain saw his ashen face and vacuous look. "I want you to stay here for a while, Mason. Go sit on the couch. Here, take your drink. Take the whole bottle. I'll come back in a few minutes. I am ordering you to stay here, is that clear, Mason?"

"Yes, sir," Mason whispered. He sat on the couch, looking out at the stars, where all looked peaceful and quiet, unlike inside the wounded ship. He took a drink of the cognac, and then drained the glass. His happy new life was shattered. Any part of him not bound in skin and bones was blown apart. His skin felt cold and clammy, and his head was pounding on the inside. They had a beautiful morning, making love; then off to work, full of life and purpose. This morning their future lay bright directly ahead; now, he had no future. None that he cared about anyway. Mason felt as empty as the blackness of space, with no stars to light up even a corner of his life.

Captain Baines came back, and offered to have Mason stay there for the night, but he declined. He took Mason to his quarters and left the bottle of cognac with him. "I'll call you later, and come see you tomorrow, Mason. Don't bother to take duty for a few days, or even a week, if you want. I'm so very sorry, John," the Captain said, and hugged his shoulders. "She was my friend, too, you know," and his eyes welled up in tears, as he left.

Mason put the bottle of cognac on the table, but didn't drink any more of it. It tasted foul to him. The air in his quarters smelled rank, and he realized it was the smell of noxious gas, fire retardant, and death all over him. He took off all his clothes, and took a shower. He gathered up his smelly uniform, and took it to the incinerator in the hall, and disposed of it. He went back inside, and the room smelled better. He put on clean underwear, and lay down on their bed. He pulled Sherrie's pillow up close to him and hugged it, and cried himself to sleep.

XXXVI

The death toll from the pirates' attack was significant: everyone on duty in the mess halls at the time of the attack was killed, a total of eleven souls, including Sr. Chief Mason. The wounded from the mess halls were those lucky enough to be sitting in the back of the main mess hall, totaling fifteen. All four engineering officers eating early lunches in the officers' mess were killed, including Ensign Campbell and Lieutenant Roshkov. Those killed while in cryonic hibernation totaled twelve, all traitorous crewmen already sentenced to die.

Captain Baines held himself responsible for the deaths of his officers and crew. He had been warned about pirates; that's why Earth Command sent the battleship escort group for them. But what puzzled him was the pirates were only two hours away from them when the slingshot maneuver completed. It was too much of a coincidence to be a coincidence. The Captain went to visit Mason later the evening of his wife's death, but he was asleep, so he did not disturb him. He was busy managing the schedules for Lt. Commander Davis' repair crews working on the outer hull of the Hesperia to seal the holes in her hull. He wanted those repairs done as quickly as possible, and get on their way to Mars, without any further pirate attacks. They could repair the interiors while the ship was in hyper-speed.

Mason's Space Marine buddies would not leave him alone the first day. They fought and sparred with their champion Mason until they were all beaten and bruised, then dragged him to dinner, such as it was, served in the main lounge. Mason wouldn't have any drinks; he didn't want to crawl inside a bottle. He was not interested in drinking to forget his beloved Sherrie.

Mason sent Dr. Hassan a message, asking to see Sherrie in the morgue. It was his right, as her husband, and he needed to say good-bye to her. He showed up for his appointment at the hospital. Dr. Hassan took him to his tiny morgue, stacked with bodies of the deceased in their black body bags, waiting to be transferred to the last remaining walk-in freezer. At least he had kept Sherrie's body in the cold drawer under a clean sheet, out of respect for her, and his affection for the lady. The Doctor pulled the sheet back to her shoulders, and her face was white and cold, but perfect. She looked like she could come out of cryo-sleep to Mason.

"She was evidently walking away from the blast, Mason. Her face and upper frontal torso are untouched, but her backside was blown away. She was killed instantly. I doubt she even knew what hit her. The force of the explosion was so great," Doctor Hassan said.

"Did she suffer, Dr. Hassan?" Mason asked in a whisper.

"No, she never saw it coming, Mason. I always think it's a blessing when that happens, when your loved one never suffers at all. Don't you?"

"Yes, Doctor. She suffered enough already," Mason said. He leaned in to kiss her good-by, and Dr. Hassan pulled the sheet over her head. Mason suddenly went white, put his hand to his mouth, and ran out of the hospital. Dr. Hassan quickly closed her drawer and went after Mason. Nurse Baines was just getting off the lift when she saw Dr. Hassan run into the men's room. She heard someone retching violently, and Dr. Hassan talking gently. He came out of the men's room, holding Mason, bringing him back into the hospital. He gave him a shot for his stomach, and another to lightly tranquilize him, as Nurse Baines watched. Mason looked at her as tears welled up in both their eyes, and Dr. Hassan led him back to his quarters.

Nurse Baines had gone to visit Mason twice, but he was not in his quarters, he was with the Space Marines. She heard about their sparring sessions, and decided it was the best thing they could do for him now. But he needed time to grieve in his own way. John and Sherrie had been a couple for over three years, and married just a few months. John was still her best friend, and she would not abandon him now. She had grown close to Sherrie, as well; they talked together almost every day. It was so unbelievably sad for Mason. She hurt for him, and his gentle heart.

Captain Baines held a memorial service for the deceased crew members and officers in the afternoon. He was too familiar with the text read for the dead on this cruise, having held three memorial services already. He was like everyone else, and wanted the whole mission to be over as soon as possible. Two months to Mars, then two weeks to Moon Base. After this cruise, he would not accept another mission on board a ship. The Captain earned the right to settle down with his beautiful wife, and start a family. He had his fill of adventure.

After the service, he went to Mason and asked him how he was doing. He was expecting to hear him request to be back on the bridge, but he instead asked for his full week off. "Of course. I will only call you if an emergency happens; is that fair with you, Mason?"

"Yes, Captain Baines, it is more than fair, sir. Thank you." Mason left before anyone else could ask how he was doing. He was doing lousy, period. For the first time in his life, he made plans for the future beyond the next promotion. He and Sherrie planned to start a family on Earth when they got off this wretched tub. Now, his only plan was to survive until he could walk away from the Hesperia. Anything beyond that was too far away for him to consider now. He changed out of his class A uniform, and went to the gym. He sparred with the bots for twenty rounds each, until he was bloody, bruised, and exhausted. He went to the showers, and straight up to bed.

"I have not been able to see John Mason but briefly since this awful thing happened. I'm very worried about him, Victor. I've gone to his quarters, and he's not there, several times. It's not good for him to hold it all inside. He needs someone to talk with now," Mrs. Baines said.

"Yes. You're right. I've also gone to his quarters, but he's gone. He's been spending a lot of time in the gym, abusing his body, and taking his hurt out on the sparring bots. He hasn't been in the lounge at all, except to pick up a sandwich to go once every day or so, according to Sammie," he said. They picked at their dinner in silence, pushing the food around the plates. He sighed, "I'll most likely be my old swim team weight when this cruise is finished. This food is deplorable." They managed to share a laugh, and decided the synthehol wine was their best bet.

"I would like you to go and see Mason, my dear. You're right; he does need someone to talk with. I know you're his best friend, and he will talk with you, if he talks with anyone at all. I'll advise Dr. Hassan to give you tomorrow off, and you spend the day with Mason. He needs you now." The Captain finished his synthehol wine.

"Will you be joining me, Victor? He's your friend, too, you know."

"I'll spend time with him another day. I have to get this ship underway as soon as possible, so this bloody mission can be over." He stood up, looked out the window and thought for a moment. "Mason is best friend to both of us, Rachel. He has saved my life at least three times and your life twice, as well. Please go to him, and spend time with him. I know he'll talk with you. The two of you have a special bond, some sort of connection. I'd like you to be with him, and comfort him. You can give him what he needs to go on living, Rachel." He kissed her, and left. She was stunned at her husband's request. He had not only given her permission to be more than a friend to John; he asked her to comfort him, and give him what he needed to go on living. He had just given her a "hall pass" to be with another man. She could not have been more floored.

She awoke when Victor's alarm went off, but he got up and reminded her she had a day off, and to sleep in. After he was showered and dressed, he kissed her cheek and reminded her to spend the day with Mason. There was no way she could go back to sleep after hearing her husband say that again. She got up, showered, put on a nice skirt and blouse, and got ready to visit John. She decided Victor didn't realize what he asked her to do. What husband would ask his wife to be with another man? Certainly not Victor Baines, who valued loyalty and trust above all qualities. Or did he? Was he trying to repay John Mason for saving his life so many times? Did he think she and John needed to have an affair before they left the ship, and get it over with? Did he want her to have an affair, so he could have one in the future with another woman? Rachel never told Victor of her feelings for John. Did he think they already had an affair? By the time she left their quarters, she was confused and angry with her husband.

She worked herself into quite an Irish huff. Her maiden name was Cohen; her father was Jewish. Her mother was a passionate Irish redhead with a fearsome temper, with bright green eyes that would ignite with fire if another woman smiled at her husband. Rachel warned Victor about her temper and jealous streak before they were married, and he accepted her as she was.

Mrs. Baines was pounding the hall in her high heels as she walked to the lift. She paced back and forth until the lift arrived, and she got inside. It was the "local," packed with crewmen, and stopped at every floor, adding to her frustration. When she finally reached Mason's door, she was fit to be tied, and knocked a little too loudly on his door. He assumed it was one of the Space Marines, and answered as he was, dressed only in a towel wrapped around his hips. "Mrs. Baines! I'm sorry, I thought it was... just a minute, please come on in!" He let her in, and ran inside his bedroom to dress. He stepped into his one-piece uniform, the first thing he could find to cover up. When he came out, he was more apologetic.

She was enjoying his embarrassment. She loved teasing John Mason. "I wasn't exactly knocking on every door until a man would answer wearing only a towel, John. Especially in the married quarters," she said, and laughed a little.

He laughed with her at the situation. "Well, at least you found a clean man, Mrs. Baines," he said. "How are you, and what are you doing here on a workday?"

"My husband wants me to spend the day with you," she answered truthfully. "I hope it doesn't interfere with any plans you may have made, John," she added. She looked at his small quarters. She had forgotten how it was to not be a senior officer, with her larger and nicer living space, and the sacrifices the crew makes to serve on board ships. She spent several years in similar tight quarters herself, before moving up the ladder.

"I have no plans whatsoever. Or, I should say I had no plans, but now I do," he said. "You look very nice today. Is it all right if I change into street clothes, too? I feel out of place next to you, dressed so lovely."

"Be my guest, John. We have the whole day." She sat and waited on him patiently. Rachel was still fuming at her husband for putting her in a position of questioning his motives, and having the audacity to give her a "hall pass." As if she needed or wanted one. She had never been in a relationship when she was unfaithful, which was more than she could say for every man she'd ever trusted to behave the same way, except Victor. She was righteously pissed off by the time John came out to her, dressed in nice black trousers, dress boots, and a black silk shirt. He was frankly a gorgeous hunk, she admitted to herself. If she was going to have an affair, it would be with someone like John, and she would choose the time and place, not her husband.

"I hope I look all right. I don't have a lot of street clothes with me," he said innocently. She assured him he was dressed just fine. Mighty fine, if she allowed herself to think about it, which she would not. "Where are we going?"

"Out!" She said. They left his quarters, walking down the hall to the lift. She pushed the button for the observation lounge, the only place she could think to go. Everywhere else was closed and sealed off, except for the main lounge, which now served as their mess hall. They first talked with each other there, so many years ago, when only twenty or so people were awake, and the mission was new, and full of excitement.

"I haven't been here since our wedding. I had a good time with you here once, remember?" She looked at him, and smiled. "Very few others were awake, and we had the whole place to ourselves, if only for a little while," she added.

"I remember very well, like it was yesterday," he said, recalling how they talked about nothing and everything, flirted with each other, and she was so beautiful. She was still beautiful, and as exciting to be around as ever.

The lift stopped, and they got off. The lounge was empty. They picked a couch close to the far window and away from looking at the injured ship, currently under repairs. Their view was glorious Saturn. Although the ship slingshot her way past the big planet, it was still huge, and clearly visible from the 360 degree view of the observation lounge; it was magnificent. "Now I know why men love going to the stars, John. There is no way to see this other than to be out here," she said, gazing in wonder at the planet. "It's good to feel small, and be a part of the whole scheme of things."

He listened to her, and looked at Saturn anew, through her eyes. The big planet truly was a sight to behold, second only to mighty Jupiter. "Would you like a glass of wine, Mrs. Baines?" He stood and brought over two glasses of red wine for them. Their couch was the perfect place to view the stars, and forget about the Hesperia for a few hours. He held her hand and sat with her, talking with her for hours, and really smiled, for the first time in days. He made her laugh out loud, and lately, he was the only man capable of doing that with her. He meant so much to her.

"Are you hungry? My stomach is growling," Mason said.

"To be truthful, I'd rather have a real glass of wine and a sandwich. Do you still have a bottle left, John? It'd be a nice treat for this wonderful day." Of course he did, and she was the one person he'd like to share a bottle with.

"Let's go," he said, and pulled her off the couch. They picked up a couple of sandwiches on the next floor's main lounge, and went back to his quarters. She decided on a pinot noir, her favorite red wine. "And let's not forget dessert," he said, picking up the bottle of cognac Captain Baines had given him, and never drunk. They went to her old quarters with their bounty.

"I'm glad I kept these quarters. I like time to myself now and then, away from the problems of the ship. It's become my sanctuary, John," she said, letting them inside. She made a luncheon out of two humble sandwiches, and they sat at her table and enjoyed themselves.

They took their wine over to her couch, and talked about nothing in particular. After the wine was gone, the cognac was poured, and the conversation continued. She was totally and completely relaxed with him, shoes off, blouse unbuttoned a bit, and he did the same. They were enjoying each other's company immensely.

In space, there is no daylight, all is night. They lost track of the time, and didn't care what time it was. She had her ambient lights on in her quarters, soft and warm. She got up and put on her favorite music crystal to play. Mason asked what she wanted to do when they got off the "Hysteria," and she thought that was the funniest thing she'd ever heard. She busted up laughing, and so did he. They were off again, laughing happy drunks on her couch. But tonight they were drinking cognac, the liquor of love, and not bourbon.

Eventually, they laughed themselves into panting and tears of joy, and she hugged him. He hugged her back, and they sat back on the couch, smiling and talking. When the laughter died down, they found themselves a little too close, and much too interested in getting closer. Mason nearly kissed her, and she wanted him to. He quickly stood up, and poured the last of the cognac into their glasses. He stretched out his arms, and she watched him. She was not only his best friend, but his nurse, and was familiar with his physique; she was very attracted to him.

He did not sit down again, and it was a wise decision. They had been flirting with each other over the years, and it was fun and harmless. Tonight was different. *She* was different. She was radiant, and had a glow about her he couldn't quite identify. He wanted her so much. She was in a soft blouse with her hair down, and she was alone with him. No uniform or silver clustered Commander's insignia blocked him now. The suppressed feelings of love and desire he felt for her were emerging once again.

"Are you going to sit with me?" She asked, patting the couch again.

"I'd better not," he said, sipping his cognac.

"Why not, John? We were having such a good time," she said, holding her drink, and trying to be nonchalant.

"We are having a good time. I haven't had this good of a time in many moons, and I never want it to end," he said, looking at her. Mrs. Baines started to look hurt, becoming red-eyed.

"Did I say something wrong, John?" She asked.

"No, you said everything right. You did everything right, all day. This was the best day I've had this year, maybe this decade." He sat down on the arm of her couch.

"Then, what made you move away from me?" She asked, slightly drunk.

"The real answer?" He asked.

"Yes. Please." She looked at him, and seemed much warmer than he'd ever seen her. He used all his self-control to not go to her.

Mason sat his drink down, and took her hand, pulling her off the couch. "I cannot sit with you on that couch any more tonight, because if I do, I'll kiss you, and we'll have a problem. Right now, you and I can look your husband in the eye, and hide nothing from him, because we are innocent. If I kiss you, and you like it, we won't stop there, I know it. I can feel your passion, and you can feel mine." He put her hand over his beating heart, and put his hand over hers. "I want to be able to laugh with you, and be with you any time we feel like it, and not have to hide from your husband. I won't make a dishonest woman out of you, and I won't be a dishonest man." He held her close, and she understood. Mrs. Baines had no intentions of using her "hall pass."

"I'm sorry. I think I'm a little drunk, John. We were having such a good time; I didn't think. I don't want to betray Victor, ever. He's upright and noble, and he's good to me. Most men wouldn't let us get together like this." She sat back down on the couch.

"And that's why we have to put on the brakes, so we can get together like this whenever we want to, and he knows it's all right," Mason said softly, sitting on the arm of the couch again.

"Thank you. You really are my best friend, John. What will we do when this mission is over? Will I ever see you again?" Her eyes got red and cloudy.

"We'll have to make sure we do, that's all. I couldn't bear not ever seeing you again, too," and he started to cry. Mrs. Baines became suddenly aware that his recent grief and pain had just surfaced, and the dam was about to break. She pulled him off the arm of the couch, and held him close, but there was no danger now. Mason cried on her shoulder, and could not stop. She moved back, taking him with her, lying on the couch with him in her arms. She held him until he stopped crying, stroking his back to soothe him. Now she understood what her husband meant about comforting him. She thanked God for her best friend John, and asked Him to give him peace. She thanked God for Victor, who not only loved her and understood his friend's needs in times of crisis, but also completely trusted them both to not cross the line.

When Captain Baines came into her quarters around 1am, he found them lying on her couch holding onto to each other, fully clothed, and sound asleep. He gently touched her, and she awoke. She slipped away from John, and went to bed with her husband.

XXXVII

Repairs on the outer hull took two days, and the Hesperia was off again at hyper-speed 4, streaking towards Mars. It would take three weeks to repair what they could of Deck 5, but the mess hall was now only half its former size. The steel kitchen was restored, not that anyone left of the mess crew could prepare a decent meal. Decks 8 and 9 were repaired satisfactorily, and the jumbled mess of cryonic containers was straightened. Several crewmen who had been put into hibernation were awakened to fill open positions from those lost in the pirate attacks.

Mason returned to duty after his week off to grieve the loss of his wife Sherrie. He used part of the time off to pack her things for shipping back to her parents. He kept her Senior Chief insignia and the wide silver bracelet he bought for her for their first date, and their modest wedding rings. He also kept her two favorite music crystals; playing them soothed his grief.

They purchased life insurance policies after they were married. It was Mason's brother in-law's idea, to provide protection primarily for Sherrie if something happened to him while on duty. He hadn't seen any need to buy some insurance on Sherrie, but Dave insisted they both be covered while serving in the military. How ironic Dave was correct; anything could happen to either one during an assignment, even to the cook. It gave Mason no comfort to know he was now a multi-millionaire. Dave asked him to come live with his family on Mars Colony III, and work on the Mars base. But no billets were open on Mars for a Prime Marine. Serving as a Prime Marine was his only purpose in life; all his other dreams were shattered.

Mason applied for Officer Candidate School and was accepted immediately, but for a class beginning three years from now. He would be the oldest Lieutenant in the Prime Marines if he actually attended and graduated. At least he had three years to consider it. Captain Baines convinced him to go ahead and apply, especially since the Chief of the Joint Chiefs of Staff, Admiral Worthington himself, and his Commandant of the Space Marines recommended him. Whatever his decision on OCS, he would not give up his Prime Marine status. He worked too hard to become one, and his chest full of medals proved him to be one of their champions.

Three more weeks to Mars. The Captain decided not to stop there, and give pirates another shot at them. Mason got to call home, at least, and talked live with his sister Sarah, Dave, and their family. Mason took his annual medical exam with Dr. Hassan, and he had lost over six kg. His face and body were as lean as could be, and he had been sparring every other day with either the Space Marines or the sparring bot. There was only one bot left; Mason killed one of the robots during one of his double sessions of masochism the week after Sherrie's death. The good Doctor had the first opportunity of his thirty-plus year career to designate someone as physically rated AAA-1, the top rating available. Mason accomplished something in the last month, anyway. To celebrate, and also to mark the next phase of his life, he grew a goatee. It gave new definition to his now-chiseled face, and even Lt. Commander Westerly told him he looked more handsome with it. It changed his appearance dramatically.

Captain and Commander Baines hosted a party for Mason's thirtieth birthday in the observation lounge, and it was a rousing success. Even the buffet was palatable; someone in the mess hall figured out how to make roast beef that night, and they were all appreciative. They were all dressed in their class A uniforms, and the Captain had many photos taken to commemorate the occasion. Mason's favorite picture was of him with Commander Baines; she held his arm, with the Captain standing behind them, his arms around them both. He would carry that photo with him for the rest of his life, along with Sherrie's portrait.

Mason was invited to the Captain's quarters after his party by Commander Baines, and he brought one of his last three precious bottles of twenty year old Woodford Reserve bourbon to share. Thanks to Captain Kouras, Mason was the owner of the last real booze on the ship, and he was more than happy to share it with his best friends. They toasted each other, and Mason's birthday; but Mrs. Baines only drank a small sip, which the men immediately noticed. She usually enjoyed her drinks, even bourbon, now. She could out-drink most men on board, as a matter of fact, and both men knew it.

"Why the tiny taste, my dear? It's very good bourbon," the Captain asked his wife.

"Yes, and I have to admit, it actually tastes good to me now, thanks to you, John." She put her glass down and smiled at them. "But I won't be drinking for quite a while. I only drank a sip to toast John's birthday." John smiled at her, realizing why she made that comment.

"Why not? Just because I've run out of cognac?" The poor, clueless Captain asked her.

"Thank you both for the wonderful birthday party. It's time I should be going," Mason said. He thanked Captain Baines, and Mrs. Baines gave him a big hug, and they shared a knowing look between them. Now they both knew why she nearly let her emotions overwhelm her the other night. No wonder she looked so different, so radiant their last night together, as well as tonight. Most pregnant women had that enhanced glow about them.

The next day, Captain Baines' chest could not have been more puffed out. He announced that Mrs. Baines was expecting, and it was now everyone's job to get her to Moon Base safely. The bridge officers cheered for him, as he took his command chair with renewed purpose.

Two more weeks to Mars. The red planet could be seen from all bridge and observation lounge windows, the small red dot growing bigger daily. Suddenly, the alarms went off, "Red Alert! Intruder Alert!" continued for several minutes, as the familiar orange cloud moved in closer to their ship. Captain Baines had Lieutenant Marston send live vid cam feed to Earth Command, and hailed the cloud. "This is Captain Baines of the mining freighter Hesperia. Please state your intentions, the ONE." Mason quickly came beside his Captain.

This time, they responded with immediate visual transmission. The bridge crew was treated to a full screen image of the Yellow Man and their large reptile leader. "Captain Baines, we require one of your species for study. We will send you one of ours in trade." Dr. James' voice was calm and crystal clear, not the translated computerized voice they heard in earlier meetings with the ONE.

"The ONE has been able to study you for over seven years now, Dr. James. Why do you need another of our species?" Captain Baines casually asked.

The Yellow Man's face screwed up in his version of a smile. "We require one of your species to study for further enhancements, to join our species together." Mason looked at Captain Baines, who gave him the nod.

"Why didn't you take one of the pirates you sent to attack our ship, instead of requesting one of our crew, Dr. James?" Mason asked. "They worked for you, yet they were one of our species."

"They were unacceptable as study specimens. They were easily corrupted, and untrustworthy. They were not worthy. We require one of *your* species to study. We will send you one of our species in trade, John Mason." Mason looked at Captain Baines, who was fascinated with their exchange.

"We will not give you one of our species to study, and we are not interested in one of your species to trade, Dr. James. We ask to pass freely, and be left in peace," The Captain stated.

319

"We will let your ship pass in peace, as you have requested, when you give us one of your species to study. One of our agents in hibernation will do," the Yellow Man said.

The Captain heard the buzz from Marston; Earth Command responded. They wished to know which traitor the ONE wanted. The Captain could not believe it. "Marston, confirm this message with Earth Command directly, and be sure to confirm the authorization codes. One moment, Dr. James," the Captain said. Earth Command's response was confirmed; they were willing to trade a traitor. He was appalled.

"How would this exchange take place?" Baines asked quietly.

"We will take his cryonic container, and give you ours in trade," Dr. James replied.

"Will your trade be of similar size, and in cryonic hibernation, as well?" He asked.

"If you wish our trade to be in cryonic hibernation, we will provide you our trade in the container, for your ease in transportation. The ONE are many sizes. You may choose which to study." Dr. James motioned with his hand, and eight reptilians of various sizes walked upright to the forefront of his monitor. "Choose now, Captain Baines," Dr. James said.

Earth Command wanted a big one, the second one from the end, most resembling their seated leader. Captain Baines was in disbelief, and demanded confirmation from them.

"Which of the traitors do you wish to study, Dr. James?" Mason asked, as the Captain waited for his confirmation.

"Sukesh is the most worthy of our study," was the reply. Captain Baines had Marston send that information over, and waited for Earth Command's response.

"Please give us two minutes, Dr. James," Baines said quietly.

Lieutenant Marston said, "Captain Baines, Earth Command agrees to the exchange of Lieutenant Sukesh for their trade, sir."

"What is the name of your trade, so we may address him properly?" Baines asked, resigned to the trade.

"You could not pronounce his name. You may call him whatever you like, Captain Baines," Dr. James said.

"Do we have your word that Lieutenant Sukesh will not be harmed in any way, while we promise not to harm your trade, Dr. James?" Captain Baines asked. He would not be party to sending Sukesh to a certain death at the hands (or claws) of the aliens.

"Sukesh will be the subject of our study. The ONE have not harmed me. They have enhanced my mental and physical attributes, and the same may be done to Sukesh, if he is found worthy. He will not be harmed," Dr. James said, a big strange smile coming to his unusual face.

The Captain made arrangements to exchange the cryonic container of

Lieutenant Sukesh for the cryonic container of the big reptilian on their cargo bay in two hours. Baines called the Space Marines to move Sukesh's container to the starboard cargo bay area, and make room for a larger container to be stored in a sealed compartment. He requested Earth Command confirm their agreement three times, just to be certain this was really happening.

Mason was on guard, standing right by Captain Baines, just in case the ONE decided to take him, as well. Sukesh was extremely intelligent, a full Lieutenant, with knowledge about the Space Forces and their methods, ships, weapons, and limitations. Mason could not believe Earth Command acquiesced to this trade. How would they communicate with the reptilian, if humans were incapable of so much as pronouncing his name?

The time for the exchange was here. The ONE were on their viewing screens. A small ship, probably one of their shuttles, suddenly appeared directly in front of the cargo bay, and a beam shone on the container. The container was raised up and out of the cargo bay to the waiting alien shuttle. As it was taken on board, a much larger container was sent by the same beam into the cargo bay, and placed on the cargo bay floor. The small shuttle disappeared.

"The trade is complete. You may now pass in peace. And, congratulations on your new son, Captain Baines," Dr. James said, making a small bow. Captain Baines went white as a sheet, watching their transmission dissolve, and the orange cloud dissipate into invisibility.

"Westerly, take the comm," the Captain said, running off the bridge. "MASON!" The two men ran down to the lift and went to the hospital. He found Nurse Baines, who had no idea why he was so agitated. Captain Baines demanded an immediate complete examination of his wife by Dr. Hassan. While the emergency examination was taking place, Captain Baines paced back and forth in the hall frantically, his worried brow so wrinkled that his entire face was askew. He was sweating profusely, and his breathing was rapid and shallow. After an eternity, or so it seemed to Mason and Captain Baines, Dr. Hassan emerged, and told him she was perfectly fine, and the fetus was developing as expected, with no complications. The baby's sex could not yet be determined. Baines rushed in to her and took her in his arms, and kissed her repeatedly, until he cried. He announced she was through for the day, and took her to her old quarters to rest.

Neither Dr. Hassan nor Nurse Baines knew what made the Captain act that way until later that day. The Captain played back the entire recorded encounter with the ONE including the cryonic container exchange for Nurse Baines and Dr. Hassan, with Mason in attendance, in the Captain's quarters. When the well wishes from Dr. James played, both Dr. Hassan and Nurse Baines were visibly startled, and the Captain no longer looked foolish. "But, how could he have known, Captain? I had not even told Dr.

Hassan until after I told you. The information was not in the ship's computers anywhere!" She asked her husband.

"The Yellow Man knows everything we do," was all he said, in a quiet voice.

XXXVIII

Captain Baines did not stop at Mars Colony III, and most of those who disagreed last week changed their minds; everyone wanted this mission over as soon as possible. The red planet was large on their view screens as they flew by, still on course to Moon Base. As they left Mars' space, they went to hyper-speed 3. The ship also picked up 4 long-range fighter escorts for the final leg of the journey. It was now less than two weeks to Moon Base.

Everyone's off-duty time was consumed by packing and sending communications home, or searching for new billets. Mason was packing his gear. He decided to incinerate his worn uniforms and destroyed mess dress, and ordered new uniforms to be ready for his pick up at Moon Base. Wherever he would be for his next assignment, he wanted new uniforms.

He made a trip to the packing stations to vacuum seal his package to his sister's home on Mars Colony III to store for him, containing Sherrie's bracelet, their wedding rings, several pictures of her and him together, and the big black souvenir rock he picked up in Section 4. As he put the items in the vacuum sealer, the computer identified the black rock as over three kg of raw platinum. Mason was amazed. He thought it was only slag rock. He was glad Captain Baines let him keep it and the other two smaller rocks. He made certain to insure his package.

Mason helped Commander Baines with her packing on his own time, to keep her from going crazy. The Captain was still working sixteen hours a day, filling out the plethora of reports required from this historic mission. Mason remembered how she felt when she was stuck making all their wedding plans and arrangements by herself. She truly appreciated his help; neither of them realized how much stuff she and Captain Baines brought on board with them and needed to remove to storage and transport. To thank Mason for helping his wife, the Captain made reservations for a suite for him at the hotel where he and Mrs. Baines would be staying for the week they had to remain on Moon Base, completing the final unloading of crew, passengers, cargo and platinum from the Hesperia.

Mason completed his Special Security Chief reports to the best of his ability. There were few answers to the questions raised on the Hesperia: no one knew who killed Dr. Reese or Dr. Wise, or attempted to murder Mason; the chief traitor who put the envelopes containing $10,000 charge crystals and gold coins under the pillows of the Yellow Man's recruits was not identified; how the contraband drugs and poisons, as well as a two meter, high-intensity laser rifle had been smuggled aboard was unknown. What was blatantly obvious was the purpose of the attacks themselves. The ONE wanted a new colony, and a "Perfect Man" to seed their DNA throughout the solar system. The Earth Command brass would fight over whether or not to treat that purpose as an invasion for years to come. Mason had no idea what part he would play in the ONE's future plans for him. They were not done with John Mason.

The remaining crew and officers were awakened from cryonic hibernation one week from Moon Base, with the exception of those who would be court-martialed, or executed as traitors. They would stay in their sealed containers and not be awakened until they reached Earth Command in Houston. The final passengers to be awakened were the civilians who operated the Esplanade concessions and restaurants, and everyone was happy to get a decent meal at the sports bar or bistro. Less than eighty miners were still in cryo-sleep, and the URE decided it was best to let them stay there until they arrived on Moon Base. They were presumed innocent.

Commander Baines hosted a farewell dinner for Dr. Hassan and Mason at the bistro the last night of the voyage, and hoped the Captain could join them at some point. She was beginning to have a little bump show on her flat tummy.

Dr. Hassan was one of the few officers who received his new assignment confirmation; he would be the Chief Surgical Consultant at the Earth Command Hospital in Berlin. No more adventures for him in deep space. Accompanying him would be the reptilian alien in his cryonic container, who was to be transported to somewhere deep in the Alpine mountains for "study."

"Have you and Captain Baines received word of your new assignments, Commander?" The Doctor asked.

"No. I thought the Captain would know by now, but so much depends on our receiving assignments together at the same base. We have very different qualifications and skill sets," she answered. "What about you, Mason? Have you heard anything yet?"

"I was accepted into OCS, but the class will not start for another three years. The Captain advised me to apply for several billets, and hold off choosing which one to take until we are on Moon Base. It's making me uneasy not knowing where I'll be next, in truth." Mason answered. "I hope I can spend a little time on Mars Colony III to visit my family before the next assignment."

Captain Baines arrived after the plates had been cleared away, but ordered his meal anyway. They kept the conversation going while he quickly ate a steak and potatoes. "There will be a ceremony tomorrow I would like you all to attend, to commemorate the end of our historic voyage. It will be held in the main pavilion at Moon Base, and there will be a dinner afterwards. The ceremony is class A, and the dinner is mess dress. Did you get your mess dress uniform replaced, Mason?" Baines asked.

"It's waiting for me at the Base Exchange, Captain Baines," Mason answered. Damn good thing he ordered it two weeks ago.

"Dr. Hassan, Captain Baines: would you honor me by letting me sharpen your swords? They were pretty beat up the last time I saw them, sirs," Mason asked. Both men were happy not to have to spend the time doing the old-fashioned blade sharpening themselves.

Mason picked up the men's swords, and went to his quarters to sharpen the blades. Dr. Hassan's sword blade was cleaned of the blood that soiled it the night of the Captain's wedding reception, but it was severely nicked from stopping the sword of Captain Baines' attacker from hacking his neck. Mason spent his last night on board the Hesperia sharpening that blade and Captain Baines' sword, while listening to Sherrie's music crystals, and enjoying some of his of bourbon. It was a fitting end to this mission. It was the warrior's way.

The next day at o-five hundred hours, the Hesperia docked at Moon Base. No one was allowed off until the precious platinum was off-loaded onto URE armored shuttles. The civilian passengers got off ship first, then the crews from all stations except engineering and the bridge. Commander Powers supervised the engines shut-down, and the engineers disembarked. The bridge crew was next. Captain Baines and Mason were the last to leave.

The hotel suite was wonderful for Mason. He filled the large spa tub and soaked for nearly an hour before dressing for the ceremony. He ordered room service, and ate a large chef salad with real, fresh vegetables, and a thick rib-eye steak. He put on his old class A uniform, and ordered his other new uniforms delivered to his suite in two hours. To kill a couple hours before the ceremony, he walked around Moon Base, reacquainting himself with the place. It was still the best space base in the solar system, with every convenience a man could want. He returned to his suite, and his new uniforms were delivered right on time. He packed most of his new uniforms and his last full bottle of bourbon in his gear bag. He decided to change into his new class A's and tall boots.

The ceremony was very pageant, and three admirals had taken the shuttle to Moon Base to welcome the Hesperia, including Admiral Tomiko.

Mason was happy to finally meet the man who promoted him on the Hesperia in person. All the Hesperia line command officers sat together on the stage, while Commander Baines, Dr. Hassan, and Mason sat together in the second row of the audience. Lt. Commanders Westerly and Davis were promoted to full Commanders; Commander Powers was promoted to Captain; and then the medical command officers were invited to the stage.

Medical Captain Dr. Hassan was awarded the Silver Star for bravery and performance above and beyond the call of duty in battle, the first living medical corps officer to receive such distinction in over one hundred years. He was speechless.

Commander Rachel Baines was awarded the Bronze Star for dedication and superior performance above and beyond the call of duty in battle. After Admiral Tomiko pinned her bronze star on her uniform, Admiral Worthington promoted her to Medical Corps Captain. She was beaming. Mason was almost in tears for her. She had not been given any hint of her medal or promotion; neither had Dr. Hassan. Their surprised faces were a joy to behold. Such promotions were expected for the bridge officers, but not for the medical officers. They surely deserved their rewards, Mason agreed.

Admirals Tomiko, Worthington, and Spencer presented Captain Baines with several medals and commendations, and promoted him to Rear Admiral. His wife, the new Captain Baines, was applauding and crying for him at the same time. Admiral Worthington announced there was one more medal to be awarded. He read the accompanying commendations for over five minutes without announcing who the recipient was. Mason was waiting for Baines' name to be called again, when he heard, "Master Sergeant John Mason, please come to the stage."

Mason was awarded the URE Medal of Honor, for a very long list of his accomplishments and sacrifices, and for repeatedly putting himself in harm's way to protect the Captain and bridge, engineering, and medical officers of the Hesperia. The pure gold medal was placed around his neck with its blue and gold ribbon. The Chief of the Joint Chiefs of Staff, Admiral Worthington, saluted him, saying, "Congratulations, Master Gunnery Sergeant John Mason." Mason returned his salute perfectly, and the Admiral pinned his new insignia on him.

Mason understood why his and the Baines' assignment requests had not been filled. Admiral Worthington held them up because of the promotions. They all met at the hotel afterwards, and celebrated with champagne. Mason stepped out to get the swords for Admiral Baines and Dr. Hassan, and the men were amazed at the sharpness of the blades, and how they gleamed. Mason put such a sharp edge on both swords that they looked new again, without any nick, scratch or imperfection.

Mason changed, put his new insignia on his mess dress uniform, measured the placement of all his ribbon medals, and put the jacket on to check them again. He finished dressing, placed his Medal of Honor around his neck, and became depressed. Yes, he saved the Captain and most of the crew of the Hesperia, but could not save his own wife. Sherrie loved him completely, and devoted herself to him. Sherrie would have been proud of his medal and promotion, he told himself, trying his best to keep from crying. Now he was alone again, burdened with an overwhelming feeling of guilt for her death. He was not responsible for her death; the pirates were. He knew if he had been there with her, he would have died, too, because the explosion was so strong. He was filled with ennui, and nearly succumbed to its throes of despair. But Mason knew that a brave man had to keep moving forward. It was the way of the warrior.

He took his hat and gloves and walked the long distance to the dinner, to clear his head. But he was introverted and distant the entire night. The formal dinner was very nice, and packed with Space Forces officers. One Prime Marine officer, Colonel Tyrone, sought Mason out to talk about OCS with him. The Hesperia officers all sat together, with Admiral and Captain Baines seated next to each other, surrounded by the other ships' officers, according to rank. Mason was invited to sit at the Admirals' table as the Medal of Honor recipient.

Captain Rachel Baines kept looking over at him, smiling at him, and her smiles made him feel more comfortable. He was happy the post-dinner festivities were few; there was dancing and live music, and no speeches. Admiral and Captain Baines danced with each other for the first two dances, and then he led her to the Admiral's table, and asked Mason to dance with her. Mason was honored to oblige; he led her across the dance floor very well, which delighted her.

"You always surprise me, John. I didn't know you could dance this well until tonight," Captain Baines said with a smile. She was radiant, fully enjoying her night of celebration and success. Mason smiled at her glowing face, twirled her around, and took her back into his arms, neither of them missing a step. It was a magical dance, or so it seemed to them. He led her around the floor like they had been dance partners for a lifetime, moving and turning and bending together in perfect rhythm, in their own world. They finished the dance and he took her back to her Admiral. He handed her back to her husband with a flourish, then bowed slightly, and left. He didn't say a word.

Mason thanked the Admirals, and took his leave. He went to the Hesperia table, thanked them all, and wished them good journeys. When Sergeants Milton and Johnson saw him leave, they quickly followed him, and caught up with their Prime Marine before he disappeared. "You didn't think we'd let you leave without buying you a drink, did you Mason?" His buddies took him away from the formal affair to a favorite Space Marine bar, the "Winged Fury," where they passed the remainder of the night away, and they all got very drunk. Obliterated, in fact. It was just what Mason needed. He finally got past thinking of Sherrie's death and feeling guilty for a little while that night, and had a great time until the bar closed. He danced with all the girls, had an outrageous time with his buddies, and even smoked a couple of cigars. They stuffed him in a cab and took him back to his hotel.

Mason slept until 9am, unusual for him. He got up with a real bitchin' hangover, took two aspirin, drank three glasses of water, and headed back to bed, when he saw a note under his door. It was an invitation from Admiral Baines for lunch that day in their suite at noon. Oh, brother. Only three hours to sober up, and get a clear head. He put sweats on and went to work out in the hotel's gym. After an hour's workout, a steam and a sauna, he was beginning to feel like he might be able to attend the Admiral's lunch. He ran the streets of Moon Base for more than an hour, until he was drenched with alcohol sweat, and went back to the hotel to clean up. He looked better than he felt, but at least he was presentable in his new class A's. He popped a couple more aspirins and went to the Admiral's suite.

"Welcome, John. We weren't sure if we'd see you this morning," Mrs. Baines said with a big smile. She was wearing a nice dress, no uniform today. "I understand the "Winged Fury" will never be the same after last night!" She had a saucy smile on her face, like someone had given her all the details. Or was about to.

"Mason! I was worried we'd missed you. Thank you for coming today," Admiral Baines said. "We're to be on the midnight transport tonight for Earth Command Central, in Houston. We wanted to be sure to see you before we left."

"Did you get your assignment at HQ, sir?" Mason asked.

"Yes. I will be at Earth Command Central, and Captain Baines will be at the medical research facility a few kilometers away. She will be addressed as "Dr. Baines," now, not "Nurse Baines." I'm very proud of her, Mason." He put his arm around her and hugged her. "And I'm also proud of you, Master Gunnery Sergeant Mason! I recommended you for promotion, but did not know you would receive the URE Medal of Honor. You are the first one I've had the privilege to serve with, and you bloody well deserve it!" He saluted Mason, and received a salute in return.

"Thank you, Admiral Baines. I didn't expect to receive anything, let alone another promotion," Mason said humbly.

"I could not have accomplished half of what we did on the Hesperia without knowing you always had my back, Mason. Well, I'm late for a meeting. Enjoy your lunch with Mrs. Baines," he said, and left.

Their lunch was delivered and set up on the patio. The time was noon, and the Moon Base artificial lights synthesized a bright sky for them, so they sat under the umbrella and ate. They both enjoyed big salads; Mason was served white wine, while Mrs. Baines drank sparkling water. "So, tell me about the Winged Fury, John. I've never been there. What's it like inside?"

He described the bar to her, its Space Marine decorations covering every conceivable centimeter of wall space; the stage for the band and the dance floor; pool tables, and clientele. "I'll wager you were the only Prime Marine in mess dress in the bar, John. You certainly made the news this morning. I received three calls about your exploits already," she said, laughing.

"Exploits? What exploits, ma'am?" He had no memory of any exploits, or what her calls could have been about. He had little memory of what happened after the seventh or eighth round of bourbon, except that he had a blast.

"Let's see. There was the tequila shooter contest, which you won; the arm wrestling contest against a dozen or so girls; and the lap dances." She looked at him, smiled an upside down sexy smile, and wiggled her shoulders at him. "Now, I want to hear all about it, John."

"Merely conjecture and hearsay, Mrs. Baines," he said, starting to remember. He'll have to get that uniform cleaned right away.

"No, no, I have it on good authority you had a fabulous time, and broke at least a dozen hearts in one evening. Now 'fess up, Marine," she insisted. He told her how his buddies wanted to help him celebrate his promotion. "So, you blew off the old stuffed shirts at the Admirals' dinner, went to party your brains out with the girls at the Winged Fury, and you didn't take me," she said, acting jealous.

"Sometimes a man's got to do what he's got to do, Mrs. Baines," Mason said, smiling, now remembering the entire night. He was totally guilty of all accused exploits, and much more. He wondered if she also heard about the two wild, hot girls who followed him into the men's room; Mason looked at her and blushed, and they both burst out laughing.

"I'm glad you had a good time, John. You seemed down at dinner. You didn't speak to me the entire evening, even when we danced, except to say good night. I was worried about you. Until my phone started ringing this morning, that is." They laughed and finished their lunches, sitting on the patio in the artificial sunlight. "Have you received any information on your requested billets? I'm sure you'll have double the offers, now," she asked.

"I haven't even looked, to be honest. I was trying to sober up to have lunch with you, ma'am," he confessed.

"Well, let's look now. I'm excited for you, John." She got up and went to get her com tablet, and they sat on the couch together, reading his transmissions. She was right; every billet request was filled, and six other offers, but nothing on Earth, or Mars. "I was hoping you'd have something in Houston, so we could see each other often, but it doesn't look possible."

She was disappointed. "There's nothing under five years. Aren't you scheduled for OCS in three years?"

"Yes, I am," he answered.

"They would hold the OCS slot open for you, I know that for a fact. The classes run once a year at Space Marine OCS. Once you're accepted, you attend the first available class. You can still make it, John," she encouraged him, patting his arm.

"You don't like me as a Master Gunnery Sergeant, Captain?" He asked her, smiling broadly at her. He had such an irresistible smile.

"Yes, of course I like you as a Master Gunnery Sergeant. It's the top of your rank. But you are a great man, and a respected leader. You deserve to be an officer, John Mason." She was completely serious with him. It made him feel good to hear her talk about him that way.

"I'd be the oldest Lieutenant in the Prime Marines, ma'am," he said. "We don't get as many promotions as you do in the Space Forces."

"I know you, John Mason. You'll be a major in no time at all," she said, suddenly smiling. "Major Mason; now that has quite a ring to it, doesn't it?" They both laughed as she got up to pour more wine for him.

"We can still talk on the vid transmission live feeds, whenever we can, ma'am. I want to stay in touch with you, and watch you develop." He looked at her belly. "I want to see your son when he's born," he gently said, smiling at her. She smiled, and gave him a kiss on his cheek.

"Thank you, John. I'm not letting you go, you know." They both leaned back on the couch and she talked about her plans with Admiral Baines to settle down in a house after the baby is born. He stayed with her for a couple more hours, talking with her, and enjoying her company, like old times. The artificial lighting soon turned to dusk, and her hotel room was growing dark.

"I'd better get going, so you can finish packing. Do you need my help with anything, ma'am?" She shook her head 'no,' holding his hand. He stood up and stretched his arms, and helped her up off the couch.

"Will you come see us off at the transport station tonight, John? It would mean a great deal to me, and Admiral Baines, as well," she asked.

"I'd be honored to, ma'am," he said. He started walking towards the door.

"Just a minute, John." She came right up to him, and put her arms around his neck. "I'd like to give you something to remember me." She pulled him to her, and kissed his mouth, gently at first, then let him have it good. He responded freely to her, kissing her with the passion that he subdued for all those years. He picked her up in his arms, and kissed her over and over again, cradling her, and she openly loved his affection. He put her down gently, and they kissed once more; then pulled apart. John's heart was about to come out of his chest, and she was nearly breathless.

That was all they could do; their romance could go no further. They smiled tenderly, and Mason walked out her door, glad he was wearing a long tunic to cover his throbbing cock. He ran into Admiral Baines in the hall, and they shook hands. I warmed her up for him once more, Mason realized, and laughed out loud as he walked back to his room.

Admiral and Captain Baines stood on the crowded transport platform as Mason walked up to them. They both lit up when he approached, and he wished them well. Mason noticed the Captain looked shamelessly satiated, and was smiling at him, her eyes twinkling in the platform lights. "You must plan to come visit us when you take your annual leave, Mason. Our door is always open to you," the Admiral said. "I mean it, we want you to not forget us, John."

"I couldn't even if I tried, Admiral Baines, Captain Baines," Mason admitted.

"Have you chosen your billet, John?" She asked.

"I think so. The Esmeralda," Mason said.

"Excellent choice, Mason. She's brand new; a gleaming titanium hull, I understand. Many more facilities and conveniences than the Hesperia," Admiral Baines said, pleased with Mason's choice. "You'll have a cruise you won't soon forget, I dare say." The Admiral had no idea how right he was.

Captain Baines hugged Mason tightly, and she gave him a little kiss; the Admiral shook his hand. Mason said, "It is an honor to have served with you, Admiral and Captain Baines," and saluted them, as they boarded the transport. The happy couple returned his salute, and he stayed on the platform until the doors closed. He watched them settle in their first class seats, and wave at him. The big shuttle headed off for Earth with a roar, taking his best friends away from him and leaving him alone. He had never felt emptier.

The streetlights glowed with their small amber orbs as the Moon Base artificial lighting overhead dimmed sufficiently for him to see the stars, where his future and destiny lie in wait for him. Mason walked the long, empty street back to his hotel, feeling lost and abandoned. His purpose was clear: to be the best of the best, a Prime Marine Master Gunnery Sergeant, and maybe an officer, someday. He went to his room, signed on to his com tablet, and accepted the billet for the Esmeralda. He removed his uniform, packed up everything lying about in his room, and requested a wake-up call for 0-five hundred. Polishing off the last two shots of bourbon, he discarded the bottle and went to bed, dreaming of Sherrie and Mrs. Baines; and the Yellow Man, who still knew everything they did.